REPLAY SEE HEAR

Robert Lilly Brewis

First published in Great Britain as a
hardback original in 2012

Copyright © Robert Lilly Brewis 2012

The moral right of this author has been asserted.

All characters and events in this publication, other than those clearly in the public domain, are fictitious and any resemblance to real persons, living or dead, is purely coincidental.

All rights reserved.
No part of this publication may be reproduced, stored in a retrieval system, or transmitted, in any form or by any means, with out the prior permission in writing of the publisher, nor be otherwise circulated in any form of binding or cover other than that in which it is published and without a similar condition including this condition being imposed on the subsequent purchaser.

Typeset in Sabon by Consilience Media

Design, printing and publishing by Consilience Media
www.consil.co.uk

CHAPTER 1

"Trevor, you make sure those strops are secure," the crane banksman shouted.

Trevor Carhill and his work mate were busy slinging a bail of timber battens to be lifted by crane to the roof top of a new building. Joiners were eagerly awaiting the timbers so they could get on; they had to get some shuttering finished by lunchtime, ready for a delivery of concrete which was due in after lunch. The site was the former multi storey car park in Gateshead Town Centre in North East England – made famous by the fact that the Michael Caine film Get Carter was filmed there. A scene in the film where Michael Caine throws a corrupt councillor off the top gave the car park iconic status. It was finally demolished after standing derelict for many years having become an eyesore and blight on the town centre. A new development to revive the town had finally begun after much protest from the people of Gateshead to save the area from becoming a ghost town.

"It will be all right," Trevor shouted back to the banksman, "you can take it away now."

The banksman looks up at the tower crane as he puts the radio to his mouth. "OK it's all yours Ernie, you can take it away nice and easy," the banksman said speaking into the radio.

Trevor and his workmate Brian steadied the bail of timber while the crane took the weight of the load. "Hold it there," Trevor said, raising his hand.

"Stop, Ernie," the banksman said over the radio. "What's wrong?" he then shouted over at Trevor.

"The strop's still slack on Brian's side," Trevor said, trying to force the loop of the strop down to make a better bite. "That's got it," Trevor said, "it's all yours again," waving his hand above his head in a circular motion. "Try again Ernie," the banksman said into the radio, "up nice and easy, keep going."

The bail of timber started to steadily rise from the ground up into the air. Trevor and Brian watched the load sail up high above their heads; the crane operator in the cab of the tower crane had a good view of the whole site: he waited until he had the load clear above the height of the building before he began to slew the load over to the waiting joiners. There were three joiners on the roof behind edge protection barriers. One of them got a length of reinforcing bar and bent a hook at one end of the bar. When the load came closer he reached out with the reinforcing bar, hooking the loop of the strop holding the load of timber. He then tried to pull the load closer to the roof.

By this time Trevor and his workmate Brian had moved closer to the building to prepare another load of timber ready for lifting. They were now working directly below the hoisted load; the tower crane driver said over the radio to the banksman, "What the hell is that wanker trying to do with that hook? I could put this load in the boot of that car down there if I wanted to. Tell him to get out the sodding way."

The banksman shouted up at the joiner: "Get the bloody hell out the way and leave it to the crane."

The joiner, who was only trying to hasten things up because they were on a tight schedule, tried to unhook the reinforcing bar. He could not free the bar so one of his fellow joiners came to help him; they both pulled and yanked the bar free. The strop must have had a length of slack jammed between the timbers – when it was lifted the strop became loose and it pulled away free of the load leaving only one strop holding the load.

The bail of timber was now unbalanced; one side of the load

CHAPTER I

fell sharply – the sudden jolt pulling the load free from the bite of the single strop. Almost everyone on site was now looking up at the lifting operation because the banksman shouting up at the joiner had attracted their attention. There were cries and screams of 'lookout' from all quarters of the site as the timber began to fall, the banksman screaming at the top of his voice through his cupped hands, "lookout below" in the direction of Trevor and Brian. Both men were now looking up at the load of timber cascading down towards them.

The closest place of safety was to get through the entrance into the building in front of them. Trevor was the furthest away from the entrance; as he started to make a bolt for safety he shouted, "For fuck sake run." There was no need for the warning: Brian was already making for the entrance.

Reaching out, desperately trying to grasp fresh air to aid his progress in his dash for life, Trevor stumbles forward, his hands shoot out digging into the ground franticly trying to pull himself upright, his hard hat flying away from his head. Trevor is on the heels of Brian – being the younger and fitter of the men, Trevor could move the quicker; they are only feet away from safety. Brian is blocking Trevor's way. He realises he is not going to make it to safety unless he pulls Brian to one side, leaving him to his death. Trevor drives his front foot into the ground and dives forward, both hands hitting Brian squarely in the back sending him head over heels through the entrance to safety.

Trevor knew he was doomed: the impact of him pushing Brian had almost stopped his forward motion. He glanced up just as the mass of timber buried him. Everyone on the site stood motionless in shock from what they had just witnessed; suddenly a cry of "get help" rang out which seemed to prompt action. Men scrambling from all directions to the scene of the accident, they began franticly removing the heap of timber off its helpless victim, revealing the lifeless body of Trevor Carhill.

CHAPTER 2

Clare Carhill, a 35 year old widow, stood in the kitchen of her two-up-two-down semi, staring out the window. The house was on the Old Fold council estate in Gateshead. Clare was busy washing the dishes when her thoughts took her back four weeks ago to when she received the call about the accident. Clare was on holiday at the time with a couple of work friends in Spain; she got the next available flight home. Wondering what she will do now without Trevor, he was the only family she had. A knock on the door startled Clare; she dropped the cup she was holding into the kitchen sink. Clare opened the door to a sombre looking man who began to weep.

"Oh Brian," Clare said sympathetically, "come on in, I will make us a cup of tea." Clare pulled a chair from the kitchen table: "Here, sit down." Brian sat down, wiping the tears from his eyes and just sat with his chin on his chest staring at the table. "Here, get that down you," Clare said, placing a cup of tea on the table in front of Brian.

"I am so sorry," Brian said sobbing.

"It's not your fault Brian – it was an accident," Clare said.

"He saved my life; he would not be where he is if I had not been in his way," Brian said.

"You must stop doing this to yourself: you will end up ill if you don't."

Brian Taylor was Trevor's best friend; they had worked together for 15 years on various construction sites. Brian felt guilty about what had happened and was struggling to come to terms with it.

"There was nothing you or anyone could have done to

prevent what happened. It was an accident and you have to get over it," Clare said, trying to comfort him. "Listen Brian, you don't have to go with me this morning if you are not up to it, you can wait here until I come back," Clare said.

"Will you be all right, Clare?" Brian asked, "I would rather not go."

"Sure, I will be fine," Clare replied.

Truthfully Clare was pleased that Brian did not want to go – she had enough to think and worry about as it was; Brian would have only added to her burden. Clare looked at her wrist watch, "Look Brian I must go or I will be late, you just wait here and I will come straight back when it is all over." Clare put her coat on and left; she really had plenty of time to get to her appointment but needed to be on her own for a while to think. As she walked Clare thought about Trevor; the last time they spoke was when Trevor dropped her off at Newcastle Airport, kissing her on the cheek and telling her to have a good time on holiday. Trevor was all she had left since her husband was killed in a car crash four years ago.

At 9-45 in the morning Clare walked into the entrance of the Royal Victoria Infirmary in Newcastle. The heavy load of the critical decision she had to make was weighing her down. She walked to the reception desk.

"I have an appointment with Dr Luke," Clare said to the receptionist. "Ah yes Mrs Bellamey," the receptionist said, "Dr Luke is waiting."

"Miss Carhill," Clare said, correcting the receptionist.

"It's all right, Gloria," a woman said as she walked towards the reception desk. "I will take care of Clare. How are you Clare?" the woman asked.

"Not good Dr Luke, I have been dreading this day."

CHAPTER 2

"That's understandable," Dr Luke replied as she led Clare down the corridor to her office. "Clare," Dr Luke said, "before we go in, there is something I need to tell you: there has been a slight improvement..."

The door of the office opened before Dr Luke could finish what she was saying. "Please come in Miss Carhill," a man said.

"Clare, this is Dr Mayo and this is Dr Lustman," Dr Luke said as they entered the room.

"What do you mean improvement?" Clare asked.

"Please sit down Clare, we will explain," Dr Mayo said, gesturing to a chair that had been placed in front of the now seated doctors.

"What is this Linda?" Clare asked Dr Luke in an anguished voice.

"Since the early hours of this morning there has been a slight improvement in your brother's brain activity," Dr Mayo said.

"So what you're telling me is that Trevor is going..."

Dr Lustman butted in: "We are not telling you anything of the sort. In this situation we are here to advise you."

"I came here this morning for us to decide whether we switch off my brother's life support, now you're..."

"Clare you must listen, all we are saying," Dr Luke said, "is there is improvement, but even if the brain activity was to even increase it does not mean Trevor is going to get better."

"As you know, Trevor suffered massive head damage as well as other injuries. We had to replace his skull with a Titanium plate during surgery," Dr Lustman said.

"But if there is the chance, I want to wait before we decide anything," Clare insisted.

"What we think Clare, is that we review this in 72 hours. Even if it were possible that Trevor improved enough to survive without life support he would never be the same," Dr Luke said.

"I don't care," Clare said, "I want to see him, I need to speak to him."

"Very well I will take you down to the I C Unit," Dr Luke said.

Clare did not wait to say goodbye, she left the office in a hurry. As they walked down to the Intensive Care Unit Dr Luke said to Clare, "Please Clare don't read anything into this; we are most probably postponing the inevitable. I don't want you to build your hopes up."

Clare stopped, turned to Dr Luke and said: "If there is the slightest chance, no matter how small that chance is, I want Trevor to have that chance, even if it means we have to delay any decision making indefinitely."

CHAPTER 3

Camp Bastion. British Army Base. Helmand Province. Afghanistan.

"Please come this way Captain," the orderly said as he walked towards the Colonel's office. The orderly knocked on the door, opened it and said: "Captain Wienwright sir." "Ah Captain please come in."

The Captain walked into the office, stood to attention and saluted. "Please sit down Captain," the Colonel said. The Captain sat down, looking at the Colonel's name plate that was strategically placed on his desk, so those who sat in front of the desk could not miss it: it read Colonel V. W. Baldwin.

"Captain," the Colonel said, looking down at the open folder on his desk, pausing before he spoke again, "well Captain, do you think we will be able to keep a lid on this?"

"I do hope we can sir, it is very important to me that I am here as an ordinary officer and do my duty," said the Captain. "There is nobody below the rank of Major who knows my secret," he added.

"That may well be the case now," the Colonel said, "but what after a few weeks or months pass and people forget themselves and let things slip out, not intentionally mind you, but they do you know."

The Colonel paused then added: "And if the Taliban get wind of who you are they will be lining up ten deep to get a shot at you. They will go all out to try and bag an officer, but a member of the Royal Family, that would bring a great victory to their cause."

"I am sure it can be kept quiet sir," the Captain said. "It is not only you Captain, it is your men as well; every officer here and his men are under constant threat of attack, even more so if the man leading them is royalty," the Colonel said.

"I am not royalty Colonel, I am a second cousin to Her Majesty – that puts me well out of reach of the throne sir."

"Do you think it is fair, Captain, to the men who will serve under you, that they don't know you could be an added risk to them?" the Colonel asked.

"Sir I am a Captain in the British Army, and if my country is at war it is my duty and an honour to fight for that country – my family links should not prevent me from performing that duty," the Captain said, pushing his chest out and flaring his nostrils.

"Very well Captain, but if I get the slightest inkling that who you really are has leaked out, you will be back on the training barracks before you can pack your kit bag. I will go right to the top to have you removed – have you got that Captain?"

"Yes Colonel," the Captain said, standing to attention and saluting. Doing an about turn he marched to the door.

"Captain," the Colonel said just before the Captain got out the door. "Sir," the Captain replied. "We will discuss your orders later. Welcome to Camp Bastion Captain Wienwright."

"Thank you Colonel Baldwin," the Captain said as he left.

CHAPTER 4

Brian Taylor was making his way around to Clare Carhill's house; he was going to go to the hospital with Clare this morning. Brian missed his best friend Trevor – Trevor used to look out for Brian, make sure that he was all right. Brian was not the brightest kid on the block; he had difficulty reading and was no good at numbers. Trevor would make sure his wages were right, fill his time sheet in for him, and keep his work sheet up to date. Trevor liked Brian and the feeling was mutual: Brian would do anything for Trevor, Trevor treated him like a mate, not like the other guys at work. They would call him Brun. Brian knew this was their name for someone they considered to be thick, and at work Trevor always called him by his proper name. Usually the men at work would take the mickey out of Brian, and Trevor would tell them to lay off him, he would not let anyone pick on him. No wonder then that Brian has been totally at a loss since the accident happened.

Brian only lived a few streets away from Clare's house; 'Patterson Gardens, Felling' Brian would say if anyone enquired where he lived. Clare was just coming out of the house when Brian came up the street: "That's what I call good timing," she said, pressing the fob on her car keys to unlock the car.

"How you feeling today, Brian?" Clare asked.

"I am a bit nervous," Brian replied, "I don't know what to say to Trevor."

"It will be all right you'll see, wait until we get there, now get in the car," Clare said.

Dr Luke asked Brian if he would mind waiting while she spoke to Clare in her office. Reluctantly Brian agreed – he did not like being on his own in public places.

"Now then Clare, we need to talk about where we go from here," Dr Luke said. "As you know, hour by hour and day by day, Trevor has been improving. His brain activity is increasing quite rapidly. My colleagues Dr Mayo and Dr Lustman and I of course are just astounded with his rate of progress. One of the nurses reported eye movement this very morning, and that alone is remarkable at this stage – in fact it's miraculous, considering that only three days ago we were debating whether to switch off his life support. But there is still a long way to go before we let Trevor try to breathe for himself. His other injuries, the breaks and the fractures will mend if he keeps getting stronger, so we are recommending no change in his treatment; we just have to give it time."

"Thank you Linda, you have been a tower of strength these past weeks," Clare said.

"And now, no doubt, you want to go see Trevor. Keep talking to him."

"Thanks again," Clare said as she was leaving the doctor's office. "Come on Brian, let's go and tell Trevor all the gossip."

Clare opened the door to Trevor's room. Brian just stood looking; he got a shock when we saw his mate just lying there helpless. Trevor's head was mostly covered in bandages, a small opening left for the eyes, tubes into his nose, wires attached to his head. There was a frame around his head. Trevor had plaster casts on both arms down to the wrists, one leg was completely plastered and the opposite ankle was plastered. A folded bed sheet covered Trevor's chest and groin. The nurse was changing a drip at the bedside.

Clare asked: "Will it be all right nurse?"

"Of course Clare," the nurse replied. "I am just about done

CHAPTER 4

here; just press the button if you need me," the nurse said, leaving the room.

"Come on Brian, don't look at all the equipment – just look beyond it, focus on Trevor." Clare pulled another chair close to the bed, "Here Brian you sit that side and I will sit this side of Trevor."

Brian was scared: he sat down looking at all the apparatus that Trevor was hooked up to. Clare could see this fear in his face. "It's all right Brian, there is nothing to worry about," she said, "but all these machines, the monitors are necessary: they are helping Trevor." Clare said she needed Brian to relax and be confident talking to her brother. "Take Trevor's hand," Clare said, as she held his other hand. Brian slid his hand over the bed sheet just touching Trevor's fingers. "It will be fine Brian, don't worry. Hello Trevor," Clare said. "I have brought someone to see you, say hello Brian."

"Hi mate, I really don't know what to say," Brian's voice was quivering; he was trying hard to control his emotions. Brian took hold of Trevor's hand carefully and sat down very slowly. "Jesus!" Brian said, jumping to his feet.

"What is the matter?" asked Clare.

"He squeezed my hand, he squeezed it."

"Are you sure?" Clare asked.

"He squeezed my hand hard, he did," Brian repeated.

The nurse came back in the room. "Is everything all right Clare?" she asked.

"Brian says Trevor squeezed his hand: is that possible with the plaster cast on his arm?" Clare said.

"Yes that is possible, it is Trevor's upper arm that is fractured on that side, but it is very unlikely he has the strength to grip," the nurse said.

"He squeezed my hand I tell you, he did, I would not say he had done so if he did not," Brian said.

"Well, if he did then that is great news," the nurse said, standing behind Brian shaking her head at Clare.

CHAPTER 5

"This is soul destroying," the soldier said looking through his field glasses; "nothing is going to happen here."

"Makes no difference," another soldier said as he tried to push his bum into a more comfortable sitting position in the hard earth.

The soldiers were on a hill top vantage point overlooking a road. It was the early hours of the morning in Afghanistan. Twenty yards behind these two soldiers were two more soldiers sitting in a Land Cruiser Buggy, scanning the terrain in all directions through their night vision glasses, looking for any signs of movement or activity. Their job was to make sure the two soldiers on the hill could concentrate on their task, without having to worry about their backs.

"Intel must have it wrong," one soldier said to the other.

"There is plenty of time yet, just keep your eyes peeled Willas."

It was pitch dark, the sky black with a million sparkling diamonds, cold and deadly silent. The four soldiers were a US Delta Special Forces Unit, the best of the best; they were out on an intelligence tip off. All four men seasoned and hardened soldiers, all four had originated in the marines.

"Holy Moly," the spotter from the hill top said, "would you believe it, it's the midnight Taliban Bomb Company."

The soldier sitting alongside the spotter flung himself into prone position, his sniper rifle already set up by his side. He guided his eye into the view piece of the powerful nightsight, cuddling the butt of the rifle into his shoulder, shuffling and squirming for a second or two, his right hand reaching around to the trigger guard. Then he lay as still as a dead body. "1500 yards one o'clock," said the spotter.

By this time the two soldiers at the Buggy were down on their knees, intensely scouring the area with night binoculars. The sniper and the spotter had to be able to do their job without any interruptions from any quarter, and two soldiers on point made sure they could. The sniper pulled his left hand away from the stock of the rifle to press a button on the telescopic sight. There were several buttons on the telescopic sight, his finger going expertly to the right one without looking. In the eye piece of the telescopic sight he could see a greenish haze appear; the terrain became clear in that green haze. The sniper pointed the rifle in the one o'clock direction. The spotter called out in a low voice, "1450 yards, still at your one o'clock." "I have got them," the sniper said, "three of them." "Yes three," the spotter said. "I will stay fixed," the sniper said. "You have a look around."

The spotter took his gaze away from the three figures to check around, a few seconds later saying "all clear, only the bomb squad out tonight."

Once again the sniper shuffled about for a short while, and then lay perfectly still; he could see three figures walking gingerly towards the road, taking their time, every step placed carefully to the ground. The figures were white in the green haze background; it looked as if they had lights on inside their bodies which were glowing through their skin and clothes. The shapes of the figures were slightly distorted, because of the backpacks they were carrying and their arms were full with bulky objects. "1400 yards," the spotter said.

The sniper then presses another button on the case of the telescopic sight, the centre figure of the three came up in close view in the eye piece; another press of the same button and three

CHAPTER 5

figures back in view, the sniper not saying a word, his breathing slow and easy.

"1300 yards," the spotter said. The top half of the figures disappeared momentarily, as they went behind a small hill. The spotter then spoke out again, "1200 yards".

The figures reach the road side. The sniper presses another button the on the telescopic sight, saying at the same time "middle". The image of the middle figure becomes closer in the view, and a red cross appears in the view, this time over the glowing white image of a man's head and shoulders. The centre of the cross is trained on the head of the figure. The sniper's finger begins to apply pressure to the trigger of the rifle, all kinds of data begins to appear in his view, numbers and letters stack up either side of the red cross. He squeezes ever so lightly on the trigger again: thoof, a sharp muffled noise from the rifle, but no movement whatsoever. Then the sniper sees the glow of the target's head fan out behind him, looking momentarily as if he were wearing a red Indian headdress, the heat from the fluid leaving the back of the man's head glowing for a split second in the thermal imaging.

"Ouch that hurt," the spotter whispered. "Left side," the sniper said, at the same time pressing buttons on the telescopic sight as he spoke, showing him a wider view, the two remaining figures still not aware their fellow bomber was dead, only the noise of his head bursting as the bullet passed through it made them look his way.

Another button pressed into mode, the head and shoulder of the left side figure appears, as soon as the cross zeros, on the figure's chest, thoof a muffled sound again. Bang an almighty blast, the whole night lights up, you could see all around for hundreds of yards for a split second. The sniper throwing himself back away from his rifle, and rubbing his eyes, as he was temporarily blinded from the massive bright flash.

"Wow the fourth of July," the spotter shouted as he threw himself to the ground, not wanting to be silhouetted by the bright flash of the explosion. The blast would have been seen for miles, the two soldiers on the buggy going to ground as well. The sniper's bullet had gone through the back of the Taliban fighter's back and stuck the IED he was carrying in his backpack, causing it to explode.

Darkness again in seconds, the spotter turned to the sniper and asked: "Did you get the third one?"

"I may have just winged him," said the sniper. "Man that is some tool," the spotter said, patting the rifle. He was right about that: this was the first time the rifle had been used out in the field. The rifle had just not long ago finished its trials and testing on the firing ranges in Houston, Texas – basically straight off the planning table.

A peep on the field phone, the spotter answered it: "Knight Hawk clear, Hawk has taken his prey." He listened for a while and then said, "Well guys, we are going nowhere until it gets light." "What do you reckon serge," one of the two soldiers that were at the Buggy said to the other. "It will be light in a few hours, and we will be out of here, so keep alert Willas, that blast would have awoke every gun up for miles."

No sleep for the soldiers tonight – they had given their position away. But their experience had taught them it would be very unlikely they would get any unwelcome visitors; there would be plenty of Taliban out there and they would have heard the IED blowing up, or even seen the blast. Most would think it was a planting gone wrong, a lot of them would know that the planting was taking place and where. And everyone on both

CHAPTER 5

sides would be watching the area but staying clear, with no one wanting to risk anything in the dark. Daybreak would be the crucial time. So the Night Hawk Unit were staying put for now.

"Extraction first light," the spotter said.

Eight miles away a small village was awoken by the noise of the blast. Akhamid Shali was sitting on the floor of a dimly lit house, in that village, discussing tactics with seven other men; they sat in a circle. When the IED went off Shali shot up onto his feet, looking in the direction of the blast and said: "This is not good."

The door of the house burst open and in rushed a man gasping for breath, and clearly in a panic, "General, General," he gasped, "it was Balli, it was Balli." Akhamid Shali took hold of the man by the hair. "What is this you are saying?" he asked.

"It was Balli, he told the Americans, and he told them about the bomb."

"Where is Balli now?" Shali said in a rage.

"Alama has him; he said he will keep him alive for you General."

By now all the men in the room were standing. "No helicopters," Shali said, "the Americans are still out there." Akhamid Shali knew the ways of the American military – he should: he was trained by them. "We must move quickly," Akhamid Shali said. "We go to avenge our brothers."

Shali was still holding the man by the hair, "Go and tell Alama to send the men to meet me," Shali said to him. Shali hesitated for a while before speaking again. Where on the road would the Americans wait, he thought to himself, then after a few seconds' thought, said to the man: "Meet me on the pass to the hills in half an hour. Tell them to bring everything."

The man left as quickly as he had come. Shali glared at the

group of men standing before him, nostrils flaring as he breathed in and out heavily. "The Americans are going to die, come we must move quickly, there will not be much time."

One of the men said nervously: "What will Ali bin say?"

"There is no time to consult, move or I go myself to avenge our brothers," said Shali.

One of the men took a lamp and went into the next room, pulling the worn carpet away from the floor. He began to scrape the ground with the heel of his foot. Soon three more of the men were in the room digging with their bare hands at the ground, one taking out a knife and stabbing it into the earth to loosen it. They dug only a few inches into the dirt and hit wood. They began digging even faster; as Shali began to get agitated, he waved his arms shouting "faster, faster". They were digging like dogs would to bury a bone.

"More light," Shali said.

One of the men brought another lamp; just as the men were lifting the wooden door from the ground, it revealed an old blanket. One of the men pulled it to one side, exposing the weapons cache that had been hidden beneath the floor. There was several Kalashnikovs, hand guns, grenades and ammunition.

"Quickly, quickly," Shali urged as the men started to remove the guns – the first AK47 out of the cache being passed to Shali. One of the men went outside; he returned after a few seconds saying it was clear. Shali turned and started to leave, first blowing the lamp out; the men, now all armed, followed Shali in haste. There were not many houses in the village; most of them had dim lights that could be seen shining through cracks in window and door covers; no one was asleep in the village – the blast from the IED had made sure of that. There was plenty of movement outside, but that did not bother Shali and his men;

CHAPTER 5

he knew the Americans would not come to the village at night. Shali had no time to be checking on anything or anyone who may be moving around. They had at least eight miles to cover on foot, in the dark, if he was to get into position to ambush the Americans before it got light. Shali knew there would not be many American soldiers out there who attacked the bombers, but he also knew they would be Special Forces, and not be so easy to take out.

In no time Shali and the seven men were at the narrows of the pass that led to the hills; waiting there was a group of about a dozen men, all armed, carrying AK47 rifles, and at least three of them shouldering LPGs, and an assortment of other small arms. These were the Taliban Fighters, brave and ready to die for their cause at any time.

"My General," a man said, "what are our orders?"

Shali turned to the man and said, "Alama, what have you done with Balli?"

"He is alive General, we keep him alive, I have had him taken to Ali Bin. What is the plan my General?" Alama said.

"I will tell you on the way, we must hurry to reach the Americans before they get help."

"General," a voice rang out, "please General!"

"Who is this?" Shali asked.

"My General, this is Hareem – he is the one that brings you the news of Balli," Alama said.

"Speak man," Shali said.

"I wish to come with you my General to fight the Americans."

Shali eyed Hareem up. "Come then," he said, "but make haste."

The band of Taliban fighters began to run through the pass

and on up the hills. They had not gone more than half a mile when Shali stopped; raising his hand, he stood motionless for a second or two. He turned and ran back down the line of men behind him; Hareem was telling his fellow fighters how honoured he was to be there with them. Shali drew his knife from its sheaf, he grabbed Hareem by the throat, pushing the knife, so that the point was at Hareem' s nose.

"You give our position away and I will cut out your tongue," Shali said to Hareem.

"Oh my General, forgive me, I am sorry my General," Hareem said as he dropped to his knees begging.

"Shut up you oaf, shut up or I will kill you," Shali said.

Hareem went quiet, reaching his hands up in a subdued manner. Shali let loose of his grip on Hareem, kicked him in the stomach before turning around and running back up to the front of the troop of men, not stopping when he got to the front of the line, just waving for the men to follow him.

CHAPTER 6

On the hill top the US soldiers are more relaxed now; an hour has passed and no signs of any trouble. The two soldiers that were on point had moved to the hill top with the others. They sat close together; only now and then one would raise a head up and take a look around through the night vision binoculars. Two of the soldiers were lying down on their backs, jackets pulled over their head and shoulders, trying to get some sleep.

"What time is it Rees?" one of the two sitting soldiers asked.

Rees pulled the cover from his wrist watch face, "2-35".

"Wake the Major," the soldier said.

"No need," a voice said as a head popped out from under a jacket. The Major sat up, slapped his hand on the covered head of the other soldier who was lying down, saying "Come on Willas, let the Serge and Rees get a bit rest."

Rees and the serge shuffled their way to the middle of the group, rolling up in a ball. The Serge said: "Wake me when breakfast is ready," Willas doing likewise. "We will wake you in a couple of hours," the Major said.

General Shali and his men moved as quickly as they could under the cover of darkness trying not to make a sound. Alama was up alongside General Shali.

"If we are quiet," the General said, "we will catch the Americans off guard," trying to keep his voice as low as possible, but loud enough for Alama to hear him. "If we can get into position before the Americans know we are there, we have them Alama," the General added. "There will be no more than six of them, and they will be on the top of the highest hill looking down on the road. And if we can get in the vicinity and locate them before first light, they will be ours. We will have to be vigilant and move like shadows; the Americans have the capability to see in the dark – they must not see us; we have to be ready before the light comes."

"It's 4-30 Willas," the Major said, "wake the guys up."

Willas poked the heap of clothes with the barrel of his M17 rifle that the Sergeant was sheltering under. "Serge, Serge."

"OK, OK," came from beneath the coat as a head popped out.

"4-30 Serge," Willas said. The sun was just starting to come up over the horizon.

"Wakey wakey," the Serge said, shaking the other heap of clothes that lay beside him.

Rees came rolling out from under his covers, unzipping his pants as he did; "I am fucking bursting," he said, as he took a leak still lying on his side.

The Major crawled forward to the brow of the hill, looking down to where the bomb had gone off; there were no visible signs of any bodies, only a big crater covering half the dirt road. The crater was about 20 feet in diameter, and about six feet deep. Rees rolled back into a sitting position, after zipping himself up.

"Not be long now," the Major said, "get on the phone Willas."

"What is wrong with you, Rees?" the Serge asked, looking at Rees just sitting staring in the direction of the buggy.

Rees shouted, "Fucking shit," as he threw himself forward. Too late: three or four bullets ripped into his chest and face; he was dead before he hit the ground. The ground all around them throwing up dirt as bullets struck. The Serge and Willas were peppered with bullets, blood and flesh flying off them and

CHAPTER 6

mixing with the dust. The two soldiers jerked violently as more bullets ripped into their lifeless bodies. The Major took a round in the shoulder, then threw himself over the brow of the hill, just as another round tore through his thigh.

The Major dug his hands into the ground and began to franticly pull himself down the hill, propelling forward like a man swimming, but with no water. The noise was deafening: it sounded as if a hundred guns were being fired at once. An explosion to his right as a grenade went off, bullets flying over his head and hitting the ground all around him. His shoulder and leg were on fire, but the fear overrode the pain. The Major looked forward: "If I could only make it to the crater for cover I may have a chance," he thought, and he drove harder pulling with his arms and pushing with his uninjured leg to propel himself further down the hill. The rain of bullets getting closer to his body, desperately he tried to get distance between himself and the Taliban fighters firing at him. He glimpsed up at the crater; too far, he thought, as bullets thumped into the ground just above his head; I am not going to make it, the Major thought, as he stopped the frantic efforts to escape. Major Christopher Bennet knew this was the end – strangely he no longer felt afraid.

The Major rolled over onto his back; he wanted to look at his killers before he drew his last breath. Looking back up to the brow of the hill, he could see about 20 men standing aiming their weapons at him. The Major reached down to get his sidearm, which was no longer there; the Major was hoping to get at least one of them before they finished him off. The Taliban fighters started to jump down the hill, in kangaroo hops; they were on top of the Major in a few bounds. They dragged the Major to the top of the hill.

The Major looked down at the bullet ridden corpses of his comrades, some of the Taliban still firing into their lifeless bodies. Two of the Taliban fighters held the Major upright, another went behind him, grabbing him by the hair and pulling his head back. The Major winced in pain, looking straight forward into the eyes of General Akhamid Shali. Shali starred back and smiled, as he pulled the knife from its sheaf in his waistband, lifting it up into the air so the Major could see it. Major Chris Bennet just smiled back at Shali. This enraged the General immensely, and he wanted the Major to beg for his life. The Major knew exactly what he was doing, he wanted it to be over quick.

Shali holding the twelve inch-long, slightly curved blade in his right hand, just under the Major's chin, then moved it slowly to his right shoulder; the Major grinned, not taking his gaze from Shali, looking him straight in his eyes. The knife shot forward as if just been released by the grip of a powerful spring, showering Shali and the two Taliban fighters that were holding the Major up, with the Major's blood, as the knife sliced through the Major's throat. The Major's head fell back over, and nearly came off completely in the hand of the Taliban fighter, who held the Major by the hair. The Major's body slumped to the ground as the men's grip on him was released. The Taliban fighters began screaming and shouting, firing their guns in the air, some of them firing into the body of the Major, making it shudder violently.

"Enough, enough," Shali shouted. The celebration stopped almost immediately. "Get everything," Shali said. "We must get away from here quickly, grab whatever will be of use to us and leave. The Americans will be here soon."

"General, General," Alama said, "look!" Alama was holding the powerful Long Range Super Rifle.

CHAPTER 6

"This is good," Shali said. "Make sure you get all the ammunitions that go with this weapon, check the vehicle, and now move – time is of the essence. Hurry, hurry. We will split up: Alama I will meet you at the hideout tonight."

The Taliban fighters gathered up as much of the Americans' kit as they could carry, and scattered in different directions, two of the men following Shali, as he ran off towards the west.

It was daylight now; Shali knew what would happen if they did not put distance between them and the Americans. The Taliban knew the area well, all the places of cover. Shali was running hard, he wanted to at least get to the mountains; he could hold up until nightfall, he would be able to move around much easier in the dark. The three men had been running for about 15 minutes when Shali stopped.

"Listen," he said.

"General," one of the men said.

"Shee," Shali said, turning around 360 degrees – there was the faint sound of a helicopter's rotors chopping through the air. There was nothing of any substantial cover for at least a mile in either direction; there was the odd hill or two, a few bushes, possible cover from being seen at ground level, but a different matter from up above.

Shali said: "Now quickly," and he fell to his knees and began to dig the ground with his knife. The two other men knew at once what Shali was doing, and began to dig as well. The three men dug a shallow trench about seven foot long, two foot wide, Shali opened the top of his knife handle, took out a small piece of pipe, put it in his mouth, then lay down in the shallow trench, pulling his head cover over his face, and put his hands on his chest.

The two men started to cover him in earth, placing a couple

of stones on top of the mound; they both looked up to the skies, hands clasped together and said a short prayer, then ran off in opposite directions. It took only a few minutes for the sun to change the discoloured dug up earth to the same shade as the rest of the earth. From high up in the air it would be difficult to pick out the mound.

    Shali lay motionless, straining his ears to try and pick up the sound of the helicopter, through the few inches of dirt that covered his head. Nothing, he heard nothing for what seemed like ages, then the constant thud of the helicopter rotor blades chopping through the air. The noise got louder and louder, the helicopter was flying very low. But as soon as the helicopter came it left, the sound getting fainter as it flew away. It had worked, Shali said to himself, I have fooled the Americans. Shali was pleased with himself and even more pleased that he had avenged his brother's death by killing the Americans.

CHAPTER 7

Mohamed Ali Bin stood at the entrance to the stronghold cave hideout, in the Afghanistan mountains. This was the headman, the leader of the Taliban in the Northern region, one of the Western world's most wanted men. For years he had wreaked havoc on the towns and cities of Europe, and the capitals of democracies. Ali Bin was feeling very proud; all the men that had gone out on the raid with General Akhamid Shali had returned; he now waited for Shali to return. There had been no reports of anyone being arrested by the Americans, so Ali Bin was confident that his favourite General would be turning up soon.

Alama came out from the cave and stood alongside Ali Bin, looking up to the mountains on either side to check that the lookouts were at their posts. A wave from each lookout made Alama feel much better.

"General Shali will be back soon, my Lord," Alama said to Ali Bin.

"Of that I am very certain," replied Ali Bin. "It will take more than what the Americans can throw at my Shali to stop him. But now Alama we need to be careful: the Americans will be looking for reprisals for the death of their soldiers. Go and make sure the lookouts are doubled up."

Just as Alama was about to move off, a lookout waved his hands above his head, then the other lookout did the same.

"It's Shali," Alama said, "he is back, my Lord."

"Forgive me my Lord," Shali said, taking the hand of Ali Bin and kissing his knuckles. "I had no time to inform you, my Lord, we had to act quickly."

"No need for forgiveness, you acted like a true General,

avenging our dead brothers by killing the Americans, and the prize of the American gun you have brought to us makes for a glorious day."

"What of Balli, my lord, is he here? I will take great delight in stripping the skin from his body."

"Balli is safe under guard, we have plans for Balli, General, leave him to me."

"But my Lord, he must pay for his treachery," Shali protested.

"Come now General Shali, tell me of your great conquest while we drink to the killing of the Americans. And then we can discuss your plan for the British. Come my hero," Ali Bin said putting his arm around Shali's shoulder, and leading him into the cave.

"Sit Shali," Ali Bin said pointing to the cushions on the carpet; there were several Taliban leaders standing, waiting for Shali to sit. Shali sat down crossed legged, pulling his ankles tightly under his thighs.

"I have news," said Ali Bin. "My sources tell me that the British have a celebrity in their ranks."

"What do you mean, my Lord?" Shali asked.

"It may be possible that one of the British officers is the son of a Lord or a Politician."

"How will we get to him?" Shali said, "He will be more protected than usual."

"The British are to treat him as any other officer, and he will be leading the patrol that you attack, my General," Ali Bin said.

"This is great news indeed, Lord."

"Drink Shali," Ali Bin said, offering a cup of tea.

"This is a good day," Shali proclaimed, "first the death of the Americans and now this news. The only thing that sours it was

CHAPTER 7

the death of our brothers. Balli and all his family will pay for that treachery, you will see my Lord."

"No General Shali," said one of the men sitting opposite him, "Balli has agreed to redeem himself, for the sake of his family, we have persuaded him to perform a task for the cause."

"Tell me more," Shali said.

CHAPTER 8

North East England, two weeks later, Clare Carhill walked up the path to Brian Taylor's house. She knocked on the door and Brian opened it.

"Hi Clare, come on in," Brian said.

"No Brian I won't come in, I just called to tell you the news: Trevor has opened his eyes today; I got a call from the hospital, I am going down to the hospital to see him."

"I will get my coat and come with you if that is all right," Brian said.

"Of course it will be all right, I will be happy with the company."

Clare went and sat in her car waiting for Brian. "I have a good feeling about this, Brian," Clare said as she drove the car. "What with Trevor breathing on his own now without the aid of a machine, and now he has opened his eyes."

Brian asked: "Will he be able to talk to us, Clare?"

"I don't think so," Clare replied, "but soon, Brian, soon."

Clare put her hand on Brian's hand, gave a gentle squeeze and said: "Trevor loves you very much Brian."

Clare and Brian walked straight passed the receptionist's office in the Royal Victoria Infirmary. They went to Trevor's room, and as they reached the room, Dr Mayo was just coming from the room. "Oh Miss Carhill, how are you?"

"I am fine, Dr Mayo," Clare said. "Good news about my brother opening his eyes."

"Very good news," the Doctor said, "but don't go in yet, Miss Carhill as the nurses are busy changing his head bandages. I have been checking to see how his wounds are healing."

CHAPTER 8

"And are they healing, Doctor?"

"They are healing extremely well, in fact better than we thought. The rate at which he is getting better has got us all amazed, it's astounding."

The nurses came out of Trevor's room.

"Is it all right, nurse?" the Doctor asked.

"Yes they can go in."

Brian and Clare went straight into the room and sat either side of Trevor's bed. Clare took hold of Trevor's hand.

"Hello Trevor," she said, "I have got Brian here to see you."

Trevor's eyes were closed, but there was plenty of movement under the eyelids. "That's called REM," Clare said to Brian, "Rapid Eye Movement."

A knock on the door and Dr Luke came into the room, "Hello Clare, hello Mr Taylor, how are you both today?"

"We are very well, thank you," Clare answered for both of them.

"Trevor is doing remarkably well," Dr Luke said to Clare, "he is no longer in a coma."

"Will he open his eyes again?" Brian asked.

"He may well do if you talk to him, but he is heavily sedated."

"I want to be here," Clare said to the Doctor, "in case he opens his eyes again, someone should be here he knows."

Doctor Luke said: "I can organise it so you can be here any time, night or day."

Clare said, "I would love that, if you would arrange it please. I must go to work – the bills have to be paid – but if I could come in any time, great."

Brian said: "I will be able to come in any time as my doctor has declared me unfit for work – he says I am suffering from depression."

"That's good," Clare said, "I mean that you can come to see Trevor any time, not that you are suffering from depression!" Brian smiled.

"I must go now," Dr Luke said, "but if there is anything you want to ask you just give me a call Clare."

Clare spoke to Brian once Dr Luke had left: "We must keep talking to him, I will read to him.He likes Harold Robbins."

Brian said, "I can't read that well, but I will watch all the wildlife programmes on the television and tell Trevor about them, he likes the wild life programmes."

"You're very sweet," Clare said.

CHAPTER 9

Camp Steadfast British Army Garrison. Maira District, 130 miles from Helmand Province in Afghanistan.

Major Brent sat in his office looking over a map of East Maira, a single knock on the door of his office. The door opened and a voice said: "Colonel Baldwin on the phone sir."

"Thank you." The Major put the telephone to his ear, "Yes Colonel, what can I do for you sir?"

"You know why I am calling, Major, how is it going down there?" the Colonel said.

"Everything is fine, sir. Captain Weinwright and his troop leave on patrol in a few hours."

"I can't help worrying about this; the suits in Whitehall should have sent him to the Falklands or kept him back home," the Colonel said.

"He has powerful friends; he obviously has pulled strings to get this posting," the Major said.

"I can tell you Major I tried everything I could to get the Captain stopped from coming here; they know it is bad enough over here as it is."

"We can only do as we are told, sir," the Major replied.

"If the Taliban get the slightest inkling that Captian Weinwright is related to the Queen, the shit will hit the fan all right," the Colonel said. "They will be on him like flies on a cow's arse, Major."

"Captain Weinwright is going to do his tour of duty here without anyone knowing his background," the Major insisted.

"I hope you're right Major, because we have enough trouble

on our plates without attracting anymore. Intel from the Americans puts a build up of activity in your area Major, and that is not going to help your situation down there."

"I have put Captain Weinwright with Captain Stoko's Platoon sir."

"That's another thing," the Colonel said, "a seasoned officer pushed to one side so some toffee nosed upstart can get his."

"Colonel," the Major butted in, "it will be fine sir, the men are all seasoned and battled hardened. The Platoon will look after itself – they have got through more scrapes than any other in the whole British Army." The Major went on, "Sergeant Parker has got more skirmishes and full on battles under his belt than any other Sergeant since we came here; he will keep Captain Weinwright out of trouble."

"Even so," said the Colonel, "I want you to get onto our boys in blue and tell them to keep an eye on the patrol when it is out."

"If it will make you happy sir I will talk to the RAF."

"Very well Major, keep me up to date," said the Colonel.

"Yes sir and thank you," the Major said putting the telephone down.

"Good morning Sergeant," the Major said. The Sergeant was overseeing the loading of equipment onto a Sarasin truck.

"Good morning Major," the Sergeant gave a salute.

"Where is Captain Weinwright?" the Major asked the Sergeant.

"He is with the Warrant officer, Sir, trying to wangle us more kit I hope!"

"How is he fitting in?" the Major asked the Sergeant – if anyone should know it would be Sergeant David Parker of the first Battalion the Rifles: twenty years' service in Her Majesty's

CHAPTER 9

Armed Forces and tours in Iraq and seven tours in Afghanistan. Sergeant Parker was especially manoeuvred into Captain Weinwright's Platoon to look out for the Captain until he got some experience under his belt.

"Well Major, I think the Captain is going to be all right, a bit green, but weren't we all at one time, you cannot fault his prowess and leaderhip skills. He is mad keen to get out there sir and do his job, I know that," the Sergeant said.

"Will he hold if it got bad?" the Major asked, "Do you think he would buckle under pressure Sergeant?"

"I have no doubt the Captain will stand his ground in any situation or circumstances," the Sergeant replied, "I am a good judge of character: I have served with a lot of Captains in my time, and if you would beg my pardon sir I do know what to expect from my Captains. And frankly sir I don't like where the conversation is leading to."

"No, you don't understand Sergeant, I am concerned that the Captain is fitting in with the squad," the Major said.

"I think the Captain is going to do us proud," the Sergeant said. "If I may Major, what's the story – Captain Weinwright coming here out of the blue, and then Captain Stoko being transferred?"

"No great mystery, Sergeant; Captain Stoko was needed elsewhere and Captain Weinwright filled the void."

"If you don't mind me saying so sir that is full of shit and you know that," the Sergeant said.

"Well that's all you're getting Sergeant," the Major said, and quickly added: "Are the men taking to him?"

"The men will take to who I tell them to, Major," the Sergeant barked out, feeling the Major was suggesting a lack of discipline and respect.

"Easy Sergeant, I am only asking."

"Well yes sir, sorry sir," the Sergeant said.

"Just keep an eye on things out there, Sergeant, will you?"

"You can depend on me sir," the Sergeant said, saluting the Major.

The Major left to go look for Captain Weinwright. The Sergeant turned to the soldiers loading the Sarasin truck and shouted: "Come on, come on you lot – we leave in a couple of hours."

Major Brent went straight over to the warrant officer's office; Captain Weinwright was just coming out.

"Good morning," the Major said to the Captain.

"Good morning Major," the Captain said, with a look that said it all. Captain Weinwright knew the Major had been speaking to Colonel Baldwin, and he knew that the Colonel did not approve of him being here. But this is where he wanted to be; he was sorry Captain Stoko had to be removed to make this post available; he was determined to do his duty as a soldier and gain the trust and respect of Captain Stoko's men in the process. He wanted to prove to everyone that he was capable of leading the Platoon, he wanted for nothing more than to get out there and show them, then maybe he would be left alone to do his job.

"I am not here to lecture," the Major said.

"Are you not?" the Captain replied.

"Come on – it is hard for me as well, being stuck in the middle," the Major said.

"I know that the Colonel tried his best to stop me getting this posting, Major, and I think you are in agreement with him on that."

"All I wanted to do was wish you good luck on your first Patrol."

CHAPTER 9

"Did you not do that at the briefing this morning, so why again Major?" the Captain said.

"Colonel Baldwin rang me; he is worried, and rightly so: if word gets out who you are..."

"Who am I, Major?" the Captain interrupted. "I am a Captain in the British Army – nothing else. And for anyone finding out who I am related to, it is conversations like this in the open that will let it spill out. Why can't you all just forget and let me get on with my job?"

"OK," the Major said, "I know this is going to happen whether we like it or not, so we will keep it strictly professional."

"Thank you," said the Captain, saluting the Major.

"Have we got everything?" the Captain said to Sergeant Parker.

"If we have not sir someone will pay dearly," Sergeant Parker replied.

"I just need to get my kit and we will be off, Sergeant," the Captain said.

"Very well sir, I will move the men up," the Sergeant said. The Captain went to sort his kit out and just as he was coming back from his billet, a voice said, "Don't forget this Captain." Major Brent passed him a flak jacket. As the Captain was walking back to the vehicles he thought to himself, I am not afraid of fighting; he was afraid of not doing the right thing – he knew he would not panic under fire; it was all about making the right decisions at the time.

"I will travel up front with you for a while if that is all right sir," the Sergeant said to the Captain when he returned.

"That will be fine Sergeant," the Captain replied.

There were five Sarasin tucks in the convoy; the squaddies called them armoured pigs. The Patrol was to be out 72 hours;

their task was to locate the Taliban and engage. The five vehicles waited, their engines running. Captain Weinwright got in the rear of the first vehicle; there were seven soldiers already in the back of the Sarasin and three up front. Sergeant Parker sat up front, the legs of the machine gunner between him and the driver; the machine gunner stood looking out the turret. All the other vehicles had the same amount of soldiers in them, three up front and eight in the back. The Captain sat down next to the radio man.

"Let's go," the Captain said to the Sergeant.

The Captain turned to the radio man and said, "Let the skies know we are leaving, Corporal."

"Yes sir," the Corporal said. "Dog Walk to Cloud Eyes, come in Cloud Eyes."

Cloud Eyes came back over the radio speaker. "Proceeding east on Patrol from Bastion, five vehicles in convoy, be advised, Dog Walk out."

"Consider us advised, have a nice day, Cloud Eyes out."

Captain Weinwright then spoke to Sergeant Parker, "When we get out about twenty miles Sergeant, get off the track. We will continue over rough ground – that will keep these boys awake."

"Yes sir," said the Sergeant.

CHAPTER 10

Mount Batten American Army Base, West Afghanistan, set back off the village of Taruffi.

The Afghans that lived in Taruffi were not loyal to the Americans – they tolerated them. The base was large compared to the British Garrison at Miara. Some 6000 marines were assigned there – a hub of military activity. Helicopters taking off and landing on a regular basis, vehicles coming and going, soldiers marching to and fro. The base was well fortified: a concrete wall surrounded it, lookout posts every twenty yards, Stars and Stripes flags flew, groups of soldiers here, there and everywhere, a walled city in fact.

A motorcycle drives through the village; there are two men on the motorcycle, and it does not go very fast, the rider trying to keep the dust down as it passes through the village heading towards the Army Base. The motorcycle still travelling very slowly pulls up some fifty yards from the Base. The pillion passenger dismounts rather awkwardly, he walks very gingerly towards the Base. The entrance to the Base is set back from five checkpoints, the first is about a hundred yards from the main entrance. The checkpoints are staggered twenty yards apart; you have to pass through all five before you can enter the Base. The man trying hard to keep upright walks towards the first checkpoint. There are six soldiers standing in the road, all eagerly watching the man approach; there are machine gun positions either side of the road behind sand bagged walls. The road barrier was down; another two soldiers stood behind the barrier. At the right of the road barrier was a pedestrian walk way which also had a barrier across it; just in from the barrier was a small hut that was protected by sand bags. All five checkpoints had similar defences.

The man shuffles towards the first pedestrian checkpoint. A soldier moves out of the hut.

"Stay where you are, don't come any closer," the soldier shouts at the man.

Other soldiers have their weapons trained on the man by now. The man stands, swaying from side to side but trying to stand still. The man looks very weak and disorientated; his clothes are nothing but rags.

"Raise your hands," the soldier says, speaking Afghan to the man, as two other soldiers move in closer. "Raise your hands," the soldier says again.

He lifts his arms as if he were lifting a heavy weight. "Keep your hands open wide," the soldier says.

"Jesus," one of the soldiers says as he moves closer to search the man. "What has happened to you?" the soldier asks as he reaches out a hand to open the coat the man is wearing. The face of the man is badly bruised and several cuts are visible to the head; his eyes are glossy – he looks as if he is in a drug induced stupor.

"I am Shaleem Balli. I have come to see Colonel Vergil Pain; he knows of me, he will see Shaleem Balli," the man says.

Balli staggers a little forward, the soldiers are nervous, they cock their weapons when Balli moves unexpectedly. The soldier moves closer and starts to search Balli; he gently pats down the torso; Balli winces with every touch the soldier makes on his body. The soldier notices that Balli's arms and legs are badly cut and bruised. The soldier presses harder with his hands now, checking there are no unusual shapes under Balli's clothes. Balli

CHAPTER 10

moans out; the soldier stands back away from him saying, "Are you all right man."

The soldier moves in closer again, Balli staggers, another soldier says "if this fucker moves again I will blow his fucking head off". The searching soldier opens the clothing of Balli revealing his chest. "Fuck me," the soldier says as he sees the extent of the wounds on the body of Balli. There are several cuts on his chest and stomach, one cut running from the throat to the groin, and it was stitched up plainly by an amateur. The soldier turns to his fellow soldiers and says: "Someone has let loose on this guy with a machete."

"I must see Colonel Vergil Pain. I am Shaleem Balli – he is expecting me."

The soldier shouts back at the sentry hut where a soldier was aiming his weapon, ready to drop Balli at the drop of hat. "Bring a chair, will you, before this poor sod falls down." A chair is brought out.

"Sit him down," the soldier says while walking back towards the sentry hut.

"Watch him," the soldier who brought the chair says as he looks at Balli's injuries.

"This guy is not capable of hurting anyone."

In the sentry hut the soldier gets on the telephone, "I have an Afghan here who wants to see Colonel Pain. His name is Shaleem Balli. He says the Colonel knows him and it is important that they speak. The man's in a bad way."

"OK Corporal," the voice says on the other end of the telephone, "I will get back to you in a couple."

The Corporal hangs up saying to himself, that's if he lasts that long. The Corporal comes out of the hut with a drink of water for Balli. "What happened to you?" the Corporal asks, as he holds the drink to Balli's mouth.

"No time," Balli says, "I must speak to Colonel Vergil Pain. It is urgent."

Back at the village the people had noticed the soldier bring the chair out for Balli. They were starting to gather into groups wondering what was going on, their curiosity getting the better of them. Normally they would just ignore the Base.

Even further away other eyes were eager to see what was happening. Up in the hills Akhamid Shali looked through field glasses that only five days ago he had taken from the Americans' Delta Force Unit.

"Are they taking him in General?" Alama said to Shali, just as the motorcycle that dropped Balli off at the American Base drove up.

"Look for yourself," Shali replied rather angrily, giving Alama the binoculars. Shali was disappointed at something, Alama could tell. Shali walked back towards the motorcycle.

"What do you think?" Shali said to the man on the motorcycle.

"I don't know General, maybe."

Alama waved to Shali to come back to the vantage spot on the hill. The telephone in the sentry hut rang; the Corporal went to answer it. "Yes," the Corporal said on the telephone.

Colonel Pain said: "What's this you have at the checkpoint?"

"There is an Afghan here sir who says you know him and you will see him, he's pretty well beaten up; someone has had a right go at him sir," the Corporal said. "His name is Shaleem Balli he says, he can hardly walk sir. What we shall do with him sir, he's stirring up some interest from the village?"

"Just one moment, let me think," the Colonel said. "Bring him to checkpoint three and I will come out."

CHAPTER 10

"He is going to need medical attention sir," the Corporal said.

"Leave it with me," and the telephone went dead.

"What is it Alama?" Shali said.

"They've taken him in," Alama said as he peered through the binoculars.

"Here," Shali said, holding his hand out for the binoculars. Shali watched while two of the soldiers helped Balli further in to the checkpoint entrance, the road barriers were lifted at the Base entrance and a vehicle began to drive out. The vehicle had a red cross on the roof.

"This is good," Shali said. The vehicle stopped at the next checkpoint and four men got out. Shali watched as they made their way up the pedestrian walkway of the checkpoint. "No, not good," he said as he sees the soldier carry the chair to the next checkpoint and sits Balli down again.

"Sit him there," the Corporal said to the two soldiers, as he made his way to meet the four men that got out of the vehicle.

"Has he been checked?" Colonel Pain asked as he approached with his aids and a doctor.

"Yes sir, he is clean, but in a bad way sir."

The Colonel moved a little closer straining his eyes to make sure it was all right before he moved even closer. The Colonel hesitated. "Is this man who brought the information that the Taliban were going to plant IEDs?" The Colonel was nervous; he turned to the doctor and said: "You wait here."

Slowly moving forward the Colonel spoke out: "Balli is that you?" Balli pushed himself unsteadily to his feet, moving his arms out to one side only a foot from his body, hands open wide. Balli opened his mouth to speak but no words came out.

"Balli," the Colonel said as he edged further forward to get a clear look, "it is you, what the hell have they done to you?"

The Colonel took another step closer; he looked at Balli trying to say something. The tears began to flow down Bali's cheeks; Balli slowly mouthed the word 'sorry' and began to shake from head to foot. The Colonel knows now he is in trouble; he begins to swing round to make a run for his life, "down," he shouts as he turns.

Shali looks through the binoculars. "Make the call Alama, make the call," Shali shouts, and he presses on a number on a mobile phone. Balli explodes in a mass of flame, blood, flesh and fragments of bone blasting outward and engulfing the Colonel and the soldiers closest to Balli. Along with the blast came shards of nails and ball bearings flying into the doctor and the aids, sending them scattering away like paper in the wind. The Taliban had packed as much deadly cocktail of nails, nuts, bolts and ball bearings with the explosives they could cram and conceal in the stomach of Balli. The villagers cheer as the bomb goes off; they know that the Taliban is watching. Alama throws his arms up in the air and jumps with joy.

"A small price to pay for betraying his brothers," Shali says. Then he looks at Alama with an evil eye. Alama stops his joyful dance at once. Shali was not satisfied with a few Americans getting blown up; he wanted Balli to get inside the Base before detonating the bomb – even if it had not killed many Americans he would have got right into the heart of the American stronghold. Shali turned and walked to the motorcycle and said then to the rider: "Kill the family of Balli; this will be a warning to any other traitors."

By now Alama was at Shali's side. "Come Alama," Shali said, "let us see if we cannot prepare the same fate for the British."

CHAPTER 11

"Can I change the point men, sir?" Sergeant Parker said to Captain Weinwright.

"Yes Sergeant, you may."

The Sergeant waved a few directional signals to the men either side of him; they began to disperse in all directions. The Patrol was on foot now, the vehicles some ten miles further back.

"The radio operator reporting Cloud Eyes wanting a status sir."

"What, again?" said Sergeant Parker.

"Those fly boys are worried about us – that is the third time today, Major Brent more like," Captain Weinwright said.

The radio crackled, the Corporal listened intensely. "That was Base, sir, the Americans have had a suicide bomber at Mount Batten Base; several killed sir, even a Special Forces Colonel."

"How the hell did they get in that place, it is like Fort Knox?" said Sergeant Parker.

"Don't know, Serge," said the Corporal, "that's all I got."

"That's the second big hit the Americans have taken in a week," said Captain Weinwright.

"Yes," said Sergeant Parker, "that Special Ops crew the other day."

"We are only thirty miles from the American perimeters," said the Captain. "Corporal let the Americans know we are here; there will be plenty of itchy fingers about."

"They already know we are here sir."

"Well let them know again, and when you are on with it let Base know again. "Sergeant, just a few more miles and then we will make camp," the Captain said as he went marching on through the barren Afghan terrain waving his hand for the Patrol to move onward. "We will bring the vehicles up now Sergeant; by the time they reach us we will have got to that raised ground area up ahead."

"Get a move on Alama," Shali said as they set off across the hills; they had only gone a few hundred yards when Shali's mobile rang. Shali listened for a while and said, "Yes, my Lord, it went well, but now we go for a greater victory against the British. All our men are ready and waiting, my Lord, they will bring glory on us. There will be martyrs among my men this day." Shali put the mobile phone away. "Not much further now, Alama, just over the ridge."

The two men got to the top of the hill; down on the road were waiting four men on motorcycles. Shali and Alama ran down to where the motorcycles were waiting; saying nothing they just mounted the back of two motorcycles and sped off.

"Good as any place," Sergeant Parker said.

"It looks fine to me," Captain Weinwright said. "Secure the perimeters, bring the vehicles up Corporal. And let those that need to know, know where we are."

"I need a drink," the Captain said, sitting down on his hunkers. Sergeant Parker passed him a water bottle.

"I will take a look around, sir, make sure we can sleep tight tonight," Sergeant Parker said.

"OK Sergeant, make sure the men are all right as well, will you?" said Captain Weinwright.

Shali and the other motorcycle riders came to a halt at a fork in the dirt road, just at the bottom of the rise before the mountains. There was a trodden footpath that led up the mountains. Shali dismounted and walked to the path. Shali

CHAPTER 11

looked up the path; some half a mile away a line of figures were coming down the mountains. These were the Taliban fighters, this was Shali's army. There were fifty or sixty men in the troop, snaking their way down the path. Every one of them carried a weapon of some sort, they either shouldered weapons or carried weapons in their arms. As they got closer you could see the firepower they had with them. Mortars and RPGs were strapped to the men's backs and all the men had small arms. The sound of a motor engine came from the right hand fork in the road.

Shali and the others looked down the road: a truck and more motorcycles come into view as a cloud of dust from the vehicles blows behind them. About a dozen more motorcycles and a clapped out old truck came to halt alongside Shali and his men.

Shali turned to look at the last of the men gathering around him; he turned back to Alama and said: "Tomorrow we will bring great glory on ourselves. We will kill many British."

The men start to gather closer as they pour onto the road from the path. Shali lifted his hands above his head; he slowly turned around three times looking at his army before he spoke. "Tomorrow, my brothers, we will show the British the teeth of the Taliban, we will make them pay with their blood for the invasion of our lands. Let us give thanks for the opportunity to avenge our brothers." Shali fell down on his knees, lowered his head and hands to the ground and prayed; every Taliban fighter does the same.

After a few minutes Shali rose to his feet and so do his army of men. Shali called out: "Abdul!"

A man approached Shali. "Shali, my General," he said.

"Go Abdul, prepare my men– make ready."

"Yes my General Shali." Abdul lifted his hand above his head and then pointed along the left fork in the road, motorcycles started their engines and began to move off. Some of the men that are on foot clamber onto the truck, they cling on werever they can. Abdul gets into the truck. It begins to drive off; the men that could not get on the truck or motorcycles follow on foot.

All the Taliban fighters had left to make ready for battle, only Shali, Alama and two men remained at the road junction. Shali watched as the army of men got further and further away.

"Now let us go," Shali said as he mounted the back of a motorcycle; Alama rode pillion on the other motorcycle. Both motorcycles' engines started up and they were away. They headed up the mountain footpath; they only rode so far up the mountain path then went to their right along a path that seemed to skirt around the mountains.

"My Lord," Shali said as he entered the entrance to the cave of the Taliban Stronghold.

"Ah Shali, my General," Ali Bin said as he offered his hand to Shali. Shali got down on one knee and kissed Ali Bin on the back of the hand. "The Americans did not appreciate the present that Balli brought them from us," Ali Bin said.

"This is true, my Lord, they all fear for what comes next, they run around like headless chickens looking to stop our onslaughts. We will drive them out of our country, or butcher them all," Shali said, then added: "And now the British will feel the wrath of the Taliban, my Lord. What do we know of the British convoy my Lord?"

"Our men are watching their every move. The new officer takes his vehicles off road in staggered formation," said Ali Bin.

"Multiple targets instead of one line of targets," Shali replied. "He goes on foot; leaving the vehicles behind, the soldiers move some five miles ahead, he then calls the vehicles forward. This

CHAPTER 11

means we may only get the foot patrol."

"Still it will be a glorious day, we will rejoice in your victory," Ali Bin said.

They head towards the Rolling Hills of Haraeffa.

"This is where they meet their God," Shali said. "Now my Lord, I must go and make ready – we have many miles to cross."

Ali Bin walks with Shali as they leave the cave, Alama and the two motorcyclists are waiting outside, another man is with them.

"Shali, this is Hareem Sadina, he is the one that brought us the news of Balli's treachery."

"I know of this man, my Lord, he is only good for bringing and fetching," Shali said.

"I want you to take him with you on the raid, as a reward for his loyalty," Ali Bin said.

"This man talks too much, my Lord, I have already had to beat him."

"It would please me if you took him," Ali Bin was insistent.

Shali did not want this man with him – he was a fool – but agreed to take him. "So be it my Lord," Shali said.

Hareem moved forward and bowed saying, "Thank you, my Lord."

Shali bowed his head taking the hand of Ali Bin and kissing his knuckle. Shali walked to Alama and said: "You look after that oaf; keep him away from me, tell him if he gives me any cause for concern I will slit his throat."

"Yes my General," Alama said as he had to squeeze tight up on the motorcycle to make room for Hareem to get on. Shali mounted onto the back of the other motorcycle, telling the driver to go. The two motorcycles sped off towards the west.

CHAPTER 12

"Good morning Sir," Sergeant Parker said as he walked up behind the Captain, who was looking out towards the direction they would be heading. The sergeant came and stood by the Captain's side and stood looking in the same direction.

"Ah, good morning, Sergeant," the Captain said.

"The Rolling Hills, sir," Sergeant Parker gestured up ahead. The Captain looked at him puzzled. "The Rolling Hills of Haraeffa," the Sergeant said again.

"Ah yes," the Captain said.

"Lots of cover there sir, we will have to be careful."

"Do you think we will encounter any Taliban?" the Captain asked.

"I don't know sir – you could go out on patrol ten times and see nothing, you could go out three times on the trot and have had a fire fight, but you have to think that every time you come out you will make contact with the enemy sir."

"Have you had contact with the enemy, Sergeant?" Captain Weinwright asked.

"Many times sir, but they were mainly skirmishes, shots from a distance, a few mortar shells falling close, and then a few times some very close and near misses. You never let your guard down sir. We will go and see if we can find Taliban sir, but it is most likely they will find us, and really sir that is what we are doing – we are inviting the enemy to come to us. They know we are here and they will pick their moment. We just have to be ready," the sergeant said.

"Have all the men in the Platoon had experience fighting the Taliban?" the Captain asked.

CHAPTER 12

"Every Jack one of them sir," said the Sergeant.

"They seem a good crew."

"Every one of them knows what to expect out there, and every one of them will do their duty, sir," Sergeant Parker said. "What are our orders sir?"

"Get the point guards in sergeant, they can stay back with the vehicles –we'll move off on foot. Corporal Harper?"

"Yes sir," the Corporal replied.

"Radio base: tell them we are moving off on foot, west the Rolling Hills."

Sergeant Parker went round barking orders; soldiers began getting ready to move. Backpacks were lifted by one soldier, while another slid his arms into the carrying straps. Weapons had already been checked and cleaned but still a final check before the soldiers gripped them in the ready stance, prepared to fire.

"All ready sir," Sergeant Parker reported.

"We will move off in two columns of eighteen men, fifty yards apart, you take the North side and I will take the South side, each column keep in view of the other at all times, we head towards west," the Captain said.

"Cloud Eyes sir, asking status," said the Corporal.

"Advise them on our position, Corporal," said the Captain. "Let's go Sergeant."

The two columns of men moved off heading west across what was mainly uneven ground. There was not much vegetation – just the odd tree now and then. The land looked like waves on the sea. As they moved off, the men left behind with the vehicles began to pack up camp and wait for the call to move up. The soldiers that had been on guard duty would get their head down for a well earned sleep.

The columns yomped on, each and every man fully alert. The Captain looked over the men as they moved forward. Every man looking for danger, all the men were ready, to just spring into action the moment anything happened. "The Sergeant was right," Captain thought, "these men are on the ball."

Now and again the Captain would change formation; sometimes he would have the men move into four columns, and then the patrol walking abreast. It was a clear day: you could see for miles in either direction. The hills ahead got wider as the troop got closer to them.

"Cloud Eyes, sir, status and local."

"OK Harper," the Captain said, "send it."

Sergeant Parker came over alongside the Captain. "Yes I know, Sergeant," the Captain said before the Sergeant could speak. The Terrain was getting a bit hillier with dips and troughs; there were a lot more places for a sniper to hide. "We will move back to the four column formation, Sergeant. Nine men in each – keep in constant sight of each other."

"Yes sir," Sergeant Parker said. The Sergeant did not have to give the order: the men were already moving into formation.

This kind of terrain went on for a couple of miles. The Captain kept the men in the same formation until they got closer to their objective; then he changed the formation back to walking abreast as the troop were approaching the foot of the much higher Rolling Hills. The Captain stopped the troop; there was about four hundred yards of clear ground ahead before the beginning of the incline of the hills.

"Not much cover at all until you get into the hills, Sergeant," the Captain said, "what do you think?"

"I don't know sir, it looks all right," the Sergeant said, scanning the horizon with his field glasses.

CHAPTER 12

"We will rest here for fifteen minutes before we cross the open ground. Harper, bring the vehicles up, they can camp at this spot while we move into the hills."

Shali looked over the positions his men had taken: there groups of three and four men lying in wait on hill tops and in shallows, some of the men in the small valleys rigging up mortar launchers in the ground, others setting up heavy machine gun nests. Shali moved forward to get a better view from the top of one of the higher hills. Shali crawled to the brow of the hill just so he could see over the crest. Shali was now looking down on the British Patrol. About six hundred yards away, four groups of soldiers sat taking drinks and at the same time looking around, very aware of their situation. Alama crawled up alongside Shali to take a look for himself.

"They rest before they die," Shali said to Alama. "We will wait until they are at the bottom of the hills, one hundred yards away then we will attack. Go Alama, make ready to slaughter the British dogs."

Shali stayed on the hill that he observed the patrol from. "This will do," he thought, "I will give the order to attack from here and watch the British dogs die."

"OK Sergeant, let's get the men moving," the Captain said. All the men began getting to their feet.

"Now watch out boys," the Sergeant said, "there could be something out there that might sting, and I don't mean scorpions; just be aware it is an ideal ambush spot – I know I would choose it."

"Four columns again, Sergeant," the Captain said, walking on in front of the men. The Captain knew they were exposed in the clear ground, but only a few hundred yards until cover. His men had the same thoughts as they moved forward, everyone looking for the nearest bolt hole to dive onto at the first sign of trouble.

"Come on," the Sergeant said, "move quickly – we don't want to be out here any longer than is necessary." Just some three hundred yards or so to go before they got to cover and relative safety.

"Dog Walk, Dog Walk, Cloud Eyes calling," came over the radio. Corporal Harper answered the Radio: "Go ahead Cloud Eyes, Dog Walk here, what is your…" and then suddenly a burst of automatic gunfire came from right of the hills up ahead; just one weapon was firing. "Take cover," the cries went out from the Captain, the Sergeant and at least half a dozen of the men.

"Too soon, too soon," Shali said to himself, looking over to his left where the firing was. He focused on Hareem, who was just firing his weapon at will in the direction of the British.

"Imbecile!" Shali shouted up to the heavens. "Fire, fire!" Shali shouted. At once all of the Taliban fighters began to open up on the British, who by now were taking cover as best they could. Captain Weinwright dived to the ground, Corporal Harper the radio operator alongside him. The rest of the soldiers scattered to find cover.

"Are you there Dog Walk?" came over the radio as mortar shells exploded harmlessly about a hundred yards in front of the soldiers. The mortars had been set for this distance ready for the ambush. But that had been pre-empted by Hareem who was so afraid of the battle to come that in his panic began shooting too soon. This gave the British time to take cover and dig in where they could.

Dog Walk came again over the radio: "Contact, said Harper, "contact, we have contact Cloud Eyes." Bullets now spat up the

CHAPTER 12

dirt around them as they struck the ground.

"Confirm Dog Walk," came over the radio.

Harper was more composed now: "Cloud Eyes we have contact, engaged with the enemy."

"Copy that, Dog Walk, I am only thirty miles to your south east, will be there in seconds, Dog Walk."

Sergeant Parker peeped over the small bit of mound he was trying to hide behind; there was intense fire from every position up ahead of them and from every hill. Shells starting to explode pretty close now, the Taliban fighters starting to find their range.

"The whole fucking Taliban army must be out there, Sir," Sergeant Parker said. At the same time the Captain was shouting: "return fire". They were taking fire from at least twenty five positions. The earth lifted up just in front of the Captain and the Corporal, coming back down and covering them in soil.

"We need to move," the Captain said, "got to get better cover."

Just then two smoke trails flew over their heads from behind. Wham! Two explosions behind the hills from where they were being fired at, then two lines of earth and dirt began to shoot up from the middle of the hill, rapidly moving to the top of the hill, the earth shooting up like geysers. Then the roar and thunder as a Tornado jet shot over head, the jet no higher than a hundred feet above the ground; it then began to climb, sharply banking to the right at the same time, turning to make another pass.

"Dog Walk, Dog Walk," came over the radio, "be advised American Apache Gunships to your south, call sign Blue Yonder."

"Copy that, Cloud Eyes," Harper said.

Captain Weinwright barked at Harper: "Get them now."

Harper was on it already: "Blue Yonder, Blue Yonder, this is

Dog Walk, do you copy, Dog Walk?"

"We are south east, your local will be coming in at your eleven o'clock. Keep your heads down."

"Copy that," Harper said.

"Get onto base: tell them our status, then get the trucks up here fast," the Captain said to Harper, bullets and motor shells still tearing into the British position. "We have to move from here – not the best of cover." A cry of agony from the Captain's right as a bullet ripped into a young soldier's chest.

Sergeant Parker was taking rounds all around him; he knew if he did not move soon he was going to be hit. He looked up ahead – a hollow in the ground, about twenty yards: much better cover. He did not hesitate: he was up and running, firing his weapon from his hip. Captain Weinwright saw the Sergeant make a bolt for better ground. The Captain arose and began firing his weapon in the direction of the Taliban – no specific target, just trying to give the Sergeant cover fire.

Sergeant Parker had only got about half way to the hollow in the ground when he took a hit from machine gun fire up to the right. A scream from the Sergeant as the bullet went through his left shoulder, sending him spinning to the ground. The Taliban machine gunner had him in his sights again: bullets splattered around the ground where the Sergeant fell. Another scream of agony from a soldier as he took a hit. Without thinking, Captain Weinwright was up and running towards the Sergeant; a tirade of bullets flew the Captain's way as he made his charge forward, firing his weapon as he ran. A cry of pain again from Sergeant Parker as a bullet struck him in his right leg. The soldiers all retuned fire to cover the Captain as made his mercy dash.

Captain Weinwright dived on top of the Sergeant, grabbing him wherever he could. Lying on top of the Sergeant, the

CHAPTER 12

Captain began to roll over, taking the Sergeant with him – over and over they went, as a stream of bullets chased them across the ground. After about three rolls, the Captain and the Sergeant went spilling into the hollow. The Captain crawled to the edge of the hollow.

"This is our chance, men," the Captain shouted. "When the Tornado makes his attack, run. We make for the hills." The Captain knew if they stayed where they were, they would just be peppered with mortars. There was no going back over – the best cover behind the soldiers was too far away.

"We are with you, sir," came a shout from one of the soldiers. The Tornado jet came from the right, once again sending a couple of rockets that this time took the top of one of the hills off, sending bits of bodies and mangled weapons blasting into the air, following up with strafe fire that ripped into the hillside and the enemy positions.

"Go!" the Captain shouted as he leapt up into a run, picking up the Sergeant's weapon as he charged forwards. He looked either side and saw about twenty of his soldiers were up and charging with him, firing their weapons as they ran. Ahead, flashes appeared through the dust clouds as the Taliban fired on the advancing British soldiers; a bullet struck a soldier at the Captain's right – the soldier fell down lifeless without a sound. Mortars exploded all around again but luckily none of them close enough to take any of the soldiers down. The machine gun that got the Sergeant began to open fire again as the Tornado jet soared up into sky, the screaming, thundering sound of its engines over the sound of the gun fire. By now some of the soldiers were hitting better cover at the bottom of the hills. To the left up ahead two dark figures appeared just above the horizon. The Captain did not see the Apache helicopters: he was too focused on the machine gun blasting away at them from the hill up to the right.

The Captain reached the bottom of the hill – there was much better cover here, but the Captain did not go to ground: he kept on going up the hill. The Apache helicopters' gun ships just hung motionless in the air. The pilots took a split second to assess the situation that greeted them.

One of the pilots spoke: "It looks like the Brits want to get among them, it's a full frontal attack. We will have to pick our targets Mac – we don't want any own goals."

"Roger that," came the reply.

The Apaches dipped their noses and started to move rapidly forward, at the same time opening up with machine guns and rockets launching from the helicopters. The helicopters disappeared behind a blast of flashing orange and white lights. By now most of the soldiers were under cover. Captain Weinwright was still running up the hill, his head down, driving on upward, not firing his weapon.

He looks to his left just as the Apaches start to let loose: he is at the top of the hill. Far to his right the ground starts to erupt, the thick dust billowing up like a sand storm in front of the helicopters as they wag their tails from side to side and spray the ground with Gatling gun speed, pushing the thick cloud of dust along as they move forward. Explosions of fire and even thicker dust clouds as the Apaches fire rockets into the Taliban positions. Flashes of lights appear in the dust as the Taliban try to fight back.

The Captain feels a sharp burning feeling in his side: he has been hit, but it has not put him down. He looks to his left – three Taliban fighters lie on the hill top; one is firing a machine gun, another feeding the gun with an ammunition belt. They were

CHAPTER 12

oblivious of the Captain. But the third Taliban fighter begins to point his AK 47 at him. The Captain dives to his right as the AK 47 starts to light up, bullets flying past the Captain's body. "This is it," he thinks, "the light will go out soon."

The Captain opened fire with his light machine gun; as he was falling the time seemed to go in slow motion. He could no longer hear the noise of the explosions and the gunfire going on around him. The Taliban fighter's head threw back as a lucky shot hit it. By now the other two men on the heavy machine gun had seen the Captain and were struggling to get into position to lay down fire on him. With the bullets hitting the ground around the Captain, he had two choices: he could roll to his right which would send him tumbling down the hill to relative safety, or roll to his left and then he would have to fight for his life.

The Captain chose to fight, keeping his finger squeezed tight on the trigger of his light machine gun and firing in the direction of the two Taliban fighters; his tirade of bullets hit home, striking all three of the enemy, their bodies shaking violently as the bullets ripped into them. Dragging himself into the dead men's position he rose to his feet looking at the awesome sight that lay before him: the noise was like a million football rattles being turned at the same time as the Apache helicopters kept on spraying bullets out, ahead of them, pushing the dust storm up in front of them. And then silence as the gunships stopped firing. The Captain still stood there, the helicopters just hanging in mid air, the muffled sound of their rotors – nothing compared to the deathly sound of the Gatling guns.

The dust begins to clear. A soldier comes diving into the position where the Captain is.

"For fuck sake, sir, get down!" the soldier shouts.

"No need now," the Captain thinks, looking over the battle

field. Smoke rises up in several places, men running in the distance, some on motorcycles going up and down the hills fleeing the terrifying nightmare they have just experienced, running for their lives. The helicopters dip their noses and give chase after the fleeing Taliban, their machine guns occasionally firing. The odd shot rings out from other directions, the Captain takes no notice.

The soldier stood up beside the Captain. "Are you all right, sir?" the soldier asked. The Captain felt the wet patch on his left side – a slight pain, but nothing too bad. "I am all right son," the Captain replied.

The Taliban bodies lay all over the hills, the Apache helicopters had chewed them up and spat them out. There was still firing in the distance as the gunships chased their prey. The Captain looked down at his men going around checking the dead. He felt proud and at the same time felt sick: proud of his men – not one of them complained about what he had led them into – and sick because for a while he had forgotten all human decency and he could kill without hesitation, and with whatever means if he had to.

The Tornado jet flew overhead back and forth a couple of times, and then flew out of sight after reporting that the convoy was only a couple of miles away. The Apache helicopters came back, one of them starting to descend on the clearing where only ten minutes ago all hell had broken loose. The other helicopter hovered a hundred feet above where Captain Weinwright stood, the pilot looking straight down at him. Harper, the radio operator, came up to the Captain handing him a radio.

"It's Blue Yonder, sir," Harper said.

The Captain took the radio: "Blue Yonder, Captain Weinwright."

CHAPTER 12

"You guys all right down there, Captain?"

"We have casualties, but e-vac is on the way."

"Mac's putting down, Captain. His Co is a medic – he will help until e-vac arrives," the pilot said.

"I appreciate that," Captain Weinwright said.

"I will stay here until support arrives," the pilot said.

"Thank you Blue Yonder," the Captain said.

"It's what we're here for. Anyway we had a few scores to settle," the pilot replied. "Your tail end is coming from the east Captain. Blue Yonder out."

The Captain looked to the east – dust was coming up from the vehicles heading their way.

"You need Green to look at that, sir," Harper said.

"No, let him see to the men first. How's Sergeant Parker" the Captain asked Green.

"Not good sir. I wish e-vac would hurry up," Green said.

Captain Weinwright began to feel dizzy and started swaying on his feet. Harper got behind the Captain and eased him into a sitting position.

"You stay like that, sir, until the boys get here," Harper said, and just then Green was by his side with his medical kit. Green lifted the Captain's tunic; a piece of flesh the size of an apple had been torn out of the Captain's side when the round went through.

"You will live, sir," Green said.

CHAPTER 13

Major Brent sat at his desk staring at the telephone; it rang once. The Major had the telephone to his ear in an instant but before he could get a word out, the Colonel spoke: "Talk to me Major."

"Well sir it looks like Captain Weinwright picked himself a fight with the Taliban. The reports are patchy, but from what I can gather it was one hell of a fire fight," said the Major. "We have taken casualties sir, we have four soldiers dead and five wounded and one of those is Captain Weinwright sir"

"For Christ's sake," Colonel Baldwin butted in, but before he could say anything more the Major went on: "Err no sir Captain Weinwright is all right. His wounds are not life threatening; he is mobile according to the reports I am receiving, but like I say sir the reports are patchy at the moment. Dog Walk is still pulling its pants up sir."

"And the enemy?" the Colonel asked.

"At least forty three dead. Could be as many as fifty sir – they cannot count the bodies as yet, too many pieces and bits in some areas," the Major said.

"Over forty dead," the Colonel said.

"Yes sir, that's what I am hearing. Looks like the Americans were involved as well sir. Cloud Eyes called up a couple of Apache Gunships that were in the vicinity."

"God help us," the Colonel said, "just wait until the media get hold of this lot, what a mess."

"With all due respect sir, is that not what we are here for, to go out and seek the enemy and engage with them?"

"You are perfectly right Major, but we don't send members of the Royal Family," the Colonel said. "I am on my way down

CHAPTER 13

there, Major. Get all the information you can, I will speak to the Americans, and I have no doubt Whitehall will be breathing down our necks."

"Yes," Major Brent said looking at the telephone and putting it down very slowly.

Captain Weinwright lay on the hospital bed starring at the ceiling. He was in Camp Bastion Army Hospital.

"How are you doing?" a voice said. The Captain looked out of the corner of his eye. Colonel Baldwin and Major Brent were standing alongside the bed.

"I will live – only a flesh wound – the bullet went straight through the meaty bit."

The Major said: "That was one hell of a thing you did out there."

Weinwright looked puzzled. "The thing with the machine gun nest and Sergeant Parker," Major Brent elucidated.

"Have you heard any news on Sergeant Parker? They tell you nothing in here."

"He is going to be all right, thanks to you."

"Thank God," the Captain said.

"The other guys are all going to be fine as well Captain, so don't you go worrying yourself there," said the Major.

"One hell of a set to you had out there Captain. Back home the papers just love it – you are a national hero," the Colonel said.

"Christ no," the Captain said.

"I am afraid so; the secret's out – you are all over the news," the Major said. "The Americans have you charging up the hill with your men like the charge of the Light Brigade, and how they came in to save the future King of England."

"Tell me this is not true," the Captain said.

"It is all over Captain; we have to get you back to the UK as soon as possible. Your military days are over – well at least at the sharp end, so to speak," the Colonel said smiling to himself. "And now it is back to Captain Stephen Weinwright, the Earl of Stanley, for you," the Colonel added.

The Captain lay with his eyes shut saying 'this cannot be happening to me'.

"If you wanted to keep your identity quiet you went the wrong way about it, dear boy," the Colonel said. "It is back to Blighty for you in a few days' time."

CHAPTER 14

Two weeks later at the Royal Victoria Hospital in Newcastle.

"What the bloody hell are they doing to him in there?" Clare Carhill asked as she sat waiting with Brian Taylor to go in to see her brother Trevor. They had been told to wait while the nurses gave Trevor a bed bath and change his bandages. The moans from the room were unbearable for Clare.

"I know they are not trying to hurt Trevor. I suppose they have to move him about to clean him," Clare thought.

"I wonder if I should go in," Clare said to Brian.

"Oh I don't know," said Brian, "that gay nurse is a bit bitchy." More moans and groans came from the room.

"I have to go in," said Clare, getting up and rushing to the door and opening it. She hardly got her foot in the door.

"Get out Miss Carhill, you will be able to see your brother shortly."

Clare protested: "If I am in the room it might be easier for Trevor."

"Get out! I will not allow you in this room while we are dealing with a patient."

Brian came over. "Come Clare and sit down, let them get on with their job," Brian said.

"But it is not as if I have not seen Trevor's injuries."

"I know you worry about him, but he will be all right – it is not the first bed bath he has had," Brian said. "

Well I don't want to be anywhere near the next time they bath him," Clare started to cry.

"Come on now, we can't have that," Brian said. "If Trevor

sees you like that what is he going to think? You said yourself when we go to see Trevor we have to be happy and cheerful."

"I know Brian, I am sorry." Clare has had a lot on her mind since the accident; it has all been building up inside her, but she has had to stay strong, she knows that if she gave up there would be no one there for Trevor: she has to be there for him.

"I will go and get us a cup of tea," Brian said.

"No it's all right, I am all right now, I just let it get to me what with all that Trevor has been through and hearing him in pain."

The door of the hospital room opens. "You can go in now, Miss Carhill," the nurse said. "But don't be tiring him out, he needs his rest, and don't you be getting him excited," he turned and said to Brian. Brian dropped his head and blushed.

"I am sorry about before, nurse," Clare said.

"That's all right, we were not trying to hurt him you know, I have not lost a patient yet," the male nurse said. "I am very gentle – not like some I can name," the male nurse added as he gave an accusatory look towards the female nurse who had just been assisting him with Trevor. The male nurse turned, looked back into the room at Trevor and said: "You have guests, now you behave and don't you be telling them any of our secrets." Clare and Trevor went straight into the room.

Trevor Carhill is conscious now – his recovery has been miraculous: he can speak, but cannot open his mouth – he has to speak through his teeth. Trevor's jaw is wired, and his jaw was fractured in the accident, along with a multitude of other injuries. His head is still in a supporting frame which holds the titanium plate in place while it bonds with his remaining upper skull. His legs and arms are still in plaster; he can move his fingers and toes, but these injuries are not the doctors' main

CHAPTER 14

worries; it is his brain they are concerned about – will there be much damage?

"What was all that noise about?" Clare said as she leant over and kissed Trevor through the head frame.

"Hi mate," Brian said as they both sat down.

"I don't know what hurts the most – hearing that gay nurse go on about his unsuccessful dates, or the bloody aches and pains I feel when they move me around. It does not hurt if I lie still, but no, they think I am enjoying myself, so they have to bloody move me," Trevor said trying to shout, but that hurts as well.

"Don't go on, Trevor, they are only trying to help," Clare said. "Now what did Dr Luke say this morning?"

"Nothing," Trevor said. "Dr Luke did not come this morning. Ramoan my friendly nurse says that Dr Luke is not coming until this afternoon; she has a meeting this morning, apparently to discuss my case with other doctors. I would have liked to have been a fly on the wall at that meeting."

"They would have been talking about how well you are doing," Brian said.

"Yeah, maybe you're right," Trevor said. "How are you two doing, anyway?"

"Never mind about us – how are you doing?" Clare asked.

"Well I was all right – I knew the doctors were worried that I may have some mental problems, but I had dismissed that because I felt fine in the head until last night," Trevor said.

"Why, what happened?" Clare was alarmed.

"Well until last night I could remember nothing about the accident. I can remember how it happened but then nothing else until I came around last week. But last night I could remember them operating on me."

"What's this you mean," Brian asked, "how you can remember something you never saw?"

"That is it," Trevor said. "I did see it. I can remember every detail of it."

Clare was now getting worried; she was thinking her worst fears were coming true: Trevor was suffering from brain damage. She thought she would have to steer him away from these kind of thoughts. "Oh no God please," she said to herself, "not this."

"It is all the drugs and medication they are giving you that makes you think these strange thoughts," Clare insisted.

"No I tell you, I can remember the operation, the actual surgery I went through, I saw it all, and what's more I can give a detailed run down on the whole episode."

"Oh don't Trevor, please," Clare said.

"It's all right, it does not bother me," Trevor said.

"It is all dreams," Clare said, "dreams filling in the blank spaces."

"I don't know, it was pretty real to me. I could hear what was being said as well."

Clare's jaw dropped: "Please Trevor, don't say these things."

"I am sorry Clare if I am upsetting you."

Trevor thought 'what am I doing? Clare has been through a lot lately and I am dropping this on her, the past four and a half years Clare has had it rough, what with her husband getting killed in the car crash, and her not talking about it. There is a lot lying heavy on her mind'. Trevor said to Brian: "Would you go and get Clare a cup of tea?"

"Sure," Brian said, getting up and leaving the room.

"Look Clare, I know in my mind I am going to be all right – please don't you worry any more about me. You have been through too much yourself without adding any more worries to

CHAPTER 14

your lot. Now you have done your job for me, now can we start thinking about you please."

"I am all right, Trevor, there is nothing wrong with me," Clare said.

"There is everything wrong with you Clare; you are so unhappy, you need to start to live your life. Kevin died."

"Don't," said Clare.

"Since Kevin died you have not spoken about him or the accident, you won't even use your married name."

"I don't want to talk about it Trevor; never mind me, it is you that needs help."

"No, you do Clare, you must face up to things; if you don't I will refuse to get better. Now let us both make a new start."

"I wish I could," said Clare, "but when I think of him in that car with her when they were both killed." Clare began to cry: "It should have been me with my husband who died in that car crash not her."

"I know Clare love but it has happened and what's done, well you know. Now let us make a deal: you try to get your life back on track and look at men again and I promise to get well again now. How's that?" Trevor said.

"I will try," Clare replied, as she wiped the tears from her eyes.

Brian came back in the room with three cups of tea on a tray. "Who is the third cup for?" Trevor asked.

"It's for you," Brian said.

"I can't drink tea you idiot! Oh never mind," Trevor said. Clare laughed; Trevor smiled.

Brian said: "Well, I don't know, you try to do someone a good turn and that's the thanks you get! That Dr Luke is in her office, Clare, I've just seen her go in."

"Trevor, I will go and have a word with her about what was discussed at their meeting; come and get me, Brian, if Trevor needs anything."

"I don't need anything. Yes you can find out what was said about me, and you tell me because those doctors tell me nothing."

Clare really wanted to see Dr Luke to discuss what Trevor had been saying about remembering the surgery. She knew in the back of her mind that Trevor was just imagining what he said he had seen. But she wanted it confirmed by a professional.

"Come in," Dr Luke said when Clare knocked on her office door. "Clare, please come in and sit down. Now just let me finish this and I am all yours." Dr Luke was reading something on the computer monitor. "Right Clare," Dr Luke said as she turned the computer off, "I have news for you Clare. we are going to move Trevor from the ICU this weekend, as we think he has improved enough to be moved into an observation room."

"That is great," Clare said, "if you are sure he is ready."

"Yes, we think he is ready to be moved. Trevor has defied medical science. His recovery rate was the focus of conversation at our meeting this morning. We have doctors from all over the country interested in Trevor's case. And how is he doing today?" asked Dr Luke.

"Well Doctor, Trevor is saying some strange things."

"Strange things Clare, what do you mean?"

"Well, Trevor says he can remember everything about the surgery he went through, claims he could even hear what was being said at the time," Clare said.

"Come Clare, you know that is impossible; it is all the medication that Trevor is getting that makes him imagine what he says he saw. Trevor has been through a great trauma," Dr

CHAPTER 14

Luke said.

"I know this Doctor, but he is convinced he was there; well I know he was there, but he is adamant he witnessed the surgery."

"Clare, with what Trevor has been through, this kind of thing is normal."

"I know Doctor, but I can't help but worry what if it is brain damage, oh I can't bear to think about it," Clare said. "I want Trevor back as he was."

"You go and see Trevor. I will be along shortly. I will finish up here and be along in twenty minutes or so," Dr Luke said.

Clare was busy telling Trevor what a medical miracle all the doctors thought he was, when there was a knock on the door and Dr Luke came in. "Hello Trevor, and how are you today?"

"I would be a lot better if you did not keep sending that gay nurse in all the time to wrestle with me!"

"Come on now Trevor we know you love it. And besides it keeps you alert," Dr Luke said. "Now what is this Clare tells me, you are frightening her with stories of your dreams?"

"I tell you what I saw."

"Trevor, you promised," Clare said. Trevor stopped short of what he was saying and gave a look of concern to Clare.

Dr Luke said: "Clare, would you and Brian give Trevor and I five minutes please." Clare and Brian left the room.

"Trevor, these dreams are normal. You have Clare worried that they are the start of a mental breakdown or even brain damage. With the head injuries you suffered, she even thinks you may be losing your mind. That may be the case – I won't know until we do further tests," Dr Luke said.

"Doctor, I can tell you I was there, I saw and heard everything, the operation on my head, the lot."

"How could you see this, Trevor, you were barely alive, in

fact at some stages you were clinically dead?"

"Doctor I can shut my eyes now and recall every moment of it."

"What are they up to in there," Clare said. "Five minutes she said – it has been twenty five minutes," Clare said to Brian.

"Maybe the Doctor is examining Trevor's brain," Brian said.

"Oh don't be stupid, Brian," Clare said, and then quickly with an apology, "oh Brian love, I am sorry, forgive me."

"That's all right," Brian said. Brian would have anyone say anything to him, as long as it did not hurt Clare or Trevor.

"Trevor, I want you to say nothing more about this to anyone but me, do you understand?" Dr Luke said.

"Well if you think," Trevor paused. "Not a word to anyone but me. I will speak to Dr Lustman and Dr Mayo about this tomorrow. Now say no more."

Dr Luke went to the door. "You can come back in now," she said.

Brian said as he walked back in to the room: "What you two been doing, making your will?", then it dawned on him what he had just said. "Sorry, sorry, I will keep my big mouth shut from now on."

"Clare," Dr Luke said, "Trevor and I have had a talk about his dreams. We are going to do some tests, but it is not a problem. I think it is as we said: the drugs and the medication. So I don't want you to worry anymore about it."

Dr Luke went straight back to her office and made a call to Dr Mayo. Dr Mayo answered. "Dr Mayo I have just had the most extraordinary conversation with Trevor Carhill. I want you to come over as soon as you have the time please Doctor."

"Can we not discuss this on the telephone, Dr Luke?" Dr Mayo asked.

Chapter 14

"I would rather we did it here Doctor – I would like Trevor to be present when we talked."

"Very well," Dr Mayo said, "I will get back to you and tell you when I can get there."

"Thank you Doctor," Dr Luke said.

CHAPTER 15

Chelsea. London. England. Military Hospital.

"Now then, how are you Sergeant?" asked Captain Weinwright.

"Look what we have here," Sergeant Parker said. "It is good to see you sir."

"No Sergeant, it is good to see you," the Captain said. "How are they treating you Sergeant?"

"They look after me fine here sir, four squares a day and all that. I see you made the headlines. I have been keeping up with events sir," the Sergeant said, gesturing to a pile of newspapers on his bedside table. "I can't wait to tell the boys I have had a real time celebrity to visit me!"

"I have had my fill of the press for the last two weeks, and if I don't see them again even that will be too soon," the Captain said.

"No sir, it is good for the boys back in Afghanistan sir, they have their Captain to read about. I have even had the press here; the sister threw them out after a while; they are coming back they say. They wanted to know about you sir, and if I knew that you were a relation of Her Majesty and all that," the Sergeant said.

"And what did you tell them Sergeant?"

"They got the facts, sir, on how my Captain saved my life and beat the Taliban army, that's what they got," the Sergeant said.

"I had a lot of help as far as I can remember, Sergeant," the Captain said.

"What I will tell them when they come back sir..."

CHAPTER 15

"You tell them whatever you wish Sergeant," the Captain said.

"Come to think of it, sir, they are a bit of a pest aren't they? They must be on your case a lot, sir," the Sergeant said.

"Believe it or not, Sergeant, but this morning I had to get the wife's brother to dress in my clothes, and the wife to take him out for a drive in the car – the press followed them thinking I was in the car, so I could sneak out to come and see you!"

"That's very good of you sir," the Sergeant said.

"So what do the doctors say, Sergeant?"

"Well sir, the leg might be all right, they seem quite confident about that, but the arm sir, it is not looking too good," the Sergeant said.

"I am sorry to hear that, Sergeant," the Captain said.

"I was more worried I was not going to be able to walk, sir, that was my main fear, but it looks like I have a good chance. I would have liked the arm as well, sir, but it is what it is," the Sergeant said. "Some of the lads have come off a lot worse. That was a very brave thing you did out there sir and I owe you my life."

"I did what any of the other men would have done Sergeant," the Captain said.

"Oh I don't think so, sir, the machine gun posts as well – that took courage," the Sergeant said.

"It scared the life out of me Sergeant."

"It did sir, and the men said you were calm under fire sir."

"It was not the actual doing of the event that scared me Sergeant – it was the fact I could do it and feel no fear," the Captain said.

"War does strange things to men sir, I just know that what you did for me was brave and you deserve the medals they will pin on you sir," the Sergeant said.

"Medals, I don't want medals, I want my command back and to be out there with men like you, Sergeant," the Captain said.

"Well we know that cannot be sir," the Sergeant said. "When will they be pinning the gong on you sir?"

"I don't know Sergeant," the Captain said.

"I would like to be there sir, all the men would; it will be a proud day sir," the Sergeant said.

Two nurses came into the room. "Sergeant Parker has to be ready for surgery shortly sir," one of the nurses said.

"Surgery?" the Captain said.

"The arm sir," the Sergeant said. Captain Weinwright could hardly control his emotions. 'Here I am talking to this man as if we were just passing the time of day, and all the time he has this massive dilemma on his mind, and not once did he give any inkling what he was about to go through and no signs of fear – that to me is courage,' the Captain thought.

"I am so sorry Sergeant, I don't know what to say."

"It's all right sir, what can you say? I will get by."

Captain Weinwright stood to attention and saluted the Sergeant saying, "It is a pleasure to know you Sergeant Parker."

CHAPTER 16

Seven months later, Newcastle upon Tyne.

Thursday, seven thirty in the morning, a man joins the queue to get on the Metro train at Gateshead Stadium Metro Station. The man travels on the Metro train, sitting near the window; he is nervous and bites his nails as he stares out of the window; he is a small man about five feet two inches in height and stocky; he has black hair and a short black beard and has an Asian appearance. The Metro train stops at the next station, Gateshead Interchange Station; the nervous man stays seated – this is not his stop – the Metro train pulls away. It travels over the River Tyne on the Metro Bridge.

'The next Station is Central Station' comes over the intercom. The man gets up ready to alight at this station; there are a lot of passengers wanting to get off at this station and also a lot of passengers wanting to get on the Metro train at this station. Central Station is the mainline Railway Station in Newcastle; the Metro link to Central Station is easy access for people of the North to get to the mainline trains – at Central Station you can get a train to almost anywhere in the UK.

The man does not follow the other passengers, who are either leaving the Metro Station to go into Newcastle City Centre or going on to the mainline Central Station. The man walks along the station platform and stops at a door. A sign on the door reads 'no unauthorised persons'. The man takes a deep breath and opens the door.

"Good morning Susie, good morning Audrey," the man says to two women sitting at a table drinking a cup of tea. The two women are wearing orange high visibility vests; it says on the back of the vests, 'Churchgate Cleaners Keeping Your Metro Tidy'.

"Good morning Shea," the two women say.

"Do you want a cuppa, Shea?" Audrey asks.

"No thanks," Shea says as he takes his coat off and puts a similar orange vest on.

"Are you all right, Shea?" Susie asks. "You look a bit under the weather."

"I am fine thanks Susie, I just feel a bit listless.

"Audrey, are you going to get on to head office to get the buffing machine fixed?" Susie asks.

"I will try again Susie, but they take no notice," Audrey says.

"Audrey can I have the store's keys to get some more cleaning fluid?" Shea asks.

"You just got some the other day, Shea. What you doing – drinking it?" Audrey exclaims.

"I cannot clean without cleaning fluid Audrey," Shea says.

"I am only kidding," Audrey says, throwing the keys over to Shea and saying, "Make sure I get those back."

Shea leaves the cleaners' office and walks along the platform and through a pedestrian tunnel that has a sign above it that reads 'To Central Station'. He goes up two flights of stairs and onto the Central Station Platform. The platform is crowded with people getting off and on trains. Shea weaves his way through the people and stops at a door and waits. At the front of Central Station a Royal Mail Mercedes Vito Van stops.

"You cannot stop here," a police officer says to the driver. "Your place is further up the road."

"Yes we know Officer," the driver of the van says, "but we have been asked by our Supervisor to try and get this Mail sent

CHAPTER 16

back to Edinburgh. It had been sent down here by mistake on the overnight train. We will be only ten minutes Officer."

"No more than ten minutes," the police officer said, "now hurry up."

A taxi driver shouts over to the police officer, "You cannot let them park there they have the place blocked off."

"Let me worry about that," the police officer says as he starts to direct the heavy rush hour traffic around the Royal Mail van. The station was very busy with droves of people coming out of the station to get to their place of work, others going into the station to catch trains to their place of work. There are two men with the Royal Mail van.

"I will go and get a barrow Alama," one man says to the other.

"Be quick Mohamad," Alama says. Mohamad pushes through the sea of people to go and get a barrow. Alama opens the back of the van and waits for Mohamad to bring the barrow. Mohamad is back in a couple of minutes with a four wheeled barrow. The two men take six large Royal Mail bags out of the back of the van and load them onto the barrow; Mohamad pulls the barrow while Alama pushes, as they take the barrow into the station. It is difficult to get through so many people.

"Come on you two, get a move on," a Railway Police Officer says. Alama puts his hand in one of the bags and brings a wire out; it has a toggle on the end of the wire.

"What are you doing Alama?" Mohamad says.

"If we are discovered I will take them with us," Alama replies.

They take the barrow along the station platform. Shea sees them coming: he opens the door he was standing next to and then the three men push the barrow inside the narrow passageway.Shea goes to the end of the passage and opens another door to the cleaners' stores. He goes inside and moves boxes to one side; the three men quickly take the Mail bags off the barrow and stack them into the back of the store room.

Alama opens one of the bags and takes out a small black box; he then takes a wire out of all six bags and plugs each wire into the black box. Alama looks at his watch; it is eight thirty; he types thirty five hours into the black box keyboard and then presses a red button on the digital display. The thirty five hour number begins to count down a second at a time.

"Quickly now," Alama says. The three men hide the bags by stacking boxes in front of them, Shea locks the stores door and the outer door when they leave onto the platform. Shea has put a couple of boxes onto the barrow to make it look like they were taking a delivery back. The three men take the barrow back outside to the van.

"Come on," the police officer says, "this place is a nightmare to keep moving." They throw the boxes into the back of the van; the police officer stops the traffic so the van can get out into the heavy flow of traffic. Shea takes the barrow back into the station.

CHAPTER 17

After his appointment at the hospital with Dr Luke, Trevor Carhill was walking down Northumberland Street in Newcastle – the main Street in the City; it was ten thirty in the morning. Trevor was feeling a bit under the weather; he was drowsy, the street was very busy with people going about their daily business, and not wanting to attract any attention to himself he slipped down a side street. He had a slight pain in his head. He pulled himself into a dark corner doorway. 'This is nice and quiet,' Trevor thought, 'I will stay here until I feel better.'

After several minutes Trevor began to feel much better. He looked down the alley; a dark blue van is parked. Just as Trevor was about to leave he heard someone talking and moving about close to him. Not wanting to cause suspicion, Trevor pulled himself tighter into the doorway. Two men appeared from out of a building just a few feet away from where Trevor was concealed; the men spoke in a foreign language. The two men went to the end of the alley; they were clearly keeping a look out for someone.

Suddenly another person pops out of the shadows, one of the men at the end of the alley waves him out, the man comes into the light; he is carrying a long slender case, and it is heavy. Then another two men appear carrying bags. One of the men who was at the end of the alley comes back and opens the van and waves to the man with the slender case to get into the van. The men carrying the bags place them into the back of the van, then they go back into the building, returning almost immediately carrying a long white box, which they slide into the van, and then again back into the building and returning with an identical box and place that into the van. They climb into the van; the van door is quickly closed behind them. Two men that were keeping watch get into the front of the van, one of them into the driving seat and starting the engine.

Trevor thought there is no doubt that something fishy has just gone down. As the van began to move off Trevor began to think hard about what he had just witnessed. He started to feel a bit of discomfort in his head; he started to get a mental picture in his head that he could see inside the van. He could see the three men sitting in the back of the van; he could even hear them talking in their language. Trying to focus even more, Trevor begins to see and hear more clearly. Trevor saw one of the men open the slender case; he was talking as he did. What he saw was a powerful rifle – one of those things you just see in movies. Larger than most other rifles, it had a telescopic sight, a long barrel with a broad piece on the end.

The next thing Trevor knows is someone is asking him if he was all right, and the vision of the men and the gun were gone.

"Ah yes thanks, I am fine," Trevor said to the concerned passer-by. "I was just feeling a bit giddy." Trevor did not know what to think, 'did I just see that, am I just dreaming. Will I be seeing things all the time now,' he thought? Troubled by this Trevor thought he needed to tell Dr Luke the next time he went for his check up.

Walking back into the main street he cannot get out of his head what he had just witnessed. He made his mind up – 'I am going back to see Dr Luke now'. At the hospital Dr Luke got someone to take her patients while she went to see what was so important that Trevor could not wait to tell her. Trevor started to explain to Dr Luke what he thought he had just seen through these eyes in his head. Dr Luke was very concerned –

CHAPTER 17

there has not been an episode like this since Trevor said he had seen the surgery taking place on himself. His recovery has been so successful the doctor wanted no setbacks. Dr Luke tried to explain Trevor's visions away. The mind is a very complex and brilliant computer, he may be just getting a glitch in his recovery.

But Trevor is convinced what he saw was real; he began to get agitated and upset. Doctor Luke decided to get Trevor to stay for the time being until he calmed down and was more at ease. Dr Luke organised a room for Trevor to lie down and gave Trevor something to relax him. Dr Luke did not want to ring Clare, Trevor's sister yet: "I will wait and see how Trevor is in an hour or so."

Trevor lay on the hospital bed with his eyes closed; he thought 'I am sure what I saw was real – the men in the van, even their voices, I could hear them speaking even if it was a language I could not understand.' And then Trevor started to think 'maybe the doctor was right, I have been through hell, my head was all smashed up, and I am bound to have problems. And if this is what I get I think I can live with that.'

Trevor lay back, trying to relax; no matter what he did he could not get what he had seen out of his mind. Trevor tried another approach – instead of trying to erase the thoughts he would try to intensify them; he began to concentrate on his vision. It was just like someone had switched the television on – an instant replay of what he had seen in his mind's eye began to play out. The three men in the back of the van with the rifle as plain as day, he could hear the words spoken just like before.

Shocked and amazed by this Trevor sat up sharply, 'this cannot be true, this cannot be happening,' he thinks. Trevor composed himself, lay back down, closed his eyes, ignoring the slight pain in his head he begins to concentrate again on the vision. Smack! There it was again just as if he pressed the replay button. Trevor opened his eyes and he began to shake. This was frightening: 'what will I do?' he lay thinking 'could I see before the men came out of the building?' He tried to concentrate on that thought, no nothing, he opened his eyes, I will try after the van leaves. He lay back down and tried to think of the van leaving, no nothing again. Maybe it is all gone even the inside the van vision. Trevor concentrated on the inside the van thought, there it is again: instant replay.

Trevor is scared – he presses the attendance button; he keeps his finger on the button until a nurse comes in the room.

"What is it Mr Carhill?" the nurse asks.

"I want you to get Dr Luke straight away," Trevor says to the nurse.

"Dr Luke is busy at the moment, Mr Carhill, is there anything I can do?" the nurse says.

Trevor gets vexed and shouts at the nurse: "Get Dr Luke for me now."

"Very well Mr Carhill I will go and get the doctor if you calm down."

Dr Luke comes at once when the nurse tells her about Trevor being so upset. "What is it Trevor?" Dr Luke asks. "Why all the panic?"

"It's back, doctor," Trevor says. "I can bring it back any time I want, I just have to think of what I saw and there it is again."

"OK Trevor we are going to sort this." Dr Luke tells the nurse to get an observation room ready. "I am going to keep you here Trevor until we can get to the bottom of this. I will give Clare a call and get her to bring you a few things."

Trevor would rather stay in the hospital: he is afraid and worried where this could lead.

CHAPTER 17

Trevor calms down a bit and Dr Luke asks him: "You said the vision's come back Trevor."

"Yes I can summon them at will, I just have to think about it and there it is, just as before every detail as before right up until that man asks me if I am all right, then it switches off," Trevor says.

The nurse comes back into the room. "We have the observation room ready, Dr Luke."

"Right Trevor, let's get you somewhere more comfortable and then we can start to get you sorted. Nurse, you take Trevor down. I have to go and sort my patients, Trevor, but I will be down to see you in half an hour I promise," Dr Luke says. As soon as she gets to her office Dr Luke calls Trevor's sister Clare, and then she telephones Dr Mayo. Dr Mayo is not answering; Dr Luke leaves a message for him to get in contact as soon as possible – it is very important.

CHAPTER 18

"Let's move," Shali said as he removed the rifle from its hard case and began to feed it into a lose fishing rod bag. The van pulled away sharply making Shali miss the opening of the fishing bag.

"Nareem, you fool," Shali said. "Take your time – there is no rush."

"Sorry my General," the driver said.

"Do not call me General," Shali snarled at the driver.

"Sorry my Gen, sorry Shali," the driver said again.

"And do not any of you lot forget, here I am Shali."

"Yes Shali," was the reply from all the men in the van.

"Goomi," Shali said, "make sure you make the others understand, they must be at the ferry before seven o'clock."

Goomi, turning back to look over his shoulder to speak to Shali, said: "I will make sure they all know and trust me Shali."

"Will you be at the ferry, Goomi?" asked Shali.

"No, my brother, I have a destiny to fulfil and an Emirates flight to catch; I will be going home another route."

"Veeri, let Goomi out here."

The van stopped; Goomi got out saying, "Mohammad be praised." Goomi made his way up John Dobson Street and headed towards Newcastle University.

The van with the four men in drove off, going south out of the City driving over the Tyne Bridge.

Shali said: "Take this," to the man sitting opposite him, handing him the fishing rod bag with the rifle in it. The man took the rifle and placed it carefully under the bench he was sitting on. Shali stretched out on the bench he was sitting on.

CHAPTER 18

Five minutes later the van was heading south down the A1 motorway. Another ten minutes later the van was pulling into the Washington Service Station.

"This is your stop, Rasheed," Shali said. The van pulled up next to a silver Vauxhall Vectra in the car park. One of the men in the back of the van got out.

"Call me," Shali said to him, "if there is anything suspicious."

"Yes, Shali, I will," Rasheed said.

Rasheed got into the silver Vectra and started the engine. He drove out of the Washington Services car park, turned left and drove off heading south down the A1.

"Give him fifteen minutes and then we go," Shali said. Nareem began to check inside the bags. "Nervous?" Shali said to him. Nareem did not answer – he just looked at Shali. "Don't be," Shali said.

"Nothing is to go wrong, now," the driver said.

"No Veeri, fifteen minutes I said, keep calm there is plenty of time it will go good Mohammad is with us."

After a short while Shali checked his watch. "It is time," he said. "We go now, Veeri." Veeri drove in exactly the same direction as Rasheed had done in the Vectra, heading south down the A1. They were only out on the road ten minutes when Shali's mobile rang.

"Yes," Shali said, after checking his mobile to see who was calling. "This is good Rasheed, we will be there shortly," Shali said on the mobile. The van driver said: "Durham half a mile," as they passed a directional sign.

"Watch your speed, Veeri," Shali said to the driver. "We do not want to bring any unwanted attention to us. Put the bags under the seats."

The van took the slip road off the motorway, took a right at the roundabout and then the road heading for Durham.

"You know where to go," Shali said. The van drove into Durham City, the driver following all signposts indicating City Centre, across two roundabouts; the Cathedral was just in front of them. The next turn off slightly to their left would have taken them straight to the Cathedral, but the driver missed that turn off and took the next one. They took the road down towards the river, following the river around a slight bend and then took a sharp right up a dirt road; a sign read Bailey Mill and then they went into a small asphalt car park. There parked in front of them was the silver Vectra. Ten yards away was the river, and just down a grass bank to the river was Rasheed: he was all kitted up for fishing, waders on he began to walk in the shallows and cast his fishing rod. And there to the left was the old mill.

The stone work on the mill looked new; it had not long ago been sand blasted. The mill stood on the river bank; at one time it had a water wheel, but this was long gone now. To the back and at one side of the mill were trees, the small car park was at the front. Nareem put the bags from the van into the boot of the Vectra. Rasheed just kept on fishing, but really he was on lookout. Veeri took a fishing rod and bait box out of the van and prepared to do some fishing, watching all around as he did. Shali got out of the van with the fishing rod bag that contained the rifle and walked straight to the mill door. Nareem hurried over to meet Shali at the door; the door had a padlock, and Nareem took a key from his pocket and opened the padlock. Both men went inside the mill and shut the door behind them.

Nareem took two torches out of the bag he was carrying. "This way," he said to Shali. Nareem knew his way around the mill – for the last three weeks Nareem, Rasheed and Veeri had been coming to the river to fish. They came in the blue Transit

CHAPTER 18

van and the silver Vectra so the locals would get used to the vehicles being parked at the mill. They had forced entry into the mill during those past weeks and changed the lock. Shali knew if anyone passed or even came close it would look like a regular scene.

The mill only had windows on the front and one side and these were boarded up. It was very dark. Shali followed Nareem up the timber stairs to the top floor. Nareem took a large lamp from his bag and turned it on; it lit the whole room up clearly. There were no windows on the top floor – they had been blocked up with stone some time ago. A ladder was already placed in position; it reached up through the main entry hatch in the ceiling into the roof space. Up the ladder Shali went with his torch, leaving the fishing rod bag with the rifle on the lower floor. The roof space was all decked out and easy to move across.

"There," Nareem said, pointing to one side of the roof. Shali moved over to one side of the roof space, bowing lower as he went, trying not to bang his head on the sloping roof. In front of Shali was a purpose built frame; it looked like a table, but was far too tall and narrow for a table.

"Which ones?" Shali asked.

"There," Nareem pointed as he moved behind the timber frame.

Nareem took out a screwdriver and began to slide up one of the roof slates; a beam of light came shooting in the roof space. It got wider as Nareem pushed the slate higher and it held in position when he released the pressure. Nareem then did the same to the next slate in line. This made a hole in the roof about one foot long by six inches wide.

"Go get the glasses," Shali said. Nareem went down the ladder and came back with the field binoculars; he gave them to

Shali.

Shali stood behind the timber frame; leaning his elbows on the frame, he lifted the binoculars to his eyes.

"Perfect, just perfect," Shali said to himself. What Shali could see was the podium that had been erected just outside the Cathedral. The podium was draped in ribbons and flags. In the centre of the podium was a microphone stand; there were people busy arranging chairs at the rear of the podium. Now and again a branch from the trees outside would blow into view. It was just under a mile in distance from the mill to the podium.

Nareem asked if he could take a look. Shali passed him the binoculars.

"Is it not too far away?" Nareem asked as he focused his view through the binoculars. "Will you be able to do it?"

"We will see," Shali replied. "Now go and get the rifle and then tell Veeri to turn the vehicles around."

Shali pulled the powerful rifle out of the fishing rod bag. He spread the stabiliser's legs at the nozzle of the barrel and rested them on the timber frame, and the nozzle of the rifle was just inches from the opening in the roof. Shali pressed a button on the side of the telescopic sight casing; lowering his head he brought his cheek alongside the rifle. Looking through the sight, it was just a blurry light in the eye view; Shali pressed another button and then the view began to become clear. Shali could see the podium very clearly; he focused again and this time in his view was the top of the microphone stand – it just looked as if it were only feet away. If you stood where the podium was you would not be able to see the mill for the trees. You had to look very hard just to see the roof of the mill just poking through the trees. There were no windows on the side of the mill that faced the Cathedral. Nareem had reported to Shali that two men in

CHAPTER 18

suits had walked around the mill last week giving it a good look over. They had tried the door of the mill and when they found it to be locked they left, clearly passing the mill off as not being a potential sniper vantage point.

Shali put the butt of the rifle on the timber frame. He then went down the ladder to the next floor. He sat down with his back against the wall and began to pray in a whispered voice. Shali sat in this position for half an hour.

"It is time," Nareem said quietly.

Shali looked up at Nareem and said: "Get everything ready. We have to be away from here in minutes."

Shali rose to his feet and went over to the bag lying on the floor; he took out the rifle magazine, looked at the long slender shells that were in it; he then went over to the rifle and slammed the magazine home. Shali then bent over the rifle, moulding his cheek into the butt, pushing his head closer to the sight. Shali switched the telescopic sight on; what Shali saw were three rows of people sitting at the rear of the podium, the Bishop was talking into the microphone, flashing over the view was the words 'safety on'. Shali pressed a button on the sight and then 'weapon armed' came up in the view for a second. Shali pressed again a button on the sight: a wider view appeared in the eye view.

CHAPTER 19

Durham City, North East England.

A police motorcycle escort pulls up outside the Cathedral. A large black limousine stops just behind the motorcycle escort. There are lots of people their waiting for their special guest. Lots of cheering and flag waving: everyone is excited. The police move forward to form a cordon around the Limousine; it is a special day indeed for the people of the North East of England. It is the opening of the newly refurbished South Wing of Durham Cathedral. The South Wing had been severely damaged by fire three years ago, and after a vigorous fund raising campaign, finally all the work has finished at a cost of two million pounds and it has painstakingly been restored to its former glory.

A red carpet had been put down from the road side to a purpose built podium for the occasion. There were state dignitaries and church officials waiting to great the honoured guest. The Bishop of Durham was presiding over the proceedings. A police officer steps forward to the limousine and opens the door; out steps a man dressed in a military uniform, at the other side of the limousine steps out a lady dressed for the occasion. Arm in arm they walk up the red carpet to the podium, then up the stairs to the floor of the podium.

Shali can now see his target walking arm in arm with his lady wife up the steps to the podium. The Bishop gestures to the man in uniform to step forward, his lady wife goes and sits down, and then the Bishop introduces him to the cheering crowds as Major Christopher Weinwright, the right honourable Earl of Stanley. The Bishop stands to one side as the Earl takes his position at

CHAPTER 19

the microphone. Shali presses a button on the sight of the rifle; the view narrows so that only the Earl is visible, and once again Shali presses another button on the sight – now only the Earl's head is in the eye view of the sight. A red cross appears; all kinds of numbers and figures appear either side of the cross. Shali looks at the numbers counting up, they stop at 1,570 yards. Shali aims the centre of the cross on the face of the Earl, there is no movement from Shali or the rifle, only the Earl's head moving slightly as he talks. Shali begins to squeeze the triggers, once again all kinds of data appear either side of the cross. "For my brothers at the Rolling Hills of Haraeffa," Shali says.

The Earl stepped forward to the microphone, making his opening speech after all the announcements had been made. Just a few minutes into his speech, when wham – the Earl's head exploded; there was no sound, just a rush of wind, blood and matter splattered on to people all around him, his lady wife directly behind him covered in the Earl's blood. His body falls back over, crashing to the floor, there is a brief silence and then all mayhem breaks loose. People jumping from the podium trying to get away from the awful sight that lay in front of them, others trying to get on to the podium to try and assist if they could. Television cameras getting tipped over in the rush of people trying to get away from the danger area. Even for the layman it was obvious the Earl had been shot, but from where? There had been no noise or indication as to where the shot had come from. And what special security men that were there, were at a loss; they were just scouring the horizons looking for a sight of someone.

The chaos ensued, the police running here, there and everywhere, but no one knew what was happening or what to do. The security forces were completely caught off guard.

People running around screaming and crying, then some sort of order began to take hold: security men trying to get people to calm down; they were really trying to keep everyone in the vicinity, just in case there were people who may be involved in the shooting so they did not leave the scene. There were no immediate buildings that close by where a sniper could take his shot from. The shot had to have come from a great distance away.

CHAPTER 20

Shali pulled the rifle away from the timber frame saying, "Nareem quickly."

Nareem threw the timber frame to one side, went to the hole in the roof and carefully slid the slates back into position. By now Shali was on his way down the ladder with the rifle, he put it on the floor shouting, "Hurry Nareem."

Nareem passed down the bag and the lamp to Shali, then came down the ladder. Shali was away down the stairs now. Nareem took the ladder and threw it against the wall; he picked up whatever kit Shali had left and made his way down the stairs. Shali was outside now. Veeri had the van running ready and the back doors open.

Shali put the rifle into the back of the van while Veeri took the bag. Rasheed was waiting for Nareem to come out of the mill; as soon as Nareem got outside Rasheed snapped the lock shut on the mill door. Shali got into the back of the van, pulling the doors closed behind him. Veeri got into the driving seat and drove off; Rasheed and Nareem got into the Vectra and followed the van. They turned along the dirt road that ran alongside the river, going the opposite way to the way they came in, Shali saying to Veeri, "Be careful." They passed a couple of men fishing in the river about four hundred yards from the mill. They kept on driving along the dirt road; the river began to narrow and get shallow.

A mile down the dirt road they came to a ford in the river; they crossed the river there. Shali was watching through the back window of the van to make sure the Vectra was keeping up with them, and also keeping a look out in case they were being followed. Once they had crossed the ford in the river they kept going along a dirt road through woods for a couple of miles, then they came to a tarmac road; they turned onto this road and headed east, and kept on going down this road. There was no sign of any police or anyone who looked as if they were looking for anybody.

Their escape route had been well planned. But now they had to travel on the main roads: they crossed over the A1 motorway, the road they had used to come into Durham, and kept going east heading towards the A19.

Shali tells Veeri to slow down; Veeri looks at Shali and asks, "Is it safe?"

"Yes," Shali says, "we have time now, the British will still be trying to work out what has just happened."

Shali takes his mobile phone out of his pocket and speed dials a number; he waits for an answer, then says into the mobile: "It is done my Lord, now the British will bear our reign of terror we will bring on them."

Shali says nothing else: he puts the mobile away. They drive for five miles, passing through Penshaw Village and onto the A19; they turn left and head north until they come to a junction, then North again along the Felling Bypass for a mile. They turn right down towards the River Tyne; a signpost reads Friars Goose Marina. The van followed by the Vectra drive down to the Marina. There is a car park with several cars parked in it before you get to the Marina. The van pulls up alongside a white Vauxhall Zafira; the Vectra pulls alongside a white Audi A4. Veeri gets out of the van and opens the Zafira. Shali takes the rifle and puts it on the back seat of the Zafira while Veeri gets the bags out of the van and puts them in the Zafira. Nareem and Rasheed put their bags into the Audi.

CHAPTER 20

"Now," Shali says, "we make ready for our guests." Shali tries to keep his men calm: "We have plenty of time now, just act natural."

CHAPTER 21

A helicopter lands in the grounds of Durham City Police Station. There are at least twenty people waiting for the helicopter's arrival. There are senior police officers, officers from the Anti Terrorist Squad, Criminal Investigation officers, and two Majors from the Special Forces Regiment SAS, Bomb Disposal officers. On board the helicopter are four men from MI5: Commander Peter Gray, his deputy Charlie Garret and two agents named Andy and Colin. Helicopter rotors have not stopped turning and the four passengers alight the craft.

A police officer comes over to introduce himself. "Chief Inspector Collingwood, sir," Peter Gray says to the Inspector. "We will have to do the introductions on the move, Inspector, time is of great value." "Have you got an operations room set up?"

"Yes sir," says the Inspector.

"Get everyone in there and we will find out who's who – a quick briefing, then I want to be out at the scene Inspector."

"The Police Station and my men are at your disposal sir and we have cars waiting," the Inspector says.

The MI5 men are at the scene of the assassination, Peter and Garret are standing on the podium. Peter said it had to come from over that way.

"All that's over that way is an old mill," Garret said, looking at a document he had in his hands. "Bailey Mill about a mile that way. There are officers down there, it is where the blue Transit and the silver Vectra were spotted. CCTV has these vehicles entering the City an hour before the shooting."

"Let's get over there," Peter said as he waved to Andy and

CHAPTER 21

Colin to follow him and Garret.

At the mill there were several police cars parked; Andy went over to speak to the officers. Colin went further down from the mill to speak to other officers who were doing a ground search. Peter and Garret were walking around the mill.

Andy came and said to the two men, "The local anglers had seen a couple of guys fishing, they said that the same guys had fished here regular for the last few weeks, and they came in the blue Transit and the silver Vectra."

"Fishing all right," Peter said, "more like giving the place the once over for their shooting spree."

"This has to be where the shot came from," Garret said, "it's the only place."

"There is no view of the podium from here; even if there was it has to be a mile away," Andy pointed out.

As they walked around the mill Peter noticed a new slate lying on the grass; there is no doubt where the slate has come from. Peter and Garret looked at each other and instantly both men came to the same conclusion: the roof of the mill. Garret said to Andy: "Get in there quick."

The mill had been opened by the officers earlier, lights were brought, all three men rushed up the stairs of the mill. Andy spotted the ladder; he placed it through the entry hatch into the roof space, and Garret went up first, followed by the other two men. Garret noticed the hole in the roof where the slate had fallen from; you could not miss it: a beam of light shone through from the daylight outside.

Peter shouted down the hatch: "Get me some glasses." By now Colin was half way up the ladder; he went back down to bring the binoculars. Peter looked through the binoculars straight through the hole in the roof.

"That is some shot, there are not many could make a shot like that," Peter said as he handed Andy the binoculars.

"Could you make that shot, Peter?" asked Andy.

"All conditions would have to be perfect and you would need the right weapon."

"Maybe," Andy said.

"This is the bench they rested the weapon on," Garret said lifting up the timber frame.

"We need to find these vehicles and fast," Peter said.

Colin said: "By the time this lot here got themselves sorted they could have got twenty miles away."

"You are right," Peter said. "It was twenty five minutes before an all points bulletin went out, and that can put them anywhere within a forty mile diameter."

CHAPTER 22

Dr Luke came into the private observation room where Trevor Carhill was to be administered to. Trevor was lying on the bed; the hospital porter was still arranging things in the room.

"Clare will be here shortly, Trevor," Dr Luke said. "Now Trevor, I want you to stay here until we have this under control. Do you agree Trevor?"

Trevor agreed saying, "I am going nowhere until I can have some kind of explanation for what is happening to me."

A few minutes later Clare came into the room. "I came as soon as I could. What's happening?"

"Clare," Trevor said, "I know I promised that I would not do this but I can't help it, I have seen things again, Clare, and this time I am more sure of what I saw than ever before."

"Dr Luke," Clare said, "what can we do?"

"I think this time, Clare, we listen to Trevor."

"Clare, I saw people in a van with a gun, I could hear them speaking in their language. I have gone over it that many times in my mind – I can nearly say the words they said."

The hospital porter was still arranging the room, while Dr Luke and the others were discussing Trevor's dilemma, when the porter turned on the wall-hung television set. Dr Luke turned to the porter and began to tell him off for being so rude. But Trevor intervened: "No, leave that," he said.

There was a newsflash on the television about the shooting of the Earl of Stanley. The news reader said how the world would be shocked by the brutal slaying of the Earl, adding that the Earl had been shot in the head by a sniper. The shooter is still on the run.

Trevor Carhill and Dr Luke looked at each other in shock; Trevor knew what he had seen this morning was somehow related. They did not hear any more of the news that was being broadcast, their thoughts now on what to do.

Trevor spoke: "What I saw in my head – it has got to have something to do with the shooting." Dr Luke knew this as well but was finding it difficult to comprehend.

"The powerful rifle I saw, it could be the one used in the shooting. The whole episode has suspicious circumstances written all over it. Dr Luke, I think they were involved," Trevor said. "The more I think of what was said, the more I believe I saw the men who shot the Earl."

"What do we do?" Dr Luke asked, telling the porter to leave the room, and the doctor shut the door behind him.

Clare by now was getting very worried and confused. "What are you two saying?"

Dr Luke came right out and said it: "Trevor believes he saw the men that killed the Earl, this very morning."

"This cannot be true," Clare said. "How could you have seen these men, Trevor?"

"The same way I witnessed what happened to me in the operating theatre. What the fuck am I going to do?" Trevor said, getting out of the bed and starting to get dressed. "This is definitely connected to this murder, I can feel it."

"There is only one thing to do," Clare said, "we go to the police."

Dr Luke said: "We have to tell the police, I agree, but how do you go about it?"

Trevor shakily putting his shoes on said, "That's what we do, get the police and quick."

"How do we do this, do we go to the police or do we call

CHAPTER 22

them"

"I don't know," said Trevor.

"We call them," Dr Luke said. "That way we can explain how we came to hear about the death of the Earl of Stanley and how we made the connection."

Within ten minutes three plain clothes officers were in Dr Luke's office and uniformed officers waiting outside the office door. Detective Inspector Furgason was the first to speak: "Doctor, you are telling us you have information relating to the shooting of the Earl of Stanley."

"Not me," Dr Luke said. "It is Mr Carhill; he has a story to tell."

"What, what have you got?" Furgason asked.

Trevor began to tell his tale; immediately Inspector Furgason's attitude began to change from a 'maybe interested' one to 'this is a major important' one. The Inspector tried to egg Trevor on to get to the end of his story, because the Inspector knew time was important. And also if what Trevor was saying was true, there were two possibilities: he is a key witness or Trevor is involved and there may still be members of the gang at the address Trevor is talking about. The Inspector pushed Trevor to tell him the address where he saw the men.

"I don't know the address," Trevor said, "but I can show you."

"Let's move," Inspector Furgason said, pushing Clare, Dr Luke and Trevor towards the door and at the same time telling one of his fellow officers to get back up and follow them to the location that Trevor was taking them to. Inspector Furgason was thinking there was no doubt what he had heard was far-fetched, but he could not dismiss it.

By now every intelligence agency in the world was scouring

the airways trying to pick up any chat that might be linked to the assassination of the Earl of Stanley. Agents from every country allied to the United Kingdom were gathering what intelligence they could. MI5 and MI6 were by now in the location, CIA and other American agencies bouncing information in secret around the globe.

On his way to the location Trevor did not have much time to think; he was terrified and Furgason kept throwing questions at him. Can you remember what the men looked like, what they were wearing, not even giving Trevor time to answer. Of course he could remember what they looked like – he just had to replay events in his mind's video player.

In no time the police cars arrived at the spot Trevor had directed them to, sirens and horns blaring so they could get a clear and fast run to the location. As soon as Trevor pointed the area out to the police officers where he witnessed the men with the rifle, one of the plain-clothed officers was on the radio ordering the area to be cordoned off.

Furgason and his men with Trevor were just going to enter the alley when one of his men said: "Sir, it's the Super," handing a mobile to Furgason. They were still walking into the alley way while Furgason was on the mobile.

Furgason stopped suddenly: "Hold up," he said, "we have to wait," turning around and walking back out the alley and telling everyone to get back as he went. Furgason called Clare over: "I want you to go with these officers," he said.

"Where to?" Clare said.

"We need to look at your house," Furgason said. "Your brother lives with you, does he not?"

"Well yes," Clare said, "but why do you want to look at my house?"

CHAPTER 22

"Just routine," Furgason said.

Clare went with two officers, kissing Trevor on the cheek before she left and saying, "I will be back as soon as I can." A black Range Rover came hurtling down the street, screeching to a stop. Two suits got out. "Special Branch," Furgason said to his men. All would be put on hold while they waited for these men, Furgason thought to himself.

One of the men got out of the Range Rover and waved Furgason over. Trevor was dazed by the speed things were moving. The guy from the black Range Rover showed Furgason his warrant and ID card. As soon as Furgason saw the men's ID he stepped to one side – he was clearly the more superior officer. One of the guys from the Black Range Rover took control, and began barking out orders to everyone; the other suit was on his mobile giving the location of where they were. And within a few seconds another black Range Rover came screeching to a halt.

Charlie Garret got out one side of the Range Rover with Agent Colin getting out of the driver's side. Furgason was led over to meet Garret by one of the first suits. Furgason pointed over towards Trevor after looking at Garret's ID. By now there were vehicles coming from all directions, police cars, unmarked cars, and even military vehicles. Garret walked over to Trevor and took him by the arm and led him back towards the Range Rover. There were still all types of vehicles arriving on the scene. Colin's arms waving first this way and then that way, as he shouted out orders to the arriving men on the scene. There were men all in black uniforms with their heads covered in hoods; they all carried weapons. Trevor could hear a helicopter in the distance, clearly approaching their location as the sound got louder.

"Get in the back seat of the car," Garret said to Trevor. Once

Trevor was in the car Garret got in and sat next to him. Trevor asked Garret who he was. Garret answered, "For the time being that is not important. What is important is what will we find when we go into the building."

"How the hell do I know?" Trevor said. "I have never been in there before."

Just then Colin opened the car door. "Everything is in place," he said.

"OK," Garret said, "no one does anything until the Specials get here, no one comes or goes."

Garret turned to Trevor and said: "Is there anyone in the building, is there anything that my men should be looking out for?"

Trevor was getting very annoyed now and he shouted his reply, "All I can fucking tell you is what I saw this morning."

By now Colin had been briefed by Furgason on what Trevor and Dr Luke had told him. Police and army marksmen were now positioned on rooftops of buildings that overlooked the building, police and armed officers evacuating nearby properties. Garret got out of the car and waved Colin over. Trevor watched as Garret talked to Colin, Collin nodding his head in agreement to what was been said to him. Then Colin gestured to two men who were standing behind the Range Rover; they came over and talked for awhile with Colin, then the two men came over to Trevor and said: "Will you come with us, Mr Carhill, into that other car over there," at the same time taking hold of Trevor by the wrist.

It was when the plain-clothed officer reached out to take hold of his wrist that Trevor saw the butt of a hand gun under his jacket. Trevor was ushered into another car. Both the men sat on either side of Trevor in the back seat of the car. They

CHAPTER 22

drove off at high speed; Trevor knew his way about Newcastle and he could tell they were making their way down towards the quayside. Trevor asked where they were going but got no reply off either man.

They pulled in just under the Tyne Bridge at the Royal Marines cadet training school on the River Tyne. A helicopter was on the helipad, its rotor blades were turning. Two men bundled Trevor out of the car and frog marched him to the helicopter; before Trevor could protest, he was bundled into the back of the helicopter, the two men sitting either side of him again. Trevor was constantly asking 'am I under arrest' and 'where are you taking me', and still getting no reply off his two escorts.

As soon as they were in the helicopter the pilot throttled up the engine and they took off. 'Funny,' Trevor thought, 'I always wanted to take a helicopter ride, but not like this, I wanted it to be my idea.' They had only been flying for about ten minutes when the pilot was talking on his headset. Trevor could feel the helicopter descending. Trevor looked out of the window; he could see Durham Cathedral, where the Earl was murdered. They were not landing there, but pretty close by; they came down in the rear of what was obviously the police station, police cars parked at the front and all around the building. A small crowd of people standing in a huddle – maybe ten or twelve. Trevor could see plainly two of the officers were armed with what looked like machine guns, two of the group were women police officers. Trevor was taken out of the helicopter by another two men in plain clothes who had been waiting with the group. The other two escorts stayed seated in the helicopter.

Trevor was escorted into the rear entrance of the police station; this time Trevor was not going to go as willingly as he had before. The escorts had to pull and push him through the doors, all the time Trevor protesting and asking 'what is happening, where are you taking me,' no one answering, only murmuring between themselves.

Trevor tried to stand still, saying, "I am going no further until somebody tells me what's going on." The escorts just looked at each other and put more effort into dragging Trevor along; one of the officers behind them started to push Trevor from the back. Trevor's feet just slid along the tiled floor as the men dragged him. Trevor held himself rigid, not wanting to relax and make the men's job of taking him into the building any easier for them.

CHAPTER 23

Garret walked to the alley where Trevor had seen the men with the rifle getting into the van; Colin was not far behind him. Garret spoke to a man who was heavily armed; the man carried a machine gun and also had hand guns, one under his armpit, the other holstered to his waist.

"What do you think?" Garret said to the man.

"I am not sure yet until I get some feedback from my men," the heavily armed man said. The armed man was dressed in black, hooded and wearing a bullet proof vest; he was in voice contact with his men, because every now and then he would speak into thin air saying 'copy'. He was dressed much the same as lot of the men at the scene now. But this man was a specialist in this field of work; this is the man in charge of the Specialist Team whom Garret referred to earlier.

"Simon," the man said to Garret, "the name's Simon." A crackling on Simon's earpiece, Simon replied saying "I am on my way."

Simon moved down the alley to the back door the suspects had come out of. The door was open and at either side of the door stood men dressed similar to Simon. Simon spoke to one of the men saying, "What you have got?"

"Nothing up to now, it looks deserted," the man said to Simon. Simon moved to go through the door; Garret began to follow him. Simon stopped and just looked at the dark passageway leading into the ground floor of a four storey building that had been rented by one of the suspects.

Simon turned back and said to Garret, "You two go and wait in the alley. I will give you a call when it is safe to enter."

Garret protested: he wanted to be one of the first in so he could protect evidence that may be present. But Simon insisted, saying no one was going anywhere until he and his men had secured the building. Garret had to withdraw because he could see Simon meant what he said. When Garret and Colin had left, Simon and his men began to edge their way along the dark passageway, their eyes getting used to the dim light, there was daylight coming in from the open doorway.

Trevor was pulled through the doorway entrance to the police station, marched along a series of corridors each with locked doors at their ends. The doors were opened by officers who could see them coming through eye slits in the doors. Down a flight of stairs they went and along three more corridors, down more stairs. Trevor thought there must be more of this building underground than what is above ground. The next corridor they went into had doors along each side; the first door they came to was opened by one of the suits. Trevor was told to go inside the room; all that was in the room was a table and three chairs Trevor was told to take a seat. Trevor took a seat saying nothing, he knew he was not going to get any answers; the door was shut behind him by the officer who had been standing at the door when they came in.

No sooner had the door shut than it was opened again; in came a couple of men Trevor had not seen among the greeting group. The two men sat down; they had folders of papers with them. The older of the two men spoke first. "Would you like something to drink?" he said to Trevor.

"I would," Trevor said; his mouth was dry as sticks.

"Coffee?" the man said.

"Yes," Trevor replied, "white, no sugar."

The younger man opened the door and spoke to the officer

CHAPTER 23

standing there; he came back and sat down. Trevor did not know what to expect; his whole body was shaking. He looked at his watch – it was only 1.45; only a few hours had passed – it seemed like more, but it was not.

The older man spoke again: "My name is Peter Gray; this man here is Andy." No other name, just Andy.

Trevor tried again, "Will you tell me what is happening or going on here".

Andy said: "We were hoping you were going to tell us because seemingly you know more about these men at Mosley Street than we do."

'Mosley Street'. This was the first time Trevor had heard the name of the street, even though he knew his way around Newcastle. A knock at the door. Peter said: "yes." A man came in with three cups of coffee on a tray. Trevor took a sip of his coffee; it was the best coffee he had tasted for a long time – it was like nectar he thought, savouring every sip; it seemed like days since he had had a drink. Peter leant over to a cupboard on the wall; he opened the door. There was recording equipment in there; Peter switched it on.

"Now Trevor, you tell us everything you know and what happened since you got out of bed this morning." Trevor began to tell his story again.

Simon and his men were moving gingerly along the passageway, the light getting a bit better now from the windows at the front of the building. Simon could see there were two doors on the same side and stairs going up to the next floor level. Four storey building, Simon thought, every floor the same as the ground floor – this is going to take a long time. He and everyone else knew that there would be none of the suspects in the building, but you could not be a hundred per cent sure. Garret and Colin were standing at the entrance to the alley at Mosley Street, Colin saying to Garret, "We should have gone in, and these big footed soldiers would mess up any evidence that may be there." Garret said the SAS knew what they were doing and anyway they had to make sure the building was safe and secure.

Simon pointed to one of the doors as he passed it. Two of the men following behind stopped at the door, one of them getting down on his knees to examine the lock. Simon nodded towards the next door as he passed that one; two more of the soldiers that were behind Simon stopped at that door and began to examine the lock and listened against the door. Simon and the other four of his men began to creep up the stairs to the first floor. This floor, Simon noted, was a mirror image of the ground floor.

The first door he came to he did not have to say or do anything to his men: two of them just got on with trying to open the door as easily and as carefully as they could. Simon and the other two men, moving as fast as they dared, went up to the next door – time was of the essence. Simon knew Garret wanted access as soon as possible into the building; they needed to see if there was any kind of evidence or information that could lead them to the suspects, and if they are connected to the assassination of the Earl they will be making their getaway, so the quicker they get through checking the building is safe and secure the better for everyone concerned. Simon knew as well as anyone they needed to get these men before they left the country.

One of the men was now on his knees, the door was eased open; Simon pulled his gun around from his shoulder and edged his head around the door. A big room well lit from light through the windows, a couple of adjoining doors, they had to move quickly, Garret and his men eager to get into this building. At a

CHAPTER 23

glance you could see this room had not been occupied for a long time. Experience had taught the SAS not to waste time. The first floor rooms must have been the same because the first pair of soldiers were now in the room Simon was in; a quick look inside the adjoining rooms showed they had not been used for a while either.

Simon moved up to the second floor level; it was the same floor layout as the floors below. By now two more of the soldiers were back in tow after checking a previous room. The passageway and the stairs had definitely been used recently; they kept on checking the rooms. The same as the ground floor and the first floor – no one had been in the rooms for a long time on the second floor either. Simon moved up the stairs to the third floor, moving quicker now they had learned the layout of the floors and rooms from the others they had checked. Simon stopped at the first door with two men, another two of his men going past him to the next door on that floor level, one man going down on his knees to the lock. Just then the soldier opened the door where Simon was; Simon was just going to move into the room, when the light coming from the room caught on something above the door that the men ahead of him were opening. Simon strained his eyes and could make out what seemed to be a spider's thread that came from the top of the door going across the ceiling to the stairs.

Garret and Colin were getting itchy feet; Garret was saying to himself 'come on guys, we have no time to waste'. As Garret turned to look up to the rear of the building to check if there was any movement on them getting access, an almighty blast ripped the roof of the building off, sending it into the air. Throwing out the walls from the two top levels of the building, bricks, glass and timber came showering down. Flames and smoke tore out through doorways and windows back and front of the building.

Garret pulled Colin around the corner away from flying debris. The front street was carnage: cars were buried under rubble, alarms were going off, and as the smoke began to clear you could make out the shape of figures lying in the road. Some just heaps of rags, others moving very slowly, one person crawling along the ground using his hands and arms only, his legs no longer part of his body. You could hear the screams and cries of the injured and the shocked over the noise of the car and shop alarms.

Colin turned to Garret in shock and dismay saying, "What the fuck has just happened?"

"Fucking booby-trap, that's what just happened," Garret shouted as they both began to run towards the wreckage of the building. Clambering over smouldering debris Garret got to the back door first – or what used to be the entrance into the building. Throwing bits of timber and broken furniture to one side they found, lying about ten feet inside the passageway, one of the SAS team; the man was charred black, the rags of clothes that he still had on his body were smoking. The man was dead. Garret tried to go further into the building. Colin stopped him – pieces of debris were still falling and there was fear of collapse. It was a disaster area; there were still fires burning in places in the wrecked building.

A police officer shouted, "Sir over here." Colin went over to the officer, a body of a man lying across a battered dustbin. Colin shouted over to Garret; Garret came over. He cannot believe what he sees: it is Simon, his body is broken – you could not lie the way he was lying without snapping the torso into some ugly deformed shape, there is blood oozing out from

CHAPTER 23

wounds in his head.

Simon's head moves. Garret moves closer to try and stop him from moving to prevent further injury, but on closer inspection of Simon's injuries Garret knows moving is going to make no difference to the outcome of Simon's fate. Simon is trying to speak, Garret puts his ear to Simon's mouth, but after a second or two, Simon gives a muffled moan and then nothing: he was gone.

"What did he say?" Colin asked Garret.

"I think he said, wire on the ceiling." Garret went round to the front of the building; the carnage that met him was a sight of utter devastation. He stepped over the charred body of what was another member of the entry team. He looked around – at least five heaps of smoking clothes that used to be human beings. Every shop window was blown out, curtains blowing in the wind. Garret's blood boiled as he stood looking at the gruesome sight; nothing he could have done would have prevented this.

People came from all angles now, trying to help the injured.

He hears someone moan to his left near the wreckage of a car. A man is wedged under the car. Garret screams for help; Colin and two police officers come running to try and assist Garret who now was trying to lift the car off the man on his own, The four men try to lift the car together; they move it a small amount, the man screams in pain. Just then a fireman says to Garret, "Leave it to us sir, we will get him out." There were more firemen and emergency service personnel all over the disaster area now.

Colin says to Garret, "We should go, there is nothing we can do here." The evidence, if there was any, will take Forensics days, maybe weeks, to find – by then it would be too late.

CHAPTER 24

Back in London MI5 and MI6 were on high alert. In the high security operations room agents sat at computer monitors, intensely working away. Everyone had the same goal, trying to get a lead on the shooter who took out the Earl of Stanley in Durham City. One of the operators let out a loud shout of, 'Jesus no way'; Carter, director of operations, was in the ops room at the time.

"What the hell is it" she said to the operator who gave out the shout. "The safe house at Newcastle has just blown up Ma'am; the SAS team were inside when it went up."

Carter dropped her head into her hands. "How many?" she said.

"Looks like all of them Ma'am, and some local police on the outside." Telephones began ringing, machines began clicking into action, and the whole room was a wash of voices. Carter kicked into professional mode. "Get me the Home Secretary, pull everything we have on any terrorist units. Also get me Washington as well; let's see what the Americans can come up with on this."

Peter Gray was looking at the paperwork in front of him. It was a copy of the statement that Trevor Carhill and Dr Luke had given Detective Inspector Furgason. It read exactly the same as what Trevor was telling them now.

Andy interrupted Trevor: "Wait just one minute – are you trying to tell us that when these men got into the back of the van and closed the doors behind them, you could still see and hear them?"

"Yes, I am telling you this, and I can still see and hear them if

CHAPTER 24

I try."

Andy turned and looked at Peter and said, "For fuck sake governor."

"Come on, calm down," Peter said. "You can describe every man and tell us what they said."

"Describe them yes, but what they said no; I could not understand what they said – they were talking in a foreign language, I think it was Pakistani and all the men looked Pakistani. And they spoke in a foreign language."

Andy said, "This guy is taking the piss," as he stood up sharply, banging his hand on the table.

"Take it easy," Peter said, "sit down."

"Get a voice recorder," Trevor said. "I can say the foreign words but I don't know what they mean."

"That will not be necessary," Peter said, "as we are already recording what you are saying."

Andy said again to Trevor: "So you can see them in your head?"

"Yes, yes," Trevor said. "How many more times do I have to tell you?"

"If you can see them in your head then where the fuck are they now?" Andy asked.

"I don't know where they are now, I can only see them from this morning for that brief time until someone broke my concentration."

Peter turned to Andy and said: "There are lots of mug shots of possibles – go and get them – and Andy, get me a language expert as soon as possible."

When Andy left the room Trevor said to Peter: "I can see and hear them as plain as day. I am not lying and I am not crazy."

"Well I think we will be the judge of that," Peter said.

"Did they have something to do with the shooting of the Earl?" Trevor asked. Peter did not answer him.

Trevor said, "I could even see the rifle when the man took it out of the case."

Andy came back in the room with albums of photographs of suspected terrorists. "We have not got much time, so you had better be quick picking these guys out of this lot." Andy was convinced this was a pointless exercise. Andy thought Trevor was in on this somehow; no one could have this amount of information about these guys and not know what they were up to. Peter Gray was an old school agent: he gathered facts and acted on them. And he knew there was no way that Trevor could be involved with these guys, well at least not in the last six months or so because Trevor had been seriously injured at work.

Peter Gray rose from his chair and left the room. He went down the corridor to the kitchen, passing a room with the door slightly open, just the same as the room he had just left. In it were two more agents, a man and a woman; they were questioning Dr Luke. Peter stood at the kitchen bench, opening his folder to read again what he had just been listening to from Trevor Carhill.

A plain-clothed officer came in. "This has just came in for you, sir," he said, handing Peter a couple of pieces of paper. Peter studied the papers for a moment then went back to the interview room.

Andy jumped up saying, "This is no good, this sap is playing games with us governor."

"I take it you have had no luck then," Peter said.

"A couple of maybes on the guys in the front of the van but nothing on the men in the back."

Trevor said, "I saw the men in the front of the van and in the

CHAPTER 24

back of the van as plain as I see you and they are not in those photographs."

Peter leant over Trevor and put a piece of the paper he was carrying on the table in front of Trevor saying, "You ever seen that before?"

"That's it!" Trevor shouted, jumping up to a standing position. "That is it, that is the rifle I saw in the van, the one the men had."

Andy looked at Peter and said: "What the hell is this, Peter?" Peter gestured to Andy to come follow him out of the room; Peter told the officer standing outside the room to go in the room and stay with Trevor.

Peter held the photograph in front of Andy saying, "The Americans lost one of these guns in Afghanistan about seven months ago. This rifle is the best on the market; in the right hands it can hit a target 2,500 yards away. An American special ops team were killed and the rifle taken."

"That's a fucking mile and a half, governor," Andy said.

"Long Range Super Rifle's not long off the test circuit, so this report tells us." Peter said: "I have no doubt that this is the rifle that did for the Earl. But now we need to know who was driving this super gun and quick before they leave the country."

Peter was getting weary – it had been a long day and it was not over yet. Andy was keen to get in and do some real interrogation on Trevor. "I really don't think he is involved," Peter said to Andy. "Yes his story is out of this world, and yes he does know a lot about the events before the shooting. But no way on this earth is he part of this team who hit the Earl. God, we are not even a hundred per cent certain it is the same guys he said he saw. Although everything points to him, I don't think so."

A loud commotion started along the corridor, making Andy

and Peter rush to see what was happening. Garret and Colin with a trail of other men behind them were coming along the corridor. Andy called down to Colin saying, "What has happened?"

"They blew the fucking building up, a bloody booby-trap in the safe house, the whole search team dead," Colin said.

Garret's eyes popping out of his head, "Where's Carhill?" he said.

"Wait a minute," Peter said. "Calm down." Peter himself really wanted to go in and have a go at Trevor, but he knew that was not going to help matters.

All the other routes of inquiry were coming up with nothing. The CCTV in Newcastle had picked up the van leaving the City by the Tyne Bridge going into Gateshead this morning. CCTV in Durham City picked up the same van entering the City, but not leaving the City, well not leaving by the route it took to enter the City. Police search teams were out looking for the blue Transit van, we even have the number of the van now. An appeal to the public to look out for the van was broadcast over local radio and television. Police forces all over the UK were trying to gather information that would help in the case, specialists in every field of police detection and still nothing. What evidence there was in the safe house was blown all over Mosley Street.

At this moment Peter knows that unless something breaks Trevor is their only lead. Peter told Andy go and get Colin and go to work on Trevor, "and Andy," Peter said as he was leaving, "no rough stuff". Peter got Garret to follow him into the kitchen.

"Jesus Peter, it was a nightmare, bodies all over the place, parts of bodies lying in the street."

Peter asked how many. "I don't know yet, all nine on the

CHAPTER 24

sweep and search team gone."

"Who's down there now?" Peter asked Garret.

"Anti-terrorist squad running the show, a guy called Kelvin Klerk has the reigns."

"Anything from London?" Garret asked.

"Carter has the whole country's resources on it, all the airports are covered, they are mostly closed down in the North East, ports, docks and ferries being watched, but what are we looking for or who, we don't know a bloody thing really. The only one that can give us a lead is Trevor Carhill," Peter said. "Garret, do you really think this guy is for real?"

"He has some kind of inner sight, a third eye, he can see through fucking brick walls," Garret said.

"Through steel actually," Peter said.

"So what do we do?" asked Garret.

"We get experts in, I have a language expert coming, see what we can make of the words he says were spoken," said Peter.

"It is his head that we want to be looking at," Garret said.

"We have a shrink to do exactly that as well," Peter said. "We have to start making progress – it is a long time since the shooting: these guys could be long gone."

Peter turned and walked along the corridor and into the interview room where Dr Luke is being interrogated. Peter looked at Dr Luke and said: "Is this possible, he can see things in his head that are actually happening?"

"I am trying to tell you but no one is listening," Dr Luke said.

"OK," Peter said, "I am asking is it possible what Trevor Carhill is claiming – that he can see in his subconscious mind actual happening events? I am listening."

Dr Luke started to explain what Trevor has been through –

his massive head injuries, and the surgery that had to be done to rebuild his skull. Dr Luke told Peter: "Trevor said he could see the surgery been carried out on himself when he was barely alive." Dr Luke continued: "Trevor told me everything that went on in the operating theatre. In the operation theatre there were eight people: myself, Dr Mayo, Dr Lustman, an anaesthetist and four theatre nurses, and of course Trevor. Dr Mayo and Dr Lustman were performing the surgery to rebuild Trevor's skull. Trevor's brain was exposed, and the top of the head was to be capped with a titanium plate. When Dr Lustman was ready to place the plate, the theatre nurse passed the titanium plate to Dr Mayo to hold in position. Dr Mayo fumbled the plate and dropped it. The surgery was held up for ten minutes while the titanium plate had to be sterilised."

Peter butted in: "Dr Luke this is not telling me that Carhill can see the things he claims he can."

"Mr Gray, Trevor told me that he saw Dr Mayo drop the titanium plate. No one else knew that – only the people that were present in the operating theatre," Dr Luke said. "We think somehow Trevor has gained the use of ESP (extrasensory perception). Don't ask me how; we don't know – we are running extensive tests. We cannot come out in the open about this until we have tangible proof. Now I know Trevor told me everything that went on in the operating theatre, Mr Gray, I say what Trevor says is true. And now I am thinking that Trevor needs a catalyst to kick-start this ability to see in his subconscious."

"A catalyst? What do you mean doctor?" Peter asked.

"I think he needs to be in deep concentration on a subject or subjects, or a situation that is so unusual that it holds Trevor's full concentration; this opens the door beyond what he can see in actual normal vision and audio. He can follow the event

CHAPTER 24

wherever it goes so to speak."

"Wherever it goes," Peter said. "If this is true the possibilities are mind boggling. So doctor you are saying I should put men's lives at risk and spend millions of pounds of taxpayers' money on the say of one man's subconscious dreams?"

"The way I see it," Dr Luke said to Peter, "it's all you have got at the moment."

"We are bringing in some top head doctors; I would like you to help – Carhill trusts you," Peter said.

"But what about my other patients and work at the hospital?" Dr Luke said.

"Don't worry about that, we will sort cover for you for the time being," Peter said.

Charlie Garret went into the interview room where Andy and Colin are speaking to Trevor Carhill. Garret said to Colin: "I want you to go to Newcastle Airport and meet an American, a Paul Bennet; he arrives on the seven o'clock flight from Tel Aviv. This guy is a weapons man, CIA, he knows everything about our super rifle."

CHAPTER 25

"Ma'am, the PM is on the telephone." Carter left the group of people she was in deep conversation with, and went into her office closing the door; this was the call she dreaded. "Yes Prime Minister," she said trying to sound calm.

"What the hell is happening Liz?" the Prime Minister said, shouting down the telephone.

"This mess is outrageous; I want answers and I want them quick Liz."

"We are working on every possible lead Prime Minister, we have all routes out of the country covered; the perpetrators will not get away," Liz Carter said.

"How on earth could this be allowed to happen? And this disaster in Newcastle – what went wrong?"

"A bomb, Prime Minister," Carter said. "The bastards had rigged a booby-trap ready for our men."

"And the fatalities?" the Prime Minister asked.

"Nine Special Service men and five local enforcement officers dead and seven badly injured, two of them are not expected to make it, Prime Minister," Carter said.

"For the love of God, I cannot believe this is happening on British soil," the Prime Minister said.

"We are leaving no stone unturned and we are pulling out all the stops, Prime Minister."

"I am going for a meeting with the Queen shortly Liz; I want to be able to tell Her Majesty that everyone responsible for what happened will be caught and dealt with."

"I can assure you Prime Minister everything humanly possible is being done to catch these terrorists. I will keep you

CHAPTER 25

informed every step of the way, Prime Minister."

"I hope so Liz, this kind of thing does not happen in the United Kingdom. Someone will have to pay."

Liz Carter put the telephone down. 'Where will this all end?', she thought, 'something has to break soon.' Carter got up and went and opened the door of her office; she looked over the operations room – a mass of bodies working tirelessly at computers, teleprompters were clicking away, people shuffling back and forth with papers and folders, people on the telephone, people shouting information across the room to other agents. Carter shouted across the room, "Come on everyone: do it, do it, get something, we need to move, come on." Everything stands still for a split second, then the room bursts into a hive of activity – everyone in the room was trying to look even more busy, if that were at all possible.

Andy got up from the table in the interview room saying, "I need to speak to Peter". He called the officer into the room to watch over Trevor. Trevor sat in the room at the table, the officer stood in front of the door. Trevor thought to talk with the officer but then changed his mind. 'What the hell am I mixed up in,' he thinks. He was feeling very tired. 'At first I was excited when I found out what I was capable of doing with my mind,' Trevor thought, 'but now I wish it had never happened'. Maybe it is gone now, he thought.

Trevor decided to check if he could still summon up the images in his mind. He began to focus and concentrate on the morning's events – click, there it was playing again. This time Trevor began to take more notice, listen more intently, look in detail – what the men were wearing, was there anything he had not noticed before? What he did notice and realise was the men in the front of the van, the driver and the passengers, were talking as well, turning their heads to talk to the men in the back of the van. Not a lot was said from the men in the front of the van but when they turned to talk to the men in the back Trevor could get a good look at their faces.

Peter Gray and Andy came back in the room. "Now then Trevor, I have had a good talk with Dr Luke and she is trying to convince me that what you say is true. Now I am going to give you the benefit of my doubt. I will interview you entirely on the basis that what you say is fact, and I hope I am not wasting precious time."

Just then Charlie Garret opened the door. "They have found the van and the silver Vectra," Garret said.

"That's good news," Peter said. "Where are they?"

Garret looked at the piece of paper he had in his hand and said, "Friars Goose Marina, it is in Gateshead on the banks of the River Tyne."

"Andy you go with Charlie," Peter said. "Make sure no one touches anything; Get the show down there, now move. At last we have some movement."

He called the officer into the room and told him: "Go and get Miss Simpson to come in here, will you please? Right Trevor, I want you to tell me everything that happened and what was said in that van again, but first tell me about these long boxes you saw these men put into the van."

"They were just boxes; two of the men carried the boxes between them," Trevor said.

"Do you think they were weapon boxes, the kind of boxes there would be rifles or machine guns in?" Peter asked.

"I don't think so," Trevor said. "If I did not know better I would have said they were concrete kerbstones, but for two reasons I knew they were not."

CHAPTER 25

"And what are those two reasons that make you think they were not kerbstones?"

"They were too long for kerbstones; a kerbstone is about three feet long, and these were twice that length, about six feet," Trevor said.

"And the other reason?"

"Well," Trevor said, "they looked like concrete, they were the same colour as concrete and looked the same texture as concrete. But if they were concrete those men would not have carried them that easily. Yes, the ones they put in the back of the van were heavy, but no way as heavy as they would have been if they were real concrete."

"Six foot long?" Peter said.

"Yes, about six feet long by twelve inches wide at the bottom and about eight inches wide at the top and ten inches high, and one side was tapered," Trevor said.

CHAPTER 26

Shali said to Rasheed, "You and Veeri take the car and go to the hideout. Wait there for the others to arrive. Nareem and I will be along later. Rasheed, make sure you are not followed, drop Veeri off first to look and see you are not followed, go away and wait until Veeri calls you, then return. Stay hidden. Come Nareem, we are to wait until the British come for the vehicles."

Shali and Nareem got into the Zafira and drove back up to the main road, turning left and heading south; they drove for about two miles, then turned down towards the Tyne Tunnel. They passed through the Tyne Tunnel and out the other side of the River Tyne, then turning north they headed for Wallsend. They drove for about two miles to Wallsend and took a road signposted 'Riverside walk'. Turning down this road they came to the river's edge. There were several small parking areas. Shali had Nareem park close to the river front. Shali took the binoculars from his rucksack. Looking through them, Shali said "perfect".

Directly across from where they were parked, on the other side of the River Tyne was the Friars Goose Marina, and Shali could see the parked van and Vectra in among other parked vehicles.

"And now we wait Nareem," Shali said.

Nareem asked, "Will they not see us, Shali?"

"We will move back when the vehicles are discovered. We will be able to see everything from the top of the road."

Shali's mobile telephone vibrated in his pocket; he answered it after looking to check who was calling. "Yes Veeri," Shali said, "very well, stay there, do not move around outside. We will

CHAPTER 26

come as soon as we are done here."

"Rasheed and Veeri are at the hideout, they have stowed the car away," Shali said to Nareem.

"Look Shali," Nareem said, "a police car has driven into Friars Goose Marina."

Shali said: "We move back to the top of the road and watch."

Charlie Garret and Andy arrive at Friars Goose Marina. There are plenty of police officers already present, cordoning off the whole car park areas, and the road into the car park is barred off at the entrance. The access road from the main road junction has a police road block in operation. A police officer comes over to introduce himself to Garret and Andy.

"Inspector Wade sir," the police officer says.

"I am Garret and this is Andy," Andy showing the Inspector his warrant card. "What's the commotion over there?" Andy asks the Inspector.

"It is the men from the marina sir, we are evacuating the area and the men will not leave without their cars."

"Go see to it," Garret says to Andy, "while I get the bomb squad down the right road this time." Garret turns to the Inspector: "Tell your boys at the road block to watch out for the bomb squad and the anti-terrorist teams please."

Andy goes to the police officers who are arguing with the men from the marina; he says to the police sergeant in a loud voice so the arguing men from the marina can hear: "Sergeant if all these men are not out of here in five minutes I want you to arrest them all and take them down the nick, and you make sure they stay there for at least one night. Now get the hell out of here and quick."

A van pulls up and a police officer gets out and goes to the back of the van and leads out a dog; this is a very special dog, a Cocker Spaniel – she is used to sniff out explosives. Not too long, armoured vehicles arrive on the scene with the anti-terrorist teams and the bomb disposal men. Andy and Garret go over to the observation post that has been set up near the car park. A wall of sandbags has been erected for the team to observe from behind. A bomb disposal officer comes over to introduce himself to Garret and Andy. "Major Peters, sir."

"Garret and Andy," Garret says to the Major. "What is your procedure, Major?"

"We need to find out if there are any explosives in the vehicles first sir. One of our guys will get kitted up and go take a look with Lucky sir."

"Lucky?" Andy said. "The Cocker Spaniel sir, she is our explosive detector; you name the type of explosive and Lucky will sniff it out."

"Lucky by name and I hope by nature," Garret said.

Looking down onto the car park there were about twenty five cars parked in various places. The van and the Vectra were alongside each other with cars either side of them; there was a row of vehicles in front of the van and the Vectra and another row in front of those vehicles. The car park was marked out in bays, and wheel buffers separated the rows.

"OK Major, it is all yours," Garret said.

"All right Captain, you can send your man in," the Major ordered.

The bomb disposal man was all rigged up in blast-proof clothes – he could hardly walk; poor Lucky only had a camera on her head. Man and dog move slowly towards the vehicles; as they were doing so, the rest of the bomb disposal men were unloading a robot from the back of a van some distance away up the road. The robot was on tracks – it was basically a couple

CHAPTER 26

of articulated arms, one with a gun in its grab claw, the other arm was just the claw and a camera built on a tracked frame, all could be manoeuvred by remote control.

The dog starts to sniff around as she approaches the vehicles. Getting encouragement from her handler, the dog gets closer to the Vectra. The dog is getting excited as she sniffs around the car, the handler cheering her on, the dog even jumps onto the bonnet of the car and underneath checks all around the car. The dog is excited but the handler does not seem too impressed.

They move away from the car and go to the van; this time Lucky the sniffer dog is more excited – her tail is wagging and she is moving rapidly, nose to that place then another, then back again to where she had covered before. The response was more animated than the reaction on the car: first the front of the van and then moving slowly towards the back of the van. As they move near to the back of the van the dog gets very excited – she begins barking and jumping up at the rear of the van.

The handler pulls the dog back close to him; he looks through the windows on the back doors of the van, checks the inside, then he goes to the front of the van and looks through the windows, over to the car and looks through the car windows. Man and sniffer dog return back to the observation post; another bomb disposal guy gives the dog handler a hand to remove his hood and jacket; the handler then starts to make a big fuss over Lucky, patting her and telling her what a good dog she is.

Andy, Garret and the Major go over to the dog handler who is still praising and patting his dog.

"What we got Sergeant?" the Major says to the dog handler.

"The car is iffy but the van – there is definitely something in the back that Lucky does not like. In the back of the van there is a bag with something inside it and what looks like a rifle case, a couple of fishing rods and other bits and pieces I can't identify. But the van is hot, the car maybe."

"I need those vehicles," Garret says to the Major.

"If what the Sergeant says is right sir, you may be getting the vehicles in a skip," the Major says. "Bring Robbie over," the Major orders.

The remote controlled robot is tracked down towards the car park, the Corporal who operates the remote controls goes and stands behind the sandbag wall, a television monitor is set up – it shows what the robot camera is looking at. Major Peters orders everyone to take cover.

Garret says to the remote control operator, "What's your name son?"

"Corporal Barry Armstrong, sir."

"Well Barry, let's have a look at the car first, can we?" Garret says.

"Yes sir," says the Corporal. The robot tracks down towards the vehicles. Andy and Garret watch as the robot gets close to the car, then they turn their gaze to the monitor. A close up shot of the lock on the boot of the car is what they see.

"OK Corporal," the Major says. The Corporal pushes a few buttons and then moves the joystick on the control panel; there is a trigger on the joystick. The Corporal squeezes the trigger, a loud bang from the gun been discharged, a large hole appears where the lock used to be on the car boot. A few skilful manoeuvres with the joystick and the robotic arm prises the boot of the car open. The Corporal manoeuvres the camera to take a look in the boot: there is nothing to be seen.

"Now the doors, Corporal," the Major says.

Garret's mobile phone rings, it is Peter Gray. "How does it

CHAPTER 26

look Charlie?" Peter asks.

"Well Peter, it looks like we have another booby-trap," Garret says. "The bomb boys say the car may be clean but the van has definitely got something in it – the sniffer dog was going bananas."

"How long?" Peter asks.

"Well the bomb boys are just opening the car doors now; there is nothing happening but when they move to the van I will be getting down behind the sandbags," Garret says.

"Keep me posted on that, Charlie."

"Will do," Garret says putting the mobile phone away.

All the car doors were open. The robot shoots a couple of rounds into the dashboard of the car, it tracks to the front of the car and forces the bonnet up after shooting the locking mechanism out; the camera shows nothing suspicious in the engine compartment.

"OK," the Major says, "let's have a look at the van, Corporal. Doors at the front first."

"Yes sir," the Corporal said. The robot fires its gun at the lock of the passenger door of the van; the door does not need to be forced open – it flies open from the gunshot blast, the camera reveals nothing in the front of the van.

The camera is manoeuvred right inside.

"Clear the dashboard," the Major says to the Corporal. The Corporal manipulates the joystick and the robot fires a couple of rounds into the dashboard of the van: no response, nothing happens. "Now the back doors, Corporal," the Major says.

"This is the one," Garret says to Andy.

The lock on the back doors of the van appear on the monitor screen and as before a loud bang as the lock is shot out; all that is left is a hole where the lock used to be. The Corporal moves the joystick very slowly, the articulated arm snakes out and begins to pry the back doors open; the arm of the robot hooks its claw in the hole on the doors, the Corporal pulls back gently on the joystick, the robot moves back over, pulling the doors open. The robot goes back in closer, the camera shows the back of the van just as the dog handler described it.

"What now sir?" the Corporal says.

The Major says: "Send a shot into the bag."

"Hold on that," Garret says, "Barry, could you pull out of the back of the van the rifle case and other bits and bobs with that arm?"

"Yes sir, I can," the Corporal says.

"Do that please," Garret says, and the Corporal looks at the Major. The Major nods his head in agreement. The articulated arm reaches out into the van, the grab on the end of the arm expertly manoeuvred takes hold of the gun case, and it gets a perfect grip and picks the case up. The robot backs off and slews around the arm, beginning to lower the case to the ground.

"No," Garret says, "drop it, and drop it from as high as you can, lift it up son." The robot arm rises up; it reaches just higher than the height of the van; its grab open, the rifle case falls to the ground hard. Nothing happens. "OK," Garret says, "let's try the bag son." The Corporal manoeuvres the robot back to the rear of the van; the robot arm reaches back into the van, the camera showing every detail on the television monitor.

Andy and Garret watch in anticipation as the arm moves forward. The grab on the end of the arm takes hold of the bag. It begins to lift slowly and the underside of the bag is revealed: the bag is a rucksack turned inside out. The robot arm lifts a bit higher and then a bright flash and an enormous loud bang. The sides of the van push out, the roof of the van rips up from

CHAPTER 26

the rear and tears down its length, the robot arm is blown off completely and the robot is thrown about twenty feet back over and landing on its side. Smoke bellows out of the twisted van, glass is blown about, all the windows of the cars in close proximity to the van are blown out, the dust and the smoke begins to clear. You can see the extent of the blast now, the back of the van torn open to the front seats, the chassis remains with wheels and tyres smouldering. The Vectra car's side facing the van is all dented and pushed in and it has been thrown tight against the car it was parked alongside, and the car parked on the other side of the van suffered the same damage and was pushed up against the car alongside it.

Garret spoke first: "Well, I hope that's it."

Andy said to the Corporal: "That was a good job mate, but I think Robbie needs a mechanic."

"OK Major, what now?" Garret said.

"Our boys go take a look." Two of the bomb disposal team started to get ready in their blast-proof clothes; once they were ready they slowly walked towards the twisted van, stepping over the pieces of debris as they went. They looked over the wreck, checking in every nook and cranny underneath, inside and out and then they did the same with the Vectra car. "It is all clear," they reported, standing back and removing the heavy cumbersome hoods they were wearing.

"Very well," the Major said.

"Can we move close now?" Garret said to the Major.

"Just give the boys ten minutes to make a final sweep," the Major said, as the Captain sent in six men to give the scene a final check over again.

Garret said to Andy: "Get Forensics and the guys down ready to move. We get what we can off the ground, then I want the car and the van taken to Durham as soon as we can." Andy went to talk to the men who were parked some distance up the road from the scene. There were two flat bed wagons waiting to cart the vehicles away to Durham when they were ready.

The Major came over to Garret and said: "It is all yours now sir."

"OK Major, thanks for that," Garret said. Garret called Andy on his mobile phone to bring the teams in now the scene was clear. Andy started to walk back towards the scene with about ten men wearing white hooded overalls and as many men again following them carrying equipment. Police officers removed the barriers to allow the forensic team to enter the car park; most of the men in white overalls began immediately to comb the area adjacent to the twisted vehicles.

Garret got his mobile phone out and gave Peter Gray a call.

"Yes Charlie," Peter said, "how is it going down there?"

"Well the van was rigged with explosives –it blew up – the blast was not as bad as I thought it would be," Garret said.

"Is there anything we can use quickly?" Peter asked.

"Not a lot in the van, nothing in the car that we can see yet."

"What was in the van?" Peter asked.

"Fishing rods, the gun case and our rucksack with the bomb in it," Garret said.

"There were no boxes that looked like elongated kerbstones then?" Peter said.

"What's these boxes?" Garret asked.

"Carhill told us there were boxes that looked like kerbstones, only they were longer than kerbstones; he had seen the suspects put them in the van, nothing like that there then?"

Garret stands looking at the van. Just in front of the van were the wheel buffers that stop the vehicles going too far into

CHAPTER 26

the next row of parking spaces when they park: these buffers are made of concrete. Garret notices two of the buffer sections are moved just in front of the car and van. He drops his hand holding the mobile phone and shouts at the top of his voice: "Get the fuck out of there, run for your lives."

There are about twenty men around the Vectra car and the Transit van wreckage; they all look Garret's way as he screams at the top of his voice for them to run for their lives, "There is another bomb, run, get out of there."

Andy, who is close to the vehicles, turns and starts to make a run for it; all the rest of the forensic team start to make a dash for their lives. The last man gets about thirty feet away from the bombed vehicles when a massive explosion goes off; the ground lifts up, sending cars hurtling into the air, bits of metal that are ripped from the vehicles is thrown in all directions at a deadly ferocity. All the fleeing men and flying debris is sent scattering across the car park; Andy is sent rolling head over heels; Garret, who is at least fifty yards away, is blown onto his back; Garret lying on his back looking up at all the debris falling back down onto everybody, the cars that were not in the centre of the blast were peppered with holes from being struck with bolts, screws and ball bearings that had been packed in with the explosives.

As the smoke and dust began to clear you could see the men crawling away from the blast, some of them thankfully getting to their feet and staggering away. All the people who were not involved in the blast started to run to assist the injured. Garret heard Peter's voice; he realises he was on the mobile just before the blast. "Yes," Garret said.

"What happened Charlie, tell me it was not bad," Peter said.

"The wheel buffers in the car park, it was them Peter, they blew up," Garret said.

"What's it like Charlie, are you all right, is Andy OK?"

"Yes, yes I think so," Garret said as he could see Andy dusting himself down.

Garret got to his feet and looked at the scene; a big area is cleared of vehicles and a large crater could be seen where the van and the Vectra once were. Garret took a deep breath and moved forward, talking to Peter as he went. "I don't think it is as bad as Mosley Street, there are people hurt but they are moving, thank God," Garret said. "Andy is bleeding," he said to Peter.

Andy shouted back to Garret saying, "It is nothing, only a scratch."

Garret said: "Peter, I think we just sussed this in time; we could have had at least twenty people dead. What Carhill tells us from now on we had better believe."

Peter said: "Get Andy and yourself seen to and get back here as soon as you can."

"Peter, that bomb was on no timer and it certainly was not rigged with a motion sensor switch; it was detonated remotely, electronically, maybe a mobile phone," Garret said. "I think our bombers and shooter are still around. There are high vantage points miles away over the other side of the River Tyne; we could have been watched from any one of those locations. I think we were very lucky, Peter. They could have detonated the device any time they wanted; they most probably were waiting for a chance of maximum casualties."

"I will get people over there just in case," Peter said. "Now make sure they get everything sorted and you and Andy checked out."

"Will do," Garret said putting the mobile phone away. There were ambulances standing by in case this emergency came about; the injured were getting prompt help. A medic was taking a look

CHAPTER 26

at Andy – he had a cut to his forehead. Garret asked the medic how Andy was. "He will live – a couple of stitches maybe."

CHAPTER 27

"All right Trevor, we are going to try a different approach – or what I should say is, the same approach but in a better environment and more relaxed atmosphere," Peter said. "Because of recent events, we are not just giving you the benefit of my doubt, we all want to listen to what you have to tell us. I want you and Dr Luke to stay with us voluntarily – you are not under arrest but I urge you to help us as much as you can. We will move the interviews into more favourable surroundings. There are sleepover rooms here in the police station – we would like you to stay the night. The rooms have an adjoining interview room which is much better than this one; there we will be able to start again. You can have the run of the building – you will be free to go anywhere you wish inside the building."

Trevor asked what has brought this change of attitude. "The boxes that you saw the men putting into the van, the ones you said looked like kerbstones, they were designed to look like that to fool us – they had been used to replace wheel stops in the car park where the van was abandoned; they had been filled with high explosives. The information you gave us about those boxes, Trevor, gave us vital seconds to react before they were detonated. That information saved a lot of lives," Peter said. "Yes there were people hurt but fortunately there were no fatalities."

A knock on the interview room door and Colin popped his head round. "I have the Yank here, Peter," Colin said.

"Will you take Mr Carhill and Dr Luke upstairs to the apartment rooms and make them comfortable please, Colin?" Peter said. Trevor asked Peter if he can make a telephone call to his sister Clare.

CHAPTER 27

Peter said to Colin: "See to that will you and get Trevor and Dr Luke whatever they want. Trevor, in the meantime, if there is anything you can think of that may help us locate these people who are doing these appalling things..." Peter said.

"I will let you know, yes," Trevor said. Peter got up and left the interview room, saying, "I will be with you in a short while Trevor."

Colin said, "Right let's get you to a more pleasant room," taking the chair from under Trevor as he stood up. "We will go next door and get Dr Luke, and you two can say goodbye to these depressing rooms."

Peter Gray is on his way upstairs to the reception area to meet the American CIA man; a plain clothes officer is on his way down the stairs. "Sir I have..."

"A Mr Paul Bennet," Peter said before the plain clothes officer can finish his sentence.

"Err, no sir I have a Mrs Joanne Martin, from Durham University, language expert sir."

"Ah right," Peter said.

I will have to stop doing that Peter thought to himself. "Come with me," Peter said to the plain-clothed officer.

The plain-clothed officer says to Peter: "Jenkins sir."

Peter said: "What?"

"Jenkins sir, that's my name."

"Right Jenkins," Peter said. At the reception a man and a woman are waiting. "Mrs Martin," Peter said, putting his hand out to be shaken.

"Joanne," the young woman said, taking Peter's hand and shaking it.

"Joanne, would you mind – we are sort of in between things at the moment – would you go with Jenkins please? Jenkins would you take Joanne to the apartment where Colin is please? I will be along soon."

Then Peter turned to the tall American.

"Paul Bennet," the American said in a low, somewhat feminine voice as he showed Peter his ID wallet. At the same time Peter reached out his hand to shake the hand of Paul Bennet, Peter knocked the wallet out of the American's hand. The wallet fell to the floor and opened at a photograph of a young man in military dress uniform. "Oh sorry," Peter said as he bent down to pick up the wallet. Peter picked the wallet up, thinking after hearing Paul Bennet speak 'this must be his, oh never mind it has nothing to do with me'.

"Commander Peter Gray," Peter said, handing Paul Bennet his wallet back. "Please come this way," Peter said, walking at a fast pace towards the stairs. He looked behind himself – Paul Bennet was limping along behind. "War wound," Peter said.

"Yes, I lost it in Iraq," Paul said.

"God, I am sorry, I did not mean it that way," Peter said.

"That is all right," Paul said as he followed Peter into a room on the next floor level.

"Please take a seat," Peter said.

"I would rather freshen up first," Paul said.

"Ah," Peter said, "once again I have to apologise, my mind is all over the place, you have just flown in from Tel Aviv."

"That's right," Paul said. "There is some kind of convention going on over there – every Rabbi in the world must be there. Our lot seemed to think something was going down, that's why I was there until I got the message to take the next flight to the North East of England."

"That will be my doing," Peter said.

Peter got up and went to the door saying, "Excuse me a

CHAPTER 27

moment please Paul." He opened the door and called a police officer over. Peter talked for a while with the officer and then returned to talk to Paul. "We have got you a room in one of the local hotels here in Durham, Paul. I suppose what I want from you can wait until tomorrow. I really want your knowledge on this super rifle of yours."

A knock at the door and a police officer comes in. "I have put Mr Bennet's bags in the car sir," the officer said.

"Thank you," Peter said to the officer. "Paul, if you go with this officer I will see you bright and early."

"Thanks," Paul Bennet said. "I am dead on my feet. Until tomorrow then."

"Yes," Colin said, "come in," when someone knocked on the apartment door. Jenkins and Joanne Martin came into the apartment room. Colin was sitting discussing the day's events with Trevor and Dr Luke.

"Colin, this is Joanne Martin – she is the language expert, Peter told me to bring her to you," Jenkins said.

"Please Mrs Martin, will you sit down."

"Joanne, just Joanne will do," Joanne said.

"This is Trevor Carhill and this is Dr Linda Luke," Colin said. "Dr Luke is here to look after Trevor who has suffered a bit of an accident lately, and Trevor is the main reason why you are here. Trevor has spoken a few phrases into the voice recorder and we would like you to interpret them for us if you can."

"I will certainly try my best," said Joanne.

"Well that's all we can ask," Colin said. "Jenkins would you go and sort some tea or coffee out for us please." Jenkins nodded and went out of the room.

"Now Joanne, like I said, Trevor has been speaking these words and phrases, and we have recorded them. Now Trevor does not know what he has said because it is in a foreign tongue. We need an exact word for word interpretation, even if we have to keep going over it and over it, we have to know it all. Now just take your time," Colin said as he pressed the play button on the voice recorder.

As soon as Joanne hears the language she says, "It is Afghan, the words are Afghanistan." Joanne lets the whole recording play and then asks Colin to replay it, and Colin sets the recorder away again. Joanne listens again, "The first two words are: LET'S MOVE." "That's what the big man with the rifle said," Trevor says.

"That's good," Colin says. "Now the next phrase."

"The next sentence is the big man with the rifle speaking again," Trevor says. Joanne listens and says, "NAREEM YOU FOOL TAKE YOUR TIME THERE IS NO RUSH." Joanne tells Colin to play the recording again.

"And the next," Colin says.

"That's what the driver said," Trevor says as he listens to his own voice of the recording.

Joanne interprets, "SORRY MY GENERAL, that's what those three words are," Joanne says. They all listen intently to the next sentence. Trevor says, "This is the big man again." "DO NOT CALL ME GENERAL, that's what is said that time," Joanne says. "Next is the driver again," Trevor says. "SORRY MY GEN SORRY SHALI."

"Shali, that's what you call the big man, the one with the rifle," Trevor says. "He says a lot this time," Trevor says as they all listen carefully. "AND DO NOT ANY OF YOU FORGET, HERE I AM SHALI, YES SHALI." "All the men in the van say that," Trevor says. "These are the words of Shali again, there is much more this time," Trevor says. "GOOMI MAKE SURE THE

CHAPTER 27

OTHERS UNDERSTAND, THEY MUST BE AT THE FERRY BEFORE SEVEN O'CLOCK." "That's what this Shali said next," Trevor says. He was intrigued to understand the words himself now.

"And the next," Joanne says. "The next sentence is what the passenger sitting closest to the door said, I WILL MAKE SURE THEY KNOW, TRUST ME." "So you call that one Goomi," Trevor says. "The next is the same passenger speaking, this Goomi," Trevor says.

Joanne interprets again, "WILL YOU BE AT THE FERRY SHALI?" "The next sentence is a real mouthful – it's that Shali talking again," Trevor says.

Just then Jenkins comes back in the room with an assortment of hot drinks. "Put them there," Colin says, "and would you go and see if Peter is free for me Jenkins?" Colin waits until Jenkins leaves the room and then tells Joanne to carry on.

Joanne listens to the whole sentence first then tells Colin to play it again. "NO MY BROTHER I HAVE A DESTINY TO FULFIL AND AN EMIRATES FLIGHT TO CATCH, I WILL BE GOING HOME ANOTHER ROUTE." "That's what all that was," Trevor says. "Is there any more?" Joanne aks. "No, that is it," Trevor says.

Colin was deep in thought after hearing that last sentence. Then he spoke: "Well it was just about seven fifteen when the bomb went off at Friars Goose Marina. Peter and Garret are convinced that the bastards were somewhere around when it exploded, so by my reckoning it was not seven o clock tonight they had to be at the ferry, it has to be tomorrow or the day after."

Dr Luke said: "Trevor that is brilliant."

"Yes, well done," Colin said. "We need to check the Emirates flights that are on the move from now. Joanne, thank you, that has been a great help to us," Colin added.

"No bother," Joanne said, "anytime."

"I will have you taken back to your accommodation, and Joanne don't be speaking to anyone about what has gone on tonight – I would hate to have to come and arrest you," Colin said. "Joanne, we will need a number where we can get hold of you at any time."

Jenkins and Peter came into the room. "Jenkins, would you see to Joanne please?" Colin said.

Jenkins said: "OK. Colin do you or anybody want anything when I am out?"

"No thanks. Is there anything that you would like?" Colin asked Trevor and Dr Luke. They both say no.

"You off?" Peter said to Joanne.

"We have got it all, word for word," Colin said. "Joanne was brilliant and she assures me it is word perfect."

"Well thank you once again Joanne," Peter said, taking the transcript off Colin and starting to read it as Jenkins and Joanne leave.

"Colin, get onto Emirates flights – all of them, North East first, then further afield. General Shali," Peter said, "this must be our main man."

"All the ferries are covered – nothing has left or is going to leave," Colin said as Peter was still looking at the transcript of the recordings. "And if you and Garret think they are still in our neighbourhood, that's if they were present at the Friars Goose Marina bomb."

"They must have detonated the bomb, and to know when to detonate the bomb they had to watching," Peter said.

"Right Colin, Andy and Garret will be here soon. We have a

CHAPTER 27

lot to go over. Dr Luke, do you have everything you need?"

"I am all right as long as I can use the telephone," Dr Luke said.

"You can both use the telephones but you must not talk about what has happened. I must warn you – the telephones that you will be allowed to use in here and only these ones will you use – they are monitored; your conversations will be recorded. I am sorry but it is a necessary precaution, you understand," Peter said.

"Now Trevor, I want you to get some rest. I also want you to keep looking in your head, if there is anything you have missed, it may seem trivial to you but could be of great importance to us. Look after him, Dr Luke, will you? He is our star witness. We will leave you now but please understand in our job there is no nine to five days, we work twenty four hours a day. So I will apologise now if I have to come and drag you out of your beds in the middle of the night," Peter warned. "OK Colin, we have work to be done, let us leave these people to get some rest."

CHAPTER 28

Nareem and Shali are driving back to the hideout; they drive back through the Tyne Tunnel heading south. When they get through the Tunnel they turn right, heading west, going towards where they abandoned the van and Vectra car. Police vehicles and ambulances pass them. Nareem is nervous; Shali is just staring out the car window.

"How did they know?" Shali said.

"How did they know what Shali?" Nareem said.

"They must have known – why else would they have reacted like they did? All was planned: they had found the bomb in the van as we expected, they were convinced that nothing else was a danger to them or why did they risk moving in on the vehicles – then they all panic and run: how did they find out we had left another bomb Nareem?" Shali said. "The dog missed the trap, just as we planned it would with all the explosive odours around the vehicles. There is something we don't know."

They had driven for a couple of miles now heading north. "Take the next right," Shali said.

Nareem nodded, "Yes Shali."

They turned down towards the riverside again; the signpost read 'Bill Quay'. Driving down towards the River Tyne, they turned off onto a side road. It was difficult to drive down the side road: trees and shrubs were overgrown either side of the road; the road had not been used for a long time, but there were small signs that the road had been used recently if you looked close enough.

"Stop Nareem, that fool Rasheed has broken a tree branch. Go and make it good Nareem," Shali said.

CHAPTER 28

"Yes Shali." Nareem stopped the car, got out and walked back to the tree which had the broken branch. He tried to pull the branch back to its natural look – he got it as best as he could and went back to the car.

Shali was talking on his mobile phone: "We are at the gates now, Veeri," Shali said then put his mobile phone away.

"Is it done Nareem?" Shali said.

"It is good Shali." Nareem drove carefully down the overgrown road until they came to some old steel gates. There was an old rusty chain wrapped around the meeting ends of the gates – a padlock secured through the chain kept the gates locked. On the gates was a sign: R & B Harrison & Sons Ship Repair Yard. The ship repair yard had been empty and derelict for some fifteen years.

Shali says, "Come on Veeri, we have a lot to make ready." Just then Veeri comes through the bushes on the other side of the old rusty gates, an AK 47 assault rifle in his hands. Veeri shoulders the weapon and opens the padlock and takes the chain off the gates. Veeri struggles and has to pull very hard to open the gates. Shali pushes Nareem on his shoulder; Nareem gets out of the car and goes to help Veeri open the gates. Shali gets into the driving seat and drives the Vauxhall Zafira through the gates; he drives through trees, their branches rubbing along the side of the car as it passes through them. At one time this would have been clear hard surface but over the years the foliage has got the better of the asphalt ground.

As the Zafira passes through the trees and the bushes, old buildings come into view; from the road you would not know the ship repair yard was there unless you knew this place fifteen years ago. A couple of fabrication sheds and office buildings still remain; they are programmed for demolition soon; windows in every building are broken from vandalism, doors are hanging off their hinges, but one of the fabrication sheds has had its doors semi repaired – they do not hang straight but they cover the entrance.

The doors of the fabrication shed open up. Rasheed waves Shali into the shed; Shali drives the car into the shed. Rasheed quickly closes the doors when the vehicle is inside. Shali parks the car alongside the white Audi A4, and parked beside the Audi A4 is a Mercedes Vito van with British Telecom markings on its sides. Down in one corner of the shed there are signs of habitation: a table with food, plates and bottles upon it, chairs and bed rolls, boxes and bags untidily lie around; there are two work benches with tools, a bottle barrow with oxyacetylene cutting gear stands beside the benches, and leaning against the benches are AK 47 rifles.

Rasheed opens the door to the car for Shali to get out. Shali says to Rasheed: "You had left broken branches at the entrance, Rasheed. What have I told you? You cannot take any chances. We must not be discovered before we have fulfilled our destiny."

Nareem and Veeri come into the fabrication shed pulling the doors closed behind them. "What was it like Shali? We heard the second bomb explode."

"The British suspected. They somehow knew about the second bomb – they were warned – we detonate the bomb too late, we did not kill as many, they were warned, from now on we must be more vigilant and cover our tracks. I suspect the British police may know something or they must be very lucky, Veeri," Shali says.

"What do we do, Shali?" Rasheed said.

"We keep to our plan, we have to, but tonight I cross the river by boat. Veeri, you take the van and meet Nareem and me

CHAPTER 28

on the other side of the river tonight. Rasheed, you come with us and row the boat back here to the hideout," Shali said. "Now, is the box ready?"

"It is all done," Veeri said. Shali walked to the back of the van; standing there was a dark green British Telecom Relay Box, the kind you find on most street corners in English cities and towns. The box was constructed with thin sheet steel so it would be robust enough to withstand knocks and being leant against, and it would be light enough for the men to carry. The dimensions of the box were about four feet high by five feet long by sixteen inches wide.

"And the ballast," Shali said.

"We have sandbags in the back of the van," Rasheed said.

"We load the box now," Shali said. The four men lift the British Telecom roadside Relay box and slide it into the back of the van. "Have we heard anything from the others?" Shali asked.

"No we have heard nothing," Veeri said.

"All must be well then," Shali said. "Veeri, you and Rasheed make sure all is ready for tonight; come Nareem, we eat and then we pray."

Rasheed and Veeri went to the work benches and began to put things into bags. Veeri said to Rasheed: "I will do this. You go and make the boat ready."

"Why is Shali going over the river by rowing boat – why does he not travel in the van with you, Veeri?" Rasheed said.

"Because Rasheed, Shali cannot take that chance now, he must not get caught or stopped before we have all done what we have set out to do," Veeri replied.

"Shali, Nareem and Alama are going to die, aren't they, Veeri?" Rasheed said.

"Be quiet Rasheed, don't let Shali hear you, now go and see

to the boat. You row Shali and Nareem over the river tonight," Veeri said.

Nareem went down to the riverside, a simple eight feet long wooden rowing boat was tied up to the old slipway jetty. Nareem untied the rowing boat and pulled it up the side of the slipway until it hit the bottom. He then tied the rowing boat off again. Rasheed went to get the bags and the kit to load into the rowing boat. As he was walking back up to the fabrication shed Shali was walking down towards the river.

As the two men met Shali said, "You worry, Rasheed."

"I worry for you my General, I think you go to your death," Rasheed said.

"That is my destiny," Shali said.

"But we need you back home to kill the infidels," Rasheed said.

"Killing many of them on their own land will help our cause, and in doing so Nareem, Alama and myself will go to a better place Rasheed, we will be martyrs. I am only worried that I am stopped before I can kill many of the British, before I die a glorious death," Shali said. "I think now they know we are still nearby," Shali added. "That is why we load our weapons and munitions in the boat and go over the river by boat and not with Veeri. The British police will check all movements over the river. Bridges and the tunnel will be watched. Veeri has a better chance on his own getting through the tunnel. Now, make sure we have everything loaded into the boat, forget nothing, as soon as it is dark we leave."

"Yes Shali," Rasheed said and went to get the bags from the fabrication shed.

Shali stood at the riverside looking up river. Just up around the bend in the river about a mile away is Friars Goose Marina.

CHAPTER 28

Shali smiled: inside he feels good, he has fooled the British and he is sitting on their lap at the same time.

"It will be time soon Veeri, you leave now. Nareem and I will see you on the other side of the river at the place we have chosen," Shali said.

"And if I am stopped Shali?" Veeri said.

"You go to work, you repair telephones!" Shali said, laughing. "Come Nareem, Rasheed put the weapons in the boat. Veeri you have nothing suspect in the van."

"Only sandbags," Veeri said laughing. "Let us go now my brothers."

Rasheed took the guns to the rowing boat. It was dark now, they had to walk carefully. Shali guided Veeri out of the fabrication shed. As Veeri reversed the British Telecom van, Nareem went to open the gates. When Veeri left in the van, Shali and Nareem made sure the gates were locked, then went down to the riverside. Rasheed sat in the rowing boat, oars in hands, ready to go. The rowing boat was stacked front and back with bags and various bits of kit. Shali got into the boat while Nareem untied it from the jetty, pushing the boat into deeper water and then leaping into the boat. Shali had to grab Nareem by the backside of his pants and pull to help him into the boat.

The river crossing at this point was about four hundred yards; it took a good twenty minutes to row across, and on the other side of the river the men unloaded the boat and then hid the bags in the bushes on the roadside.

"Rasheed, you hide and wait for Veeri to come. Do not be seen." Shali and Nareem hid in the bushes at the roadside with the bags and waited for Veeri to come in the van. They only had to wait about ten minutes then Veeri came with the British Telecom van. The men quickly loaded the kit into the van.

"Did you get stopped?" Shali asked Veeri as they put bags into the van.

"Yes I did get stopped," Veeri said. "They checked the back of the van and asked where I was going."

"What did you tell them?" Shali asked.

"I go back to the depot after my day's work, I tell them, and they say go," Veeri said.

When the men had all of their equipment loaded they drove off towards the north. They got on the A19 motorway and kept going north for about four miles, taking the turn off for Ponteland and Newcastle Airport. Staying on this road for half a mile, they took another turn off towards the airport. They keep on going for another half mile and drove past the vehicle entrance into the Airport. There was a heavier police presence than usual at the entrance to the airport car parks. All three men look as they passed.

"They suspect something, Shali," Veeri said.

"They know nothing, keep going," Shali said.

They drove for two miles then took a turn off that led them into a little industrial estate; they drove along a road that had a chain link fence along one side and commercial buildings along the other side of the road. "This will do," Shali said.

Veeri pulls the van over to the side of the road that has the chain link fence and stops. All three men get out and go to the back of the van. Shali has a quick look around – there is no one about. Without saying a word, Shali opens the back doors of the van. All three men pull the British Telecom Relay box out of the back of the van; it is heavy for three men; they struggle but manage to lift the box and place it down on the footpath tight up against the chain link fence. Shali opens the two doors on the front of the British Telecom Relay box. Nareem and Veeri get the

CHAPTER 28

sandbags out of the back of the van and place them inside the British Telecom Relay box floor to weight it down. Shali reaches through into the back of the box and opens the doors on the opposite side, revealing a portion of the chain link fence that the box stands in front of.

Nareem quickly cuts a hole in the chain link fence with wire cutters then puts the cutters in the back of the van. Veeri has already taken the bags and equipment out of the van. Shali goes through the box and out through the hole in the chain link fence on to the other side. Veeri passes the bags through to Shali. When all the equipment and weapons are on the other side of the fence, Veeri goes through the box. Nareem locks the van and then he goes through the box, pulling the roadside doors closed and locking them on the British Telecom Relay box. Nareem then goes through the box and taking one of the bags places it back in the box before pulling the doors closed on the chain link fence side of the box.

"Now Veeri," Shali says, "you come with Nareem and me, and you help make us ready for our glorious victory, and prepare the way for Alama. I depend on you, Veeri, to get the others to the ferry and home safely."

"Yes, I will make it so, my General," Veeri said. All three men take hold of the equipment and set off over the large mowed grass area and up over a hill.

Half an hour later Veeri returns to the British Telecom Relay box; he pushes the doors open and goes inside the box. He takes a length of wire out of the back that he had left there earlier and he weaves it through the chain link fence and repairs the hole. Veeri then closes the doors shut and locks them with a bolt on the inside. Veeri, now inside the box, looks through small peep holes that have been specially drilled in the box. He checks to make sure the coast is clear before he comes out of the box onto the footpath. The way is clear.

Before coming out of the box Veeri takes two bottles, one small, the other large. The small bottle is labelled nail varnish remover. Veeri sprinkles the contents of the bottle inside the box, and then, taking the larger bottle, he goes through the doors of the box onto the footpath and, leaving the bag and an AK47 assault rifle inside the box, he shuts the doors and locks them. The larger bottle is filled with human urine; Veeri pours the urine around the bottom of the British Telecom Relay box.

Veeri then goes to the van and unlocks it and gets inside. Veeri starts the engine and drives off, doing a u-turn in the road and heading back the way they came. Veeri only drives about three hundred yards along the road; he turns left at a junction and then drives another three hundred yards and turns left again, this time through some open gates. The sign above the gates reads 'Ponteland Golf Club non-members are welcome'. Straight ahead of Veeri is the Golf Clubhouse. Veeri pushes hard down on his right foot: the van accelerates forward up over the neatly manicured lawn and crashes through the double glass doors into the reception area of the clubhouse. Immediately alarms start to go off. Veeri climbs over the seats into the back of the van and opens the back doors. He jumps out of the van and runs out through the gates he has just driven through, across the road and into the grounds of a printing firm. Veeri clambers over a fence and runs around the back of the Printers; he then climbs over another fence and off into some woods.

After running for about five minutes Veeri stops in the woods and sits down on the grass. He takes out his mobile phone and presses a couple of buttons on the phone. There is an almighty loud explosion as the van blows up inside the clubhouse, ripping

CHAPTER 28

the roof off completely and sending it into the car park area, glass and debris are thrown all over, all over the well looked after gardens; what is left of the clubhouse instantly bursts into flames.

Veeri gets up from his sitting position and begins to jog through the woods; at the edge of the woods is a clearing, and then the gardens of some houses. Veeri runs over the clearing, the lights coming on inside the houses that were not already lit up. The noise from the bomb going off brings people out of their homes. Veeri keeps on running towards a house that is not lit up; he leaps over the back garden wall, running up alongside the house to the detached garage.

Veeri unlocks the garage door and goes inside, turning the light on and closing the door behind him. There standing ready is a motorcycle, a motorcycle helmet, gloves and a jacket on the seat of the motorcycle. Veeri puts the helmet, jacket and gloves on, he turns the light off and opens the garage door. He wheels the motorcycle outside the garage, puts it on its stand and then shuts the garage door. Veeri starts the engine and then speeds off heading south.

Rasheed is crouching down in some bushes near the riverside; he has had a long wait and is worried the others have met trouble. But then he hears the sound of a motorcycle approaching and feels much better. Rasheed does not move out from his hide until the motorcycle stops and he is sure that it is Veeri riding the motorcycle. Veeri stops at the side of the road and removes his helmet. Rasheed comes out from his place of hiding, and the two men push the motorcycle down the bankside into the river.

"Quickly," Veeri says, "let us get out of here." Both men go to the riverside and get into the rowing boat.

Rasheed says, "Did all go well Veeri?"

"Sheee," Veeri said, "talk quietly – your voice will carry in the open river. All has gone as planned Rasheed, the General and Nareem are ready to unleash terror on the British. Now we have to make ready to do our part." Rasheed pulled as hard as he could on the oars – he did not want to be out in the open on the river even though it was dark.

CHAPTER 29

"All right gents, what you have there is a copy of the transcript of what Trevor Carhill heard the men in the van say," Peter said, talking to Charlie Garret, Colin and Andy. "Most important thing that hits us with this information is there is at least one other gang of terrorists operating in this patch. And what is even more important is what they are up to."

"We need to find one of these guys," Garret said.

"Well at least we have three names now: Shali, Nareem and Goomi," Peter said.

"This Shali – Goomi called him General Shali," Colin said.

"I don't think there is any doubt that he is their leader. We have all our resources looking into our General Shali," Peter said. "And with the photofits that Carhill did, we have a better chance now of coming up with something."

"At least with the names maybe now we can obtain real photographs," Andy said.

"I hope so," Peter said.

"We had Trevor look at all the photographs we have on our files of known terrorists and he did not come up with a match," Colin said.

"We will see what we come up with now that we have names to go on," Peter said. "What do we have on Emirates flights?"

"We have an Emirates flight due into Newcastle International Airport at 7-40 pm tomorrow night and it does not depart until Saturday afternoon at 2-30 pm," Colin said.

"That Saturday afternoon has got to be a big possibility," Andy said.

"I agree," Peter said. "We have to check on what the other

local airports have on Emirates flights departing; the arrivals are not much of a major concern at the moment. Where is the one that arrives at Newcastle coming from, did you say Colin?"

"It is due in from Tel Aviv at 7-40 pm Friday night."

"Just in case, Colin, get in touch with Israeli intelligence and let them know what we are up against here," Peter said. "My immediate concern is the others they speak about and what they are planning – there has got to be a lead to them somehow. We will have to make sure Trevor Carhill has told us every little detail."

"I will talk to Carhill tomorrow," Andy said. "I need to give that man my apologies for giving him a hard time, and thank him – he saved my life among many others."

"Has our American friend come up with anything?" Garret asked.

"Not as yet. I really have not had a chance to talk much to Paul Bennet – he was tired after his flight from Tel Aviv; he had been on duty for twenty four hours, then he had to drop everything and leave to come straight here," Peter said.

"What was he doing in Israel?" Garret said.

"Some Jewish festival or holiday – Bennet called it a convention, I think," Peter said. "Bennet's bosses were expecting something to happen – that's why the CIA were there and still there in force I believe. I don't think he was happy being pulled out – at least that is the impression I got."

"What's he like, this Yank?" Andy said.

"Well I don't know," Colin said, "I think he may be a bit gay."

"What makes you think he is gay?" Andy asked.

"Well he stands about six feet two inches tall and about sixteen stone in weight and he talks like a teenage girl," Colin

CHAPTER 29

replied.

"That will do," Peter interjected. "The American is here to help us no matter what side he bats for. Paul Bennet is a veteran – he lost his lower right leg in Iraq during the service of his country."

"In that case the American deserves our utmost respect," Garret said. Andy and Colin nodded in agreement.

"Now that we have the American here, what do we tell him about Carhill?" Garret said.

"We tell Paul Bennet Carhill is a witness and nothing more; he saw the van with the suspects at the rear of Mosley Street. We do not tell him that Trevor saw them in his mind," Peter said, "no way does that get back to the States, not yet anyway. I will have my work cut out trying to convince Liz Carter. Now back to business."

Just then a plain-clothed officer came into the room. "Sorry sir but I thought you would want to see this straight away."

The officer passed Peter a piece of paper. Peter read it and got very annoyed, saying to the officer, "Why were we not told this earlier?"

"What is it Peter?" asked Garret.

"A witness from the Friars Goose Marina has seen the cars that our suspects may have left in."

"The woman had gone off duty sir well before the bomb went off. She did not know anything about it until one of her work colleagues got in touch with her," the officer said.

"Where is this woman now?" Peter asked.

"She is at Gateshead Police Station sir," the officer said.

"God love me," Peter said. "Colin get straight down there and see what we have.

"I am on it," Colin said.

Colin had no sooner gone out the door than in came Jenkins. "Sir, we have reports of an explosion at a golf clubhouse not more than five minutes ago," Jenkins said.

"Where?" Peter asked. "Ponteland Golf Course – this is two miles from Newcastle International Airport," Jenkins said.

"Andy you will have to take this one. Take Jenkins with you and use the helicopter – there will be plenty space to land on a golf course," Peter said.

"You heard the man Jenkins," Andy said. "Go and wake the pilot in the day room and I will go and get some gear," Andy said on his way out the door with Jenkins close behind.

"What the bloody hell has a golf club got to do with this lot," Garret said.

"It may have no bearing at all on this case, we will have to wait and see what Andy comes up with," Peter said.

Peter's mobile phone rings. "It is Colin," Peter says to Garret. "Yes Colin."

"Peter, this woman, a Mrs Marjorie Stanton, she is the receptionist in the hotel at the Friars Goose Marina, she said when she was going off duty she had seen four men taking bags out of a van and car and putting them into two other vehicles. The men, she said, all looked Pakistani – her own words – one of the men was much taller than the other three, they all had beards and were all pretty much dressed similar to each other and that is her description of the men, but the vehicles – at least one them it is good Intel – now she is sure one of the vehicles was a white Vauxhall Zafira with a 60 plate, no number; the other vehicle she is not so sure about, it is white as well and could be BMW three series and possibly with a 60 plate as well," Colin said.

"Did this Marjorie Stanton not think it suspicious – men taking bags from one vehicle and putting them into another?"

CHAPTER 29

Peter said.

"Come on Peter, it is a hotel – that is pretty normal practice, would you not say? Bags getting moved about?" Colin protested.

"Yes you're right Colin, it's just I am grabbing at straws. Tell me Colin, the witness – did she see what direction these vehicles went?" Peter asked.

"They passed her as she walked up to meet her lift. They went straight up to the main road, they could have turned east or west – the witness would not know which way as the vehicles were out of sight," Colin said.

"Thanks Colin, give our witness my thanks and tell her we may be in touch, and you get back here as soon as you can," Peter said putting his mobile phone away.

As Peter was listening to Colin's report he was writing it down; Garret was reading it as Peter wrote the report down.

"Well at least it is something. I will put it up on the board with the rest," Garret said.

"This is our guys, no doubt. Where are you now though?" Peter said.

"Most probably gone to ground for now," Garret said.

"I don't think so if this golf course blast has anything to do with them," Peter said. "Is this the other group – if it is them or the same ones from all of today's events, we have to get these people soon, Charlie, because if we don't I have a feeling we need to be stocking up on body bags."

By the time Andy came out of the police station the helicopter was warming up and Jenkins was already on board. Andy jumped into the back seat next to Jenkins and put on the headset that was hanging next to him. "Let's go," Andy said. The pilot throttled the helicopter up and they rose into the air, a slight manoeuvre on the stick and the helicopter turned and began to head north. As soon as the helicopter flew over the River Tyne Andy pointed out the fire in the distance: "There's our golf course."

In no time the helicopter was descending onto the fairway of Tee one on the golf course. As they were coming down to land Andy could see firemen fighting the blaze. There were several police officers waiting for the helicopter to land. As soon as the helicopter touched the ground Andy was out and running, bent over until he cleared the spin radius of the rotor blades, and then he stood up straight.

"Who is in charge?" Andy asked.

A police officer stepped forward and spoke, "Inspector John Devine, sir."

"Get me the fireman in charge quickly, will you?" Andy said as they walked towards the burning shell of the clubhouse, stepping over debris as they went. A police officer went running to get the fireman on the instruction of the Inspector.

"It looks like a ram raid sir," the Inspector said. "There is a vehicle inside the building."

"A ram raid does not make that much damage, Inspector, the bloody roof is lying thirty feet away from the building – that was caused by an explosion Inspector," Andy said.

"Yes sir, but the vehicle could have severed a gas pipe which caused the explosion."

"Why is there no gas fire then?" Andy retorted.

By now Jenkins was up alongside Andy. "Jenkins, go and see what you can find out," Andy said. "Inspector I want you to get everyone, and I mean everyone, back away from the fire – at least fifty yards – do you understand?"

"Yes sir," the Inspector said.

CHAPTER 29

"Sir, the fire chief," a police officer said.

"Regional Chief Fire Officer David Summers – how can I help?" the Fire Chief said.

"Chief Summers, I want you to get your men moved back about fifty yards away from the fire," Andy said.

"I can contain and eventually put the fire out, but I cannot do that from fifty yards away," the Fire Chief Summers said.

"And then, sir," a police officer said, "this is the secretary of the Golf Club, Kevin Robson."

"Mr Robson, I will be with you shortly. Now take Mr Robson way back over there officer and keep him there," Andy said. "Now Chief Summers I want you to get your men back, leave the hoses trained on the fire if possible if not just let the fire burnout; I want no one within fifty yards of that fire."

"I cannot do that," Fire Chief David Summers said.

"I am afraid you will," Andy said. "It is possible there could be another explosion."

When the Fire Chief heard this his reaction was swift. "My men will be out of there before you know it," Fire Chief Summers said as he began to run towards his men, ordering them to back off.

Andy looked around: there were six fire engines, at least ten police cars and about the same number of unmarked cars, blue flashing lights in the darkness, members of the public sightseeing – some of them in their bed clothes. Andy looked at the tyre tracks the van made in the grass lawn; he looked along the tracks following them by eye, up into the inferno. He could just make out a shape through the flames and smoke – it was what was left of the van.

Andy took out his mobile phone and called Peter. "What you got Andy?" was the instant answer he got to his call on his mobile phone.

"It is definitely a car bomb Peter, it looks like a van, going by the tyre tracks it left on the grass lawn. It had been driven at speed through the main doors into the reception area. Now whether the driver is still in there, of which I very much doubt, we will not find out until the fire burns itself out," Andy said. "The way I see this, Peter, I think the driver legged it and detonated the bomb from a safe distance."

"Why a golf clubhouse, Andy?" Peter said.

"It beats me – I cannot see what our bombers can get out of it, blowing up an unoccupied building. Maybe it is not connected," Andy said.

"It was a bomb so we cannot rule it out Andy, we must consider it connected with today's events," Peter said. "Be careful Andy. If this is our boys they leave surprises as you well know."

"I will keep everyone away until it is light," Andy said.

Andy walked over to the entrance where the police were keeping a cordon; the club secretary Kevin Robson was actually being held back by a police officer.

"Why are you not letting the Fire Brigade put the fire out?" Kevin Robson asked.

"I will not let them put the fire out because there is danger of a further explosion," Andy said. "Anyway, if they did put it out it would have to be demolished, so what difference is it going to make if is put out or left to burn?"

"Chief Summers," Andy shouted. The Fire Chief came over to Andy. "Just let it burn Chief, it is not worth the risk, keep everyone back until daybreak," Andy said loud enough for everyone to hear. "Our people are on their way – they will take control."

"Yes sir," Fire Chief Summers said.

CHAPTER 29

"Now Mr Robson was there anything of importance in the clubhouse," Andy said.

"I should say there was: twenty years of hole-in-one trophies and members' personal golf."

"Jenkins!", Andy shouted, cutting Mr Robson off in his flow of pointless twaddle. Jenkins came over from talking to the people on the roadside to Andy and Mr Robson.

"Yes Andy," Jenkins said.

"Take Mr Robson's statement would you? I want to take a look around," Andy said as he went over to the Inspector. "No one gets near Inspector, we have had enough people hurt today. Get your men to go and check around the perimeter of the golf course. Anything that is suspicious I want to know about it."

"Yes," Inspector Devine said. Andy went for a look around.

CHAPTER 30

"Sir, Liz Carter is on the telephone for you," the officer said.

"Thank you," Peter said, "I'd better take this in the other room. Hello Liz."

"Bloody hell Peter you were supposed to keep me informed," Liz Carter said.

"I know Liz, I am sorry, but things have been happening so fast here."

"I know you're busy Peter, but I have the Home Secretary and the Prime Minister breathing down my neck. We have to put a stop to this," Liz said.

"We are doing what we can with the information we have at hand. I think things are starting to move pretty quickly now," Peter said.

"What is this about the car bombs, Peter? They tell me another booby trap – two bombings in one day," Liz said.

"The terrorist had left their get away vehicles rigged for us; the first bomb was pretty obvious, we found it no bother; the second, a larger device, was designed to catch us off guard and kill as many of us as possible," Peter said. "If it had not been for our witness Trevor Carhill the terrorist's aim would have become a reality."

"Your witness Trevor Carhill – I thought he was a suspect Peter. What is going on?" Liz Carter said.

"Trevor Carhill is a witness Liz and he is our key to stopping these men. Because of the information we obtained from Carhill we know now there is more than one group of terrorists operating in this area and they are working together with our shooter and bombers," Peter said. "We also have names now Liz

CHAPTER 30

that Carhill gave us."

"How does he know so much Peter? That to me is a concern," Liz said.

"It is something I don't want to go into now but I can guarantee you that Carhill is on our side and he is helping us with vital information," Peter said.

"But two bombs in one day Peter – the murder of the Earl and at least fourteen people! This has to stop and soon," Liz insisted.

"Three bombs today, I am afraid Liz. We have just got a report of an explosion at a golf clubhouse near the Newcastle International Airport – no one hurt, the building was unoccupied at the time of the blast," Peter said.

"Why a golf clubhouse?" Liz asked.

"That's the big question," Peter said.

"I cannot make head nor tail of it, it serves no purpose to terrorism to blow up an empty building, unless it is a warning of some kind."

"It has my full attention this one Liz," Peter said. "We also have a lead on the threat to an Emirates flight."

"And you are certain about this, Peter?" Liz said.

"This is good information Liz, we have to act on it."

"This Emirates flight – do we know when?"

"All indications point to an Emirates flight that is due to depart Newcastle International Airport on Saturday afternoon. Now the terrorists don't know we have this information, and I think this will be our chance," Peter said.

"You're talking about allowing them access to this flight?"

"I don't know yet that we have a problem you will have to make a decision on, Liz."

"And what is that, Peter?"

"The Emirates flight in question arrives tomorrow night at Newcastle International Airport from Tel Aviv – do we let it land at Newcastle and carry on letting the terrorists think we don't know there is a threat to an Emirates plane, or divert this flight to a safe airport and, by doing this, show our hand?" Peter clarified.

"Do you think the incoming flight from Israel is at risk?" Liz asked.

"All indications say it is not – they would have to get something on the plane at Tel Aviv," Peter said.

"Have you been in contact with Israeli Intelligence, Peter?"

"Yes we are in full discussion about the situation. There is no chance the terrorists will get anything on the Emirates flight leaving Israel – it has the best airport security in the world," Peter said.

"And do you want me to go along with you that we let the plane land at Newcastle as normal to try and flush our bombers out?"

"Tomorrow is another day, Liz. The way things are going we may end up with another set of problems, but I think we should be looking at letting the plane land at Newcastle for the time being," Peter said.

"I will have to talk to the Home Secretary on that, " Liz said.

"This other gang has got to have a surprise for us as well Liz. We have to find out what they are up to; we have heard nothing from them yet and I cannot rest until I know what they are planning. Only our General Shali group has been making the play so far," Peter said.

"General Shali – he is our main target?"

"Looks like he is pulling all the strings at the moment Liz. It is all in my report. I must be getting back Liz."

CHAPTER 30

"Peter, you know I will back you all the way on whatever you decide to do, but we need some fast progress. If it keeps going the way it is the whole country will be on lock down," Liz said.

"We are doing our maddest, Liz."

"Just give me the word Peter if you need more resources and I will make it so," Liz said. "I will speak to the Home Secretary first thing in the morning – he will have to deal with the media."

"OK Liz, I will speak to you soon," Peter said putting the telephone down.

"Please come this way Paul and meet the others," Peter Gray said to Paul Bennet, the American CIA man. Peter walked into the conference room with Paul Bennet.

"I would like to introduce you all to Paul Bennet," Peter said, "Paul, this is Charlie Garret my deputy, Colin one of our field men and this is Dr Luke."

Dr Luke looked at Paul Bennet and said 'yum' quietly as she got up to shake his hand. Before she got to her feet Colin leant over to her and said, "I think I would have a better chance then you Doc."

Dr Luke replied: "Now isn't that a shame, a waste in fact!" Dr Luke took Paul's hand and shook it.

"Where is Andy?" Peter said.

"He has gone to get Carhill," Garret said.

Andy knocked on the apartment door and walked in. Trevor Carhill was just coming out of the bedroom in a rush.

"Carhill I would like to say I am sorry about–"

"Never mind that," Trevor said, "it was that language woman that did it, Joanne Martin."

"Did what?" Andy asked getting worried at Trevor's excited behaviour.

"The blouse she had on," Trevor said.

"Yes I noticed that as well," Andy said.

"No," Trevor said, "well yes, I know what you mean, that's why I was looking at it."

"Yes she certainly filled the blouse," Andy said, "but that is not what I came to see you about Carhill."

"No, the blouse that Joanne wore – on the left breast it said Durham University on her blouse," Trevor said.

"And so?" Andy prompted.

"Goomi in the van had a shirt on – it read Newcastle University on the left side of his shirt," Trevor said.

Andy was silent for a second and then said: "You are a fucking marvel, now quick we need to see Peter."

Andy and Trevor Carhill rushed into the conference room.

"Oh Andy," Peter said, "we are pleased you could make it."

"Peter I must talk to you now," Andy said as he looked at Paul Bennet. Andy was thinking how he would phrase what he wanted to say to Peter.

"Yes what is it?" Peter said.

"The shirt that Goomi was wearing – it had a Newcastle University logo on it. Trevor saw it," Andy said.

"Is this true Trevor?" asked Peter.

"Yes I am sure of it," Trevor replied. Peter thought for a moment.

"All right, Andy you and Colin take Trevor with you. Trevor is the one who can eyeball this Goomi, and make sure you two look after him out there," Peter said. "We need to keep a low profile – the University will be packed inside and outside the campus. I don't want any confrontations in public if we can avoid it – the last thing we want is for these men to know we are onto them. If we can latch onto Goomi without him knowing,

CHAPTER 30

maybe he can lead us to Shali or the others."

"I will get backup sorted and ready to go when and if," Garret said.

"Keep in constant contact. Trevor you do exactly what Andy or Colin tell you, you understand?" Peter said. "There will be the potential for real danger so I do not want you putting yourself at risk at anytime – have you got that Trevor?"

"I will be careful and do as I am told," Trevor said. Trevor was excited at the prospect of going out with Andy and Colin to do police work and also he needed to get out of the police station and breathe some fresh air.

"All right then – get out there and find me this Goomi," Peter said.

Trevor Carhill, Andy and Colin got up and were out the door as soon as Trevor got his coat on.

"Let's hope this is what we have been waiting for," Peter said. "If Goomi is at Newcastle University they will have records and addresses."

Garret came back into the conference room and said: "We are all set to move when we get the word Peter."

"Good, fingers crossed," Peter said.

"I should be out there Peter," Garret said.

"Andy and Colin will handle it, Charlie. I need you here for the time being," Peter said. "Dr Luke, this meeting we have with Paul will be boring for you. We have people coming today to look at Trevor's case. I will have someone run you to the hospital and you can get your records on Trevor."

"Oh very well then," Dr Luke said.

CHAPTER 31

"OK Paul, tell us about this Long Range Super Rifle of yours," Peter said.

"I can tell you this rifle is like no other sniper rifle on the planet," Paul Bennet replied. "This rifle can read weather conditions and it will adapt to operate in any weather conditions. It will function in extreme temperatures of hot and cold; it compensates for wind speeds and fluctuations in wind speeds. It will adjust elevation for distance to a target, it reads all situations before it is fired and will adjust to those situations. As soon as the trigger is squeezed, the rifle has acquired the target and it will hit that target within a distance of 2,500 yards."

"That confirms the point even more that this was the weapon used to kill the Earl of Stanley," Peter said.

"A complete amateur could hit a target at 1,000 yards – all you have to do is aim and pull the trigger. Skill is only needed when there are several targets that have to be taken out in quick succession," Paul said. "There is no recoil from the weapon, all the shock produced when the rifle is fired is dispersed equally back into the weapon and holding it perfectly still, the rifle will only move itself fractionally to compensate for target movement and weather conditions."

"Are you trying to tell me that when the round has left the rifle it will still hit the target even if the target has moved?" Garret asked.

"Yes to a certain degree," Paul said. "That is the real beauty of this sniper rifle – once it has acquired a target and the target moves steadily in one direction the weapon will adjust and hit that target when it is fired."

CHAPTER 31

"For that to make sense, the bullet would have to be smart," Garret said.

"Let us say for the sake of argument," Paul continued, "a target is 1,500 yards away, and the target is moving to the left, say two feet a second: the split second before the round leaves the rifle, the sight analyses the data and adjusts, so if the round takes two seconds to reach and hit a target 1,500 yards away the target has moved four feet to the left by the time the round reaches it, the round will hit that position the target has moved to. Where this ability to compensate for slight target movement comes into play, it is ideal for takng Chopper pilots out who are just hovering at the time. At one time a good sniper would predict target movement and adjust his sighting and elevation himself and only hit his target with a limited degree of success. This sniper rifle does that automatically for him and with more accurate results."

"Very interesting," Peter said. "We need to get this weapon back or destroyed before Shali uses it again."

"Shali?" Paul Bennet said.

"Yes General Shali, he is our chief suspect."

"Surely this cannot be the same Shali who killed the US Special Forces Unit and liberated the rifle from them?" Paul said.

"Tell us more," Peter said.

"It is starting to fit now," Paul Bennet said. "General Akhamid Mohammad Shali, he was killed at the fire fight at the rolling hills of Haraeffa in Afghanistan. It was your Earl of Stanley and his men that were in that battle along with our US Air Force Apache Helicopters. General Shali was killed with about another fifty Taliban fighters."

"Go on," Peter Gray said.

"I cannot believe it can be the same man but it would tie in with the rifle; no, it can't be – your Earl received the Military Cross for defeating the Taliban at Haraeffa. General Akhamid Mohammad Shali was killed at that fire fight," Paul said.

"Well it looks like General Shali has risen from the dead," Garret said.

"If this is him you have a ruthless and devious killer on your hands," Paul Bennet said. "Shali was or maybe still is Ali Bin's right hand man."

"We have to get this off straight away Charlie – maybe now we can get a mug shot instead of Carhill's photofit of Shali," Peter said.

"There are no known photographs of Shali – the CIA have been tracking him up to his demise and we did not obtain a photograph in all that time. May I ask how you come to the conclusion it was General Shali that was involved in the shooting of the Earl when you only have an eye witness of these men getting into the van?" Paul Bennet said.

"You're good," Charlie Garret said.

"Not only did our witness see the men but he heard the name Shali mentioned," Peter said.

"If you had told us earlier that you had the name Shali, maybe we could have come up with some more concrete information," Paul Bennet said.

"Our witness did not reveal this information to us until late into our inquiries," Peter said trying to avoid any mistrust that Paul Bennet was hinting at.

"And how do you have so much knowledge about Shali?" Garret said to Paul Bennet.

"I became interested when I was seconded to try and retrieve the Super Rifle – all our inquiries led to Shali," replied Paul Bennet.

CHAPTER 32

Trevor Carhill told Andy to take no notice of the Sat Nav – it was taking them into the rush hour traffic. Trevor knew a short cut and he was giving directions. All three men were in the black Range Rover driving towards Newcastle University.

"Hey Carhill, I think your doctor has got the hots for our American," Colin said.

"No way," Andy said.

"Well not now," Colin said. "I sort of dampened her ardour."

"How did you do that?" Trevor asked.

"I hinted that our American was gay," Colin said.

"You did not, did you? Peter will not like that," Andy said.

The black Range Rover drove into the University car park. They parked the Range Rover and went into the reception area.

"Yes, can I help you?" the receptionist asked.

"Yes, we would like to see the Dean please," Colin said, showing the receptionist his warrant card.

"Certainly," the receptionst said. "I will give his office a call. Would you please wait?"

Two minutes later a young lady came down to reception and said, "You wish to see Dean Lunt?"

"Yes," Andy said.

"Follow me then please," the young lady said."

Colin said to Andy: "I would follow her to the ends of the earth – she is gorgeous."

The young lady knocked on the Dean's office door and walked in. "These gentlemen from the police wish to speak to you, Dean Lunt."

"Thank you Miss Brewis," the Dean said.

"Lorraine," Trevor whispered to Colin.

"What?" Colin said.

"Lorraine – that is her name – it is on her desk," Trevor said.

"What can I do for you then officers?" the Dean said.

"I am not a police–"

Andy cut Trevor short. Andy asked the Dean if he has any students he would consider militants, radicals especially in the ethnic groups, mainly Asian or Middle Eastern. The Dean took offence at the questions at first, but then he realised the gravity of the situation after recent events in the North East.

"Really I am not the one you should be asking, it is the tutors who have their fingers on the pulse around this University – not me, I am the one they come to when that pulse misses a beat," the Dean said. "Now Mr Ramsey, he is your man," the Dean added, looking out of his office window into the car park below.

Colin looked out of the window and observed a man walking towards the University building after using his peepers to lock his car. "Have you photographic identification of all your students?" Andy asked the Dean.

"Yes, we have," the Dean replied. "It is necessary for their ID cards and the security of the University."

"We would like to take a look at them please, only the male records." Colin turned to Andy and said, "Do you want to take Mr Ramsey or should I do it?" Andy nodded back in the direction of Colin.

"OK I will take Mr Ramsey," Colin said.

The Dean took Trevor and Andy into his secretary's office. "Miss Brewis would you get student photographic records up for these gentlemen please?"

"From what date, Dean Lunt?" Miss Brewis asked.

CHAPTER 32

"I don't know," the Dean said, looking at Andy, hinting for a clue to what date period or year. "All this year's students." Andy was looking at the logo on the blouse that Miss Brewis was wearing – it read Newcastle University.

Andy pulled a chair alongside Miss Brewis and asked Trevor to sit. Andy said to Miss Brewis, "We have a few names we want you to try first."

"Very well, what are they?" Miss Brewis said. "Ah, the first name is Goomi," Andy said.

"Christian or surname?" Miss Brewis said.

"Try both."

"We have no male students with that name – Christian or surname," Miss Lorrane Brewis said.

"What about Nareem, both first and second names?" Andy tried.

"We have three students," Miss Brewis said.

Trevor looked at the photographs carefully and said: "It is none of them Andy."

"Try Shali," Andy suggested, getting frustrated.

"No one with that name either," Miss Brewis said.

"Shit," Andy said, "this is a sodding wild goose chase. Do all your students have that logo on their shirts and blouses?"

"No not at all, these are only worn by staff, people who work at the University," Miss Brewis said.

"And do you have records of people who work here?" Andy asked.

"Yes we do," Miss Brewis said.

"Try Goomi on the staff records."

"There we go," Miss Brewis said, "we have one."

Trevor glared at the photograph: "That is him, I have no doubt it's him all right."

"You are positive?" Andy said, wanting more reassurance it was Goomi.

"Without a doubt it is Goomi."

"He is on the maintenance staff – he works in the boiler room," Miss Brewis said.

Andy jumped into overdrive. "Get everything you have on this man and quick as you can," Andy ordered Miss Brewis, at the same time taking his mobile phone out of his pocket, two button touch, then someone answered. "Because we have just made one at the University," Andy said into his mobile phone, and snapping his fingers at Miss Brewis and also saying "Come on woman, come on," to get a move on with the information he requested.

Miss Brewis promptly rose from her seat, went to the printer and got a piece of paper out of it and then slapped it into Andy's hand, giving him a look that would strip paint.

"Carhill has made a match on Goomi, he is positive on the ID." Andy looked at the information on the paper he was holding. "Victor Goomi, his address is in the West End of Newcastle. I will have the details sent to you. We are on our way to check it out," Andy said.

"Is Victor Goomi at work today?" he asked Miss Brewis.

"I will check," she said. "According to the shift rota he should just be finishing night shift."

Andy turned to Miss Brewis. "I want you to send these details of Goomi to Durham Police Station for the attention of Peter Gray." Andy pressed another button on his mobile phone, he waited a second or two. "Come on Colin," Andy said talking into his mobile, "where the hell are you mate?" He waited a while, still no answer. "Come on," Andy said to Trevor. "Where's Ramsey's office?"

CHAPTER 32

"It is in the East wing," Dean Lunt said.

As they were leaving Andy turned to the Dean and said: "There will be more police on their way. You are not to say anything to anyone until they arrive."

Andy was moving with great haste now. "This is it," he thought, "a break at last – we have a target now, something to move on." Andy and Trevor were making their way towards the East wing across the University car park when Trevor stopped in his tracks. "Come on," Andy said to Trevor, "We have not got all day."

"There he is, over there," Trevor said.

"There is who over where?" Andy said.

"It's Goomi," Trevor said, "there," pointing at two men talking about fifty feet away. Goomi was talking with his hands, gesturing and waving his arms about; the other man stood nodding his head now and then. Andy took out his mobile phone and unclipped an ear plug from it. He put the earplug in his ear and at the same time, not taking his eyes off Goomi and the other man, pressed a couple of buttons on the mobile phone.

"Colin, Colin," Andy said into thin air and then saying 'shit'.

Goomi and the man he was talking to began to part company slowly. It was obvious they were in a hurry because they were still talking when they were fifteen feet apart.

"Colin come in," Andy said again talking into fresh air – still no reply. "Shit," Andy said, "you are going to have to follow the other guy, I will take Goomi."

"What?" Trevor said.

"Now fucking listen: keep well back, don't let him see you. If he is one of the terrorists he will kill you sooner then look at you, have you got that clear?"

"I think so," Trevor said.

"Just follow him – do nothing else. See where he goes and call me." Andy passed Trevor a card with his details on it. "Quickly, they are going. Have you got your mobile phone?" Andy said.

"Yes," Trevor said feeling in his pockets for his mobile phone as he was moving off to follow the other man.

Andy put a bit of a run on to bring himself back up to viewing distance between himself and Goomi who was just now leaving the car park area. Andy tried once again to reach Colin, "Colin come in Colin." Nothing again.

Trevor Carhill took off after his target, keeping back just far enough so as to keep his target in sight. Andy wanted to keep Goomi in sight at all times. He moved as close to him as he dared without been spotted – no way was Andy going to lose Goomi. Andy looked all around himself trying to get street names and reference points. He tried Colin again speaking into thin air: "Are you there Colin?" Still no reply. Andy got his first reference: the City Library. The streets were very busy with people out shopping and going about their daily business.

Andy took a mental picture of what Goomi was wearing. Hancock Museum – Goomi was just passing the Museum. Andy tried Colin again: still no reply. Goomi stood at the roadside waiting for the traffic lights to change. The traffic lights turned to red, the traffic stopped, Goomi began to cross the road. Andy had to put a step on – Goomi was getting too far ahead. Andy began to jog a bit – he wanted to get across the road in the same traffic light change as Goomi.

Colin's voice rang out in Andy's earpiece. "Colin, where the fuck?" Andy said.

Colin replied: "I have been in the bowels of the earth – that Ramsey guy took me to the boiler room to see Goomi."

CHAPTER 32

"Never mind," Andy said. "I am on the trail of Goomi. I have had to send Carhill after another target as you were not there Colin."

"I cannot hear you, Andy," Colin said. "Where are you now?"

"I am just passing the Hancock Museum," Andy said.

"Where the fuck is that?"

"Wait," Andy said as he saw a street sign: "Percy Street, we are going down Percy Street, get back up for Carhill he is on another guy."

"Carhill is doing what?" Colin said.

Just then Andy was crossing the road. Beep – a car horn – Andy had walked straight onto the road; the traffic lights had changed in the traffic's favour to move on. Andy stood motionless with the car tight up against him, a man's head sticking out of a car window, shouting abuse at him. Andy was just standing there taking no notice of the driver's outrage. Everyone in earshot of the car blasting its horn turned around and looked at Andy stuck in the middle of the traffic – including Goomi. Andy just stood; his gaze was fixed on Goomi. The whole world stood still for a second in the minds of Andy and Goomi.

Goomi assesses the situation quickly, this man has nearly been run over and all he is interested in is me. Andy knew he was sussed. Goomi turned, bumping into a woman and pushing her out of the way. Goomi was running, Andy shouted, "He has made me Colin. I am in pursuit on foot."

Andy took after Goomi. Andy blurted out a description of Goomi as he ran: "Asian guy, five foot eight inches to five foot ten inches, black short hair, a trimmed black beard, dark blue jacket, blue tracksuit bottoms, white trainers and a white shirt."

Andy gasped for words as he was in hot pursuit, popping and weaving through the people.

The streets of Newcastle are bustling at summer time. It is a historic City with all its old and new buildings; the tourists flock to it during the holiday season, especially to see the fantastic bridges that cross the River Tyne in close proximity to each other.

Andy had to run on the road to get a clear run at times; because there were so many people on the footpaths it was easier running on the road. Goomi was showing no respect for anyone who was in his way, he would just barge them out of the way even knocking them to the ground to get past them. One guy took a punch at Goomi but missed him and then shouted 'arsehole' at him. Goomi fled around a corner taking most of the road as he went: cars and buses slamming their brakes on to avoid knocking him down. Andy thought if those drivers only knew who and what Goomi was would they be so keen to brake so hard and so quickly.

Andy followed; the stopped traffic making a clear path for him. "Blackett Street," Andy shouted out.

"I am onto it," Colin replied.

Andy looked just ahead of Goomi. He could see a policeman coming in their direction. "Stop him!" Andy shouted as loud as his empty lungs would allow. "Stop him now," Andy screamed. Everyone in the street was aware of what was happening. The police officer immediately grasped the seriousness of the situation; pulling out his truncheon he began to move quickly towards Goomi. Goomi just kept heading straight for the policeman. The policeman stood in the middle of the footpath stretching his arms out truncheon in one hand as if he was trying to block the whole street off. The people in the street were diving

CHAPTER 32

out of the way to make way for the oncoming collision.

Goomi was about twenty five or thirty paces from the policeman, closing down on him fast. Goomi reached into his jacket and brought a hand gun out and then, stretching his hand, holding the gun out in front as he ran. People were now diving for cover in all directions. Bang, bang, bang: three times, one after another. He was only ten feet away from the policeman when he fired the first shot; all three shots hit the policeman square in the chest, sending him spread eagled back over. The policeman was in mid air when the third shot hit him. The police officer slammed to the ground, Goomi running straight past the dying policeman.

"Fuck sake, he has just shot a copper," Andy said.

"Be careful," was the only reply from Colin. Colin knew Andy would need all of his wits about him and he did not want to add to his lot by asking questions.

"Goomi going around another street corner," Andy said, desperately trying to get reference points to relay to Colin as he followed Goomi. "He's turning again," Andy spurted out. "Nelson Street," Andy said, going down Nelson Street. Andy was in two minds whether to pull his gun – far too many people about and he knew they needed Goomi alive: he was the only link to the others.

Goomi was running towards what looked like the entrance into a big store. Andy read the sign above the glass doors: Eldon Square Shopping Centre. Andy shouted, "Oh God no." He thought if Goomi got in there, confined place and all those people, and Goomi armed and already has shown he will kill without hesitation... Andy breathed out heavy with relief when Goomi took a sharp right just before the entrance into the Shopping Centre. The street sign read Clayton Street. Andy barked, "Clayton Street, Goomi is in Clayton Street."

"We are nearly on top of you, Colin said.

Down one side of Clayton Street was a timber hoarding to keep members of the public out of a construction site. Goomi jumped up and over the hoarding, Andy in close pursuit. Goomi hit the ground running on the other side of the hoarding, turning to look back to see if he were still being chased. No way was Andy going to let an eight feet high hoarding get in his way now: one foot on the board, hand on the top of the hoarding pulling him level with the top of the hoarding. Whoosh then bang – Goomi let off a shot at Andy. Andy threw himself over the hoarding, a slight stinging feeling to his left cheek. Andy wiped his cheek, blood on his hand. "Shit I have been shot," but no pain. Andy's blood pumping, he drew his firearm from his shoulder holster. The last thing he wanted to do was kill Goomi but if he had to defend himself there would be no hesitation.

It was hard enough to run and try and pull oxygen into the lungs but to make a constant running commentary on where he was and what he was doing only added to his lot.

"Looks like we are in a construction site, no – demolition," Andy said over the mobile phone. Goomi was heading towards the door of a derelict building – in fact no doors and no windows either, they had all been removed. Andy was up and running after Goomi, gun in hand.

There seemed to be no one about, so if it did come to a shoot-out, no members of the public to worry about. Andy got to the door. He had to stop and check before he entered. Goomi could just be standing ready to shoot him as he came through the doorway, but he had to move quickly – the target must not get away: he was their only way of finding out where the others were before things get worse.

CHAPTER 32

As soon as Andy entered the building he heard a muffled noise up to his left. A stairwell, a bare concrete stairwell – everything had been stripped from the stairwell just leaving it bare concrete. It was not dark; there was dim light from the stripped out windows and doors. With all the timber doors and windows gone there was enough natural light shining into the building to make it light enough to see. Demolition contractors strip buildings of all the wood and furnishings before they pull them down. Only the concrete and brick shell are left. This would be pulled down and crushed and reused for backfill to roads and foundations for new buildings.

Andy moved up the stairs quickly. The noise he heard had come from a way ahead of him, so he knew he could move a bit faster before caution would slow him down again. "Where, Andy?" came over his earpiece.

"I am in a derelict building," Andy spoke out as he popped his head around the wall on the first floor entrance. The place was huge – it went on forever. Andy looked down the building, shafts of bright sun light shone in through the windows all the way down the full length of the empty shell of the building. Rows of concrete columns ran down the centre of the floor area. Goomi could be behind any one of them – nowhere else to hide, the place was bare.

Andy made for a column to use as cover. He just got behind the column when a crack let out and a piece of concrete splattered off the wall behind him. Crack, another – this time Andy saw where the flash of the gun firing came from, the bullet going anywhere – there was no indication it was even close to him. "Is that gun fire?" came over the ear piece.

"The bastard is shooting at me Colin," Andy said as he returned a couple of shots, sending the bullets close but not too close to its target.

Goomi was about sixty feet down the building behind a central concrete column. Just as Andy took a look Goomi made a dash for it. He went to what looked like a little room to the left side of the building. Andy looked to his left: a room similar to the one Goomi had made a bolt for. Andy had just come through that small room – it was the stairwell landing; each floor must have two identical stairwell landings on each floor.

Andy went back the way he had just come and went up the stairs to the next floor level. Andy hoped that Goomi had gone up over into the stairwell; he had made a dash too. Andy poked his head around the wall to see Goomi just leaving the stairwell and heading down towards the end of the building. Andy was away after him; he could see Goomi running towards what looked like another stairwell entrance at the end of the building on the side. Goomi turned just before he got to the stairwell entrance and fired a shot at Andy; Andy made a dive for cover into the stairwell Goomi had just made a dash from; the bullet ricocheted off the concrete walls.

Andy went up the stairwell thinking 'I will get him on the next floor level up'. What Andy had noticed was that all the floor levels were exactly the same. Andy spoke out: "Goomi going up to the third floor; I am still in pursuit." Andy slowly peeped around the corner, his gun automatically guided around the corner at the same time and pointed in the direction Andy was looking. Andy looked for a second or two: nothing. Goomi had not come up the stairwell to this floor level as Andy had hoping he would. Andy had to make a gamble and quick: should he move over the floor to the stairwell where Goomi is or was, or should he go up to the next floor level or down again?

Andy chose up. As he turned to go up, a loud crushing noise

CHAPTER 32

and the whole building began to shake. "A fucking earthquake!" Andy cried out loud.

"What did you say? Come back Andy," came over the earpiece from Colin.

"It's a fucking earthquake," Andy said as he rushed up the stairs, the light nearly blinding him as he turned the corner and out onto the roof of the building. A quick glance to his left. He had guessed right: Goomi was just coming out the end stairwell onto the roof; he looked as bewildered as Andy. What was that ear-splitting noise and the violent shaking of the building? It could be nothing else but an earthquake. Looking past Goomi the answer to the noise and the shaking of the building was there, and over his earpiece at the same time came Colin's voice: "They are knocking the building down, you must be in the building that they are knocking down."

Goomi was just standing there, looking back at Andy. Andy could have taken him out with a shot, and Goomi had a quick look to his left and then back at Andy. Why was Goomi not making a run for it, because to his left an almighty pair of steel jaws was eating away at the concrete roof? Every bite the steel jaws made the whole building shake and the noise was deafening. Goomi had made his mind up: he took aim and fired off a shot. Andy heard the whoosh of the bullet fly past him. Andy lifted his gun and aimed higher, much higher than the target, and fired well above the head of Goomi. We need him alive. Andy did not have time to take a more accurate aim and try to hit Goomi in the legs and anyway he dared not take the chance with the whole building shaking like it was.

Goomi turned to his left and began to run towards the steel jaws and the massive machine they were attached to. "We are on the roof," Andy said.

"I can see Goomi," came the reply. Andy made chase after Goomi. 'Where is this going to end,' he thought, looking at the massive steel jaws biting great lumps of the concrete roof away like a prehistoric monster chewing at its food. Big long booms hinging in and out, pushing the jaws into the building and with ease taking large pieces of the concrete roof away.

As Andy got closer he could see that the building extended as long again; there was another building joined to the one Andy and Goomi were in by a link structure. The other building was a mirror image of the one the two men were in. The machine was breaking out a link floor between the two buildings. The machine jaws were just about to chew through the last piece of concrete span linking the two buildings together – Goomi ran, making for the last strip of concrete. He was not going to make it.

Andy shouted: "No, stop, stop," just as the steel jaws grabbed around the last piece of concrete. Only a few reinforcing steel bars holding the section up from the other building, the jaws closed shut and began to pull away. Goomi put his foot on the back of the top jaw just as it was pulling away; he jumped from the jaws and onto the concrete link strip, which by now was being pulled away from the building by the massive machine and was starting to fall from its hold in the other building. Slowly the concrete section began to drop. Goomi was now running up a slight gradient – he had three or four steps to go before he was safe.

"He is a goner," Andy said, still running towards Goomi.

Colin shouted over the earpiece: "He has had it," as he looked up from the roadside.

"Jesus, what the fuck?" the machine operator said, as he looked up the long boom of his machine and saw Goomi jump

CHAPTER 32

off the machine jaws and onto the concrete section the machine was pulling away. The 360 degree Long Reach Demolition Machine is equipped with a camera on the end of the boom to aid the view of the operator; the men that operate these specialist machines never take their eyes off the working end of the boom. The operator must be aware and be ready to react in any situation. But that is a situation that is involved with the structure of the building he is tearing down at the time. And if he were to have an unplanned collapse in the building he was always ready to pull his machine to safety. But always being alert does not prepare you for the situation that this machine operator was encountering now.

Fortunately for Goomi, the machine operator was one of the best in the business, realising if he made the slightest movement on his control handles the man on the roof was dead. In a split second the operator changed from the action of pulling the concrete link section out to one of lifting it slightly. That gave Goomi that valuable second of time to get a foot on the solid roof of the building before the concrete link section came crashing down.

Now the machine operator had to think very quickly again, because he still had a hold with the jaws of the machine of the very large and very heavy lump of concrete. It was far too heavy for the machine – the operator had to release his grip fast or the weight of the concrete section would tip the massive machine over. The whole machine began to tip forward as the weight became too much for the machine to balance out at that height. But this was a situation that happened quite a lot in this business. As the machine lurched forward the machine operator coolly just manipulated one of his control sticks. The jaws on the end of the boom opened; the machine was now at a very dangerous angle: the concrete fell free from the jaws crashing to the ground in a pall of dust. The operator lifted his bottom off his seat and braced himself for the shocking thud as the machine sat back on its tracks; if the operator had stayed seated the shockwaves would have ricked his back. Seventy tons of machine thudding back to the ground shook the area; people in the adjacent streets could feel the shock through the ground.

'The drama was not over yet,' Colin was thinking and then said over the earpiece: "He is one lucky son of a bitch." Andy was still in full stride as he got closer to a large opening between the roofs of the two buildings; he was thinking, could I make it; not slowing down any, Andy was even pushing harder.

Colin who was standing in the street looking up, shouted: "Don't do it." By now the busy main street was at a standstill as crowds of people were looking up at the drama unfolding in front of their eyes. Colin shouted up again: "You will kill yourself for God's sake Andy, don't do it."

Andy looked down to the right as he was running, gun in hand and looking into the cab of the machine, the machine operator was still looking up. These men never take their eyes off the dangerous end of the machine when the boom is up in the air. The machine operator saying out loud, "This guy has got to be joking." Andy and the machine operator made eye contact with each other. Andy was thinking, 'I hope you know what I want mate because I am going for it'.

As if they were in one mind and one brain in control of both thoughts, the machine operator began to move his control sticks at the same time sitting back onto his seat, his eyes fixed on the end of his boom and Andy. The boom of the machine began to rise up and at the same time the steel jaw attachment on the end of the boom started to close and rotate to the horizontal

CHAPTER 32

position. By now Andy was coming to the end of the roof at the point of no return – his forward motion sending him into mid air, the gasps from the crowd of people down on the street below, some of them covering their eyes with their hands unable to look.

"Christ Andy," Colin said. Like someone just reaching out their hand to catch a ball, the machine operator placed the jaws of the machine in front of Andy offering him the broadest side of the tool possible for Andy to land on. The jaws came to rest at the roof level of the building about ten feet away from the edge Andy leapt from. Wham! He landed smack in the middle of the now closed jaws of the tool. Andy going to his knees as soon as he made touchdown, grabbing out with his one empty hand to grip the jaws to stop himself falling forward, the machine operator was ready for the forward momentum from Andy's leap. As if it had been rehearsed a million times, the machine slewed to the right towards the other roof top, just before the jaws slammed into the building the operator stopped them dead in the air; this added more forward momentum to Andy sending him head over heels onto the roof. Andy rolling over a couple of times and then into a crouching position: it was precision. Andy was not going to muck up by falling over from what he had just been through. Not only for Goomi but for Andy, today was the day they had come across one of the best High Reach Demolition Machine Operators there is.

Adrenalin now really racing through the veins Andy was in hot pursuit again. Goomi had gone down the centre stairwell of the building. In all that had gone on Andy had never lost sight of him. Colin's voice came over Andy's earpiece saying, "I just cannot believe what I have just seen."

This time Andy followed Goomi down the same stairwell;

there was still thundering noises of concrete being crushed in jaws and the building shaking. Surely the High Reach operator has not gone back to work after everything that had just happened? Missing the third floor out Goomi kept on going down the stairs and came out on the second floor. Andy could just muster the breath to say, "Goomi is on the second floor." For an instant Goomi looked around to the right – it was solid walls and plenty of windows but he knew himself that he was still thirty feet up so going out of a window was not an option.

Goomi looked to his left – he could see the whole of the far side of the building was gone. The thundering noise was smaller machines than the High Reach Machine with singular jaw attachment tools on their booms and these machines were demolishing the building that Goomi and Andy were in now. The demolition crews at this end of the building had not witnessed what had happened just before at the other side of the buildings and were oblivious of what was going on.

Colin said: "You are going back into danger Andy."

Andy said back to Colin, "I was in danger as soon as I jumped over the fence." Goomi ran head on towards the machines, one of which was breaking through the walls at the very time Goomi ran by. Andy was not letting him get out of sight. Goomi ran to the wide open space that the machines had made in the end of the building, concrete and bricks falling down only feet away from him. Andy could hear Colin say "the Eldon Square Demolition Site, as quick as you can," followed by "the cavalry is on its way, mate just keep him cornered".

Goomi came to the edge of the building where the machines had demolished up too – nowhere to go now but down. He looked about: ten feet below him was heaps of concrete, bricks and wire ramped away to where more machines were busy

CHAPTER 32

working. One had a muncher attachment on and was munching the concrete into small pieces; another, a grab attachment, was pulling large lumps of concrete out of the heap while another machine was scraping through wires and concrete with a steel bucket attachment; beyond that more machines, their booms going up and down like pumps on an oilfield, heaps of concrete and wire were all over this end of the site. Men wearing hard hats and high visibility vests dotted all over the site, hosepipes spraying water everywhere to suppress the dust.

Goomi looked back at Andy who was just coming onto that floor level. Goomi lifted his gun and took aim at Andy: bang, he fired again and again, the bullets striking the wall just behind Andy, sending sparks and concrete chippings flying. Andy had no cover – he had to dive on the floor. Bringing the gun up in both hands and taking aim, Goomi fired again, rapid fire this time, three or four shots, bullets whooshed over Andy. Andy was just squeezing the trigger on his firearm to that point when the hammer would slam down on the bullet casing when over the noise of all the machines he heard the click, click, click of an empty gun: Goomi was out of bullets. Turning, Goomi threw his gun away and jumped onto the heap of concrete and wires below him. Andy shouted out: "Colin he is out of bullets, Goomi is no longer armed."

Andy jumped up to his feet and set off to where Goomi had just leapt from. Andy came very close to being pulled out of the building by one of the machines as its big jaws came crashing through the wall and pulling the arising rubble outwards. Andy looked over the edge: there was Goomi struggling to get through steel wires and concrete, panicking and squeezing his way past large pieces of concrete he tears his clothes and at one point uses both hands to pull his leg free from where it had got wedged between the rubble.

Andy looked at all the machines working just ahead of him; not the best terrain for a jog, he thought. Andy jumped into the mangled mess immediately getting hung up on wires, holstering his firearm Andy ripped his coat free off all the wires.

"You still got him?" Colin said.

"I am chasing him across a minefield now," Andy said. Goomi was finding it very difficult to move through the tangled mass of wire and concrete. Andy, once he had got himself free, was finding it much easier to move across the rubble; he was gaining on Goomi.

Goomi could see an easier route that one of the machines had made: the machine had tracked over the concrete to gain access to the building, flattening the wires and the concrete down and making a reasonable path. Goomi made for this path just as the machine was returning to get more material to process. Just avoiding the machine's implement by inches, Goomi shot past the jib and onto the machine's tracks and then onto the running board. From the running board he clambered up a four rung ladder and then onto the back of the machine. Just then another machine that was working alongside the one Goomi was on the back of was slewing around to pick concrete up. As the back of the slewing machine got closer, Goomi jumped onto the back of that machine. Almost immediately the machine slewed in the opposite direction, sending the rear of the machine heading towards a large heap of crushed and much smaller pieces of concrete. Goomi jumped onto the heap of concrete; it was a much better landing then his last leap of faith.

Andy thought, well if he can do it so can I. Andy took exactly the same route as Goomi. If Goomi had not gone this way Andy was sure he would have caught up with him – he had

CHAPTER 32

been gaining on him all the time; Goomi was getting weaker and slowing down. Goomi was scrambling up the heap of crushed concrete when Andy was just leaping off the back of the second machine onto the heap of concrete – it was hard to get a foot hold on, the smaller pieces of concrete would push away under foot as you tried to move quickly but Andy dug in and on all fours scrambled up the heap after Goomi. By now all the machines had stopped working – all their operators were out of the machines waving and shouting in protest at Andy and Goomi putting their lives at risk with the stupid stunts, leaping from machine to machine.

Goomi was at the top of the crushed concrete heap; he could see freedom: the busy street beyond the hoarding if he could only get there he had a chance to escape. But there was still some distance to go: just a few feet behind him Andy was pulling himself up to the brow of the heap. At that moment a massive rubber tyres machine with a bucket capable of scooping up five tons of crushed concrete in every bucketful came driving into the heap. It scooped up a huge bucketful of the crushed material. As the bucket of the machine began to lift, Goomi ran towards it and jumped onto the heap of concrete in the bucket. The bucket was that big and the amount of concrete it had scooped up was so great the operator could not see Goomi on it. As the bucket was raised the machine backed off, turning from the heap of crushed concrete at the same time. As the machine backed off what came into view was a long green machine that was vibrating and shaking violently. Andy was only feet away from Goomi before he jumped onto the bucket; the machine moving at a pretty fast pace put distance between Andy and Goomi.

Goomi blew air out in a sign of relief: he knew he was caught if he had not jumped onto the bucket. The big rubber tyres machine, with its bucket full, went into forward motion, its bucket high above the cab of the machine turned towards the long green vibrating machine and emptied its load into the hopper of the long green vibrating machine. Goomi falling into the hopper first, before the bucket load of concrete came down on top of him. The long green vibrating machine was a concrete crusher and it was crushing the already crushed concrete to a finer grade.

Andy watched in disbelief as the vibrating hopper sent the material towards the crushing jaws. The large heavy steel jaws clamped together, every second crushing the concrete between them, dropping the finer product out of the bottom onto a conveyor belt which then spewed it out at the other end onto the finer grade stockpile. The machine operator had seen something other than concrete fall out of the bucket and he was promptly out of his machine to investigate, looking into the crusher machine's jaws. By now Andy was at the crushing machine with plenty of members of the demolition crew. The crushing sound changed for a split second to one of a more muffled sound. Everyone looked at the jaws; the concrete that dropped out onto the conveyor changed colour from a whitish gray to a dark red at first and then a much brighter red. It spewed out onto the stockpile heap looking like you had just put strawberry flavouring relish on top of an ice cream cone.

Just then Colin and a dozen police officers came running into the site. "Where is he?" Colin said, trying to pick Andy up from his sitting position.

"Minced meat," Andy said, pointing at the heap of concrete, the red concrete gradually disappearing under the whiter gray concrete now spewing from this end of the conveyor belt.

Colin said, "Carhill?"

CHAPTER 32

To that all Andy said was: "Oh God no."

Colin pointed at the blood on Andy's cheek and, trying to ease the tension of the moment, said: "You want to change your razor mate."

Just then a man came up alongside Andy and Colin. Andy looked at him and put his hand out, saying, "The big machine – you drive it?"

"Yes," the man said, taking Andy's hand to shake and saying "Peter Aymod".

"Andy," was the reply the man got and then Andy said "that was some impressive machine driving!"

Peter Aymod replied saying, "It was nothing compared to your trapeze act."

CHAPTER 33

Peter Gray, Charlie Garret and the American Paul Bennet were still in the conference room at Durham Police Station discussing the case. Paul Bennet was still not at all convinced about Peter's explanation as to how they came by the name of General Shali, when Jenkins knocked on the door and came in.

"This just in from Newcastle University, sir," Jenkins said, handing Peter Gray a slip of paper. Peter took the slip of paper from Jenkins and slowly began to stand up from his chair as he read the report.

"Carhill has identified a photograph of Goomi, Victor Goomi is his name," Peter said.

"This is great news," Garret said, rising to his feet to look over the shoulder of Peter to read the report for himself – but Peter began to walk around the room reading the report unaware that Garret had tried to read over his shoulder.

"He works as a boiler man at the University," Peter said.

"Is he there now?" Garret asked.

"It does not say, all it has is the address for Goomi in the West End of Newcastle and that our officers are still at the University," Peter said.

"Colin and Andy will call for back up if they need it. Charlie, I want you to go to Goomi's address in the West End of Newcastle and take Jenkins with you."

"What about the University?" Garret said.

"If need be I will go there," Peter said. "Get back up to meet you in the West End and make sure the local boys are kept informed, but don't let them anywhere near, you know what could be there waiting for us."

CHAPTER 33

"I understand," Charlie Garret said as he was opening Jenkins's coat to see if he were armed. Jenkins was not armed. Garret told him to go and draw a firearm from the arsenal.

"It will take time, a lot of paper work to fill in sir," Jenkins said.

"I will sort that, now go down and get a weapon. I will phone down and clear it, now move," Peter said.

"Peter, may I go along please just as an observer? I will do exactly as Garret tells me," Paul Bennet said. Peter looked at Garret for his approval. Garret was not too sure, what with Paul Bennet's leg and all.

"What if there is rough stuff?" Garret said.

"As long as I don't have to run I can handle myself in any situation or tight corner," Paul Bennet said.

"Well in that case, what are you waiting for?" Garret said.

The three men left the conference room, Garret on his mobile phone organising teams of anti-terrorist men to meet them at the address in the West End of Newcastle as they left.

As soon as the men left Peter went to the door and said to an officer that was sitting at a table: "Get me Liz Carter on the telephone as quick as you can please."

Five minutes later the officer popped his head around the conference room door, "Liz Carter sir, line one."

"Liz, how are you doing?" Peter said.

"I have been much better Peter," Liz said. "What have you decided Peter?"

"Liz I would like you to set up a video link between George Coagour, the CIA Director, Abe Cowan, the head of Israeli Intelligence, myself and you Liz within the next half hour – can you do that, Liz?" Peter asked.

"I can Peter, but what is this about?"

"I don't want to go over it twice Liz, we have not got the time. You will find out at the video link if you don't mind."

CHAPTER 34

Trevor Carhill began taking mental notes of the man he was following: shoulder length dark hair, a goatee beard, easily six feet tall and dark clothing. Trevor kept his distance as he followed his target thinking this is exciting but also this is very important. He said to himself, I will not lose this guy.

Trevor had a good knowledge of the Newcastle area; he said the street and road names to himself as they went along them. Trevor made sure he was far enough behind the target, about fifty yards, so he would not be suspected of following him. The target came out of the University grounds onto Durant Road and then crossed the busy roundabout into New Bridge Street. Trevor concentrated deeply as he followed.

"Hi Trevor, what's happening?" a voice said and then a hand on his shoulder stopping him going any further. It was just as if Trevor had been awakened from a sleep.

"Who, what?" Trevor said as he looked at the man who had just stopped him.

"How are you doing?" the man said. Now Trevor was getting to grips with the intrusion of his concentration.

"Oh Stan it's you, Stan, look I'm sorry I can't stop and talk – another time," Trevor said pulling away, leaving Stan gobsmacked.

Trevor quickened his pace to gain back the distance he had lost when his old friend Stan had stopped him. Still got him, Trevor said to himself; where could he be going to, he thought. The target turned down Argyle Street; Trevor waited a second to let the target get a little further in front – he did not want to blow this, he is going to the Metro, Trevor thought, as the target headed towards Manors Metro Station. Sure enough the target went into the Metro Station. Now Trevor put a spurt into his step – he would certainly lose his target if he got onto a Metro train. Down the stairs the target went; Trevor stayed at the top of the stairs watching which side of the platform the target would choose. The target went right: platform one for Metros to Pelaw and South Shields, Trevor said to himself as he came down the stairs to the platform area.

Trevor rushed to platform two on the left side and ran around it and then walked slowly out onto platform one on the right side. There was the target standing waiting for the Metro train. Trevor looked up at the information sign: it read next Metro train in three minutes. Trevor stood just looking straight ahead but taking a quick glance to his left every few seconds to make sure the target was still standing there. A rush of wind came along the tunnel blowing the target's hair over his face; the gush of wind was an indication that the Metro was imminent. Trevor took a couple of steps towards the platform edge, the target doing the same about twenty yards away along the platform. The target looked to his right towards Trevor; Trevor just kept looking straight ahead, taking his handkerchief out of his pocket and blowing his nose. Cool Trevor thought to himself. Then the noise of the Metro train pulling into the station as it slowed down and came to a stop.

Trevor began to think of all those films he had seen where someone is being followed at a train station and they get on and off the train. Trevor drops his handkerchief on the platform and bending down slowly to pick it up and glancing to his left to make sure the target does not double back and get off the Metro train. 'Doors closing' came over the Metro train's intercom. Trevor stepped forward into the train just as the doors were

CHAPTER 34

closing and, wiping his nose, looked down the Metro train to check that the target was there. The target was just sitting down with his back to Trevor some fifteen rows of seats down the carriage car. 'Good,' Trevor thought, 'I will be able to watch the target at ease now for a while at least.'

The Metro train pulled away. Trevor looked up at the station map on the carriage car wall: Central Station was the next stop, and Trevor watched the target like a hawk looking out for prey. Within only a couple of minutes a voice came over the intercom, 'the next station is Central Station'. Trevor kept his eyes firmly on the target. The Metro train came to a halt, 'doors opening' came over the intercom. No one got off the Metro train, but plenty of passengers got on at Central Station. The train was not full but it soon would be, going by the amount of people that got on at Central, Trevor thought. 'Doors closing,' came over the intercom; the Metro train pulled out of the station.

Trevor checked the map again: Gateshead was the next stop. The Metro Train System runs mainly underground in the Newcastle City area; inside the Metro trains are well lit and Trevor had a good view of the target. Daylight, as the train came out of the tunnel and onto the Metro Bridge going across the River Tyne. Trevor looked down the river at all the splendid bridges that spanned the river. 'The next station is Gateshead Station' came over the intercom. Trevor looked at the target to see if he was going to get up. A couple got up and made their way to the doors. Trevor could see that further down the carriages more people were standing up and moving to the doors to get off the train; he had a clear view right down all the carriages.

The Metro train began to come to a stop, 'doors opening' came over the intercom when the Metro train came to a halt at

Gateshead Station; the target remained seated. There were plenty of passengers waiting to get on the Metro train at this station. Trevor kept his eye on the target – if he was to get up to get off the train at the last moment he wanted to be ready to get off as well. The people getting on the train were making for the few seats that were unoccupied. Trevor just stood at the area near the automatic doors – he could see everything from there.

'Doors closing' came over the intercom; the Metro train started to move off again. Trevor just remembered Andy, 'I will have to give him a call.' Taking his mobile phone out with the card that Andy gave him, he punched the number from the card into his mobile phone. It was ringing; Trevor waited but no answer. Trevor was just putting his mobile phone away when it began to ring. Trevor answered it after the first ring saying into the mobile, "Andy I have–"

"It's Brian," came the reply before Trevor could finish what he was about to say.

"Brian I thought you were someone else," Trevor said.

"What's that noise?" Brian said. "Are you on the Metro, Trevor?" Brian said.

"Yes I am Brian, but I am terribly busy at the moment mate, can I talk to you later?" Trevor said.

"Come on Trevor mate, I want to see you. Clare and I, we are worried sick about you – where are you going on the Metro? I thought you were at the Police Station – Clare told me that's where you were," Brian said.

"I am heading for Gateshead Stadium Station," Trevor said.

"If I hurry up I will be able to catch the same Metro Trevor, I am only on Sunderland Road, two minutes away from Gateshead Stadium Station," Brian said.

"No Brian, I will give you a call later mate," Trevor said and

CHAPTER 34

then ended the call on his mobile phone.

Trevor looked down the carriages – what he saw made his heart miss a beat. Two men in black overcoats and black peaked hats: they were ticket inspectors. This is terrible – Trevor had not got a ticket to ride on the Metro train. The inspectors were moving quickly up the carriages checking to see if people had valid tickets to ride the Metro. "Tickets please," the inspectors were saying as they moved up the aisle between the seats in the carriages cars. One inspector checking tickets on one side, the other checking the tickets on the opposite side. Passengers were getting their tickets out ready to be checked; in no time the inspectors were up to the target, "tickets please," the inspector said to the target – the target reached into his pocket and pulled out a wallet and flipped it open. One of the inspectors examined it and then nodded once and said 'thank you'.

'The next station is Gateshead Stadium Station' came over the intercom. The inspectors were nearly at Trevor. Shit, shit, shit, he said to himself. The inspector looked at Trevor, the Metro train was coming to a stop, and the target stood up and began to move to the doors. "Not you again, Brewy," one of the inspectors said. This made the inspector who was going to ask Trevor to produce his ticket turn around to see who his colleague was talking to. "I will be surprised if he has a valid ticket," the inspector said. 'Doors opening' came over the intercom.

The target stepped out onto the station platform, Trevor pressed the green button on the doors and when the doors opened he stepped out onto the station platform. "What a piece of luck," he thought, looking up and mouthing the words 'thank you'. The target started to walk towards the exit. Trevor walked over to read the Metro train timetable on the station wall, giving the target a bit of time to get ahead of him. As soon as the target started to go up the exit stairs Trevor was after him. Up and out of the station, turning to his left, the target was going east along Sunderland Road. Trevor was as familiar with Gateshead as he was Newcastle. Trevor lived with his sister Clare not that far from here.

Trevor crossed the road to try and make it less obvious that he was tracking the target, but to Trevor's surprise the target crossed the road as well. Sunderland Road is a long road, Trevor thinking – if the target got off at Gateshead Stadium he must be going to somewhere close by. Still heading east Trevor kept his distance. "Trevor!" A loud shout came from behind Trevor. The target turned to see who was shouting; Trevor could not believe it when he looked back behind, it was Brian, and the target looked at Trevor and waited to see what was going to happen.

Trevor stood still until Brian caught up with him. "Trevor, where are you going?" Brian said.

"Brian listen," Trevor urged, "don't say anything please, just do as I say."

"Why Trevor? What is the matter?" Brian said. Trevor, taking a quick glance towards the target, saw he was on the move again.

"Trevor you have got to tell me what is wrong," Brian said.

"There is nothing wrong Brian, now listen, please do as I say or we are going to fall out, now. Do you hear me?" Trevor pleaded.

"Yes OK Trevor, whatever you say."

"Now Brian, just walk with me and don't speak," Trevor said.

Trevor and Brian followed the target for about five hundred yards. The target turned up a side street. "This is it, it has to be,"

CHAPTER 34

Trevor said.

"It has to be what?" Brian said. Trevor's mind racing with all kinds of thoughts, he did not answer Brian. Just then the target turned to look back. Trevor had to think quickly – do we keep on walking and have to go past the target? Trevor pulled the ID card he got off Andy out of his pocket and stopped and looked at it, turned to his right and looked at a door number of a house in an inquisitive way and then looked back at the card, and then walked to the door of the house and knocked on the door.

Brian said: "Who lives here Trevor?"

"Be quiet Brian," Trevor said glancing along at the target who had begun to walk up the street.

"Yes, can I help you?" a woman said when the door was opened.

Trevor was stumped for a second, looking back at the ID card. Trevor said, "Can I speak to Andy Redman please?"

The woman said: "I don't know – can you speak to Andy Redman?"

Trevor looked puzzled at the woman and said: "Not here?"

"No," answered the woman.

"Sorry," Trevor said, now looking in the direction the target had gone. He had turned up East Hill Road. Trevor knew this place – this is where the council housed the immigrants. There were two blocks of flats, six storeys high, one behind the other.

Trevor eased himself around the corner of East Hill Road, keeping Brian behind him. The target was just passing the first block of flats; he turned and headed for the second block of flats. Trevor rushed up the road with Brian in tow, just getting to the road end in time to see the target enter the flats. "Which one?" Trevor said. "I must know which one – I have to find out which flat he goes into."

By now even though Brian was not the brightest he had worked out they were following this man. "Who is it, Trevor?" Brian asked.

"Listen Brian, I want you to do something for me: I want you to go to the back of the flats and keep a look out for this guy – if he comes out the back I want you to ring me. God, I must ring Andy. Brian please listen, I am in a hurry. Do not do anything – if he comes out the back just call me on the mobile, promise me Brian, you will do only that."

"All right Trevor, no problem, I can do that."

Trevor ran to the entrance of the flats as Brian went around the back. Trevor thought, 'I will have to go in, I must know what flat he goes into; if I am confronted I will think up some excuse for being there. Anyway I have got through a few tight spots to get this far. I have to find out what flat number the target goes into.'

When Trevor got to the entrance, he looked up just before he entered. He could not believe it but there through a window on the second floor Trevor could see the target entering a room. A man stands up to meet the target who is moving towards the window, Trevor jumps into the entrance doorway. Did he see me? Trevor thought I will soon know. Trevor strained his ears to listen for doors opening and someone coming down the stairs: nothing. Trevor stepped back outside to take a peep – the window was covered now, the curtains had been drawn. Great, Trevor thought, staring up at the window, I've got him. Trevor closed his eyes tightly and thinks to himself 'what if', click – there it was, the flat in his mind just like what had happened yesterday morning, it was just as if he were a fly on the wall.

Trevor scanned the room: there were four other men in the room all asking the target for information. "Where is Goomi?"

CHAPTER 34

asked one of the men. "He will be along later Abdul, don't worry." "Is Shali coming to the ferry, Alama?" another asked. "No he is not, Shea," Alama said. Shea spoke again: "Is Shali going to die, Alama?" "We may all die before this day ends, but if all goes to plan we will take hundreds of the Capitalist British Pigs with us," Shea spoke again. "Shali will be a martyr, we will all be martyrs," said the third man. "Will we see the station blow from the ferry Mohamad?" Shea asked. "No, we will not see the glorious sight of the Capitalist British Pigs' City being blown up; we will not be able to leave our place of cover until we have sailed," Mohamad said. "Our great General Shali and our brother Nareem will feel the great blast," Alama said. "Now is everything ready – did you remember extra batteries for the torches, Nesta?" "Yes, yes," said Nesta. Mohamad went to check the bags; he opened one of the duffle bags – inside were five AK47s – and then he opened a back pack – torches, food, grenades and ammunition. "Good," he said. "Now Nesta, what time does your shift start?" Alama asked. "Five o'clock," Nesta replied.

Trevor focused on Nesta: he wore a navy blue uniform; it had writing on the back – all that Trevor could see were the letters 'Po'. Nesta would not turn enough for the rest of the letters to come into view. Behind Trevor, in the other block of flats a man comes to the third floor window and looks out across to the block of flats that Trevor is observing the terrorist in. Just above the terrorist flat on the third floor and two rooms to the right a woman is getting dressed – she can be seen through the window. The woman is topless and just preparing to put her blouse on. The man sees the woman getting dressed; he turns to his son who is sitting watching television and says, "There's Metcha giving a show again." The man lowers his gaze down to

Trevor looking up; the man says out loud: "The dirty bastard." Trevor tries to force his vision around the room in the terrorist's flat; his mind's eye begins to move slowly around the back of Nesta, it's working: it is coming into view. Wham – darkness!

"You dirty fucking pervert," the man from the opposite block of flats said as he landed a punch square on Trevor's jaw. Down Trevor went in a bundle onto the ground just outside the entrance to the flats. There were two other men and a woman with the man who threw the first punch at Trevor; they all started to lay into Trevor, kicking and punching his unconscious body, and then came shouts and cries of 'get the Police for the dirty peeping Tom' and 'that's too good for him – string the bastard up'. A woman came to the window across the street and shouted out: "Cut his balls off," and another woman shouted: "Yes do that and give them to my husband because he has got none."

The noise from the commotion of Trevor being beaten up brought the terrorists to their window. "We will have to leave quickly," Alama said.

"The police will come, get everything, leave nothing," Mohamad said. The four men scattered around the room, picking bags up and going into other rooms, getting papers and whatever they thought they would need.

"Quickly," Alama shouted as he put a large duffle bag on his back and went out of the door, the other three men hot on his heels.

"The back way," Nesta said. All four men with bags on their backs and carrying bags in their hands, with Mohamad leading the way, went along the corridor and down the back stairs and to the back door. Before they went out Mohamad stopped and said to Shea: "Did you set it?"

CHAPTER 34

"No," Shea said, "no time."

"I will do it," Alama said. "You go and wait for me." Alama rushed back up the stairs while the three other men went out the back door; parked just on the roadside was a red Mercedes Vito van. The three men ran to the van, Shea fumbling for the keys with his hands full, the hazard lights flickered on the van. Mohamad opened the back doors and threw in the two bags he was carrying and then Abdul threw the big duffle bag with the AK47 assault rifles into the back of the van. Nesta went to the front of the van and got into the driving seat saying, "Come on Alama."

Brian Taylor was standing watching the men piling into the van. He moved from his place of cover and over to the block of flats to get a better view. He had not taken much notice of the van because he thought it was unimportant, but not now – now it seemed very important. Trevor wanted to get the number of the van and to get a closer look to see if one of the men that got into the van was the man that he and Trevor were following.

Brian was at the back of the flats now; creeping along beside the wall, he goes past the back door that the men had rushed out of. Just then the back door opened and out came Alama. Brian spun round quickly, both men were standing face to face. Brian instantly noticed Alama as the man they had been following, Alama instantly recognised Brian as one of the men he had seen at the bottom of the street; the other one must be the man at the front being beaten up, Alama thought. Alama, without hesitation, head-butted Brian on the bridge of the nose, at the same time dropping the bags he was carrying. Brian's nose burst all over his face, blood streaming from a deep gash on his forehead. Brian's hands immediately going up to cover his face as his knees begin to buckle. Alama follows up with a left and right punch into the left and right side of Brian's head; Brian falls to his knees.

Alama brought his knee up sharply and hit Brian smack under the chin, sending him flying onto his back. Brian was knocked out. By now Abdul had noticed Alama striking Brian and was on his way back to assist Alama who had floored Brian with the greatest of ease. "Get him into the van. We need to find out what he knows," Alama said to Abdul as he waved Mohamad over to help.

Abdul and Mohamad dragged Brian to the van and tumbled his limp bulk into the back, then the two men jumped into the back of the van. Alama had gathered his bags up and threw them on top of Brian as he jumped into the back of the van.

"Go, go Shea," Mohamad shouted. Shea began to drive off at speed.

"Steady," Alama said. "Go easy Shea, we are away."

"Who is he?" Abdul asked.

"I noticed him and another man as I came," Alama said. "They must have been following me."

"But why? How did they know?" Nesta said.

"We will find out," Alama said, kicking Brian in the head.

"Did you get it done Alama?" Mohamad asked.

"It is done," Alama replied.

They drove down to the end of the street and looking along at the ruckus that was still going on just ou side the entrance into the flats, they drove straight past. "We do everything as planned," Alama said. The Mercedes van turned right at the bottom of East Hill Road and headed south along Sunderland Road.

"But where do we go Alama? The plan was that we stay at the flat until it was time to leave," Shea said.

CHAPTER 34

"We go to the boatyard. Veeri was expecting me in a few hours anyway – we will hold up there until it is time," Alama said.

CHAPTER 35

Andy checked his mobile phone. "Carhill has rung me," he said to Colin. Colin was busy giving a verbal report to the police inspector who would be left with the aftermath of Andy's pursuit of Goomi.

"You will have to call him back," Colin said to Andy. Andy pressed the call back button on his mobile phone; it rang a couple of times and then a strange man's voice answered.

"Hello, who is that?" Andy said.

"This is PC Squires. Who is it I am talking to please?" the police constable said.

"Is Trevor Carhill there?" Andy asked the police constable.

"We have a man."

"Listen," Andy said, "I am a senior police officer – my name is Andy Redman, and if you are with Trevor Carhill I want you to tell me now, Constable."

"Ah sir, this must be your card that was in the pocket of the gentleman's coat," the constable said.

"Is he all right?" Andy said.

"I need to know what relationship you have with this man, sir, before I can divulge any further information," the constable said.

"Just stay on the line," Andy said to the constable. "Colin, go and get that Inspector for me quick. This copper will tell me nothing."

When Colin went to get the police inspector Andy tried again with PC Squires: "Listen Constable, I need to know if you have Trevor Carhill with you and if he's all right."

"Sir, it is you who should be giving me information, not me

Chapter 35

telling you about this incident," the constable said.

"Incident!" Andy shouted down the phone at the constable.

Just then Colin came over with the Inspector. "Your name Inspector?" Andy asked.

"James, Inspector Walter James sir."

"Inspector James, I have one of your officers on the other end of this mobile. Now you talk to him and you tell him he must tell me what I ask him," Andy said.

"Very well, the Inspector said, taking the mobile phone from Andy. "Hello, who is speaking?"

"PC Squires – who is this please?"

"Constable Squires, this is Inspector James of Newcastle division. I want you to listen to me," the Inspector said. "It is very important that you tell the man I'm putting back on the phone what he wants to know – do you understand, Constable? Because if you don't, let me make one thing clear... do you like your job Constable?"

"Yes sir, I understand," the constable said.

Andy took the mobile back off the Inspector. "Now Constable, do you have Trevor Carhill with you?" Andy said.

"Sir, we have a man who is unconscious. He has been beaten up. This man had a card in his pocket with your name on, sir. We are waiting for the ambulance to take the man to hospital sir."

"How bad is he, Constable and where are you this very moment?"

"He has taken a few blows to the head and around the body sir, it is hard to tell how bad he is sir. We are at Emerson Court, East Hill Road, Gateshead sir, but we will take the injured man to the Queen Elizabeth Hospital in Gateshead as soon as the ambulance gets here."

Andy and Colin were in the Range Rover now; Andy had

been rushing Colin on as he listened on the mobile phone to the Constable.

"Just one moment," Andy said to the Constable, as he opened the door of the Range Rover after gesturing to Colin to stop. "Do you know the Gateshead district?" Andy said to a policeman who was on duty, keeping the crowds of people back from the demolition site.

"Err yes sir, I suppose I do," the Constable said. "Jump in," Andy said to the Constable. The Constable looked at Inspector James.

"Well go on son," the Inspector said to the Constable.

Andy was back on the mobile phone to Constable Squires: "Have you any idea who beat Trevor up, Constable?"

"Yes sir, we know that."

Andy waited for an answer; there was nothing. "Well, who the hell beat him up?" Andy said.

"Apparently sir, it was the Kosovo Community, dishing out their brand of justice."

"Kosovos, fucking Kosovos, what the hell are you talking about?" Andy said to the Constable.

"Apparently this man was looking through a window watching a woman getting dressed sir," the Constable said.

"Listen: the property you are at now I don't want you or anyone to enter it, do you hear me?" Andy said.

"We have the injured man out in the lobby entrance sir," the Constable said.

"We will be with you in five minutes," Andy said. "I want you to just to stay on the phone with me and tell me everything, but also I want you not to let anyone in the building."

"The building is full of families, sir," the Constable said.

Andy looked at Colin. "We need back up at that address

CHAPTER 35

Colin – it may be another safe house."

"I am on it," Colin said, pressing a button to activate his hands-free set.

Andy leant back in his seat to talk to the policeman sitting in the back saying, "Get on your radio to your office and tell them the officer at East Hill Road needs assistance quickly." Andy then spoke on his mobile phone to Constable Squires: "We have back up on its way to you. How many officers are there with you?"

"Only myself and Constable Davidson, sir," the Constable said.

"As I thought," Andy said. "How far now?" he said to the Constable in the back of the Range Rover.

"Two minutes and we will be there. Take a right at the roundabout and we are on Sunderland Road," the Constable said.

Just as Colin was about to turn right an ambulance came racing around the roundabout, blue lights flashing and two tone horn sounding out. "He has got to be going our way," Colin said and pulled out behind the ambulance and followed him. The ambulance took them straight to the East Hill Road incident.

"We must get all these people out of the way," Andy said as they came to a halt behind the ambulance. Andy told the Constable in the back of the Range Rover to go and help get the people back. Andy and Colin went straight over to Trevor who was lying in the recovery position with Constable Squires knelt over him. The paramedic from the ambulance beat them to Trevor.

Andy looked at Trevor – his face was covered in blood and blood was also coming from a wound on his head. Andy went down on his knees and punched the ground.

"There was nothing you could do. You had no choice: you

had to send him after the target. There was no one else or we would not be here," Colin said.

"Here? Where is here? It may be nothing for all we know," Andy said.

"Andy, you must call Peter," Colin said.

"I know, I know," Andy said, taking his mobile phone out and pressing one button.

"Let's have it Andy," Peter said when he answered.

"Sir, Carhill has been hurt; he is unconscious and needs hospital treatment urgently. It could be serious; we have an ambulance at the scene," Andy said.

"How has this happened Andy?" asked Peter.

"I had to send him to follow a target, Peter," Andy said.

"You did what? Why did you send Carhill, Andy?"

"Colin was tied up with something else at the University. I know I should not have put Carhill at risk but we would have lost the target. I had Goomi, so I sent Carhill after a guy that Goomi had been talking to at the University," Andy said.

"And this guy, the target, where is he now?"

"Looks like he is gone, Peter," Andy said.

"Gone like Goomi, Andy. And Carhill: was he injured by the target you sent him after?" Peter said.

"No, he was attacked by Kosovos at an address in Gateshead, we are looking into it now Peter."

"Andy I want you to stay with Carhill, do you hear me? You go to the hospital with him and keep me informed. I will send Dr Luke there to meet you there. Now tell me what hospital it is," Peter said.

"I will let you know as soon as I know, Peter."

Trevor Carhill was on a stretcher being lifted into the ambulance by the two paramedics.

CHAPTER 35

"Colin I have to go with Carhill. Let me know what goes down," Andy said.

"Sure thing, Andy, you let me know how Carhill gets on," Colin said. Andy jumped into the back of the ambulance and sat next to Trevor. Andy looked at Trevor's face – a black eye, the nose was burst, lips were cut and bruising on both cheeks: he had had a good kicking. As the ambulance started to pull away Trevor's head began to roll from side to side and Trevor began to moan. "Excuse me sir," the paramedic said to Andy when he heard Trevor moaning. The ambulance sped off to the hospital, blue lights flashing.

"Where are the ones that beat Carhill up?" Colin said to Constable Squires.

"They have done a runner sir, or they could be just standing among the crowd. No one is going to tell us," the Constable said. "There is this man sir, he lives in the bottom flat – it was he who called us in."

"Can I ask you your name?" Colin said to the man.

"Alan Hauxwell," the man replied.

Just then more police cars and anti-terrorist vehicles began to arrive at the scene. "Just one moment Mr Hauxwell," Colin said to the man. "Constable Squires I want you to go and get me the man in charge of this lot who just came and bring him to me. Mr Hauxwell, could you tell me who lives in the flat that the injured man was looking into through the window?"

"It is that woman's flat, her there," Mr Hauxwell pointed to a plump woman.

"And who lives in the flat above her?" Colin asked.

"Bloody Kosovos," Mr Hauxwell said.

"And the second floor flat?" Colin asked.

"Pakistanis – they come and go all the time," Mr Hauxwell

said.

"Are they in there now, the Pakistanis?" Colin asked Mr Hauxwell.

"I don't know. Almost everybody is out of their flats to see what is going on," Mr Hauxwell said.

"Captain Atkinson sir, Anti-terrorist Squad. What we got?" the Captain said.

"What we have got, Captain, is a whole load of trouble. I want you to get everybody out of these flats both sides Captain; this flat in particular we think may be hot. Tread carefully – get everyone out before we find out," Colin said.

"Mr Hauxwell, can you go with the police officer please and just wait way over there until I come and speak to you again sir, thank you," Colin said leading Mr Hauxwell over to Constable Squires. Colin then got on his mobile phone to Peter.

"Yes Colin, go," Peter said.

"Sir, a witness said a second floor flat was frequented by Pakistanis often. I think this is where Carhill followed the target to, Peter. It has got to be a safe house. I will need the Bomb Squad as soon as. I could do with speaking to Garret – what has he found at Goomi's place?" Colin said.

"I will talk to Garret. You keep everyone away from that flat until we know for sure it is safe," Peter said.

"Will do," Colin said.

Colin went back over to speak to Mr Hauxwell. "The Pakistanis you said that come and go – would you recognise them again if you saw them?"

"I don't know, maybe. I try to keep myself to myself," Mr Hauxwell said.

"Did the Pakistanis come in cars or did they walk when they came to the flat?" Colin asked.

CHAPTER 35

"They usually came in a red van but now and then the odd one would come by foot," Mr Hauxwell said.

"The red van – what make was it?" Colin asked.

"A Merc I think."

"You did not happen to get the number of this red van, did you Mr Hauxwell?" Colin asked hopefully.

"No sorry."

"And how many of these Pakistanis did you see?"

"There were four or five of them; like I said they would come and go," Mr Hauxwell said.

"Thank you Mr Hauxwell, I will speak to you again later," Colin said as he rang Peter again.

"Yes Colin," Peter said.

"Peter, the witness reckons there were four or five different faces at the flat. They came and went all the time and they had a red Mercedes van," Colin reported.

"Very well Colin, we will get that out there. Have the Bomb boys arrived yet?" Peter said.

"I think this is them coming now Peter. I will get back to you."

Two black vans that were speeding up East Hill Road behind a police escort car screeched to a stop. A man instantly got out of one of the vans and came straight over to Colin.

"Major Brian Errington," he said, putting his hand out to Colin who took the Major's hand and just said: "Colin. Major we need to be in this flat as soon as it is possible. We have not got a second to waste; we are very sure it could be rigged with a booby-trap."

"OK Colin," Major Errington said, "let us go and take a look see."

Colin and the Major went up the stairs to the second floor;

just along the corridor was the door to the flat in question. The Major walked up very slowly towards the door. He put his ear up against the door to listen. Colin thought you will not hear anything over this din: the noise from people outside, most of the residents leaving without protesting but some making life hell for the police officers who were trying to evacuate them. Just then Colin thought about Mosley Street in Newcastle and what Simon, the SAS Major, had said to Garret. Colin looked all around and up at the ceiling of the corridor.

"You sly fuck," Colin said, "wait Major, look above you."

The Major looked up and what he saw were two wires running across the ceiling; on closer inspection it was one wire fastened onto a small curtain hook that was screwed into the top of the door; it ran over the ceiling and was threaded through another small curtain hook that was screwed into the top of the wall opposite the door; the wire ran back over the ceiling, over the top of the door and into the flat.

The Major came back along the corridor and said to Colin: "I think you are right about the booby-trap. I will get my men ready."

Colin got back onto the mobile phone to Peter. "Yes Colin, what you got there?" Peter said.

"It is a live one Peter, we have some sort of trip wire rigged up above the door," Colin said.

"Colin, I want you to wait. Garret has a problem at the bedsit where Goomi resided – it may be something similar. His guys are on with it now. Just get things ready there and I will get back to you as soon as we know."

Colin went back out into the road to check that the police had moved everyone well back out of the way. The area was pretty well clear of the public and residents. Collin's mobile

CHAPTER 35

phone vibrated in his pocket. "Hello Garret," Colin said answering his mobile.

"Colin, don't let the Bomb boys cut that wire – if it is the same set-up as at Goomi's bedsit it cannot be disarmed by cutting the wire," Garret said. "The one we have here is a fishing line – it runs through hooks and goes over the top of the door and back to a spring."

"Our wire runs back over the top of the door as well," Colin said.

"It works both ways," Garret said. "The fishing line is pulling on the spring and the spring is under tension – if you cut the line, the spring recoils and triggers the explosives. And if you open the door the line pulls through the hooks and pulls on the spring; the line is fastened to the spring with a weak cord. The cord will snap and the spring recoils and triggers the explosives – it is a no win going through the door."

"How did you get past it then?" Colin said.

"We are eight storeys up in a ten-storey block," Garret said. "One of the Bomb guys had to abseil down from the roof and kick the window in. You can only disarm it quickly from inside."

"Could you not hold the tension on the line and then cut it?" Colin suggested.

"Just needs for that thin line to slip Colin and you are a goner. The way in is the windows – tell the Bomb Squad," Garret said.

Colin looks along the road – a fire engine is parked ready to act in case the worst happens. "Major, tell your men to get a ladder from the fire engine that will reach up to the second floor window," Colin said.

The Major sends two of his men to get a ladder from the fire engine. "What is the score?" Major Errington said to Colin.

"The door is a no go – we have an identical set up elsewhere. Our entry is through the window," Colin said.

A couple of the firemen came back carrying the ladder for the Bomb boys. "No you don't. You boys leave this to the Army," Colin said just allowing the firemen to place the ladder up against the bottom of the window. Major Errington wasted no time – he was away up the ladder. The Major looked through the window carefully studying the whole room; he then loosened his chin strap on his helmet and took it off and smashed the window with it. He then reached in through the broken window and lifted the latch lock and pulled the window open. The Major climbed inside.

One of the other Bomb Squad men was just about to go up the ladder to assist the Major; Colin pulled him back and said: "You hold the ladder while I go up."

Colin then went up the ladder and in through the window to the flat. As soon as the Major saw Colin he was none too pleased. Colin just said, "I am here now so let us just get on with it."

"It looks pretty crude," the Major said, "but effective."

The wire came over the top of the door and down to a spring just like Garret said. The spring was anchored just in front of the light switch so if the spring was set free it would recoil into the light switch and turn on the room light. The bulb had been removed from the light socket in the room and replaced with a bayonet socket with a wire that led down into a big duffle bag lying on the floor.

"What now?" Colin asked.

"Well," Major Errington said, pulling the table into the centre of the room and getting onto the table, "we unplug the wire from the light socket."

CHAPTER 35

The Major reached up and began to twist the bayonet fitting loose. Colin just cringed; nothing happened. Both Colin and the Major let out a sigh of relief. "That's it," Colin said.

"Seems so," the major said opening the duffle bag and adding, "there is enough Cemtex in here to cut this block of flats in half."

CHAPTER 36

The red Mercedes van pulls up just outside the gates at the R&B Harrison's redundant ship repair yard. Alama gets on his mobile phone; he knows that their plan was never to use the mobile phones unless it was totally necessary but he feels that their plan may have somehow been discovered. Veeri answers his mobile phone. "Alama, what makes you call?"

"Come and open the gates Veeri. I am with the others; we have some trouble."

Brian Taylor is beginning to come round; he moans and groans with pain. Alama strikes Brian on the head with his fist; Brian curls up in agony. Two minutes later Veeri and Rasheed come nervously out of the bushes on the other side of the gates, brandishing AK47 assault rifles.

Alama leans out of the van window. "Quickly, Veeri, open the gates," he says. Veeri and Rasheed swing their weapons behind their backs and open the gates to let them in.

Shea drove the van through the bushes and into the open fabrication shed. Abdul, Mohamad and Nesta jumped out of the back of the van. Nesta and Abdul went to close the doors on the shed just as Veeri and Rasheed came back into the shed.

"What is wrong Alama?" Veeri asked.

"Alama was followed this morning back to the safe house," Shea said, getting out of the front of the van.

"British police," Rasheed said.

"We will soon find out," Alama said, dragging Brian Taylor by the hair to the back doors of the van. Brian Taylor's mobile phone fell out of his pocket when Alama dragged him; it fell down into the corner of the van, down by the wheel arch. Brian

CHAPTER 36

Taylor was semi conscious.

"What is happening?" he said.

"You will find out," Alama said. "Get him out." Rasheed and Abdul dragged Brian onto the fabrication shed floor. "Get some rope," Alama said, "and bring him down here."

Mohamad and Shea dragged Brian down to the area where the work benches were. Alama pulled a chair over. Veeri and Shea sat Brian into the chair; Shea tied Brian to the back of the chair and pulling Brian's hands around the back of the chair tied them with cable wraps. Then Shea put cable wraps around Brian's ankles and fastened them to the front legs of the chair. Alama grabbed Brian by the throat and said: "You, the Police," as he squeezed his throat for a few seconds, and then relaxing his grip to give Brian a chance to answer.

Brian gasped for air saying, "Please why are you doing this, what have I done?" Veeri punched Brian in the stomach and winded him. Brian gasped for air again.

"You are police," Alama said.

"No I am not. Please, you're hurting me," Brian cried as Alama twisted his ear so hard it began to tear and bleed heavily from the lobe.

"Search him," Alama said. Shea, Abdul and Mohamad practically ripped the clothes off Brian to get into his pockets. All Brian had in his pockets was a little bit of cash and a wallet. Alama opened the wallet; inside the wallet was a card with a photograph of Brian on his CIU membership card.

"A policeman," Alama said pointing at the photograph of Brian on his Club Institute and Union membership card. "Nesta, you and Abdul go and keep a lookout." Alama was worried when he seen Brian's Club Card not knowing it was a harmless social club membership card. Nesta and Abdul grabbed weapons and went outside. Alama began to hit Brian around the head with a spanner he had picked up off the work bench. Brian screamed in pain; he pleaded with them to stop; the blood was running freely from wounds in Brian's head from the spanner blows.

"Who was the other man with you?" Alama said poking the spanner into Brian's groin. Brian could take no more; he had nothing to tell them so they would stop hurting him – he did not know why Trevor was following Alama. "You are a policeman – you tell me why you follow me, tell me now." Alama swiped Brian across the face with the spanner, knocking Brian's front teeth into his mouth. The blood was flowing that fast from his gums it made Brian choke on it. "Tell me," Alama shouted into Brian's ear when his mouth was only an inch away.

"Please I beg you, stop," Brian pleaded.

"Shea, the torch," Alama said. Shea pushed the bottle barrow over with the oxyacetylene burning gear on it. Veeri sparked the cutting torch alight. Alama took the cutting torch and turned the cutting flame higher, he held the cutting torch in Brian's face and said, "You tell me why you were following me and who sent you."

"Please, please, I beg you, no more." Alama turned the cutting torch so the flame made contact with Brian's hair, and the parts of Brian's hair that were not soaked in blood just sizzled up into black cinder.

The screams and yells of agony from Brian were that loud that Veeri put a bag over Brian's head to muffle the sound. Alama turned to Veeri, Mohamad and Shea. To make him talk he was going to phone Goomi.

"Alama you cannot, General Shali said we must not use the phone," Veeri said.

CHAPTER 36

"We must know. If I was followed from my meeting with Goomi then maybe Goomi was followed as well." Alama dialled a number on his mobile phone: nothing, not even a ringing tone. Alama put the mobile away saying, "Goomi is not replying, this is not good."

Abdul said: "They know of this place, Alama."

"The British do not know of this place," Alama said, "or they would be here by now, but we have to be cautious and leave this place. We keep to the plan but we go to our destinies earlier. I will hold up somewhere before I go to see our General Shali. Nesta will have to hold up with me until it is time for him to go to his place of work." Brian was unconscious but they still kept on hitting him in his stomach and about his swollen, black, burned head.

CHAPTER 37

Peter Gray walked in on Dr Luke and a couple of doctors from London; they were discussing Trevor Carhill's case. "Excuse me please," Peter said. "Something has come up. It is very important I speak to you, Dr Luke, right away."

"Of course," Dr Luke said getting up.

"No," Peter said, gesturing to the doctor to stay seated and then saying, "If you don't mind, gentlemen." The two doctors got up and left the room.

"What is it Mr Gray?" Dr Luke said.

"Call me Peter. We have a problem with Trevor Carhill, doctor," Peter said.

"What kind of problem?"

"Trevor has been beaten up."

"Beaten up by who and how bad is he?" Dr Luke asked.

"By who does not matter at this moment, but how bad does. I have spoken to the doctors in charge at the Queen Elizabeth Hospital in Gateshead – that is where Trevor is at the moment – they cannot tell me anything, it is too soon, he has only just been seen to," Peter said.

"I must get over there quickly," Dr Luke said.

"I will get you there soon enough but first we must talk, doctor."

"What is there to talk about if Trevor is hurt? I should go to assist the doctors treating him."

"I have spoken to the doctors who will be looking after Trevor and I have told them not to administer any drugs that would keep Trevor unconscious any longer than it would take naturally for him to come to. I have told them no sedatives at

CHAPTER 37

this moment," Peter said.

"What medical qualifications have you got that gives you the right to tell doctors how to treat a patient? You have not got the authority," Dr Luke said angrily and got up to leave.

"Please doctor sit down, I am afraid I have every right and I do have the authority to tell the doctors looking after Trevor what to do, doctor," Peter said. "I don't like what I am doing but I have no choice."

"Choice – what are you talking about choice? This is a man's life."

"We don't know yet if it is bad as that doctor," Peter said. "I am going to ask you to do something doctor that you are not going to like but first of all I want you to listen to what I have to say. Sometime this evening before or just after 7 o'clock there is going to be something terrible happen where a lot of innocent people are going to be killed. It is my job – no, our job doctor – to try our utmost to prevent this from happening with whatever means we have at our disposal. Now, all I have is an approximate time and a possible target."

"But what could I do that would possibly help you?"

"I have nothing concrete to go on at the moment – the leads we have may or would eventually take us to these men if we had the time and time is what we don't have," Peter said. "These men are going to kill as many people as they possibly can tonight, doctor, and we have to stop them from doing that."

"How can I help?"

"Trevor Carhill may be our only hope of stopping these terrorists carrying out their murderous deed," Peter said. "I don't know if Trevor saw or heard anything at the place where he was injured, doctor, but I have to know if he did and I must know soon."

"And so?"

"And so, doctor, I need to speak to Trevor Carhill as soon as I can," Peter said.

"And that will be when he recovers enough to speak to you – that's if he does recover," Dr Luke said, "so what are you suggesting?"

"I want you to bring Trevor here from the hospital. We will have other medical staff present," Peter said.

"And what if he cannot be moved?" Dr Luke said.

"He will be moved doctor."

Peter was running out of time – he had to take the kid gloves off. "And further more I want you to bring him and give him whatever it takes so he can talk to me," Peter said.

"What you're asking could kill him. I could kill him," Dr Luke said.

"It may not be that bad doctor, but if it is I have no choice: we must know if there is a chance we can stop these people – I have to take that chance, so if it means that I doctor, not you, put Trevor Carhill's life at risk, then I will do that," Peter said. "In my job doctor, I sometimes have to make life and death decisions. I really do hope in this case I have made the right one for everyone concerned. Now Dr Luke, if you're not going to give me your cooperation, and I mean your full cooperation on this, I will get someone else."

"I will do it because I don't want anyone else to be looking after Trevor, but when this is over I should be going to the Medical Board with this, Mr Gray," Dr Luke said.

Peter pressed a button on the telephone and a few seconds later a woman police constable popped her head around the door saying, "You wanted something sir?"

"Yes, could you see to it that Dr Luke is taken to the Queen

CHAPTER 37

Elizabeth Hospital in Gateshead immediately and tell the driver to bring back Andy with him from the hospital? Thank you," Peter said.

Dr Luke got up and left the room. Peter sat down thinking, this time tomorrow – how bad is it going to be? A buzzer went on the telephone; Peter answered it. "I have Mr Garret on the line sir," a lady's voice said.

"Yes, Charlie, what you got?" Peter said.

"Not a great deal at the moment, Peter. The boys are still going over the bedsit. We have Goomi's passport, which no doubt will be a forgery," Garret said, "and an address we found with the passport."

"Address?" Peter said enthusiastically.

"Don't get your hopes up, Peter," Garret said. "It is an address in Holland," Garret said.

"Holland or Norway – that is where most of the ferries that leave the River Tyne go," Peter said. "Wait a minute – they don't think that they are just going to get on a ferry to Holland do they?"

"We also have Goomi's packed and ready to leave backpack," Garret said.

"What we got in that?"

"This is interesting," Garret said. "We have 9 mm hand pistols, a couple of clips to go with it, there are a couple of full clips for an AK47, food and a torch with extra torch batteries."

"It must be dark where he was going if he needed a torch,"

"And basically that is it for now. I was hoping we would have come across a mobile phone but no signs, not even a charger."

"I have no doubt if Goomi had a mobile phone it went through the concrete crusher with him," Peter said. "All right

Charlie, get what you have got and get back here – the time is going fast. I will get that address checked out by the Dutch Authorities."

"How is Carhill?" Garret asked.

"I am having him brought here, Charlie. We need to talk to him."

"Is he fit enough to be brought to the office, Peter?"

"I don't know Charlie, but what do I do? I will speak to you about it when you get back."

CHAPTER 38

Andy sat in the Queen Elizabeth Hospital waiting room. He had Trevor on his mind but he also could not stop thinking of his main objective which was to stop the terrorists before it was too late. Has Trevor got vital information on their whereabouts? I should be out there at least trying to do something, Andy thought.

"Hi Andy," Dr Luke said, "I got here as soon as I could. Have they said anything?"

"No nothing, they seem a bit busy. I did not want to interfere just yet," Andy said.

"I will move them along, just give me a few minutes," Dr Luke said.

Andy went outside to give Colin a call to find out how things were going at Emerson Court. As Andy was getting his mobile phone out he observed a woman coming up the footpath to the Accident and Emergency entrance to the hospital; she is distressed and upset. Andy has never met this woman before but he cannot help but feel she is in some way connected. Andy watched the woman go into Accident and Emergency and then followed her in.

The woman went straight to the desk and said to the receptionist, "I am here to see Trevor Carhill. I am his sister."

"Shit!" Andy said to himself. "His sister."

"The doctors are with Mr Carhill at the moment. If you would just take a seat Miss Carhill, I will get someone to see to you," the receptionist nurse said.

"Can you tell me how he is and what has happened?" Clare Carhill said to the nurse.

"I am sorry, I don't have that information. You will have to wait until the doctor comes to see you," the nurse said.

Clare Carhill went and sat down. Andy moved straight over and sat down next to her and said: "Miss Carhill, I am the officer who brought your brother Trevor into hospital."

"What is going on here? This morning Trevor was in police custody and then he was on the Metro following a man and now he is in hospital," Clare Carhill said.

"Trevor has been beaten up, Miss Carhill," Andy said.

"Oh my God! How bad is he?" Clare said. "We don't know at the moment. Trevor was knocked out, but when I came in with him he was moving and mumbling," Andy said.

"How did you know Trevor was here, Miss Carhill?"

"I rang him on his mobile and a police constable answered and told me Trevor had been brought to this hospital," Clare said, starting to cry.

Andy gave her his handkerchief saying to himself, Constable Squires has still got Trevor's mobile phone. "How did you know that Trevor was following a man on the Metro this morning, Miss Carhill?" Andy asked.

Just then the driver that brought Dr Luke to the hospital came in and said: "Sir, I have to bring you back to the station, Mr Gray said."

"Yes all right I will be with you shortly," Andy said. Andy asked again: "Miss Carhill – Trevor on the Metro – how did you know?"

"Brian rang me and told me," Clare replied.

"Brian – who is Brian?" Andy said.

"I want to know how Trevor is." Clare got up and went to the desk and said: "Please can you get someone, I want to know how my brother is," pleading with the nurse on desk duty.

CHAPTER 38

"I will go straight and find out now, if you will just take a seat," the nurse said to Clare.

Andy got up and went to get Clare to bring her back to sit down. "Miss Carhill," Andy said as he led Clare to her seat, "it is very important that you tell me what this Brian told you."

"I am telling no one anything until I have seen Trevor is all right," Clare said.

Andy got up, going to the desk saying, "I will see what I can do. Nurse, can you tell me where I will find the Administrator please?"

"He is in theatre at the moment sir, but head Nurse Barns is coming up the corridor now," the nurse said.

Andy went to meet the head nurse but before he could speak the head nurse said to Andy: "Are you Andy waiting to see how Mr Carhill is doing?"

"That's right," Andy said puzzled at how the head nurse knew his name.

"Mr Carhill is being moved at this very moment," the head nurse said.

Andy asked, "Where to?"

"I should think you would be able to tell me that," the head nurse said to Andy. "Dr Luke said you knew all about it."

Andy put two and two together. "I need to speak to Peter. Nurse, can you get someone to look after Miss Carhill please? I will only be a moment," Andy said rushing outside to make a phone call.

"Yes Andy," Peter said.

"Peter, are you having Carhill moved?"

"Yes I am Andy, he is being brought here," Peter confirmed.

"Peter, I have Carhill's sister Clare at the hospital. She had rang Trevor on his mobile phone, Police Constable Squires answered it and told her Trevor was at the hospital," Andy said.

"What the bloody hell is a police officer doing telling her that in the middle of this case? I will have his badge for this," Peter said.

"I think it is just as well he did Peter because Miss Carhill may have information about what Trevor was doing.,"

"Bring her in Andy, use any excuse you have to but bring her in," Peter said.

"Will do Peter," Andy said putting his mobile phone away.

Andy went straight back to Accident and Emergency. "Miss Carhill. Look, I can't keep calling you Miss Carhill – what is your name?"

"Clare is my name."

"Clare, Trevor is being moved right now," Andy said.

Clare began to panic – she knew if one patient had been moved from one hospital to another it was because the hospital did not have the expertise to cater for the injured patient.

"Calm down, Clare, Trevor is all right," Andy said.

"But why are they moving him?"

"He is being moved to Durham Police Station – now do you think he would be going there if he were badly hurt?" Andy said.

The head nurse who was with Clare looked daggers at Andy. Clare started to calm down because it did make sense – they would not take Trevor to a police station if he were hurt, but Clare still needed answers. "Why take him back to the police station when you just let him out this morning?"

"Your brother Trevor has been helping the police – that's why he was following someone on the Metro," Andy said.

Clare sat and thought for a few seconds and said: "I want you to take me to Trevor now."

"I have a car waiting," Andy said.

CHAPTER 38

Andy and Clare got into the waiting police car. Andy said to the driver: "Step on it, use the noise if you have to but get us there quick." The Queen Elizabeth Hospital in Gateshead was a good eight miles from Durham Police Station. Andy wanted to waste no time.

"Clare, could you tell me about this Brian?" asked Andy.

"I told you – when I see Trevor."

"I am taking you to see Trevor, that is a promise. You must tell me about Brian – we have very little time to stop a bad thing from happening."

Clare thought for a while. "All right. Brian is Trevor's friend – they have worked together for years. Brian will do anything for Trevor."

"Yes Clare but how did this Brian know Trevor was following a man on the Metro?" Andy probed.

"Brian rang me and told me he had met Trevor coming off the Metro at Gateshead Stadium Metro Station and Trevor was following some Asian guy."

"I need you to tell me everything that Brian told you – it is very, very important."

"Brian said they followed this guy into some flats just off Sunderland Road and Trevor watched the front of the flats while he had Brian watch the back of the flats in case the guy came out the back."

Andy thought for a short while and then rang Colin. "How is Carhill?" Colin asked when he answered Andy's call.

Clare heard Colin asking this. "Is Trevor really all right?" Clare asked.

"Yes he is fine," Andy said.

"What's wrong Andy?" Colin said.

Andy did not want to make the conversation any longer then

it had to be so he did not answer Colin. "Why you running on two tones Andy?" Colin asked.

"No time at the moment Colin," Andy said. "Colin, I think Trevor had someone with him when he followed the target to Emerson Court."

"How could he?"

"Colin, to cut a long one short, Trevor had run into a mate called Brian and had this Brian help him," Andy said.

"How do you know this Andy?" Colin asked.

"Trevor's sister is with me now, it is what she is telling me. I think this Brian took the back while Trevor watched the front. Now, according to Trevor's sister, this Brian is a good friend of Trevor's and he would not stand back doing nothing if Trevor was taking a kicking."

"Meaning what, Andy?"

"I don't think Brian knew Trevor was being set upon – he was at the back and I think our target went out the back way. Now maybe this Brian is still following the target or... you know Colin, I have Trevor's sister sitting next to me," Andy said.

"I will check the back now Andy and get back to you," Colin said.

Andy put his mobile phone away. "Clare, have you got Brian's number in your mobile phone?"

"Yes I have. What is going on with you people?" Clare said.

"Listen Clare, I want you to phone Brian but I want you to be very careful what you say; Brian may be in danger. I will tell you what to say," Andy said.

Clare was even more worried now; Clare rang Brian's number saying to Andy it is ringing but no answer.

"OK Clare, leave it for a couple of minutes and then try again," Andy said.

CHAPTER 38

Clare tried again: it is still ringing but he does not answer. Andy's mobile began to vibrate in his pocket. "Yes Colin," Andy said.

"Can I talk Andy?" Colin said.

Andy swapped his mobile phone over to his other ear and leant his head away from Clare. "Yes go ahead," Andy said.

"Yes outside the back entrance into Emerson Court we have blood Andy and it is very recent."

Andy took a sharp intake of breath and said, "All right Colin got that. Are you coming back to the office?"

"I will leave right now," Colin replied. The car that Andy and Clare were in was now racing into Durham City, blue lights flashing and two tone horns sounding alerting other traffic to pull over and give them a clear road.

CHAPTER 39

Peter Gray was in the operations room at Durham Police Station looking at all the evidence and pictures they had stuck up on the walls. There were two walls covered and not one pick of that evidence was leading them any closer to the terrorist than they were at this time yesterday.

"There has to be something," Peter said to himself. The door opened and in came Charlie Garret. "I am worried Charlie," Peter said. "This is getting away from us."

"That's not like you Peter, you are the one who said you never give up," Garret said.

"I won't ever give up Charlie, no way, I can't let my men even think that, but we have always had something to move on."

"Something will break, you will see," Garret said.

"As long as we have enough time to react, that's all I want Charlie. Maybe Carhill's sister can come up with something."

"His sister? What has she got to do with it?" Garret was feeling worried seeing it was him who sent her home yesterday even if he had her supervised.

"Andy is bringing her in – she seems to know something about Trevor Carhill following the target to Emerson Court."

A knock on the door, a policewoman's head popped round. "You said let you know the minute the ambulance arrived sir."

"Thank you," Peter said. "That is Dr Luke and Trevor Carhill now. I hope this is going to work."

"He may have nothing at all to tell us," Garret said.

"One way or the other we have to find out Charlie."

"What are you really going to do Peter if we cannot get to these people?"

CHAPTER 39

"Short of locking down the City of Newcastle and the town of Gateshead there is nothing else I can do Charlie," Peter said. "I have the Army at Catterick Garrison and Otterburn standing by to move at the drop of a hat."

"Will we be able to shut these two main areas off and maintain order?"

"I don't think we will be able to do that, there will be panic and all we are doing is removing members of the public out of what we think are danger zones and replacing them with Army personnel and putting them in the danger zones," Peter said. "We had better go and meet Dr Luke."

"How is she taking it, having to bring Carhill here?"

"She is not happy and rightly so – I would have thought less of her if she were not against it."

"She put up a fight?"

"Well, let's just say I am off her Christmas card list," Peter said wryly.

Both men went out to meet Dr Luke. The paramedics were just wheeling Trevor Carhill on a stretcher along the passageway. Peter looked at Trevor; one of his eyes was open, the other was closed tight with the black bruised swelling; he had small cuts to his face that were butterfly stitched, red and black 'n' blue bruising covered most of his face. The paramedics were just taking Trevor into one of the apartments that had been prepared to take him; medical staff were waiting in the apartment ready to receive Trevor Carhill.

Dr Luke followed the paramedics as they took Trevor into the apartment.

"Dr Luke, can we talk?" Peter said, pointing to a room opposite the apartment. Dr Luke, Garret and Peter went into the room and sat down. "How is Trevor, Dr Luke?"

"He is alive, no thanks to you," Dr Luke said.

"I noticed his eye open – is he fully conscious?"

"Trevor is awake but he is in shock and that is a very dangerous situation for him."

"Can Trevor hear if I were to talk to him?"

"Trevor is responding to us when we talk to him but only in a limited way; he will need time," Dr Luke said.

"How bad are his injuries?" Garret asked.

"Trevor has no broken bones fortunately, apart from cracked ribs; our major concern is the blows Trevor took to the head. He has two lesions that were open to the titanium metal plate protection in Trevor's head," Dr Luke said.

"Do you think he has suffered any brain damage, I mean with your medical expertise without doing extensive tests doctor?" Peter asked.

"It is hard to tell, but I am leaning to the side that he may have been very lucky and not suffered any permanent damage," Dr Luke said.

"Dr Luke I don't want to push but I must – as you know it is imperative I speak to Trevor as soon as possible," Peter said.

"It will take time," Dr Luke said.

"You know we don't have time doctor. I want you to get Trevor lucid and responsive as soon as you can," Peter said. "Now, I would rather have you do this because Trevor trusts you Dr Luke but if I have to I will use one of the other doctors."

"What if I cannot get Trevor to respond and even if he does what if he has lost his inner sight?"

"Well if you cannot get Trevor to respond it will make no difference if he has lost his unique capability will it?" Peter said.

Jenkins came in the room. "Sir, Andy is back," he said.

"All right," Garret said to Jenkins waving him back out of

CHAPTER 39

the room.

"I have another problem I have to lay at your feet doctor," Peter said.

"And what can that be? It cannot be any worse than the problem you are putting at my feet now," Dr Luke said.

"Trevor Carhill's sister is here."

"Oh no, Clare! What am I going to tell her we are doing to Trevor?" Dr Luke said.

"Charlie will you stay and talk to Dr Luke? I must talk with Andy," Peter said.

"Dr Luke," Garret said when Peter had left the room. "I know you are dead against having to do this but you must understand Peter would not ask this of you if there was another way."

"How can that man do this job and have no feelings or human decency in his body?"

"That's where you are wrong, doctor, it is because of his feelings that he does this job. Peter has to make some life or death decisions in his job and he has to be right all the time, because if just once he makes a mistake and he does it is all on his shoulders and he will bear the burden; he will not try and fob it off onto someone else. Now, if it were not for people like Peter Gray, the enemies of this country would destroy it and kill and maim. Now, Dr Luke, what you have to do is against your medical ethics I know, but every day Peter Gray has to do things that are against all human reason and decency, so doctor, I am not asking that you agree with Peter's decisions but that you try to understand them and why he has to make them."

Andy and Clare Carhill were just coming to the top of the stairs when Dr Luke and Garret were leaving the room where they had had their talk. Clare looked along the corridor and saw

Dr Luke.

"Linda!" Clare shouted and ran along the corridor to meet Linda Luke. Clare Carhill put her arms out to embrace Linda Luke and the doctor did the same. The apartment door was opened at that very moment by a nurse who was on her way out. Clare Carhill looked into the apartment and saw her brother Trevor propped up in a wheelchair, all his facial injuries evident.

"Trevor!" Clare shouted.

Dr Luke tried to usher Clare into the room that she had just come out of with Garret saying, "It is all right Clare, Trevor is going to be fine."

Trevor Carhill heard Clare's voice call out his name; he lifted his head and said, "Clare is that you?"

Clare was hysterical now and screaming down the corridor at Andy: "You lying bastard, you told me Trevor was all right – I hope you rot in hell."

Peter Gray came out of the operations room to see what all the noise was about. "Dr Luke, take Miss Carhill and calm her down, please," Peter said.

"Clare, Clare," came from the apartment room from Trevor, "is that you Clare?"

"Maybe that is just what we needed," Peter said as he acknowledged the sound of Trevor Carhill's voice.

Andy was feeling as low as anyone could at that moment. "I am sorry Peter," Andy said as Peter took hold of him and brought him into the operations room and out of Clare's sight. "I am sorry," Andy said again. "I should not have sent him after the target."

The operations room was full of analysts processing data and people moving around. "Not here," Peter said to Andy, "downstairs."

CHAPTER 39

Both men left the operations room. Andy stood in the corridor and looked along it – he could still hear Clare Carhill crying, he wanted to go along and try and talk to her, to try and make her understand why he had to lie to her.

"Come on Andy, we have work to do," Peter said. Andy and Peter went downstairs to an empty room.

"I should not have sent him after the target Peter, he could have been killed and now his mate Brian could be dead," Andy said.

"No you should not have sent Trevor to follow the target Andy, but if it is any consolation I would have done the same thing under the same circumstances," Peter said. "Now snap out of it Andy. What's this about Trevor Carhill's friend Brian?"

"Brian Taylor. Trevor ran into him when he was following the target. Trevor had this Brian Taylor keeping a watch on the back of Emerson Court while Trevor was at the front," Andy said.

"And where is this Brian now?"

"When Trevor was taking a kicking at the front I think the terrorists legged it out the back knowing the commotion outside would bring the police. I think the terrorists ran into Brian Taylor, Peter," Andy said. "Colin told me they found traces of fresh blood at the back of Emerson Court."

"And this Brian Taylor rang Clare Carhill on his mobile phone?"

"Yes Peter, we tried ringing this Brian on our way here – the mobile was ringing but we got no answer. The mobile phone Peter, maybe this Brian Taylor still has it with him wherever he is."

"What network is the mobile phone on?"

"I don't know. Clare Carhill has still got it – I dared not take it off her on the way here, she was suspicious enough."

"OK Andy I will see to that; have you had that looked at?" Peter pointed to the cut on Andy's cheek.

Andy had forgotten all about it. "Yes at the demolition site."

"Get yourself sorted Andy, just in case this mobile phone comes back trumps. I will get Colin back here ready as well."

"Colin is on his way," Andy said.

Peter Gray went straight up to the room where Dr Luke and Clare Carhill were. He knocked on the door and went in, Dr Luke and Charlie Garret were sitting talking to Clare Carhill.

"May I come in?" Peter said.

"Clare this is Peter Gray, he is in charge around here," Garret said.

"So it is you who brought Trevor here when he is hurt and he should be in hospital," Clare said.

"Your brother will receive the same, or if not better, treatment here, Miss Carhill, I will see to that," Peter said.

"Why should I believe you? All you lot do is tell lies."

Peter sat down next to Clare saying, "Miss Carhill, in our line of work sometimes we have to tell lies to get the truth. Now why Andy lied to you was because he needs to get to the truth like I do to stop these evil men from hurting a lot of innocent people."

"I want to see Trevor."

"I will let you see Trevor, Miss Carhill, but first I want you to do something for me, I want you to give me your mobile phone," Peter said.

"My mobile phone? Why do you want my mobile phone?"

"I won't lie to you again Miss Carhill, I need your mobile phone to help me locate Trevor's friend Brian Taylor. We think Brian could be in grave danger."

CHAPTER 39

"Will you let me see Trevor if I give you the mobile phone?"

"I promise you I will," Peter said gesturing to Dr Luke to go across to the apartment.

Dr Luke got up saying, "Excuse me Clare I shall not be long, I will just go and check on Trevor."

"Now Miss Carhill, your mobile phone please," Peter said. Clare took her mobile phone out of her handbag and gave it to Peter. "Could you get me Brian Taylor's number up on the mobile phone please Miss Carhill?"

Clare took the mobile phone and punched in Brian Taylor's number and gave it back to Peter. "Get onto the network Charlie, I want to know where that mobile phone is straight away."

Garret took the mobile phone and left the room hastily.

"Thank you for that Miss Carhill," Peter said. "Don't worry Miss Carhill, I will not let Trevor come to any more harm, from now on he stays where I can see him."

"Why did those men beat Trevor up Mr Gray?"

"Call me Peter and I will call you Clare if I may. The men that beat Trevor up are the men we are trying to stop from doing this evil act; the men that beat Trevor up mistook him for someone else," Peter said.

"But Trevor could have been killed – that Andy had Trevor doing a dangerous job," Clare said.

"Andy had no choice Clare, your brother was the only one who could help us at the time and he did so willingly. Your brother is a very brave man and he has saved the lives of a lot of people. We owe him very much, you should be proud of your brother, Miss Carhill."

A knock on the door and Dr Luke came in.

"How is Trevor Dr Luke, can he receive visitors yet?" Peter

said.

"He is ready to see you Mr Gray," Dr Luke said.

Clare jumped up and said, "But you said I could see Trevor!"

"And you will Clare, I promise you, I will just check with him," Peter said leaving the room and telling Dr Luke to look after Clare.

Peter Gray went along the corridor to the operations room and went straight in. Garret, Andy and Colin were there. "Anything Charlie?" Peter said.

"Not yet, Peter," Garret said.

"You two come with me," Peter said to Andy and Colin. The two men followed Peter down the corridor. Peter knocked on the apartment door and walked in. Andy and Colin followed him into the room.

What the men saw was a surprise to them all: Trevor was sitting in a wheelchair unsupported and what did surprise them more was when Trevor turned to look to see who was coming in the room. "Well you are a sight for sore eyes," Andy said. Trevor tried to smile.

"Something funny?" Colin said, and then what did amaze the three men was when Trevor said, through swollen lips, "sore eyes", then all three men smiled.

"How are you feeling Trevor? Are you up to talking?" Peter said.

"Where is Brian?" Trevor said. "About Brian, Trevor–" Peter did not finish.

"What is wrong? Where is Brian?" Trevor said.

"Listen Trevor, about Brian, it is a bit–"

Trevor interrupted again: "Someone better tell me what has happened – why is Brian not here?" Trevor was getting frustrated.

CHAPTER 39

"Calm down Trevor, OK the truth," Peter said. "We don't know where your friend Brian is. When you were knocked unconscious the terrorist ran for it out the back. We do not know if they saw Brian or not, but Brian cannot be found."

"Do you think these men have taken Brian?" Trevor asked. "We must go and find him." Trevor was trying to stand up and would have done so if a doctor and Colin had not stopped him.

"We think it is possible the terrorist could have taken Brian," Peter said. Trevor was really getting worked up now. "If they have hurt him I will kill them," Trevor said.

Peter, Andy and Colin were quiet. Trevor took their silence to mean the worst had happened. "I will kill them all; give me a gun and I will kill them all," Trevor cried.

"Tell me where they are Trevor and I will kill them for you," Andy said.

"You let me get them Peter, you let me get them or I will tell you nothing," Trevor said.

"Do you have something to tell us Trevor?" Peter said.

"I will tell you nothing if you will not let me get them, if they have hurt Brian," Trevor was sobbing with anger.

"Trevor, you have to try and keep calm – if you get yourself all upset it will not help," Peter said.

"If anything has happened to Brian I will never forgive myself."

"Trevor, I have your sister here, do you want to see her?" Peter said.

"Yes, of course I do."

"Well you must try and keep calm – if Clare sees you in this state, it is bad enough with all your physical injuries, she will be upset with them, now just try Trevor," Peter said. "Trevor I must ask: did you see or hear anything at Emerson Court?"

Trevor just stared into space for a while and then said: "I did see something but I won't say unless I can help get those bastards."

Charlie Garret came into the apartment. The American Paul Bennet stayed outside at the door. "We got it Peter, the mobile phone is at a disused ship repair yard on the River Tyne, R & B Harrisons," Garret said.

"Operations room, you lot, quick!" Peter said.

"What is happening?" Trevor said.

"I will bring your sister in to see you Trevor, now please keep calm," Peter said.

Peter went straight over to the opposite room where Dr Luke and Clare were. "Dr Luke I want you to take Clare in to see Trevor now please, and Dr Luke–" Peter called her close so he could speak quietly, "Trevor is getting very emotionally upset –see if you can calm him."

"OK Charlie, what we got?" Peter said in the operations room that was now a buzz of activity.

"Like I said Peter, it is a disused ship repair yard on the River Tyne. Aerial photos show it having a few derelict buildings," Garret said pointing to the aerial photos of the yard up on the large wall-mounted monitor. Andy and Colin were checking their weapons, Paul Bennet reached his hand up to his armpit feeling the bulge there just reassuring himself.

"What we got ready Charlie?" Peter asked.

"We have the anti-terrorist boys, armed response and there is a Royal Marines Cadet training base on the river – they will have boats, we could use those and come in from the river as well."

"That we will. I want these guys. No one gets away. We come in from every visible angle, all sides covered," Peter said. "Get

CHAPTER 39

the SAS Units involved – they will want to be there after Mosley Street. Now, we are on, let's get moving."

"Can I go as before, Peter?" Paul Bennet asked. "I will stay back unless I am needed."

"He is true to his word," Garret said.

"All right you can go," Peter said. "Charlie I want you to stay here. I will need you to help cover in the operation from this room. I will have my work cut out on other things."

Charlie Garret was a bit annoyed he was not going on the raid at the disused ship repair yard but he did as he was told.

CHAPTER 40

Peter Gray was leaving the operations room. He needed to think: it would be a short while yet before the teams were ready to move in on the ship repair yard. "Jenkins," he said before leaving, "get me that language teacher Joanne Martin as soon as, please."

Peter walked down the corridor to the apartment; he listened at the door – he could hear muffled voices. Peter went into the room opposite and sat down at the table. He was weary; he put his elbows on the table and his head in his hands. Peter thought: it has started the run down to the end. Peter was deep in thought – he did not hear the door open and Dr Luke come in.

"Oh I am sorry," Dr Luke said.

Peter lifted his head sharply and rubbed his face with his hands. "That's all right doctor."

"When was the last time you slept?"

"Oh I don't know, two maybe three days ago," Peter said.

Dr Luke sat down next to Peter saying, "You should get some sleep, you will keel over if you don't."

"Sleep," Peter said, "if I go to sleep will this all stop and stand still doctor until I awake again?"

"I suppose not," Dr Luke said.

"I will rest when this is all over."

"But you will be no good to anyone, you're an exhausted man," Dr Luke said.

"Anyway I am always like this when my men go out with their safety turned off on their guns. I will feel better when they are there," Peter said. "In a few short hours' time this will all be over, one way or the other."

CHAPTER 40

Dr Luke looked at Peter. For the first time she could see the pain and anguish behind his eyes, the enormous weight of responsibility he carried and kept it all shut up inside, locked up behind all those memories and pains the job brings with it. "Listen Peter, can we start again? Can we be friends?"

"I am all for that, doctor, I need all the friends I can get at the moment," Peter said getting up saying 'coffee?'.

"No, I will get it," Dr Luke said, getting up and going over to the sink unit.

Peter sat back down and began to think again.

"Can I ask you something Peter?" Dr Luke said.

"Yes anything, but I must warn you I have a tendency to lie."

"The American, Paul Bennet, do you think he is gay?"

"Well, I don't know, I am not quite sure." Peter was sort of knocked off his stride by the question. "He does carry a photograph of a man in uniform, that could be his son – no, too old; it could be his father – no, too young. Have you got an eye for our American friend, doctor?"

"No I am just interested," Dr Luke said. Peter smiled to himself.

A knock at the door, Jenkins popped his head in. "Joanne Martin is on her way in sir."

"Thank you Jenkins," Peter said. Jenkins lingered a bit.

"Is there something else, Jenkins?" Peter said.

"Sir, could I go on the raid with the guys?"

"I am afraid not." Peter did not want Jenkins, an inexperienced agent, going where there may be shooting, but not wanting to make Jenkins feel he was inadequate Peter said, "I can't have all my best men there – I need people here I can trust."

"Very well," Jenkins said feeling appreciated.

"What about Trevor?" Dr Luke said.

"You know I have to put him under pressure doctor and I want you to help keep him calm. I must know what Trevor knows – you do understand that don't you, doctor?" Peter said.

"Yes I do now Peter, but go careful please," Dr Luke said.

"Trevor at the moment is very angry doctor, he wants revenge. He thinks his friend has been hurt or is in danger."

"And is his friend in danger?"

"If these people have got this Brian Taylor he is in grave danger. These people will kill him without any remorse if they think he is a risk to their plan," Peter said. "Now I may have to use the fact that these people might have got this Brian Taylor to open Trevor up, doctor, and that may not be nice. I will use whatever means I have to doctor to get Trevor to talk to me."

"I do understand why you have to do these things Peter, now I do, but is there no other way?"

"If we had the time maybe we could tread carefully but the time is against us," Peter said. "Now doctor, I need your help all the way on this even if it gets unpleasant."

"I will do what I can, I promise Peter," Dr Luke said.

"Even if I have to use Trevor's sister Clare to get what I want doctor?"

"Even that."

"Well in that case Dr Luke, I thank you now because I will not have the time later."

CHAPTER 41

A white Audi A4 pulls over to the roadside.

"I will let you out here Nesta," Alama said. "We will meet again in another life, my brother," Alama said to Nesta.

Alama drove away after Nesta had got out of the car; he headed towards the South entrance to the Tyne Tunnel. Alama wanted to be on the other side of the River Tyne, the North side. Traffic was heavy moving towards the Tunnel entrance. He could see plenty of police officers with dogs as well as the normal Tunnel security officers. Alama leant over to the footwell on the passenger side and brought out a plastic container; the container had yellow liquid inside it. The traffic was moving slowly. Alama opened the plastic container and poured some of the liquid onto his lap; he put the top back on the container and put the container on the passenger seat.

The Audi was instructed to pull into the search lay-by by the Tunnel Security. When the Tunnel Security Police Officer saw that Alama was of Asian appearance he called over a police officer who had a dog on a lead with him.

"Would you step out of the car please sir?" the Security Officer said. Alama got out of the car. There were four police officers and two Tunnel Security Police Officers. They began to search the Audi A4 car; the police dog was having a grand old time sniffing and jumping about in the car.

"Where are you going sir?" the police officer asked as he looked at the wet patch on the groin of Alama's trousers.

"I am going home officer. I live in North Shields," Alama said.

The police officer turned and said to his fellow officer: "This guy has pissed himself."

"What is your name?" the officer asked.

"Nueri Alama, sir. I work in Deli at Gateshead, sir," Alama said.

"What is in the container?" the officer said, looking into the car which had all four doors and boot open now and the police dog still sniffing around inside.

"It is piss sir," Alama said.

"Piss? What are you doing with a container of piss?"

"I have a weak bladder sir, I have to go often but there is not always a toilet sir."

"Dirty bastard," one officer said to another.

"Nothing here," the dog handler said.

"Let him go before he pisses himself!" one of the officers said.

"All right sir you can go," the police officer who was asking all the questions said.

"Thank you," Alama said getting into the Audi A4 and driving off through the Tyne Tunnel.

When Alama came out of the Tyne Tunnel he turned left and headed down the A19 Road towards Newcastle International Airport and Ponteland. Alama drove for about fifteen minutes along the A19 Road and then took a left again heading still towards Newcastle International Airport and Ponteland. Alama drove past the Airport vehicle entrance – there was heavy police security.

He kept on driving for about a mile and a half down the road; he took a right. The roadside sign read Ponteland industrial estate and Ponteland Golf Club. Taking another right Alama could see the remains of the golf clubhouse still smouldering away; in the golf course grounds there were plenty

CHAPTER 41

of police officers around as well. Alama kept on driving – he drove past the green British Telecom Relay Box. There were two police officers and a police dog just walking past the British Telecom Box as Alama drove by.

Alama kept on going past all the Industrial Units and around a long bend to a T-junction at the bottom of the road. He went left into the residential area; two hundred yards down the road Alama stopped outside a house. Alama got out of the Audi A4 and went up the drive of the house. He opened the double doors on the garage and then went and got into the Audi A4 and reversed it up the drive and into the garage. Alama switched the engine off and left the key in the ignition. He picked the plastic container up and he went and closed the garage doors. Alama then began to walk back the way he had just drove into the housing estate.

Alama left the housing estate. He could see the heavy police presence as he walked up alongside the high fence of the golf course; there were armed police officers patrolling the golf course grounds. Alama looked up – about three hundred yards ahead of him was the green British Telecom Relay Box. Alama kept on walking, looking all around: there was no one to be seen at this moment. He had to move quickly before the police on the golf course came by on another patrol.

When he reached the British Telecom Relay Box Alama stood still and put the plastic container down on the ground. He pretended to fasten his bootlace; while he was bent over Alama pushed a key into the lock on the Relay Box; he turned the key. One more quick look around, he opened the doors and went straight inside the box, pulling the doors closed behind him. Alama crouched quietly for about five minutes before he moved. When he was sure he had not been seen he arranged himself more comfortably, sitting in the corner of the box with his back against the side. When his eyes got used of the dim light he looked around inside the box. There was the AK47 Assault Rifle that Veeri had left standing in one corner and a duffle bag alongside the rifle.

Alama opened the plastic container and emptied the contents out around the bottom of the British Telecom Relay Box. After about twenty minutes Alama could hear voices in the distance. He looked out of one of the peepholes and coming up towards the box were two armed police officers – but if that were not bad enough they had a large black Labrador dog with them. Alama reached over and pulled the AK47 rifle close to him, clicking the safety mechanism off as he did so. He sat waiting for the officers to get close.

Alama thought for a moment. He stood the rifle back in the corner of the box; he then reached into the duffle bag and rummaged around. He pulled out what looked like a toggle – it had a wire coming out of the bottom of the toggle and going back into the duffle bag. Alama flipped a plastic hinged cover off the top of the toggle; it revealed a button that Alama poised his right hand thumb over. The officers and the dog were at the box now. Alama could hear the Labrador sniffing around the bottom of the box.

"It bloody stinks of piss around here," one of the officers said.

Beads of sweat were forming on Alama's forehead; the dog was still sniffing around the box. There were more beads of sweat forming on Alama's brow –they amalgamated and sweat ran down into his eyes.

"Everybody and his mate must take a leak at this box when they come out of the clubhouse," one of the officers said. The

CHAPTER 41

Labrador cocked a leg and took a leak against the box as well. When the dog had finished the dog handler officer gave the lead a quick jerk saying, "Here boy."

Alama let out a sigh of relief as he slowly pushed the cover over the button on the toggle with his left hand, his right hand thumb still poised over the button as he did, he clipped the cover shut and then pushed the toggle back into the duffle bag; he then wiped the sweat out of his eyes, trying to relax back into the corner of the Relay Box.

CHAPTER 42

"Peter, the boys are ready to go in," Garret said.

"I am on my way Charlie," Peter said. Peter came into the operations room, Garret was waiting for him. Up on the south wall were six large screen monitors and at present they were all blank screens.

"Have all the men been briefed, Charlie?" Peter asked.

"Every group knows what to expect Peter, they have all been told there may be a friendly in the ship repair yard," Garret said. "We will try and keep it as quiet as we can until the final entry."

"All right Charlie, tell me how."

"We are going in from all four sides Peter, from the north we are going in from the River Tyne; we have seconded a couple of fast boat landing craft from the Royal Marines Cadets training school. There will be four SAS soldiers in each boat; they will land a couple of minutes before the other groups move in. From the east and west we have two teams of six anti-terrorist officers in each, one team will come in from the east; the other will come in from the west. Andy and Colin go in through the front gates with are boys. The Bomb Squad are on stand-by and waiting for the word."

"If we are lucky Charlie we may have targets on site," Peter said. "We must keep it a surprise as long as we possibly can Charlie; if our friendly is on site and he is still alive I want to keep him that way. OK Charlie, let's get this show on the road."

"OK gentlemen, fire it up, we are a go," Garret said. At once all the large screens on the south wall of the operations room light up showing all different views from the head mounted cameras on the raid soldiers' helmets.

CHAPTER 42

Andy and Colin pushed through the trees and bushes of the overgrown approach road to the entrance into the redundant R & B Harrison's ship repair yard at Bill Quay, Gateshead. Half a dozen heavily armed men dressed in body armour followed them through the trees. They reach the gates to the Ship Repair Yard; the gates are secured with a padlock and chain. Andy hears over his earpiece that the raid is a go. He looks at his watch and waits a few seconds and then waves one of the heavily armed men over to him.

"Yes sir," the agent said.

"Get the gates and for God sake be careful, make sure there are no surprises," Andy said to the agent.

The agent moved to the gates, another agent followed him. Both men had light machine guns slung behind their backs, they both look over the gates, running their hands over them, trying to locate anything that would alert them to a booby-trap. When both agents were happy it was safe one of them called another agent over. The agent had bolt croppers with him; he promptly cut the chain that was holding the gates locked; as soon as the chain fell from the gates the other two agents pushed the heavy gates open. Andy and Colin went through the gates and into the trees and bushes, all the time Andy and Colin were looking out for trip wires or any other traps that may have been waiting for them.

Andy came to the asphalt road that was hiding under the overgrown foliage. He crept forward and peeped through the trees. There were four derelict buildings in front of him. Colin came up behind Andy; the two men did not speak. Andy looked to his left – he could see anti-terrorist officers carefully lowering from a boundary wall; to his right anti-terrorist officers moving into position. Andy could not see the river landing SAS soldiers

– the derelict buildings were between him and the River Tyne. Although Andy could not see every team on the raid, he was in voice contact with the team leaders. The rest of the agents moved up alongside Andy and Colin, and creeping up behind them all was the American Paul Bennet. The plan was for each group of men to begin to search the buildings as they approached them from all four sides.

Andy spoke saying, "moving up to the buildings north side". Andy got three responses of 'copy that' through his earpiece. Andy followed that with: "Are you getting this Garret?" "Copy that," came back to Andy over his earpiece.

Andy and all the agents moved together to the building front and spread out along the length of the building. Andy and Colin went to the big doors and carefully crept to the middle of the doors to look through a slight opening between the doors. All they could see was the back of the red Mercedes Vito Van – nothing else.

"What do you reckon?" Colin said.

"No way are we going in through the doors," Andy said.

Andy stepped back from the building and looked up – there were windows to the left and right of the doors about twelve feet from ground level. Andy was just going to call for a ladder when the American Paul Bennet limped to the right side of the doors and stood with his back against the wall; he cupped his hands in front of him and held them at groin height. Andy needed no more invitation then that. He holstered his hand gun and took a couple of steps back over and one two fast steps forward putting his forward most foot into the American's cupped hands, as soon as Andy's foot was in the American's hands Paul Bennet hoisted Andy up so Andy could reach and grip onto the window sill. Colin stepped back from the wall as Andy was pulling himself

CHAPTER 42

through the broken window.

As soon as Andy was inside Colin took a couple of fast steps and then his foot into Paul Bennett's hands – one quick hoist from Paul Bennet and Colin was hanging on the window sill. Colin pulled himself up through the window and then inside onto a timber floor that was pitted with holes and rotten. The two men had to be careful, the floor creaked under both their weights. Colin looked at Andy who was crouched on his hunkers with his gaze fixed forward. Colin turned to look at what had Andy transfixed.

"My God," Colin said.

"Are you getting this, Garret?" Andy said.

"Copy that Andy, you lot be careful out there."

What both men could see and what could now be seen in the operations room back at Durham Police Station was a man suspended from the ankles by a rope, the rope came over a roof truss and was anchored to a wall column; the man's head was about six feet from the floor.

"Poor bastard," Andy said quietly. The man's head was black – it had been burnt; his clothes were torn to shreds. Andy and Colin had a good look around all areas, checked all angles they could see from where they were.

"Seems deserted," Andy said, "apart from this poor sod."

Colin went to a hole in the floor and lowered himself down onto the ground floor while Andy kept a lookout. As soon as Colin hit the floor he moved into cover behind a loading dock. Andy dropped down onto the same place and jumped up alongside Colin. Both men looked over the loading dock.

Andy pointed to an oil drum that was over to one side; wisps of smoke were coming from the oil drum.

Andy said to Colin: "The doors." Colin nodded. Andy moved

to the doors while Colin covered him. Andy checked all around the doors; he could not find anything that gave him any concern. Andy slowly opened the double doors into the fabrication shed – instantly agents poured in, spreading out and taking cover. Andy moved back alongside Colin. He was just going to move forward when they heard a moan from the suspended man, a slight movement from his head.

"My God, the poor bastard is still alive," Andy said. The two men jumped onto the loading bay and slowly moved forward, Colin going to the left and Andy to the right. Andy had only gone five steps when he signalled to Colin to stop.

"The guy's rigged," Andy said. Andy moved more to his right for a better view. "Can you see this, Garret? Andy said.

"I have it Andy – it looks too straightforward, it cannot be that simple." Another moan and a little bit more movement from the suspended man sent Andy diving to the floor.

"What you got?" Colin said. He did not have the view that Andy had; what Andy could see was a piece of cord tied to the man's chest and the other end was tied through the pin of a hand grenade that was cable tied to the oxyacetylene bottle barrow.

Andy got back up off the floor and crept a little closer this time to the dangling pathetic figure. His head was black as charcoal; Andy thought the last time he had seen something like this was at bonfire night when the kids burnt the guy on the bonfire. Andy could remember the guy's head was made from a turnip and it burnt on the fire until it was just a black featureless cinder. That was what Andy was looking at now except this is a man's head and the poor bastard was still alive. Andy wanted to take his gun and shoot this poor man in the gruesome head. This most probably was Trevor's friend Brian Taylor who only this morning was going about his daily routine not bothering a soul

CHAPTER 42

– now look at this poor man. Andy was raging inside but he had to keep calm.

At the operations room in Durham Police Station over thirty people stared at the screens in disbelief at the horrific sight of this poor helpless barely alive man just hanging there by his ankles and no one could do a thing to help this man.

Garret turned to Peter and said: "What kind of sick fuck could do that to another human being?" Peter never said a word – he just stared at the sickening sight.

"What you got, Andy?" Colin asked again.

"This poor bastard has got a grenade rigged up to blow the bottle barrow if he were to move too much," Andy said. By now most of the agents had checked the building and found no terrorists present; the other teams were still going through the buildings.

Andy shouted over to Paul Bennet who was standing near the doors of the fabrication shed: "Make sure no one touches anything."

Paul Bennet nodded his head at Andy, the American feeling sick to the stomach at the terrible sight dangling in front of everyone. Andy moved a little more closer. Colin began to move closer as well.

"No," Andy said, pushing the flat of his hand towards Colin. "Stay there." Andy was six feet away from the suspended figure; he could smell burnt flesh now. The man groaned and began to move his head. Andy was too close now, he thought if this poor retch has got enough strength to move and swing a little on the rope the cord will pull the pin on the grenade. Andy, instead of diving for cover, took two steps forward and took hold of the suspended body. As soon as Andy had the body still Colin rushed forward. Andy just stood there while Colin assessed the situation. "Quite simple," he said to Andy. Andy looked all around – he could see nothing that gave any hint that there was any other trap than the grenade on the bottle barrow.

He looked up at the rope – it came over six by six inch timber that ran across the full span of the building that was the bottom of the roof truss; the rope went back to a wall column and was just tied off.

Andy turned to Colin and said: "Go for it." Colin simply walked to the bottle barrow and untied the cord knot off the grenade Colin cut the cable ties freeing the grenade from the bottle barrow and picked the grenade off the bottle barrow and threw it underarm to Paul Bennet who caught it in both hands.

"Now everyone, be very careful," Andy shouted. "Get that out of the way," Andy said to Colin.

Colin pushed the bottle barrow away from the dangling figure. Paul Bennet walked over to the smouldering oil drum and looked inside it. "They have been burning evidence," he said.

"Tip it out, we may get something," Colin said.

Andy spoke out: "What do you think, Garret?"

"It looks all right to me, maybe they did not have enough time to rig up anything elaborate," Garret said.

Andy had to make a decision. "Get the Bomb Squad down," Andy spoke out to thin air. "All right, you get this poor bastard down." Two of the agents went and supported the dangling figure while two more went to loosen the rope from the column.

Colin and Bennet were kicking the charred remains of the fire they tipped out of the oil drum hoping to find something that would help in the pursuit of the terrorists. One of the two agents who was loosening the rope from the column had it free and he and his partner were now holding the weight of the man.

"All right, are you ready?" one of the agents said. The two

CHAPTER 42

agents who had hold of the man's body began to help take the weight as the other two began to lower the rope. The man started to moan as his body was folded by the agents so his charred head would not hit the fabrication shed floor; slowly they began to lower the rope.

Thud, thud! Two hand grenades hit the floor, pins were out of the safety clasps; the grenades had been on the timber truss beam that the rope ran over, the safety pins simply tied to the rope. When the rope was lowered it pulled the grenades off the beam and their own weight pulled them free of the pins. Everyone who was present in the fabrication shed looked at the grenades and for a split second they were all mesmerised.

"Grenade!" Andy screamed as he dived for cover. The two agents who were lowering the rope left loose of it and dived to the floor. The two agents who had the weight of the dangling man were in the thick of it, one of them threw himself as hard as he could to the right, the other was pulled to the floor by the weight of the man's body falling. Bright white flash and then the deafening bang as both grenades exploded together. The agent who fell to the floor and the charred figure were instantly blown to pieces. The agent who dived to the right was flung through the doors of the fabrication shed, landing some ten feet outside; both his legs had been ripped off his torso. He lay in a lifeless heap; shrapnel thrown all around the babrication shed but fortunately for the rest of the agents none of the flying shards of metal had hit any one of them.

Andy stayed face down on the floor. He had had enough, he was ready to explode himself.

"The fucking bastards!" he screamed as he pummelled the floor with his fists. Colin jumped to his feet and rushed over to Andy; once he had seen there were no physical injuries he ran outside to the lifeless heap lying on the ground.

"We want medics in here fast," was the cry. Men came running in from all directions. At the operations room everyone was up on their feet, gasps of disbelief and cries of 'oh God no, those men'.

"Come back, Andy," came over the earpiece from Garret. Peter and Garret were waiting in anticipation for some kind of report, they could see plenty of images of mayhem but no coherent talk back.

"Come in Andy," Garret said again.

"Colin here, Garret. Andy is a bit preoccupied at the moment." Andy was standing over the remains of the agent and Brian Taylor.

"How bad is it, Colin?" Garret said. Peter was standing next to Charlie Garret, his head bowed low waiting to hear the worst.

"Mitchell and the friendly are dead; Joslyne is in a very bad way, sir, his legs have been blown off. He is still alive but only just. We have no other casualties – the shrapnel from the grenades tore into everything around, sending the van over on one side, but as far as I can tell everyone else is unhurt – but Joslyne needs to be out soon," Colin said.

"All right Colin, hold the situation until I can get you and Andy out of there," Peter said. Peter wanted to scream at the top of his voice but he knew he had to hold it together; he had heard and seen Andy losing control and he knew exactly how he felt. "Charlie you go down there; take the helicopter. Put Andy and Colin on the return flight and you get me something down there Charlie," Peter said grinding his teeth with temper.

Peter had to leave and go and compose himself. He rushed out of the operations room before he lost control in front of everyone; he knew Mitchell and Joslyne personally – so did all

CHAPTER 42

the team. Peter went into the room opposite the apartment – it was empty. He needed to be alone for a while.

The helicopter landed back at Durham Police Station. Andy and Colin got out of the helicopter; both men looked distraught and drained. Peter had heard the helicopter coming in to land; he got up and opened the door and stood in the corridor waiting for Andy and Colin to come in. Andy got to the top of the stairs first; he looked along the corridor and saw Peter.

"Peter," Andy said, "I am–"

"Inside," Peter said softly, stopping Andy from his display of emotion out in the corridor. Andy said nothing now, he just walked into the room. Colin tried to follow. Peter stopped Colin and just said 'later'.

Andy looked at Peter stopping Colin from entering the room. Andy stood up to say something; Peter turned to him and said: "Don't say a word Andy, please just sit down. Andy, I know at this moment you just want to throw all this in. Now you made a call and it went sour; now I don't know if anyone else had've been there the outcome would have been any different, but what I do know is I sent the right man for the job."

"But Brian Taylor, Mitchell and Josylne, Peter," Andy protested.

"What you do Andy is you wrap them up, and you pick them up, and then you put them in that little room in the back of your mind and you lock the door and then you throw away the key, and at night when you shut your eyes the key is hanging on the rack again, you will take that key and throw it away again, and each night you will do the same thing with that key, and then one night you will take that key and unlock that door Andy, and you will stand up and face your demons and you will come to a compromise with them," Peter said.

"And is that what you do, Peter?"

"Me, Andy, is that what I do? My rack is full of keys – the only problem is I don't know which key fits which door now, Andy," Peter said. "What you have do now Andy, is help me make sure we are not throwing any more keys away. I need you, Andy, to be focused on the job at hand now. Go and get a shower, then come and help us get these bastards."

A knock on the door and Colin came in. "Sorry Peter, but I thought you would want to see this straight away."

"What is it, Colin?" Peter asked.

"That address in Holland, the one found in Goomi's bedsit, it is in the suburbs of Amsterdam. It was rented for three months by Naffia Veeri," Colin replied.

"Veeri – that's one of our men from the blue van yesterday," Peter said.

"We are running it now Peter," Colin said. "How you doing mate?" Colin asked Andy.

"He is doing fine, aren't we Andy?" Peter said.

"I will get there, Colin," Andy said. "Now you two go and freshen up because we have work to do."

"Yes Peter," both men said getting up to leave the room.

"What do we tell Trevor, Peter?" Andy asked. "We tell him the truth Andy," Peter said. "Colin, ask Dr Luke to come and see me when you pass, will you please?" Peter said.

Peter pressed a button on the telephone.

"Yes sir," came the reply.

"Get me Charlie Garret will you please?" Peter said.

"Peter, the van was clean, nothing rigged up in it. The Bomb Boys cleared it. We have a couple of things. These guys cover their tracks well," Garret said.

"What is it you have, Charlie?"

CHAPTER 42

"They had been trying to destroy whatever evidence by burning it in a oil drum. We found a piece of orange nylon, the type used for high visibility clothing. I don't know if it means anything."

"It must mean something, Charlie, or why would they try to destroy it."

"The other thing, Peter, is thanks to our American."

"What's that, Charlie?"

"The van, Peter, it has had stickers on both sides and the back doors – they have just been removed recently," Garret said.

"How do you mean Charlie?"

"The adhesive that held the stickers on the van is still tacky, Peter."

"What do you think, Charlie? The van was used for a drop or something?"

"The first thing that comes to mind, Peter, is the Post Office – it is the right colour for Royal Mail."

"OK Charlie get yourself back here and we will push the clothing and the van as far as it will go," Peter said.

Dr Luke knocked on the door and came in. "You wanted to see me Peter?"

"Yes doctor, I have bad news about Brian Taylor: he is dead; there was nothing we could do to save him," Peter said.

"My God, Trevor will take it bad."

"About Trevor Carhill, doctor, can he get up and move around?" Peter said.

"He could enter a marathon if we put enough drugs in him but how far he would get in that marathon only God knows," Dr Luke said.

"I will have to talk to Trevor, Dr Luke, there is very little time and what I have to tell him will upset him greatly. I want you to take Clare out of the room until I have spoken to Trevor, and I also want you to tell her about Brian Taylor – it will be better coming from you, doctor, but what I don't want is for Clare to be in the room with Trevor or to come back in the room where Trevor is when she finds out about Brian Taylor."

"This could backfire on you, Peter. What if Trevor clamps up and refuses to say anything?"

"We will see, doctor. I also want you to talk to Clare about how important it is that Trevor tells us what he knows, and she should help us get that information to catch the men who killed Brian Taylor. Will you do that, doctor?"

"I will do my best. What do you intend to do about Trevor if he still insists you let him go after these men with you?"

"Maybe I will allow him to do that to a certain degree. Now doctor, I want you to go and get Clare and take her into the other apartment room until I call for you," Peter said.

Peter pressed a button on the telephone. "You want something sir?" came a reply.

"Yes, would you tell Jenkins to come and see me please," Peter said.

"Yes sir, right away," was the reply. Within a few seconds Jenkins was in the room.

"You want me sir?" Jenkins said.

"Yes Jenkins, is that language teacher here yet?"

"Joanne Martin has been here for a while sir, do you want me to fetch her?"

"Yes Jenkins, bring her to me please," Peter said.

Peter thought about how he would get Trevor to open up and tell him what he knew about what he had heard and witnessed at Emerson Court. The lab boys had found nothing of any valuable evidence at Emerson Court. Charlie Garret was

CHAPTER 42

right – these terrorists cover their tracks well, the red Mercedes Van may come up with something especially if it was used for a drop or a plant.

A knock at the door. "Mrs Martin, sir," Jenkins said.

"Joanne, please call me Joanne," the language teacher said.

"Joanne, would you sit down please?" Peter said.

"Do you want me to translate something for you again?"

"Yes, but not here and not at this moment. I need to talk to you first Joanne. This time it will be a bit different from the last time – the man you translated the words from will speak them again I hope," Peter said. "It is just that this time the man may be irate and upset – he has lost a very dear friend and he may not want to tell me the words I want you to translate so I will have to try and coax them from him."

"All right," Joanne said.

"He has a few facial injuries that are not pleasant to look at and there are medical staff present in the room to look after Trevor. Now, I want you to try and ignore all that and just concentrate on what Trevor says. Can you do that for me, Joanne? We have not prepared a recording like the last time but we will record the words as soon as Trevor says them in case you need to have them repeated."

"I can do that," Joanne said, "but can I ask – how can this man speak a foreign language and not understand it? I mean everybody can remember phrases but he tells it from several people speaking in a conversation. How does he do that?"

"I wondered when you would get to that," Peter said, "and I have no real answer for you but to say Trevor's unique ability has to be kept a secret, Joanne. Do you understand what I am saying?"

"Yes of course, I do understand, I was just curious."

"That is only natural, Joanne. Now, I want you to wait here. I will send someone to be with you, and then we will come and get you when we are ready," Peter said.

Peter shouted: "Are you there, Jenkins?" towards the door. Jenkins popped his head inside the room.

"Yes sir," Jenkins said.

"Go and see if Andy and Colin are ready will you, and if they are to come and sit with Joanne please until we are ready for her."

"Right away sir," Jenkins said.

Peter Gray went into the apartment room. Trevor Carhill was sitting in a wheelchair; there were two female nurse and a male doctor present.

"About time," Trevor said, "I thought you had forgotten about me."

"Forgotten about you, Trevor? I could not do that. I have had nothing else on my mind but you, Trevor, for the last hour," Peter said. "Why you have been on my mind Trevor is because I have been trying to think of an easy way to tell you bad news, and the truth is there is no easy way to say it Trevor. I have to tell you your friend Brian Taylor is dead."

"No, no oh my God no, what have I done to him," Trevor started to sob uncontrollably. "Was it them? I will kill everyone of them, I will do it with my bare hands if you don't give me a gun. I know every one of them, I know what they look like and I know their names," Trevor said through gasps of sobs squeezing his fists that tight his hands turned white.

"Yes, it was them Trevor, and we have to get them soon before they kill anyone else."

"I will tell you nothing unless you promise me I can kill them," Trevor said.

CHAPTER 42

"You know I cannot do that Trevor, these men would kill you if you went up against them – they are ruthless killers Trevor. You are not like that," Peter said.

"I can turn like that, you can show me, Andy will show me. I will kill them for what they have done. When I get out of here I will search for them and kill them one by one."

"That will be too late, Trevor. They will be well gone and they will have got away with what they did to Brian."

"It was that Alama, he was the leader, I will get him first," Trevor said.

"Alama. Trevor we can get him quick before he gets away. We know how to do that; you don't Trevor, it will take you too long to find them. Now, you tell us Trevor, and we will get them for you, I promise you that."

"No, no I need to get them for Brian, I will shoot them like they did to Brian. I will get my own gun and shoot them all in the head."

"They did not shoot Brian."

"What do you mean?" Trevor said through his rage and tears. "What the fuck did they do to Brian? Tell me." Trevor held onto his wheelchair arm rest and began to shake violently.

"Brian suffered terribly for a long time before he died. They tortured him to tell them something he did not know, Trevor," Peter said.

Trevor screamed out that loud, Clare jumped up saying, "Trevor, I must go to him."

"Not yet Clare," Dr Luke said. "You must let him be for a short while."

"You see Trevor, that is why I cannot let you go after these men; this is what they are capable of and for us to make them pay for what they did to Brian you have to tell us how to get to them," Peter said.

"But I have to," Trevor sobbed. "I was all he had, he depended on me and I killed him."

"That is not true Trevor now, Brian would not want you to go up against these men, he would be frightened for you. Now you tell me how to get to these men and I will show you. We will get them for what they did to Brian."

"How can you do that if you will not let me be there?" Trevor said crying, "please, please."

"I have a big screen that will show you everything when we catch up with them, Trevor. You will be able to see them taken out," Peter said.

"No, no that's not enough, that is not what I want."

"OK Trevor, I will make a deal with you. If you promise to tell us everything you heard and saw at Emerson Court I will allow you to be with me all the time of the operation and only if you also promise to do all I say or I will have you removed and you will know nothing. Now, will you agree to that?" Peter said.

"I will be there all the time?"

"Yes, all the time with me Trevor, wherever I go you go as well, but if for one moment you don't do as I say I will shut you out. Is it a deal, Trevor?"

"It's a deal."

"Good, Trevor. It is the only way this is going to happen. Now you have to try and calm down. I know that is easier said than done with what you have been through and what awful news you have just been told, but if we are to get these bastards you have to be calm and concentrate, Trevor. I will send Dr Luke in and give you a few minutes to tidy up because Clare will want to see you, but we must begin soon Trevor," Peter said.

"Clare does not have to know what happened to Brian, does

CHAPTER 42

she?" said Trevor.

"No, no Trevor, no way. Brian died a swift and painless death."

Peter left the apartment and went into the apartment next door. "Dr Luke, would you go in to Trevor now please?"

"But I want to see Trevor," Clare said wiping the tears from her eyes.

"You can see Trevor in a moment, Clare, I want you to go and wait with Andy and Colin just for a couple of minutes while Dr Luke sees to Trevor."

Dr Luke went next door. Peter took Clare to be with Andy and Colin and introduced her to Joanne. Clare just sat saying nothing. "Look after her. I will be in the operations room. Come and get me, Andy, when Dr Luke is ready," Peter said.

Peter went into the operations room. He wanted to check on the name that Trevor had mentioned. Alama, he thought, I have seen that name on a report. It was not long before one of the analysts brought a piece of paper over to Peter.

"Ah Alama, he was Shali's right hand man in Afghanistan – another one presumed dead from the battle at the Rolling Hills of Haraeffa."

Peter thought for a while. His conversation with Trevor Carhill had gone well. He did not want to tell Trevor about Brian suffering before he died but he had to use that to get Trevor to agree to talk to him. Peter knew that in the back of Trevor's mind he knew himself that he could not go after these men, so if Peter made him want the killers of Brian to pay he would have to compromise their fate and talk to him. The time was going so quick now and it would not be that long before Peter knew if he was going to stop these men.

The door to the operations room opened and Andy came in.

"Dr Luke said Trevor is ready, Peter," Andy said.

"How are you feeling now, Andy?" Peter asked and then added: "that's a stupid question – don't answer it, you feel fucking awful like the rest of us."

"I feel ready to go out and catch these people and make them pay for all the pain and suffering they have caused, Peter, that's how I feel."

"That's the Andy that I want back by my side. Now, let us go and find out what Trevor can tell us."

CHAPTER 43

Peter and Andy went into the apartment. Dr Luke, Colin, Clare, Joanne the language teacher and of course Trevor were present. Trevor was dressed now and sitting at the table with the voice recorder in front of him; Joanne was sitting next to Trevor with pen and paper in her hand.

"Are you ready to do this, Trevor?" Peter asked.

"As ready as I will ever be. Let us get on with it," Trevor said.

"All right Trevor, start from the very first time you heard or saw the men in the room at Emerson Court," Peter said.

"The man I was following went into the flat. There were four other men in the flat. As the man I followed came into the room one of the other men said..." Joanne listened.

"It is Afghan again," she said. "WHERE IS GOOMI, that's what the man asks," Joanne said. "And then the man I followed said, 'HE WILL BE ALONG LATER ABDUL DON'T WORRY', that was his reply," Joanne said.

Peter was watching Joanne. She was staring at Trevor, sitting with his eyes closed tight. She was puzzled – how is he doing this?

"Joanne please," Peter said to her.

"I am sorry," she said and went back to writing on her piece of paper. Then Trevor said: "and one of the other men said this, 'IS SHALI COMING TO THE FERRY ALAMA'. "And that is what was said there," Joanne added. "And the reply from Alama, NO HE IS NOT SHEA, Alama."

"Trevor, that is the name of the man you followed," Peter said.

"The same man said these words, 'IS SHALI GOING TO

DIE ALAMA', and that is what was said there," Joanne said. "And then this Alama said, there is a lot of it this time, Trevor said, 'WE MAY ALL DIE BEFORE THIS DAY ENDS, BUT IF ALL GOES TO PLAN WE WILL TAKE HUNDREDS OF THE CAPITALIST BRITISH PIGS WITH US'. What the hell is this?" Joanne said after she had translated that section of what Trevor said.

"Please Joanne, just tell us what Trevor says. We will discuss later what this is all about," Peter said. "And now Trevor?" Peter prompted Trevor to carry on.

"This Shea spoke next he said, SHALI WILL BE A MARTYR, and then one of the other men spoke, he said, WE SHALL ALL BE MARTYRS, and that is what was said there," Joanne said. "And the next words were spoken by this Shea, he said, WILL WE SEE THE STATION BLOW FROM THE FERRY MOHAMAD?, and that is what was said."

Peter butted in, "Are you sure those are the exact words, Trevor?"

"Yes," Trevor said.

"And you are certain Joanne that is the right translation?"

"No doubt about it," Joanne said.

"Please go on, Trevor," Peter said.

"There is a great deal said this time by that Alama he says this, NO WE WILL NOT SEE THE GLORIOUS SIGHT OF THE CAPITALIST BRITISH PIGS' CITY BEING BLOWN UP, WE WILL NOT BE ABLE TO LEAVE OUR PLACE OF COVER UNTIL WE HAVE SAILED MOHAMAD, and that is an exact translation of that mouthful," Joanne said.

"This is good Trevor, just keep it nice and easy," Peter said.

"And again this Alama said, OUR GREAT GENERAL SHALI AND OUR BROTHER NAREEM WILL FEEL THE

CHAPTER 43

GREAT BLAST, and once again that is what was said," Joanne said.

"Is there any more, Trevor?" Peter said.

"Yes, Alama speaks again," Trevor said, "he says, DID YOU REMEMBER EXTRA BATTERIES FOR THE TORCHES NESTA, that's what was said that time," Joanne said. "And this Nesta said, YES YES, just two replies of yes yes that time," Joanne said. "And again Alama spoke, Trevor said, NOW WHAT TIME DOES YOUR SHIFT START NESTA, just as it was said," Joanne said. "And this Nesta said, 5 O'CLOCK, 5 o'clock, that is the reply," Joanne said. "And this is the last thing I heard, then I awoke in the hospital," Trevor said.

"That is excellent Trevor, you did very well," Peter said.

"You promised me, Peter," Trevor said.

"And I will keep my promise Trevor, as long as you stick to our deal," Peter said. "Now Andy, get copies of that transcript ready. We need to analyse this information fast and get Garret on to it as well."

"What is this promise you are talking about, Trevor?" Clare asked, suspicions of an underhand deal coming to mind.

"Peter is going to let me be with him while they do their investigation," Trevor said to Clare.

"You have to be joking," Clare protested to Peter. "Do you not think he has been through enough that you still want to put him in danger?"

"Clare," Peter said, "I made a deal with Trevor that he could stay with me during this operation; now I am the man running this show and this show cannot happen without me, and if Trevor is by my side and I put him in harm's way, does that not mean I put myself in harm's way too? Now I cannot take that risk of myself being injured. It is important I am around to coordinate this investigation. Now does that make sense, do you understand that, Clare?"

"Well I think so. I suppose that will be all right," Clare said.

"Well I am pleased about that," Trevor said, "because I could not understand a thing what Peter meant."

"Joanne would you go and wait next door please, Colin will you see to Joanne, thank you," Peter said. "Now Trevor, you come with me and remember our deal. Is that all right with you, Dr Luke, and you, Clare?"

Peter and Trevor went out into the corridor. Charlie Garret and the American Paul Bennet were talking to Andy just outside the operations room. "Charlie, Andy, along here now.

"We have not got much time," Peter said, opening the door into the room opposite the apartment.

"Peter, can I?" Paul Bennet said he could help Peter.

Garret said, "Very well, come in."

"Andy, give Colin a shout to get himself in here," Peter said, taking a bundle of papers from Andy before he went to get Colin. "Paul, I don't think you have met Trevor Carhill, he works for me," Peter added. Trevor liked what Peter had said – 'worked for him'.

Paul Bennet said: "What is it he does, Peter, a club doorman?" pointing at Trevor's facial wounds.

"Now gentlemen," Peter said as Andy and Colin came in and took a seat. "We need to find out what we can gather from this transcript as soon as we possibly can. Now somethings on this transcript seem to be pretty obvious but we still have to make sure."

Paul Bennet was looking at the piece of paper in front of him and said, "Where the hell do you get this information from?"

"That is a long story Paul and one I have not got the time to

CHAPTER 43

tell, so for now will you just go along with it please?" Peter said.

"As you say, Peter," Paul said.

"Peter, I have just remembered something," Trevor said.

"What is that, Trevor?" Trevor looked at the American.

"It's all right Trevor, go ahead and say what you have remembered."

"Nesta, the one Alama asked what time his shift started, the one that said 5 o'clock."

"Yes, what about him, Trevor?" Peter asked.

"He had a uniform on, it was navy blue."

"That's good, Trevor," Peter said.

"No, it had writing on the back of the jacket."

"Could you read the writing?" Garret asked.

"Only the first two letters. I was just moving around the back of him – well, I think I could have moved around the back of him, but then I was knocked out," Trevor said.

"What the hell is this? If your man was in the room with these terrorists, why did you not take them?" Paul Bennet was feeling rather annoyed at the fact that the Brits had these guys under observation and did nothing, in fact let them take a civilian and that civilian was horrifically tortured before he died.

"It was not like that Paul, if we had the slightest chance of taking these bastards we would have done so. Now Paul, just listen to the information. I will value your input but you will have to wait for answers to your questions," Peter said.

"You were saying, the uniform?" Andy prompted Trevor.

"Yes, the uniform this Nesta had on there were the letters p o on the back of the jacket," Trevor said.

"How do you mean, Trevor? Just p o or was that part of a word?" Garret asked.

"It was the beginning of a word; the first letter was capital P and the o was small case lettering. There were a few more letters or even more words, there had to be," Trevor said.

"What makes you think there were more letters or words, Trevor?" Peter asked.

"The letter P started close to this Nesta's left shoulder – that's what makes me think there was more because the rest of the letters or words would go across the shoulders, and for it to make sense and look good it would have to be central – you would not just have one word at one shoulder, and the lettering was too small to be one word, it would be thirty letters long to be one word," Trevor said.

"That's why he works for me," Peter said. "Well done Trevor, now what we got here Charlie?"

"Well, the most obvious is the station, will we 'see the station blow'. Most obvious is a railway station, but we have a multitude of other stations, Metro stations, police stations, petrol stations and fire stations, and no doubt plenty more," Garret said.

"Our priority is the railway stations. We start with the busiest and work our way back. I want all the railway stations in the Newcastle and Gateshead area checked, their security questioned – has there been any unusual thing happened in the last few days? I want all CCTV footage for the last three days looked at on every station and anything suspicious brought to light. And then we work our way back through the list of stations," Peter said.

"Andy."

"Yes, Peter?"

"The ferry – there cannot be any doubt that they intend to leave the country by ferry. The ferries that leave the River Tyne go to Norway – there is a one docked at Willington Quay on the

CHAPTER 43

North side of the River Tyne. The Norseman – it is due to leave dock on Monday morning; there is another ferry due to dock on Monday afternoon when the Norseman has left, that ferry is the King of Norway. Now these ferries go to Norway, like I said. The address that was in Goomi's flat was for an address in Amsterdam, Holland."

"Yes I know you could drive to Holland from Norway, but these guys for one moment cannot think we are going to allow them to get on a ferry and sail away," Andy said.

"That's exactly what it sounds like to me," Peter said.

"The backpack in Goomi's bedsit – it had a torch and extra batteries for that torch. Extra batteries and torches were mentioned at Emerson Court, in fact they were made a point of," Garret said.

"Are there any goods containers going onto this Norseman ferry?" Paul Bennet said.

"Good point," Peter said. "It is dark in containers hence the torches – it is something to look at. Now we have no doubt that these people expect to detonate an explosive in a station and if they expect to kill hundreds of people it is going to be a pretty substantial device. Now the only time that is of any significance is these men were told to be at the ferry before 7 o'clock so we have to take it to be 7 o'clock this evening as our deadline, gentlemen. That gives us two hours. The rest of the stuff will have to go on the back burner, gentlemen. Our priority is this bomb. If anything definite comes in on any of the other points then we move on them, but nothing diverts us from locating this bomb."

"All these stations, Peter – will we have the resources?" Colin asked.

"I will bring in more help, Colin. We have to get these

priority areas empty of people."

A knock at the door. "Yes, what is it?" Peter said.

Jenkins came in the room and gave Peter a sheet of paper. "You wanted this?"

Peter took the paper and read it. "This is all I need – more people coming into the area."

"What is it, Peter?" Garret asked.

"At 8 o'clock tonight there is a rock concert at the Newcastle Arena and at the Sage Gateshead Sir Simon Rattle is conducting the Northern Philharmonic."

"Maybe our bombers knew of these events and that's why the bomb may be scheduled to go off tonight, with the maximum number of people around," Andy said.

"It would be my plan," Garret said if I wanted to get as many as I could."

"Friday night in Newcastle – it is bursting at the seams on any Friday night," Trevor said.

"I can't empty the city in two hours – we go with the hot spots, the stations. OK let's move; we'll pick up the other stuff later," Peter said.

Everyone got up on the double and went to do their jobs.

"Paul, would you get onto your colleagues in the Pentagon and run those names passed them please – and the phrases – they may come up with something we have missed," Peter said.

"I am on it right away, Peter," Paul said.

Peter was just going to make a call when Garret came back into the room holding a piece of paper. "Just come in this second, Peter. They have a white Vauxhall Zafira 60 Reg at a truck stop at Boldon just off the A19 highway; it has been standing there for a couple of hours apparently. The local boys are down there now. What do you want to do about it?"

CHAPTER 43

"Shit!" Peter said. "I could do without that at this moment."

"Should I just seal the area off for the time being?" Garret asked.

"I dare not, Charlie. If this is one of our cars it could be rigged. I can't take the chance. Get Colin onto it straightaway. Get him there fast Charlie, blues and twos. I want him to assess it as fast as he can and get back to me pronto. Get him in touch with the local police so he can advise on his way there," Peter said.

"It is done, Peter," Garret said.

When Charlie Garret had left the room Peter pressed a button on the telephone. "Yes sir, what can I get you?" came over the telephone speaker.

"Get me Liz Carter in Whitehall will you please?" Peter said.

"Right away, sir," came the reply. Peter had a moment to think on his own; his thoughts were about the men that had died and how many more before this all comes to an end.

"I have Liz Carter on the line, sir," came over the telephone speaker.

"Thank you."

"Peter, what's the status up there?"

"It is coming to zero hour fast, Liz, and I am worried. What we have, Liz, that is imminent, is the threat of a bomb in a station. Now we don't know if this is a railway station or police station or any other station but our instincts tell us it is a railway station."

"Instincts, Peter? We work on facts," Liz said.

"It is a fact that a station of some sort is going to be blown up at 7 o'clock or just after. Our sources tell us the terrorists in the second group have to be on a ferry before 7 o'clock – that's where our deadline comes from for the bomb, because our targets wanted to witness the bomb going off from their ferry but were advised against it by their leader," Peter said.

"Peter, how the hell do you know this and have not taken these targets?"

"Like I said before, Liz, it is a long story and that is one I will tell you when we have the time. Now we are looking at and will be closing down the busiest of the rail stations. I have called in the Army from Catterick and Otterburn to help in the evacuations. I only hope they are not helping in a mop up, Liz," Peter said.

"The Emirates flight is coming in on schedule, as you asked, Peter."

"That has me puzzled as well Liz – I cannot see how they are going to get on that flight going out. There are lots of things I can't fathom about this whole affair; a lot of it does not make sense. Why blow up an empty golf clubhouse? Why risk going on a ferry so close to their bomb drops?"

"Are you sure about these men going onto a ferry, Peter?"

"It all points to that, Liz. We have our witness, Trevor Carhill. He saw and heard them plotting this escape route. We know for a fact they have stored food in their bags and torches for the ferry journey."

"Torches? Where do the torches come into it, Peter?" Liz said.

"I don't know, Liz. Maybe they are going to stow away in the bowels of a boat – it's obviously somewhere dark and for a period of time, hence the food."

"Peter, I am sorry," Garret said, "but you need to hear this from Colin."

"Yes Colin, what you got?" Peter said.

"Peter, I have just talked to the waitress from the café here

CHAPTER 43

at the Truck Stop and she assures me she saw five Asian looking men heavily laden with bags get out of this white Vauxhall Zafira about two hours ago but she does not know where they went," Colin said.

"What is all the noise, Colin?"

"It is the people not wanting to leave their meals. What was that you said, sir? Wait sir. Peter, I will get back to you."

"Very well Colin, as soon as you get anything else let me know," Peter said.

"What is that about the white Vauxhall, Peter?" Liz asked.

"We are looking for a white Vauxhall Zafira that was seen leaving the bomb site of the Friars Goose Marina and I think Colin has just located it, Liz, and I think this is the beginning of the end. It is starting to move from all sides now. I think very soon, Liz, we are going to know something substantial one way or the other."

"And you are getting all this information through this witness Trevor Carhill?"

"That is correct, Liz, if it were not for him we would be completely in the dark about this whole affair."

"Peter, like I said before, no one can have that much information about what is going on unless they have first-hand knowledge," Liz said.

"You don't know how true that statement is Liz," Peter agreed.

"Peter, you be careful. Anything you need just say the word and it is yours."

"Another forty-eight hours would give me a fighting chance, Liz. I have my back to the ropes and I have tried every counter punch I know to get off those ropes," Peter said.

"Time is the only thing I can't give you, Peter, but you keep on punching and good luck. And Peter, I am sorry to hear about Mitchell and Joslyne and of course the friendly – how did that happen, Peter?"

"Another long story but a horror one I am afraid, Liz."

"What is the score with the friendly, Peter?" Liz asked.

"They had tortured him, Liz, with a oxyacetylene burning torch; the poor bastard may have hung suspended for hours in agony before we got there, Liz. The booby-trap grenades that done for Mitchell got him as well. It must have been a blessing for him," Peter said.

"That is terrible, Peter, I am sorry."

"Joslyne is not expected to make it, you know Liz."

"I know, Peter, once again I am sorry Peter."

"Now I have to get back with it, Liz."

"All right Peter, I will leave you to it. I am praying for you," Liz said.

"Thank you, Liz. I will let you know as soon as I know, Peter out."

"Sir, I have Colin back on the line for you."

"Yes, go ahead Colin, what you got? I hope it is good news for a change," Peter said.

"Peter, you are never going to believe this. I have one of the lorry drivers at the Truck Stop here. He was complaining because we would not let him leave, he said he has to unload today before 7 o'clock or his load is on his lorry until Monday morning," Colin said.

"How does that help us, Colin?" Peter said.

"This lorry driver drives one of those articulated lorries, a car transporter. They have two decks; they carry about eleven cars every lorry load. There are five of them parked at the Truck Stop waiting to go and get unloaded, Peter. These cars are brand

CHAPTER 43

new – they are straight from the Nissan Factory at Washington, new Qashqai cars, Peter."

"Yes Colin – so what is the link?"

"These new cars go to Tyne Dock to be put on a ferry and that ferry takes these cars to Amsterdam, Holland to be unloaded," Colin said.

"And you think this is the ferry our targets are going on?"

"It has to be, Peter. The lorry driver tells me you are not allowed into Tyne Dock after 7 o'clock – the gates are locked and the place is shut down until Monday morning and that is when the ferry is due to leave with three thousand new Qashqai cars on board."

"You need to get to this Tyne Dock straight away, Colin. Make sure that the Vauxhall Zafira is secured until the Bomb Squad get there and give control to the local police officer in charge. Now get to this Tyne Dock fast, Colin," Peter said.

Peter pushed a button on the telephone. "Yes sir, what can I get you?" came the reply.

"Tell Charlie Garret to come and see me now please."

"Right away, sir."

Two minutes later Garret came in to see Peter. "What is it Peter? I was just running those station queries."

"I think Colin's onto something, Charlie. It may be he has hit on the route our terrorists intend to leave the country," Peter said.

"That's great news," Garret said. "How do they intend to do it then?"

"Colin seems to think that they are going to get on a car ferry and it is the logical solution at the moment. Tyne Dock loads new cars on a ferry bound for Holland. Colin is on his way to Tyne Dock now, Charlie. I want you to get what you can on the operation at Tyne Dock and quick – we have to know for sure pretty soon," Peter said.

"I am on it now," Garret replied.

CHAPTER 44

Twenty minutes later. "Sir, I have Colin back on the line for you."

"What you got, Colin?" Peter said.

"I am parked just opposite the gates into Tyne Dock, Peter. These car transporters go in to be offloaded through one gate and come out through another empty. This place has very high security, by the looks, Peter, but will you look at that– bingo!"

"What is it Colin? What have you got?" Peter said.

"Peter, I am looking at one of the security guards; he is looking under the lorry and he has his back to me and guess what I can see on the back of his jacket?"

"Tell me, Colin," Peter said.

"Port of Tyne Authority – those are the words on the back of his jacket, Peter. Trevor was right, P o Port of Tyne Authority."

"That is good, Colin. Now we need to think how we are going to play this if this Shea who Trevor saw with that jacket on does work there. We will have to be careful, he could suspect if we just went in and warn the others," Peter said.

"So what do you reckon we do then, Peter?"

"Colin, just sit there. We will get in contact with the manager at Tyne Dock, discreetly of course. I will have him come to you, sit tight and just keep a watch for the time being."

Five minutes later a man comes out of the side door of the three storey high office block that is part of the Tyne Dock building complex. He walks straight over to the black Range Rover that Colin and another agent are sitting in. Colin sends the door window down.

"Are you Colin?" the man says.

"That's me," Colin says.

"What is going on here? I have a call to come over to see you. I am a very busy man; we have a lot to do before close tonight."

"What is your name, sir?" Colin said to the man.

"My name is Frank Ullo. I am the Day Manager here at Tyne Dock."

Colin showed his Warrant Card to Mr Ullo and said: "We need to get inside without anyone knowing we are there."

"I can take you into the offices but if you go out into the yard you will be covered by CCTV from all angles," Mr Ullo said.

"All right," Colin said. "Get us into the offices first and then we will take it from there."

Colin and the other agent Riley followed the Manager into the office block. The Manager took them into his office; it had glass walls so the Manager could see the whole floor where there were desks set out and people sitting at these desks working; along one side of the Manager's office was a bank of monitors showing all different views of the yard. You could see every angle and every gate – it was all covered by CCTV cameras. Colin stood staring at the monitor screens. "Mr Ullo, who is that man there?"

"I am not sure of his name, he has not been here long. I will check," the Manager said.

Colin grabbed the Manager by the arm and said: "No one is to know we are asking, do you understand?"

"Yes sir," the Manager said.

Colin got straight on his mobile phone to Peter. "Go Colin, what have you got?"

"Peter, like I said this place has got very high security the whole yard down to the dockside has a double fence perimeter

CHAPTER 44

and the inner fence is electrified. It is covered in CCTV cameras, Peter."

"And you think this is it, Colin?" Peter said.

"Most definitely Peter, I am watching the CCTV monitors at the moment and what I see is perfect: the transporter lorry comes in with the new cars on its back, there are two decks of cars, there are six cars on the top deck and five on the bottom deck. I am watching an Asian Security Guard who fits our description of Nesta. He is going up onto the top deck of the car transporter lorry and opening the doors and the boots of the new cars to check and make sure there is nothing in the cars that should not be there. I have a good view of the cars on the monitors and I can see inside the cars, but when the security guard opens the doors and boots of the cars on the bottom deck of the car transporter the view is restricted by the top deck – you cannot see into the cars by camera, it is left to the security guard to say they are clear.

"Now, down in the Security Office there is a bank of these monitors as well and the other security staff just go on the say so of the guard checking the bottom deck of cars to say they are clear. Peter, these cars, once checked are driven off the transporter by Port of Tyne Authority drivers and they go through security gates into the yard and they are driven down the yard by a team of eleven drivers and onto the ferry that is moored at the dockside. They park the cars on the ferry; the drivers are brought back by minibus to get another load of cars and drive them onto the ferry. There are two teams of car drivers, the car transporter does not go into the yard – it is kept in an offloading bay and when it is unloaded it drives back out a one way system and out another gate," Colin said.

"And that's how they get on the ferry?"

"It is perfect, Peter. They hide in the boot of the new cars when the car transporters are at the Truck Stop at Boldon just off the A19 highway. Almost all of the transporter drivers go there while the queue at Tyne Dock goes down. The drivers are in CB Radio contact with each other so when the queue goes down they call each other. That is why our terrorists had the torches and the food in their bags – they are expecting to stay hidden in the boots of the cars until the ferry sails on Monday," Colin said.

"They must be on board the ferry now," Peter said.

"That's for sure," Colin said. "Now they stop loading the cars at 7 o'clock. The gates to the yard are closed, no personnel are allowed onto the yard apron after 7 o'clock, not even Security or the Ferry Crew. The Ferry Crew are not allowed back on the ferry until five hours before they sail, so the whole yard and dockside is lit up at night and covered by security cameras and motion sensors. Their security is very tight."

"But not tight enough if you have an inside man," Peter said.

"Now Peter, we would have checked the ferry before it left or even held it up for a few days, but when we saw how tight the security was here, would we have checked three thousand cars on board the ferry? Maybe, I don't know, but they would have had a good chance of getting out of the country," Colin said.

"Colin, I want you to get the Manager to fax us photographs of the security staff for Trevor to look at pronto."

"All right Peter, but I will put everything I own on this man I am looking at on this monitor being our Mr Nesta."

While Colin was still on the mobile phone to Peter, the Manager came back into his office and gave Colin a piece of paper with the name of the security guard on: the name read Rika Nesta.

CHAPTER 44

"It is him, Peter, the Manager has just confirmed his names as Rika Nesta, we have them Peter," Colin said.

"We may have the second group Colin, but this is good. Now Colin, we need to get Nesta out from where he is without alerting the rest of the targets," Peter said.

"I will get the Manager to make some excuse up to bring Nesta up to his office and then Riley and I will take him."

"Colin you must be careful, he most probably will be armed and he is not going to be taken easily. Now you have civilians working there, you must take their safety first – do you understand?"

"We will get him before he has any chance of making a fight of it, Peter."

"Colin, we need him alive. We may be able to make him talk. Now I am putting back up in motion but it will be very low key so as not to arouse suspicion, but I need Nesta alive, Colin," Peter repeated.

Colin thought for a moment. "Right," he said to the Manager, "can you get us some of those long overall coats the guys are wearing?"

"I suppose so," the Manager said and added: "there is not going to be any trouble is there?"

"I hope not," Colin said. "Now please hurry up with the coats."

The Manager came back into his office with two overall coats. "I don't know if they will fit but it is the best I could do in such short notice," the Manager said.

"Now this is what I want you to do, Mr Ullo. I want you to go downstairs yourself with Riley here and you take him into the security office and you unplug one of the monitors. Riley, I want you to get your hands full of whatever is there that would be associated with the CCTV monitors – wires, plugs, anything – so you don't have to carry the monitor back up here. Now Mr Ullo, you get your security boss to get Nesta to carry the monitor back up to your office to replace the one that is broken there – do you understand?"

"Well, yes, I guess so," the Manager said.

"Riley, I want you to stay behind Nesta all the time and be ready to take him the moment he twigs onto us. You got that?"

"I have it, Colin," Riley said.

Colin began to pull some wires from the monitor board and turn one of the monitors around to make it look like he was attempting to repair it. The Manager and Riley went down to the security office and they both went inside.

"Is there something wrong, Mr Ullo?" the security supervisor asked.

"Yes Norman," the Manager replied, "one of the monitors is broken upstairs. I want to replace it with one of these ones."

All the time Nesta was watching what was happening; he knew it was unusual for the manager to come down to the security office; he would call the supervisor up if there were a problem.

"But Mr Ullo, you can't do that; we will have to get the maintenance company in to do that," the security supervisor said.

"Norman, you do as I say without argument please," the Manager said, winking his eye at Norman. Riley thought just as well the Manager had his back to Nesta because it was so obvious, the eye winking.

The supervisor unplugged the monitor and pulled it out from its frame. Riley grabbed a few wires and a couple of tools; he also picked up the supervisor's bag saying, "You will get it back,

CHAPTER 44

don't worry."

Then the Manager told Norman the security supervisor to shout Nesta in to carry the monitor up to his office for him.

"But Mr Riley, Nesta is on the cars."

"Do it, Norman," the Manager said.

"Very well Mr Ullo," Norman said. Norman opened the security office door and shouted to Nesta, "Nesta, come and take this monitor upstairs for Mr Ullo."

"But I am on car duty. Who will check the cars?" Nesta said.

"I will check the cars, Nesta. You don't think I am going to carry that bloody monitor, do you?" the security supervisor said.

Nesta seemed to take that explanation but was still very suspicious when he came and lifted the monitor off the desk. The Manager left the office first. Riley kept the door open with his foot so Nesta could go next. Up the stairs they went; the Manager kept the door open as Nesta and Riley came through.

"Just take it to my office along there, would you please?" the Manager said.

Riley waited a moment so as to let Nesta lead the way. "Just that one there, mate," Riley said stopping, nodding his head towards the office where you could see Colin messing on with a monitor through the glass walls. Colin turned to face Nesta. The overall coat that Colin had on was far too small for him. Colin had buttoned the coat up and it was pulled tight around his body, the bulge and shape of Colin's firearm was plainly visible through the coat.

Nesta knew at once he was in a trap. Both Colin and Riley knew Nesta had sussed them. Nesta threw the monitor he was carrying at Colin, Colin sort of catching the monitor and falling back onto the floor with it in his arms. Riley wrapped both his arms around Nesta, clasping his hands together on Nesta's chest.

The Manager began to run back along the corridor the way they had just come in. Nesta promptly threw his head back, striking Riley in the mouth; at the same time Nesta sent an elbow into the stomach of Riley making him lose his grip around Nesta. Nesta turned as Riley fell against the corridor wall pulling his firearm from his trouser waist band and pistol whipping Riley across the face, sending him flying up towards the entrance doorway they had just came through.

Colin had tossed the monitor off himself and was getting to his feet, ripping the buttons of his tight fitting overall coat to gain access to his firearm. The office staff were running for the exits or hiding under their desks. There were screams and shouts of people in a panic; some of the male office staff just stood and wondered if they should intervene – that was until the first shot was fired and then their minds were made up: they were making a run for it or diving for cover.

Nesta was making a run for it; as he set off he turned and aimed his gun at Colin, letting off a shot. Colin rolled to one side, the bullet striking the office floor. Nesta was running across the wide open plan office space floor now; Colin took aim and fired through the glass wall of the Manager's office, hitting Nesta in his right shoulder. Nesta screamed in pain and instantly dropped his gun from his right hand as the agonising pain shot around his body from the hole being pierced in his shoulder from the red hot bullet. Nesta fell to the floor and rolled over onto his knees and then back onto his feet.

Colin was standing now, taking aim and shouting at Nesta to stop or he would fire again. Riley had staggered to his feet, mouth bleeding, and now with his gun in his hand, Nesta spun around and jumped onto a office desk and then began to leap from desk to desk and when he could go no further he dived

CHAPTER 44

head long through the office window, smashing through the glass and landing on the road three storeys below, where he was instantly ran over by one of the articulated car transporter lorries leaving the Port docks – the driver of the transporter lorry only having enough time to stop after he had completely passed over the squashed body of Nesta. Colin and Riley looked out of the window that Nesta had just taken a dive from, both men looking shocked as they peered down at the red heap of rags that was once Nesta. Colin then snapped out of his shock, saying that would ruin anyone's day and then realising their man was gone, 'fuck Peter is going to go ape shit' Colin shouted.

"What has happened?" Peter said when Colin rang him.

"It is Nesta, Peter, he took a dive out of the office window and was run over by an articulated lorry," Colin said.

"I suppose that would kill him," Peter said sardonically.

"I am sorry Peter, we tried but he sussed us just at the last second."

"He is gone – there is nothing we can do about that now," Peter said. "Now Colin, I need one of the others if you can. The anti-terrorist teams and the SAS Squads are on their way. Now, we have been looking at the situation down there and if it is as you say and the terrorists are already on the ferry in the boots of these new cars they will not know what is going on outside – especially now that Nesta is not around to warn them."

"That is the way I see it, Peter, we could be on top of them before they knew we were there, but they are not going to let us take them alive if they can prevent it," Colin said.

"I have to agree with you Colin, do not put yourself or any of the team at risk. You liaise with the SAS Commander and the Major from the anti-terrorist teams. Let me know what you have come up with and get back to me as soon as you are ready to

move."
"All right Peter, I have people just arriving now."

CHAPTER 45

Peter Gray sat thinking that maybe he should send Garret to Tyne Dock to organise the assault on the ferry. It was not that he did not trust Colin – he had the utmost faith in all his men, it was he who picked them for his team – Colin just did not have the experience of Charlie Garret. Just then Charlie Garret came into the room.

"Peter you have to come and see this right now, the operations room," Garret said.

Both men hastily went along the corridor and into the operations room. Everyone's eyes were glued to one of the large monitors on the wall.

"What are we looking at Charlie?" Peter said.

"That's our van Peter," Charlie said pointing at the big screen on the wall. "This is CCTV footage taken just before 8 o'clock yesterday morning just outside the Central Railway Station in Newcastle."

What Peter could see was the red Mercedes Vito van, the same registration number as the van at Harrisons Ship Repair Yard, where Brian Taylor and Mitchell were killed, pull up outside Central Station. The van now had Royal Mail markings on both sides and on the back doors. They watch as two men get out of the van, a police officer goes over to the men, they talk for a second or two and then one of the men dressed in Royal Mail uniform goes into the station and comes back out with a four wheeled luggage barrow. Taxies and other vehicles are causing a traffic jam trying to get past the parked Mercedes van, the police officer starts to direct the traffic around the van.

"The bloody copper is helping them," Andy said in disgust.

Peter shouted over the operations room: "Will one of you people find out who that police constable is who was on duty outside the station yesterday morning and get him here now."

The men open the back of the van and take six very heavy Royal Mailbags out of the back of the van and load them onto the barrow, both men – one pulling the barrow, the other pushing – take the barrow into the station. They can hardly get past the hoards of people coming out of the station.

"Have we got coverage of inside the station?" Peter asked.

"Yes we have," Garret said. But what the CCTV footage showed inside the station sent a shiver down Peter's spine: the station platform was awash with people.

"This is the main railway station in the Newcastle City Centre, Peter," Garret said. "We have six platforms and trains arriving from all over the British Isles –thousands of people an hour use the Central Station."

The men pushing and pulling the barrow were swallowed up among the people – you could not see them in the crowds without going over the film slowly.

"Charlie, get that station shut down and everyone out of there now," Peter said.

"We are already on it, Peter. I have the Army and the Bomb Squad en route now, moving in to help," Garret said.

"Peter, do you want me to go and help Colin?" Andy said.

"No Andy, I need you here. This is going to get tricky."

"Another thing, Peter, look at this," Garret said, pointing back up to the screen. "This is nine minutes after the van arrived."

Peter looked up at the screen and saw the two men come back out of the Central Station, pulling the barrow with a couple of boxes on it but this time they have another man with them

CHAPTER 45

who is wearing an orange high visibility vest. The men open the back doors of the van and just throw the boxes into the back of the van. The two men wearing the Royal Mail uniforms get back in the van and it drives away after the police officer makes a space in the traffic for them to move out into the road and the mainstream of traffic.

"What is that on the back of the orange vest?" Peter said.

"We have checked it Peter, it says 'Churchgate Keeping Your Metro Clean and Tidy'," Garret said. "The Metro System is interconnected by pedestrian tunnels from the Metro Central Station to the Central Railway Station, Peter."

"Get onto the Metro Rail people, Charlie, and run those names we got off Trevor and see if we have one of their employees that match any of those names. I suspect we will because they have not used any aliases up to now," Peter said.

"See to it," Garret says to one of the analysts in the operations room.

"Have we got live CCTV of Central Station now?" Peter said.

"Coming up sir," one of the analysts sitting at a desk said, while tapping a few keys on his keyboard.

"Oh my God," Peter said when the live view of Central Railway Station came up on the monitor screen. The platforms were still awash with people but this time police officers and soldiers were trying to clear the station.

"It is this busy every Friday evening Peter, but there are even more people than usual coming into the City Centre with the Rock Concert at the Arena and the Northern Philharmonic Orchestra playing at the Sage," Garret said.

"If anything were to happen there now Charlie there would be hundreds of people killed. I want this station shut down and empty Charlie. You take Jenkins and get there Charlie and waste no time. Take the helicopter, leave now," Peter said.

"I am on it, Jenkins, with me pronto," Garret urged.

"Peter," Paul Bennet said.

"No Paul, not this time. I need you to do something for me," Peter said.

Andy was biting at the bit, he was thinking Peter was keeping him out of the action because of what happened this afternoon at the ship repair yard.

"You wait here as well Andy with Trevor and me."

"This is just starting to unfold now, sir," one of the analysts said, handing a piece of paper to Peter.

Peter looked at the paper and then said: "That figures, Careima Shea was employed as a cleaner for the Metro System by Churchgate Cleaning Company. He has only worked for them for three months; he did not turn in for work today, telephoning in sick – that also figures."

"Sir, I have Colin on the line."

"Go ahead, Colin," Peter said.

"Commander Graeme and Major Davies and myself have come up with a strategy," Colin said.

"OK Colin, let's hear what you've got."

"The only way any of these targets are going to get away, Peter, is by river, so we have used the boats we got from the Royal Marine Training School and we have the River Tyne staked out. Anyone goes off this ferry into the water, we have them."

"And what have you decided on entry onto the ferry?"

"There is no way these guys are going to give up, so we intend to get into position on the bottom deck of the ferry – that is where the last hundred cars that went onto the ferry are

CHAPTER 45

parked, Peter. When we are in position Commander Graeme and his SAS soldiers will fire a volley of Thunder Clap Stun Grenades onto the deck then Teargas Canisters. We hope to flush the targets out of the cars. We don't want to be going and trying to pull them out of the car boots, Peter, we know what kind of arsenal these guys are carrying," Colin said.

"Very well, Colin, it seems like you guys have got this worked out between yourselves. I will go with that," Peter said. "You remember, Colin, I want no casualties. You be careful and get these people."

Peter was getting very worried – there was not much time if the bomb is scheduled to blow at 7 o'clock would we have enough time to evacuate the Central Station in time? Get there Charlie, Peter said to himself. If anyone could clear the station it was him.

"Andy, Paul and Trevor, you come with me. As soon as the helicopter gets back, we go to Newcastle Airport," Peter said. "Andy, get our boys on their way to the airport now."

CHAPTER 46

Colin and the assault teams were moving into position. They had a free run up to the ferry – the terrorists had no idea they were moving into position on the boat. Two Royal Marine Fast Dinghy Landing Craft slowly moved up the River Tyne and took position opposite the ferry at its stern and the bow. Each dinghy had four heavily armed anti-terrorist officers aboard them. Colin and the team leaders were all in audio and voice contact with each other.

Colin and Commander Graeme and a dozen SAS soldiers crept up the Ramp Drive Bridge onto the bottom car loading deck of the ferry. The deck was lit up, the generators were running on the ferry, there were hundreds of new cars parked on the bottom deck. Two or three hours loading cars on Monday morning and the ferry would be fully loaded and ready to leave Port. Colin had spoken to the loading supervisor and been told exactly where the last loaded cars would be parked.

Commander Graeme gave a few meaningful hand signals to his men and they started to spread out throughout the bottom deck of the ferry.

Colin spoke out over his transmitter that was fastened to his collar: "Are you there, Peter?"

Peter lifted his head from a folder he was looking at in the operation room and clicked his fingers to one of the analysts who promptly pressed a couple of keys on his keyboard and views of what the head mounted cameras were pointed at on board the ferry and a view from one of the dinghies came up on the wall mounted monitor screens.

"Yes, go ahead Colin, I am here," Peter said.

CHAPTER 46

"We are ready to move, Peter," Colin said.

Peter could hear the helicopter on its way back to the police station after dropping off Garret and Jenkins at the Central Railway Station in Newcastle.

"Colin, I will be leaving the operations room to go to the airport. I am leaving Commander Walters to coordinate your movements to you. Copy Colin?"

"I have that Peter," Colin said.

"OK Colin, you have a go on the assault on the ferry. Good luck," Peter said.

"Commander Walters, if you will please."

Peter moved from his place of superior view in the operations room and gestured Commander Walters to take his place. "Please keep me informed on every stage of the assault on the ferry, Commander," Peter said.

"Yes sir," Commander Walters said.

"Right, let's move," Peter said. Andy, Paul and Trevor started to follow Peter out of the operations room. As they were leaving the operations room Peter held Paul Bennet back by pulling his coat sleeve. Peter said nothing to Paul Bennet until Andy and Trevor got ahead a few paces.

"Paul, I want you to do something for me if you would," Peter said.

"If I can Peter I will. What is it?"

"I want you to keep an eye on Trevor Carhill. I don't want you to let him out of your sight – even if you have to restrain him if it gets heavy. Can you do that for me?"

Peter did not want Trevor to get in any danger and he saw the big strong American keeping Trevor out of trouble and harm's way.

"As long as he stays in football tackle distance, Peter, I can do that," Paul Bennet said.

"Thank you, Paul that is a lot off my mind."

As the men were leaving and walking towards the exit stairs Clare Carhill came to the apartment door.

"Trevor," she shouted and ran along the corridor to Trevor. Clare put her arms around Trevor and gave him a cuddle saying, "You be careful" and as Clare was pulling away from her brother she looked at Andy and said, "You be careful as well". Andy felt a lot better knowing that Clare no longer despised him. The four men began to walk down the stairs and out to the waiting helicopter.

CHAPTER 47

Garret looked down onto the City of Newcastle from the helicopter. It was bustling.

"Where are we going to put down?" Jenkins said.

"I think the only safe place is going to be the football ground," Garret said, speaking over the headset, the pilot saying 'I have got that sir', St James's football ground – the home of Newcastle United Football Club. The helicopter landed smack in the middle of the football pitch. Jenkins had radioed ahead to have a car meet them; as they came out of the football ground there were people moving away from the downtown area, and as Garret and Jenkins drove closer to the Central Station there seemed to be even more people.

"We have to get these people out of here," Garret said.

The car had to move very slowly through the hoards of people, some moving away but groups just standing and watching the police and Army trying to move the people on. Garret told the driver to stop the car when he saw an Army Officer directing his men.

"Captain," Garret shouted to the officer, showing the officer his Warrant Card.

"Yes I know," the Captain said. "You don't have to tell me, this is bloody chaos."

"We need to get this sorted, Captain. We are running out of time," Garret said.

"We have more men on the way," the Captain said.

A man came over to Garret and said: "Are you in charge here?"

"Who are you?" Jenkins said to the man.

"I am the manager of Central Station. Is someone going to tell us what is happening?"

"What is your name, sir?" Garret said to the man.

"My name is Chris Dobson."

"Well Mr Dobson, I am going to tell you exactly what is happening," Garret said, "but first – how many staff have you still got in the station?"

"Most of them, I guess," Mr Dobson said, "and we have trains due in from all areas of the North-East."

"There are no more trains coming into the station tonight, Mr Dobson," Garret said.

"I think you will find there will be several trains coming into this station," Mr Dobson said.

"We have stopped all trains coming here," Garret insisted.

Just then another man came over and said, "It is true, Mr Dobson, all the trains are stuck on the East Coast line; it is chaos."

"OK Sid, I will see to it," Mr Dobson said.

"Now Mr Dobson, I am going to allow you to go back into the station to get everyone out and I want them out in ten minutes," Garret said looking at his watch.

"I can't get everyone out in ten minutes without a good reason," Mr Dobson said. "If I told you the station was going to blow up, Mr Dobson, would that be good enough reason?" Garret said.

"I am onto it now," Mr Dobson said, rushing back into the station to get all his staff out.

"Mr Dobson, you stay close at hand, I may need you," Garret said. "Jenkins, find me the man in charge with the bomb disposal men, will you, and get me a megaphone."

A minute later Jenkins was back. "Sir, this is Major Brian

CHAPTER 47

Errington from the Bomb Squad," Jenkins said, "and the Major has a megaphone sir."

"You guys certainly know how to stir things up," the Major said to Garret as they watched the people running this way and that.

"Major," Garret said, "you have a megaphone."

"Stephens," the Major said to one of his men, and Stephens came back with a megaphone from their vehicle. Garret took the megaphone and went over to the Bomb Disposal Squad's van and climbed onto the roof of the van.

"Listen up everyone please," Garret's voice echoed over the streets from the megaphone. Some of the people stopped to listen.

Garret tried again: "Listen up everyone please now." Most people stopped to hear what Garret had to say. "Listen up, I want everyone to vacate the station area and move as far back as the police and the Army tell you. Now will everybody move swiftly and orderly please," Garret said.

The people started to move but no quicker than they were before.

"You are going to have to tell them," the Major said.

"Listen up people," Garret said, "We must have everyone moved away from the Central Station. We believe that there is a bomb inside–"

Garret did not get his sentence finished – all hell broke loose, people began to run for their lives people getting knocked over in the rush; it was pure panic.

"Well that did not go down well," Garret said.

"It has got them moving sir," the Major said. "Rather a few broken bones from being knocked over than these people being blown to pieces, sir."

CHAPTER 48

"All right Commander, you heard the man – let us do this," Colin said.

The Commander pulled his mask down over his face and, speaking through the transmitter in the mask, said: "All right men, remember our lads at Mosley Street, let them go."

Almost immediately there was firing from all side of the hull of the ferry; Thunder Clap Stun grenades dropped, banging onto the steel deck floor, some half a dozen of them, and then the bright flashes as they went off and then the thunderous bangs as the deafening clap of the grenades exploding. The soldiers were prepared for the noise and were wearing ear protection and then a volley of tear-gas canisters were lobbed into the cars.

Colin lifted a megaphone to his mouth and pulled his gas mask up. He shouted 'Armed Police Give yourselves up'. Colin and the Commander knew this was a pointless exercise because the terrorists would be deafened by the Thunder Clap Stun grenades but they thought it should be done in case there were awkward questions later. The tear-gas canisters began to leak out their eye stinging smoke – it bellowed up, running along the steel ceiling, rolling along to the bulkhead walls and then cascading down onto the floor again. Inside the boot of a brand new red Qashqai Rasheed's eardrums burst when the Stun Grenades went off. The sound amplified in the steel box of the car boot; he began to shake from head to foot. He was sweating profusely and he was terrified – he did not want to die. The pain in his head was unbearable; the tear-gas began to leak into the boot. His eyes began to water – he knew it was the end for him. He began to pray.

CHAPTER 48

Rasheed reached a shaking hand into the duffle bag and pulled out a grenade. He lifted the grenade onto his chest and with his other hand shaking he poked his index finger into the pull ring on the safety pin. With both hands shaking, holding the grenade he prayed even faster and then pulled the pin free of the grenade. The red Qashqai car seemed to lift into mid-air before the explosion ripped the boot of the car off and sent it smashing against the steel roof and then the almighty bang and the blast of dark red liquid and matter splattered in all directions. The whole car still in mid-air, its shape starting to distort as the car hit the roof of the bottom deck, the cars either side sent flying into their neighbouring cars as the tyres burst and paint work peeled from the heat of the blast.

Colin and the soldiers went diving for cover – this was something they did not expect. Veeri and the others saw this as their opportunity to make a move. Veeri pushed the boot of the car he was hiding in open. His head was throbbing with the Thunder Clap Grenades and now with Rasheed setting the grenade off he was completely deaf. He jumped out of the car boot, weapon in hand and into an aisle between the rows of parked cars.

Shea had the boot of his car slightly open and was waiting for a chance to make a run for it. Shea had seen Veeri making a dash for it and decided he was going to follow Veeri. Shea, who was struck deaf as well, could just see Veeri through his stinging water-filled eyes moving bent over using the parked cars as cover as he went. Shea grabbed his AK47 and was away, following Veeri. Abdul did not know which way to go, he was so disorientated. He just jumped out of the boot of the car he was hiding in and just headed in the direction he was facing and began firing his AK47 in all directions. Mohamad rolled out of the boot of his car and just began to crawl up between the parked cars with his AK47 in front of him. He scattered along on elbows and knees – he was totally blinded and gasping for air. Mohamad had had his boot slightly open to get some air in when the Thunder Clap Grenades and gas canisters went off – he got a full dose of everything.

By now Colin and the soldiers were coming up from their cover. Abdul, who was still firing haphazardly and running towards the car ramp, was practically cut in half by the amount of bullets that ripped into him, sending him back over, doing a grotesque break dance of death as lumps of flesh and blood spouted from his body as the soldiers kept on firing until his dance of death came to stop and his limpless frame just collapsed to the floor. Colin just caught sight of Veeri and Shea making a dash up between the cars. Colin was over the barrier he had just used as cover and away after Veeri and Shea.

"Don't get in the crossfire," the Commander shouted, lifting his gasmask off his face and throwing it to one side.

One of the SAS soldiers saw Mohamad scramble up between the cars. The Soldier ran forward from his place of cover and dived onto the ground, peering under the cars looking for the terrorist. Mohamad was crawling as fast as he could, his rifle striking the cars either side of him and the noise it made giving his position away. He had no idea where he was going – he could not see a thing. The soldier heard the banging of Mohamad's AK47 hitting the cars as he crawled along. The soldier trained his gaze – there was the dark figure slithering along the steel deck up between the cars.

The soldier pulled his light machine gun in front of him and pointed in under the parked cars and in the direction of the crawling figure and let blaze, the bullets hitting the steel deck

CHAPTER 48

just inches from Mohamad, shattering the bullets into shards of piercing white hot steel and sending them rocketing into Mohamad's head and then working their way down his body. As the soldier slowly moved his light machine gun from left to right peppering the target, Mohamad was just about shredded by the myriad of pieces of white hot metal tearing into his body, the only movement from him was made by the impact of the metal hitting his lifeless carcass.

Veeri had made his way to a steel vertical ladder that went up to the next deck; he slung his AK47 on his shoulder and then began to scramble up the ladder. Colin got Veeri in his sights, jumped onto a car bonnet and fired his hand gun at Veeri climbing the ladder. Four shots he fired, the first just catching Veeri on the leg, the other three wide of their target. Colin took aim again. Shea popped his head up near the bottom of the ladder and sent a burst of bullets at Colin, making him dive down between the cars for cover. This gave Veeri a chance to get onto the upper deck and now Shea was not far behind him. The round Veeri took in the side of his right leg from Colin took a piece of the muscle out as the bullet passed through his leg – Veeri was slowed down to a sort of shuffle now, dragging his injured leg along behind him as he went along the steel corridor of the upper deck. Shea could not climb the ladder quickly with his rifle in his hand, he threw his rifle down and was up the ladder in a instant and only fifteen paces behind Veeri.

Colin was back up on top of the car and leaping from one car to the next and from the last one leapt onto the ladder, climbing from his first foot contact on the ladder, he was up to the top of the ladder in no time. He pulled himself through the bulkhead doorway – there was Shea – he could not miss him in the narrow corridor. Colin fired once, hitting Shea square in the back, pushing him forward from the impact of the bullet piercing into his back and sending a spurt of blood back out of the entry hole. Shea stopped and turned, dropping to his knees and rolling a hand grenade towards Colin, the grenade clinking down the corridor. Colin had nowhere to go – all he could do was curl up as close to the steel bulkhead as he could.

The grenade exploded, sending deadly shards of flesh tearing metal in all directions in the corridor, Shea taking much of the blast himself. He was still up on his knees, the blast tore into Shea sending his body back up the corridor, the flying shards ripping him to shreds. Colin felt sharp burning sensations in his back, his head hit against the steel wall. Veeri felt the blast – it pushed him onto his knees. He was beat; he could go no further. He turned and saw Colin rolling onto his back. Veeri knew he was going nowhere, he was dead but he wanted to take a British Pig with him. He shuffled back down towards Colin, dragging his injured leg through the bloody mess of Shea's remains. Colin was lying on his back; he was stunned from hitting his head and his back bled from several small wounds. Veeri pulled himself up to Colin and stood over him. Colin opened his eyes – he could just see the blurred shape of a man standing over him and pointing the AK47 at his head, and smiling.

Colin began to focus his sight – he could see Veeri now, the man that was going to put an end to his life. A large black clad figure drops down behind Veeri with the softness of a cat, a forearm shoots around Veeri's neck and a hand darts forward sending an eight inch long blade through the right temple of Veeri's head, the point of the blade coming out of the left temple. Veeri goes limp.

The SAS Sergeant held Veeri suspended for a few seconds in his powerful left forearm grip, Veeri dangled like a puppet that

CHAPTER 48

has just had its strings cut. Colin looked up at the large dark figure and just mouthed the words 'thank you'. Colin lay on his back thanking God as well as the Sergeant who had saved his life. Commander Graeme and other soldiers came rushing along the corridor.

"OK Sergeant, you can put him down now," the Commander said. The Sergeant began to lay the body of Veeri down onto the deck.

"Come in Colin, are you receiving? Come in Colin, this is Commander Walters. Do you receive? What is your status, Colin?"

"Commander Graeme here. Colin is down at the moment but not out. He will need a bit of time to recover."

"Commander Graeme, what is the status of the mission?"

"All hostiles eradicated and one minor casualty sustained. Commander Graeme out."

CHAPTER 49

"Major, we have an approximate location of the suspected bomb," Garret said. "When we have everyone out of harm's way and if there is enough time we will take a look."

There were the beginnings of order coming into the evacuation of the station now. The Army Captain came back over to see Garret.

"At what distance would we deem to be safe?" the Captain asked Garret. Garret looked at the Major for some kind of answer.

"I am afraid I don't know," the Major said. "I have not seen the device."

"Six bags, about thirty pounds of weight in each bag, six times thirty, maybe one hundred and eighty pounds in weight of explosives," Garret said.

"And if that is CEMTEX," the Major said, "Captain, you want your perimeter cordon at least five hundred yards away and that is only essential personnel that close."

"You heard the man, Captain. Get your perimeter back five hundred yards and no one in that perimeter without my authorisation," Garret said.

"We will go and take a look," Major Errington said, "when the station is clear."

"You are keen, Major," Garret said.

"It has to be dealt with one way or the other so we may as well find out if it is this way," the Major gestured an explosion with his hands, "or it is that way," and then the Major scrubbed a cigarette butt out with the heel of his boot. "What time are you expecting the fireworks?" the Major asked Garret.

CHAPTER 49

"Seven o'clock or maybe sometime after," Garret said.

"That's what I like about you Whitehall boys, you are so precise," the Major said.

"Will you be looking at the bomb yourself, Major?" Garret asked.

"I will, Mr Garret, I will," the Major said.

"Are you not going to put on any protective clothing?"

"If there is as much explosives as you described Mr Garret, no protective clothing in this world will be of any use, so why make the job uncomfortable with cumbersome equipment? That's what I say Mr Garret."

"Looks like the stragglers are coming out of the station now," Garret said.

"What makes you think that?"

"The police and the Army are following them out," Garret said.

"Well Mr Garret, it looks like we are on. I will just go and see which one of my men wants to accompany me on this jaunt," the Major said.

"Jenkins, you stay back here and keep me informed of anything that happens out here, you understand?"

Garret, the Major and two of the Major's men went into the station.

"The CCTV showed them pushing the barrow up to the right," Garret said.

Garret could feel his mobile phone vibrating in his pocket. "Yes Jenkins?" Garret said answering his mobile.

"Sir, the dog handler is here with the sniffer dog. Should I send him in?"

"Yes, right away Jenkins," Garret said. It was the same dog handler with the cocker spaniel Lucky from the Friars Goose bomb. Dog and handler went into the station. Garret and the three men waited until the dog handler caught up with them.

"All right," Garret said when the dog handler caught up with them. "Let's get this done."

Lucky was let off her leash. The dog immediately began to run from side to side of the platform sniffing every inch as she went. The station was eerie – it was so busy just twenty minutes ago and now it was empty and silent.

One of the Bomb Disposal soldiers said: "I don't think this station has been so empty in its entire history."

Lucky had worked her way up the platform and was just coming to the pedestrian tunnel that led into the Metro System when she stopped and barked at a door about thirty feet away from the pedestrian tunnel entrance. The Major tried the door – it was locked. The Major gave the door a checking over and when he was happy there were no surprises waiting he said to his two men 'open it'. One of the Bomb team reached in his bag and brought out a crowbar and he forced the door open. Lucky ran straight into the narrow passage and straight to a door at the end of the passage. Lucky was very excited – her whole body was waving from side to side and she jumped up at the door and began barking.

The Major asked the dog handler to take Lucky back out of the way and wait. The Major seemed to sense that this was something. He got down on his knees and looked through the keyhole.

"Looks like a store room of some sort; boxes, plastic containers, brushes and mops – it is the cleaners' store," the Major said.

"What do you think?" Garret asked.

"Well it would be about the right place going by what you

CHAPTER 49

said the CCTV showed and I don't think the door is rigged," the Major said, running his hands carefully all over and around the door. "Do you want to leave" the Major said to Garret, "while we open the door?"

"No, I am staying," Garret said.

"OK lads, open the door but try and be careful. Let us at least see what is going to blow us to Kingdom Come instead of us being surprised eh?"

The two soldiers began to carefully prise the door open; the lock that held it was only a flimsy thing – the main security door was the one at the entrance from the platform – the men had it ajar in no time. The Major held the door ajar just enough so he could reach around behind it. One of the soldiers passed the Major a mirror that was attached to a flexible rod. The Major carefully guided the mirror behind the door looking for any signs of evidence that there was a booby-trap.

"That looks clear to me," the Major said and he began to open the door slowly until he was happy it was safe, and then pushed the door as wide open as it would go. There were boxes of cleaning fluids, boxes of detergents and new brushes and mops stacked in front of the Major. The Major began to take the boxes away, passing them to the soldier behind him who would then pass them back to the other soldier, who gave them to Garret. Garret stacked the boxes in the passageway.

"Here we go," the Major said, peering over the boxes.

"What you got?" Garret said.

"It is your mail bags all right. Let's get this lot out of here," the Major said, passing a bundle of mops back to the soldier.

"Now let us see," the Major said, passing the last box back out of the store room. The six Royal Mail bags lay on the floor under a ramp section of the roof.

"There must be a staircase above here," the Major said.

"There is sir," one of the soldiers said, "it leads up to the restaurant."

The Major knelt down and carefully opened the bag closest to him. Garret moved slowly into the store room so he could see.

"Oh my God," the Major said. "If all these bags are the same there are enough explosives here to level this station, Mr Garret."

A wire came from the first bag the Major had looked into and went into another bag; this bag had wires going into it from all the other bags.

"This one here is the Baby," the Major said, carefully opening the bag. Garret cringed as the Major's hands slowly pulled the top of the mail bag open. Inside and on top of the explosives was a black box about eight inches long by six inches wide and four inches deep. On the top of the box was a digital display of numbers – one set of numbers were counting down: it had thirty seven minutes to its zero point.

"What time is it now?" the Major said.

Garret looked at his watch. "It is nearly five to seven."

"This little beauty is primed to go off at seven thirty prompt," the Major said, carefully lifting the black box to examine beneath it. That made Garret slide down the wall and onto his hunkers, putting his hands over his ears.

"This is good," the Major said.

"Can you disarm it?" Garret asked.

"This is a very sophisticated device; it is state of the art Mr Garret. These boys know their stuff. This will take time," the Major said.

"I thought you just cut the wires and that is it – safe," Garret said.

"You cut any one of these wires, Mr Garret and this Mother

CHAPTER 49

senses the slightest loss of contact with its Babies and it will send an electrical pulse instantly into every bag and detonate the explosives in them," the Major said, carefully placing the black box down inside the bag. The Major stood up saying to the two soldiers: "Go and get the X-ray kit quickly."

"Can you disarm this bomb, Major?" Garret repeated, wanting a definite answer.

"Yes I can, Mr Garret, but whether I have enough time to disarm it I don't know, so if you will get out of the way, we will try our best," the Major said, ushering Garret out of the store room.

CHAPTER 50

Peter Gray sat in the helicopter; he was not looking forward to what this day's end could bring.

"We have permission to land at Newcastle Airport, sir," the pilot said over the headset.

"Very well," Peter said.

"Sir, Durham is trying to reach you on the radio, just press the green button on the panel next to the headset line, sir," the pilot said to Peter.

"Peter here, go ahead."

"Peter, it is Commander Walters. The raid on the ferry was a success: five terrorists dead and we took a minor injury. Colin has taken a shrapnel wound but he is going to be fine."

"Thank you for that, Commander," Peter said, turning the headset back to on board transmission.

Peter turned to Andy and the others and said: "You will all be pleased to know that the raid on the ferry was a success. Unfortunately we did not get any of the terrorists alive."

"No one hurt?" Andy asked.

"Colin has taken what was described to me as a shrapnel wound but he is going to fine."

"Was Alama on the ferry?" Trevor asked.

"I don't know yet, Trevor, but we have seven down and if you had seen all of them we have still got at least three more to go and I wish to God I knew where they were," Peter said.

"Newcastle Airport up ahead, sir," the pilot said. "We have to land at the far side of the apron, we will touch down in five minutes. Sir, we have Mr Garret on the line for you now."

"Yes Charlie, what you got for me?" Peter said after pressing

CHAPTER 50

the green button on the headset console.

"We have found it, Peter, it is big – about two hundred pounds in weight of Cemtex high explosives. Major Errington says the bomb is big enough to level the Central Station and also take out the adjoining Metro Station with it as well. The bomb is on a timer and is set to detonate at seven thirty. There would have been three mainline Inter City Trains arriving here at different platforms at seven twenty and also the Metro Trains are unloading passengers every five minutes.

"The bomb is placed under a staircase leading up to the main station restaurant. With all the venues happening tonight in Newcastle City Centre the Central Station would have been filled to overflow with people, Peter, there would have been hundreds slaughtered. Carhill has done a fantastic job," Garret said.

"I agree with that, Charlie wholeheartedly. What does the Major think about the bomb?" Peter asked.

"Major Errington said he could disarm the bomb, but he does not know if he has enough time. The device is a clever one; he reckons it is not that straightforward. He is on dealing with it now," Garret said.

Peter looked at his watch. "It is seven o'clock now, Charlie. I don't want any more fatalities. If the Major cannot disarm the bomb in time you know what to do."

Andy looked at Trevor and Paul Bennet and said to Trevor: "You may need a new railway station after tonight, old son, but at least there will be no one hurt, eh?"

"That's good news Charlie, one disaster averted, now let us see if we can avoid another one. I am landing right now at Newcastle Airport. Charlie, you keep me informed of any developments at that end," Peter said, turning the headset equipment back to internal use again. "Trevor, I don't know if you got that conversation I just had with Charlie Garret, but because of you hundreds of people's lives have been saved, the North-East of England and the whole country owe you a debt of gratitude."

"Well done," Andy and Paul said patting Trevor on the back. At that moment Trevor did not need a helicopter to fly – he felt he could fly on his own by just flapping his arms.

The helicopter began to descend onto the Police Helicopter pad that was at the East end of the Airport apron. Police cars were waiting to take Peter and his men to the main Terminal Building. As soon as the helicopter landed the men were out of the helicopter and into the cars and they were driven straight across Runway One and over to the Terminal Building. Waiting to meet them was the Airport Manager.

"This is Nick Shilling, sir, he is the Airport Administrator," a senior police officer said to Peter.

"Peter Gray. How are you, Mr Shilling? Have you got constant contact with the Flight Control Tower?" Peter asked.

"Yes sir. Do you expect trouble, Mr Gray? Is there going to be any trouble?" Nick Shilling asked.

"I sincerely hope not, Mr Shilling. Who have we got from security?" Peter said.

"Here," Andy said leading a giant of a man over to Peter. "This is Inspector Paul Georgeson of the Armed Response Unit – he likes to be called Geordie."

"What you got for me, Geordie?" Peter said.

"We have forty plain-clothed officers as well as the usual armed police officers on duty inside, sir. The whole Terminal Building is covered outside with more armed officers."

"I want every parked car for two miles around the Airport accounted for. If there is any car where their owners cannot be

CHAPTER 50

traced I want that car removed –do you understand Geordie?" Peter said.

"I will make sure that is done sir," Geordie replied.

"Also, do you have an officer that knows the Airport Terminal Building I can use?" Peter said.

"There is no one who knows the Airport better than me, sir. I know the Airport and the Newcastle area like the back of my hand, sir," Geordie said.

"Well you are my man then, Geordie. Pass on your orders and then get back to me please," Peter said.

"Mr Shilling, is the Emirates flight from Tel Aviv on schedule?" Peter asked.

"Echo Foxtrot 312? I think so but I will check," Mr Shilling spoke through his headset and then stood listening for a short while.

"Echo Foxtrot is on time, it is twenty five minutes out, it is due to land on time at seven forty on Runway One," Mr Shilling said.

"Are you in touch with the controller of the Emirates flight?" Peter asked.

"We have eight Air Traffic Controllers – I am in contact with them all. Anderson has flight control of Echo Foxtrot 312," Mr Shilling said.

"Are all airport emergency procedures on standby, ready to go?" Peter asked Mr Shilling.

"As always they are ready, and you are expecting trouble aren't you, Mr Gray?"

"I am just a very cautious man, Mr Shilling."

Andy came over to Peter with a piece of paper and while looking at it said: "Peter, have you seen the passenger list for this Emirates flight from Tel Aviv? There are some fifty rabbis among the two hundred and forty passengers."

"Yes, I know Andy. Do you think I would not have checked?"

"But Peter, does that not make it–"

"It makes it what it is, Andy. We go with what we have got," Peter said, cutting Andy off before he could finish his sentence.

Andy's mobile rang just then and he walked away to answer it. Geordie, the Armed Response Officer, retuned saying, "I am all yours, sir," to Peter. Geordie was hoping to get in with Peter and his team – he was getting bored with airport duties.

"Our guys have just arrived from Durham," Andy said putting his mobile phone away.

"Now Geordie tell me about your airport and Mr Shilling stay close please," Peter said.

Peter stood looking out through the window of the Terminal Building. He could see across the runway – it was a beautiful summer's evening, the sun still shining. Peter's mobile phone rang; he answered it and then stood listening for a while and then said, "All right Charlie, you get in touch with the hospitals within a ten mile radius and anyone else that you think should know. We tried, Charlie, now you know what to do. Get back to me when you're done."

Peter then turned to Andy and the others and said, "They cannot disarm the bomb in time at Central Station. Mr Shilling, from which direction will the Emirates Flight 312 be approaching?"

"Echo Foxtrot 312 will approach from the west," Mr Shilling said.

"I want you to get on to your Mr Anderson in Flight Control and tell him that Echo Foxtrot will report a large explosion to the south of the City as he approaches. He is not to pre-warn

CHAPTER 50

Echo Foxtrot of this explosion but when Echo Foxtrot reports it to him he is to carry on with the landing procedures as normal unless he hears different from you, do you understand Mr Shilling?" Peter said.

"I do understand, Mr Gray. I will take care of it straightaway."

Peter stared out of the window again, looking over the runway, saying to himself, 'where are you General Shali?', and then he heard Geordie explaining the ins and outs of the airport to him. Peter looked at his watch; it was seven twenty nine. He then looked at all the people that were in the Newcastle Airport Terminal Building. He started thinking, 'my God am I doing the right thing here? Surely this incoming flight from Tel Aviv cannot be in danger'. There were a lot of things that did not add up in this case – but it has been like that from the beginning and it was not until things began to unfold that things did add up, and he supposed that was the way of any situation.

Suddenly a shockwave shot through the floor of the Terminal Building; even though they were standing on the second floor it was a very obvious movement of the building. Peter looked at the people – they were in shock and wondering what had just happened to shake the airport building so much. Those people who were sitting stood up with fright and looked bemused. Peter and a few others at the airport knew exactly what had happened; even though Central Station is over three miles away the shock of the blast was felt greatly in the airport. Peter said to himself, 'did you feel that General Shali?'.

CHAPTER 51

Charlie Garret and Jenkins stood on the new Redheugh Bridge, one of the many bridges that crossed the River Tyne and watched the massive explosion take place harmlessly on the former Lead Works site, half a mile from the Central Railway Station. The only damage it caused was a few broken windows on properties some distance away from the blast as it threw debris an enormous distance, and left a crater sixty feet across and thirty feet deep. That was all there was left to remind you of the deadly load of Cemtex.

Garret and Major Errington had decided after the control mechanism of the bomb had been X-rayed there was not enough time to disarm the bomb. Major Errington had deemed the bomb could be moved with the greatest of care, so he and fellow Bomb Disposal team members volunteered to move the bomb some half a mile away from the station to the former Lead Works Site on the river. The site had been cleared of all buildings last year and was awaiting redevelopment. The bomb was allowed to run its time out and explode as the terrorists expected it to happen but not in the place they expected and without any injury to civilians or emergency personnel. There was no damage to the historical Central Station building and it still stands in all its glory.

On the flight deck of the giant 747 Boeing jet the flight crew were making their preparations for their approach to Newcastle Airport; at the controls was Captain Geoff Bows, his Co-pilot Captain Nickolas Aymard and behind Captain Bows was Flight Lieutenant Wayne Emery on navigation and flight control.

"Jesus, Mother Mary and Joseph, what the hell was that!"

CHAPTER 51

Captain Bows said as he saw the massive explosion through his port side window. "Newcastle Tower, this is Echo Foxtrot 312 do you copy?"

"Echo Foxtrot 312 this is Newcastle Tower, we copy."

"Newcastle Tower be advised we have just witnessed a very large explosion in the City Centre near the riverside to our south."

"Echo Foxtrot 312 we copy that. Keep your approach as scheduled Echo Foxtrot 312, you will be landing on Runway One and will be advised on your final approach. Newcastle Tower out."

The Co-pilot Captain Nick Aymard said to the Pilot, "What do you think that was, Geoff?"

"I don't know. A gas explosion or a bomb maybe?" Captain Bows said. "Newcastle Tower this is Echo Foxtrot 312, permission to start final approach."

"Echo Foxtrot 312, you have permission to begin your final approach. You are clear to land on Runway One."

"Newcastle Tower clear to land on Runway One. Roger that. Echo Foxtrot 312 out."

"Are you nervous?" Peter asked Trevor. Trevor was pacing up and down.

"Nervous? I am shitting myself Peter, in fact I need the loo now," Trevor said.

"Well make sure you don't go to that one over there, buddy," Paul Bennet said, "someone has dropped a stink bomb in there, it is out of bounds."

Peter said: "A stink bomb? Out of bounds? My God, that is it!"

"What's it?" Andy said.

"That is why you blow up a golf course clubhouse – to put

the golf course out of bounds. He is on the golf course Andy, he is on the golf course. Stop that plane from landing, Mr Shilling. Abort the landing. Geordie, get your police helicopter up right now. Andy, the golf course, quick!" Peter was shouting orders.

Andy started for the doors.

"No, this way," Geordie said, "across the runway." Andy and Geordie made a dash for the stairs.

"Get my car," Peter shouted. Mr Shilling was franticly shouting into his headset to the Tower to abort the landing of Echo Foxtrot 312. The golf course lay at the east end of Runway One – the airport boundary fence and the golf course perimeter link fences were one and the same.

Just to the side of the putting green on hole nine was a large sand bunker. The sand in the bunker began to ripple and slide and suddenly a hand appeared from beneath the sand, and then a head covered in cloth. Shali pulled the cloth from his face and spat out a long plastic tube from his mouth which he had been using to breathe through while he was buried under the sand. He was holding in his hand a Radio Frequency Scanner; a wire from the scanner went to Shali's ear. He had been listening to the conversation between Newcastle Tower Air Traffic Control and Echo Foxtrot 312. Shali rubbed his eyes, the brightness of the sun blinding him. In the bunker next to him the sand began to mound up and then fall away. Nareem's head poked out of the sand, he pulled the cloth and the plastic pipe from his face in one swoop and sucked in air and then began to cough.

Shali and Nareem had been buried in shallow graves, in the sand bunker, since the early hours of this morning. The two men, with the help of Veeri, had dug two shallow trenches in the sand, and after wrapping the Super Rifle in cloth to protect it, Shali lay down in one of the trenches, He had placed an earpiece that was

CHAPTER 51

connected to a Radio Frequency Scanner into his ear so he could listen to the conversation between the Pilot of the incoming Emirates flight and Newcastle Tower. Shali wanted to know if there was any deviation in the Flight Plan that would alert him that they had been discovered. Shali placed a long plastic tube in his mouth from which he would breathe through and then lay back in the sand trench. Veeri covered Shali's face with a cloth and Nareem lay the Super Rifle down beside him. Nareem and Veeri covered Shali completely in sand, then Nareem lay down in his shallow trench. Veeri put the AK47 rifles alongside Nareem with his duffle bag and then covered Nareem with sand. Veeri sprinkled nail varnish remover liquid around the sand bunker and then Veeri raked the sand bunker smooth as he worked his way out of it, taking care not to cover the buried men's air tubes that were concealed just under the brow of the sand bunker where it met the grass green of Hole Nine on the golf course.

The golf course was patrolled regularly after the clubhouse was blown to pieces. The police and dogs would pass the bunker several times during the day and night and the keen dogs would pull on their leads to go and sniff around the bunker but the handler would just restrain them; you could see there was nothing of any importance in or around the bunker. The police officers had been told by Inspector Devine not to let the dogs off their leads, unless it was an emergency. The Inspector had taken an ear bashing off the golf course manager Kevin Robson about the dogs running loose and crapping on the greens and how he would be made to clean it up if they did. The Inspector's instructions to his dog handler officers to keep the animals on their leads aided the terrorists in their deception.

"Quickly Nareem," Shali said as he took the Super Sniper Rifle out of the sand and unwrapped the cloth protection from it. Both men crawled to the brow of the bunker and looked straight up Runway One. Just above the far end of the runway on the horizon was Echo Foxtrot 312, the Emirates 747 Boeing Jet approaching to land. Shali pulled the Sniper Rifle up in front of him and placed the bipod legs on the end of the rifle barrel onto the brow of the sand bunker. Shali shook himself off and settled down next to the rifle, Nareem kneeling at his side, an AK47 Assault Rifle in his hands ready to use.

Shali cuddles up into the Sniper Rifle, pushing his eye up to the view finder; he presses a button on the sight and the view finder lights up, 'safety on' is flashing on and off in the view. Shali presses another button and then 'weapon armed' is displayed. Shali gets a fleeting glimpse of the Boeing 747 jet in the viewfinder and then loses sight of it again. He presses anther button on the Rifle Telescopic Sight and then a wide angle view of the horizon appears. Shali can see the Boeing Jet now and he begins to centre onto it, another button is pressed on the sight and the Jet appears much closer in the view finder. The button is pressed again and then the nose of the Boeing 747 seems to be so close you could reach out and touch it, the big Jet looked like it was just hanging in mid-air.

With the approach being head-on the Jet's descent was gradual and practically unnoticeable – if you were looking at the Jet from the side its descent would be more exaggerated and steeper. Shali pressed another button on the Sniper Rifle Sight – he was looking straight into the cockpit windows of the Jet now; he could see both pilots' faces. Shali centred the cross in the view finder on the pilot to his left, the centre of the cross became static on the face of Captain Bows – he was that close in the view finder you could see Captain Bows' mouth moving as he talked through the headset.

CHAPTER 51

"Echo Foxtrot 312, Newcastle Tower declaring an emergency. Abort your landing, it is not safe for you to land. Echo Foxtrot 312, do you copy? I repeat: abort your approach and do not attempt to land, you are in danger."

"What the hell is going on here, Nick?" Captain Bows said, then the crack of the windscreen and Captain Bows' neck exploded into a ball of red blood and matter, his head fell forward onto his chest, only a few pieces of skin and sinew stopping it from falling off altogether. The shattered bullet carried on through the headrest on the Captain's chair and struck Flight Lieutenant Wayne Emery in the shoulder and the chest, sending him back over, crashing his head against the Flight Deck bulkhead wall and knocking him unconscious instantly. The huge Jet began to veer to the port side. Captain Nickolas Aymard grabbed the wheel firmly and began to pull back on it with all of his might.

The Jet was still descending and banking to the port side. Captain Aymard pulled as hard as he could and tried to level the aircraft, pulling and trying to turn the big Jet to the starboard side. The Boeing Jet would not respond to the efforts of Captain Aymard – when Captain Bows was hit he pushed down on the wheel port side. The only way to try and save the Jet, Captain Aymard knew now, was to go with it and turn to port side, but he had to level the Jet and stop it descending and to do that he had to throttle the four big engines back up. Captain Aymard dared not leave loose of the wheel to reach over to the throttle levers, he needed all his strength to pull back on the wheel to level off and at the same time try a steady turn to the port side.

Captain Aymard took a quick glance out of his port side window and what he saw only added to his nightmare: he was turning into the fifteen storey high Newcastle Airport Hotel. His only chance was to get more power to the four massive Rolls Royce Engines, every vein in his body was bulging, his muscles were ready to burst. He held onto the wheel with his left hand pulling the wheel back and at the same time trying to hold a steady banking turn to the port side. He reached out with his right hand and grabbed the four throttle levers and pulled them back; more fuel was released to the engines and they gradually began to gain power as they throttled up.

    Shali was taking aim again, he was zeroing in on the Co-pilot fighting with the controls, trying to gain control of the big Jet, the centre of the cross just beginning to settle on the head of Captain Nickolas Aymard, when all of a sudden Shali sees another man's face in the view finder of the sight and then a bright light that temporarily struck Shali blind. Shali pulls his head away from the Rifle sight and looks up at a police helicopter hovering between him and the Boeing 747 Jet. Shali squeezes the trigger of the powerful Sniper Rifle and keeps the pressure on, letting off four rounds. Four shots spat out of the nozzle of the Super Gun, one hitting the pilot of the police helicopter in the shoulder and taking his arm off completely; another hitting a police officer in the chest who was sitting behind the pilot, punching a hole in him big enough to pass a cricket ball through; another hit the control panel in front of the pilot bursting a hole in the casing; the forth bullet went through the roof of the helicopter cab and hit the centre shaft of the rotors, splintering sparks and small shards of metal. The helicopter leant to one side and then it began to drop fast; it smashed into the ground between the airport and the golf course, hitting bang on the fence line, the rotors still turning and catapulting the helicopter along the ground and ripping up the chain link fence, dragging it into its rotor blades, then it finally

CHAPTER 51

came to a stop, motionless and smouldering and suddenly it exploded into a ball of flames, sending pieces of the helicopter in all directions.

Andy and Geordie were running flat out down Runway One towards the golf course. Andy looked up and could see the massive 747 Jet turning just above his head.

"It is not going to make it," Andy shouted at Geordie as the two men ran as fast they could, their firearms drawn and ready to be used. Both men were stopped in their tracks when the police helicopter came crashing to the ground just ahead of them. Andy watched in horror as the helicopter spun itself along the ground ripping up the earth and throwing it up into the air and then coming to a halt and then the big fireball as the helicopter exploded.

"Let's get these fuckers," Andy shouted as he was off running again down the runway, and now the emergency vehicles tearing up behind the two men towards the crashed helicopter, the big Jet above them still struggling to gain altitude and level out from its tight turn. Geordie began to shoot his gun in the direction of the golf course.

Shali was screaming with rage because he had been prevented from shooting the Co-pilot as well.

"Nareem," he shouted, "Quickly, Nareem."

The two men jumped out of the sand bunker. Nareem stands up and as still as possible, Shali leant the Super Rifle on Nareem's shoulder. Shali took aim at the Jet again – he had not much time: the massive aeroplane had nearly completed a half turn and the cockpit was going out of view. Shali could just see enough of the left window where Captain Aymard was fighting with the controls to try and level the Jet. Shali began to steady himself; he could see the head of Captain Aymard through the view finder of the telescopic sight, the cross was just centring on the Captain's head.

Two armed police officers came running over the golf course from the east; one of the officers had a large black and tan German Shepherd Alsatian dog on a lead with him. The dog handler sees Shali taking aim with the Rifle over Nareem's shoulder; he lets the big powerful Alsatian off the lead saying 'seek him Agustus'. The German Shepherd dog needed no more prompting – his ears were back over his head and his tail was straight out behind him; the dog dug its front paws into the ground and pushed with its back legs; he was off like a rocket, the shape of him just a blur he was travelling that fast. In a split second the brave canine was airborne, his gums rolled back and his teeth jutting out in his wide open mouth; the bear of a dog slammed into Shali, sinking his teeth onto Shali's right forearm, taking him and the Sniper Rifle tumbling across the grass. Shali and the German Shepherd dog landed in a heap; the dog shot up onto his feet, Shali's forearm still in his powerful jaws. The dog began to shake his head, trying to tear the arm off the shoulder of Shali.

Nareem rushed over, swinging his AK47 Assault Rifle, hitting the dog over the side of the head with the barrel of the gun, sending the animal yelping in pain tumbling over into the sand bunker. Nareem levelled the Rifle at the dog and fired a burst of bullets into the courageous animal. The dog began bouncing in the sand as the bullets tore into his body, the dog handler screaming 'Agustus'. Nareem turned to face the two oncoming police officers, both of whom were armed but had never been in a situation where had had to shoot their weapons at a person. They pointed their guns but held back from firing – their hesitation cost them their lives. Nareem levelled his weapon and

CHAPTER 51

let fire a burst hitting both officers in the upper body, sending them sprawling back over and both men rolled to a deadly stop.

Shali jumped up to his feet and dived back into the sand bunker and grabbed an AK47 Rifle and then he and Nareem began to run across the golf course. Andy and Geordie had seen the two police officers getting shot. Andy let off a couple of rounds, but he knew at that distance between him and the targets if he had hit one of them it would be pure luck.

Andy shouted over his transmitter: "I have targets in sight. They are on foot, I am in pursuit."

The massive Boeing 747 Jet was still struggling to level out above the two running men.

Captain Aymard had both his hands firmly on the wheel now; the massive Jet was beginning to respond to his instructions but the Newcastle Airport Hotel was coming closer and closer to his starboard side now. The Captain looked out of the window – the huge building was now towering over the Jet, people up on the higher floors were now looking down onto the Jet and could see into the cockpit and see Captain Aymard struggling to gain command of the big Jet. They watched in horror and shock, not being able to escape the oncoming collision. Captain Aymard was screaming at the aircraft 'come on, come on, you can do it, come on baby, you can do it', and then looking out of the window and saying, 'I am not going to make this' as he tried to keep the port turn controlled. The huge Jet was beginning to level off and turning to the port side, but every second it was getting closer to the hotel building.

The Jet was sixty feet off the ground and above the main road, just outside the hotel; cars were screeching to a halt and people were scattering in all directions, terrified that the huge Jet was going to crash on top of them. There seemed nowhere to go for safety, the impact was imminent. From the ground the massive Jet looked and was as wide as the hotel building. People from the airport car park watched in horror as they waited for the Jet to slam into the hotel, the screams and the yells for help from people inside the hotel as they knew any second they were going to die. The Jet seemed to drift sideways towards the hotel, two hundred tons of metal travelling at a hundred and fifty miles an hour hurtling towards them and sudden death. Some of the older people just accepted their fate and dropped to their knees and prayed.

 Captain Aymard was not giving up; he was not only fighting trying to keep control of the Jet but he had to keep control of his own emotions and feelings which were now telling him to make peace with his maker because he was going to die and hundreds of innocent people with him. A strange feeling of calm suddenly came over Captain Aymard; his senses were alert, he had to try and keep a steady and controlled turn on the wheel; he knew if he over compensated the turn he and a lot of people were breathing their last breaths. The big Jet was level and now began to straighten out from the turn but is it in time? Everyone watching from a safe distance and those in the line of impact were praying it was. The huge Jet's starboard wing tip came within ten feet of the hotel building and just sixty feet off the ground, gliding over the tops of roadside lamp-posts. The gigantic aeroplane began to turn away from the hotel building, gasps of relief and people breaking down and crying and giving thanks; they had just been spared from death.

 Captain Aymard's troubles were not over yet. He had manoeuvred the big Jet from the Newcastle Airport Hotel building but now he was heading straight for the Airport Terminal Building. The Boeing 747 Jet was flying straight and

CHAPTER 51

level at sixty feet off the ground, a thousand yards ahead the Airport Terminal Building stood eighty feet high. Captain Aymard needed more power to the four big engines. He reached over with his right hand and grabbed the four throttle levers and pulled them back; the four big engines powered up, the roar of the engines getting louder as they throttled up, the nose of the Jet began to lift, people in the Terminal Building began to run for their lives, some people actually were struck numb and just stood staring at the huge aircraft speeding towards them.

Captain Aymard gave a gradual pull back on the wheel; the massive Boeing 747 Jet gave in to the Captain's commands and its nose started lifting. The huge Jet sailed over the roof of the Terminal Building, its undercarriage just touching the edge of the roof – the big Jet was back under control of Captain Nickolas Aymard.

"Echo Foxtrot 312, this is Newcastle Tower, do you copy?" Captain Aymard heard in his headset.

"Echo Foxtrot 312, copy Newcastle Tower," the Captain said.

"Echo Foxtrot 312, what is your status?"

"Echo Foxtrot 312 back in control but Captain Bows is dead and I don't know about Flight Lieutenant Emery, Newcastle Tower," Captain Aymard said.

"Echo Foxtrot 312, Tees Valley Airport has been advised of your status and are preparing for an emergency landing at that airport, do you copy, Echo Foxtrot 312?"

"That's a Roger, Newcastle Tower, Tees Valley Airport that's a copy," Captain Aymard said.

"Echo Foxtrot I will be handing you over to Tees Valley Tower, God be with you and good luck Echo Foxtrot 312, Newcastle Tower out."

CHAPTER 52

Alama had the back of the British Telecom Relay Box open and the link fence was cut and ready for Shali and Nareem to get through if they had survived the gun battle and the explosions; if they had not, Alama was ready to die alongside his brothers. Alama sat crouched with his AK47 pointed over the hill ready to cover Shali and Nareem when they made their approach.

"Two targets running north over the golf course," Andy shouted out between gasps of air as he and Geordie ran towards the burning helicopter. "Geordie," Andy shouted, "what is over that side of the golf course?"

"Ponteland Industrial Estate," was the reply Andy got.

"Both targets heading towards the Industrial Estate," Andy blurted out.

Andy could see Shali and Nareem just going over the top of the neatly trimmed grass hill. "They have got flak jackets on," Andy shouted out, "they must be expecting a fire fight."

As Andy and Geordie hit the golf course, Andy shouted to Geordie who was just ahead of him, "be careful when you get to the top of the hill."

"They are trapped," Geordie shouted back. "This place has an eight foot fence around it, we have them."

Both men dived down to the ground just before they got to the hill top and crawled as quickly as they could to look over the brow of the hill. Andy could see Shali and Nareem making for the green Relay Box and there was Alama kneeling on the ground and raising his rifle towards him and Geordie. Alama fired a burst of bullets Andy and Geordie's way, the bullets hitting the grass bank in front of them and kicking dirt and grass

CHAPTER 52

up into the air.

"There are three targets now," Andy shouted as he watched Shali and Nareem go through the Green Relay Box and out onto the road.

"What the hell! How did they do that?" Geordie said.

Just then a police car came hurtling around the bend and down the road. Shali lifted the AK47 in his left hand; he let loose a volley of shots towards the car, his right forearm still bleeding heavily from the ferocious biting attack from Agustus, the police dog; several of the bullets hit home into the front of the police car, the driver swerving to his right to avoid the gunfire and going straight through the boundary fence of an industrial unit. Nareem was at Shali's side, also firing at the police car as Alama fired another burst towards Andy and Geordie before he went through the Relay Box and onto the road.

"This way," Alama shouted to Shali and Nareem as he headed towards one of the factory units on the other side of the road.

"Be advised," Andy shouted out, "three targets now heavily armed and suited up in flak jackets."

Almost every officer was tuned into Andy's transmitting frequency and could hear his instructions broadcast; most were heading towards the airport.

Peter Gray, Trevor and Paul Bennet were driven at speed up the runway behind the emergency vehicles which were dashing to the burning helicopter. The men were in a black Range Rover, driven by Edgar, a junior member of Peter's team.

"There," Peter pointed, telling Edgar to drive past the emergency vehicles that were coming to a stop at the burning helicopter. The Range Rover drove straight over the flattened chain link fence that was lying spread all over the end of

Runway One and onto the golf course.

"Stop!" Peter shouted, the Range Rover skidding to one side and chewing up the grass on the putting green of Hole Nine and coming to a stop.

Peter, Trevor and Paul Bennet jumped out of the car. Peter looked at the sand bunker; he could see the two grave-like holes in the sand, the corpse of the brave police dog that had stopped Shali making that vital last shot at the Emirates Jet. Also Peter could see the bodies of the two police officers lying on the fairway grass, the Super Gun had been discarded onto the putting green of Hole Nine, its usefulness passed.

"What is that way?" Peter shouted to a fireman. The Industrial Estate was the answer. Peter told everyone to get in the car; he was raging and fired up now after seeing the bodies of the police officers. Peter jumped into the Range Rover, saying to Edgar, "that way quick". The Range Rover sped up to the top of the hill. On the other side of the hill was an eight feet high chain link fence between the golf course and Industrial Estate access road.

"Go through it, Edgar," Peter shouted.

"If I go through the fence, sir, we will be fouled up in all the chain link," Edgar said.

"Stop!" Peter shouted and jumped out of the car and ran down the bank to the emergency vehicles and barked an order to a fireman.

"Get in that fire engine," Peter shouted, "and drive it through that fence over there."

"I can't do that sir," the fireman responded, protesting at Peter's request as the Station Master came over.

"I am ordering you to drive that fire engine at that fence," Peter said again to the fireman.

CHAPTER 52

The Station Master, realising the urgency and importance of the outrageous order from Peter, shouted, "I have got it, sir," as he ran to the fire engine.

The Station Master revved the Eight Wheeled Red Monster up and drove it straight over the putting green of Hole Nine and then over the hill. Peter was back in the Range Rover.

"Now, as soon as he punches a hole through the fence, you go," Peter said to Edgar as he listened to Andy on his earpiece. The Station Master sussed if he drove straight at the fence it would all stay linked together and stretch; he came at it from an angle, putting his foot down, the neatly trimmed grass spewing up from the rear wheels of the fire engine as it sped towards the fence. The Station Master drove into the fence and along its length snapping the fence at its joining point and dragging about forty feet of the fencing with him leaving a large gap for the Range Rover to pass through.

Nareem ran across the road to the boundary fence of the Printing Works Factory. He stood at the factory fence and kept a look out for Andy and Geordie coming over the hill on the golf course.

"Over the fence and around the back, General," Nareem shouted. Andy had to make a decision: the targets were getting too far in front of him. Andy was up on his feet and began to run down the hill towards the Relay Box. Andy weaved from side to side to make himself a difficult target to hit. Geordie was having none of it; he was up and after Andy, bobbing and weaving as he ran. Shali and Alama scrambled over the fence; Alama waited, keeping cover while Nareem let off a couple of bursts of gun fire from his AK47 at Andy and Geordie, not aiming but just firing in the general direction before he scrambled over the fence. Then Alama fired in the direction of

Andy and Geordie until Nareem was safely over the fence. Andy could hear the bullets whistling past as they ran down towards the Relay Box. Geordie wanted to dive straight through the Box and get after the targets; Andy was more cautious saying, "Hold up until I check and make sure it is safe."

Andy could not believe it when he stuck his head into the Relay Box: the outer doors were open to the roadside. 'These people have done a lot of preparation for this mission,' Andy thought, 'God if we had not come across Carhill the terrorist would have got away with the murder of hundreds of innocent people. 'It has to be safe, Andy thought, 'the targets just piled through the Box'. Andy went first through the Box and ran straight over the road and vaulted over the fence, landing into the yard of the Print Works; Geordie was only a few paces behind him.

Andy stopped at the corner of the Print Works Factory and peered around the corner of the factory wall; he could see the targets climbing over the fence of the back yard of the Print Works. Andy stepped out from the cover of the building and stood taking aim, holding his gun in his right hand and cupping the handle of the gun with his left hand and then pulling the trigger; he fired three shots rapidly. Andy could see the sparks fly off one of his shots as it ricocheted off a steel fence post near to the targets but not near enough.

Shali turned and using one hand fired a burst at Andy, making him jump behind the corner of the Print Works Factory building for cover. Shali then turned and began to run across a short clearing and then into trees; the terrorist had temporary cover.

Geordie slammed his massive frame against the Print Works Factory wall puffing and panting. He asked Andy: "Did you get

CHAPTER 52

any of them?" Geordie had seen Andy taking aim and thought he would be lucky.

"I don't think so," Andy said.

"Where are you now, Andy?" came over his ear piece receiver.

"Where are we?" Andy said to Geordie.

"At the back of Palmers Print Works, Stain Road, Ponteland Industrial Estate. Did you get that, Peter?" Andy said.

"Copy that, Andy, we got it but we are none the wiser."

"Come on," Andy said to Geordie, "we cannot let these bastards get away."

Nareem, Alama and Shali ran straight through the woods; Nareem and Alama knew exactly where they were going – they had done a dummy run of the route before.

"This way, my General," Alama said as they came out of the woods and then into a clearing. Beyond the clearing were the back gardens of a row of detached houses. "That one there," Alama pointed to the end house. The three terrorists ran over a hundred yards of clearing and then scaled a wall into the back garden of the house.

"Nareem, the car," Shali said as he and Alama aimed their AK47 Rifles over the garden wall and then waited for Andy and Geordie to show.

"We are chasing the targets through a wooded area now," Andy shouted. Andy could see the clearing up ahead beyond the trees. "Wait," he shouted to Geordie. It was too late: Geordie was straight out into the clearing. Shali and Alama let loose with a volley of shots, Geordie let out a scream as three bullets slammed into his chest sending him flying backwards onto his back. Andy fired haphazardly in the direction of the terrorists.

Shali and Alama ran round to the front of the house; Nareem

was opening the garage doors.

"Nareem, you drive," Shali said taking over the task of opening the garage doors from Nareem. Geordie rolled about in the clearing screaming, "fuck that hurts." Andy ran over to him. Geordie was lying on his back now frantically trying to pull his shirt open. Andy ripped Geordie's shirt open for him. Geordie had a bullet-proof vest on; the flattened bullets could clearly be seen stuck in the vest. "It must have been like getting hit in the chest with a mallet," Andy thought. The Giant of a man was not giving up; he was still ready to give chase.

"They are burning me," Geordie shouted.

Andy could not hang about. "Where does that lead to?" he said to Geordie, pointing beyond the row of detached houses.

"Brook Street," Geordie said through gritted teeth as he tried to bear the pain of his chest being burnt from the red hot flattened bullets that were stuck in his bullet-proof vest.

Andy made a run for it across the clearing and leapt over the garden wall in his stride and rolling over the garden to the back of the house before getting to his feet and taking a look around the corner of the house. The white Audi A4 was just speeding out of the drive and turning north. Andy ran out into the street; he lifted his gun and aimed at the fleeing car but did not fire.

"Targets are in a white Audi A4 60 Reg heading north on Brook Street. Did you get that, Peter?" Andy shouted.

"White Audi, Brook Street heading north, copy that Andy," Peter said.

Andy caught a glimpse of something moving to his left; he spun around levelling his weapon ready to fire.

"Steady on," the massive bulk of Geordie said, "I am on your side." Geordie was standing gasping to breathe, his jacket was off and he had it stuffed down the front of his bullet-proof

CHAPTER 52

vest. "I cannot get the bastard thing off," Geordie said pulling at the vest. Andy had to laugh – he was that high on adrenalin, something had to give and the vision of the big Tynesider did it for him.

The screeching of tyres made both men turn and look up Brook Street; a black Range Rover came tearing down the road and skidded to a halt next to Andy and Geordie.

"Edgar, let Andy drive," Peter said pushing him out of the driving seat. Peter knew that when it came to fast driving there were not many that could match the skills of Andy. Peter was sitting in the back of the Range Rover with Trevor. Paul Bennet quickly got out of the passenger seat and jumped into the back and sat next to Peter. Edgar ran around to the front of the car to get into the passenger seat while Andy got in the driver's seat and took the wheel.

As soon as Andy's backside hit the seat the back wheels of the Range Rover started spinning and belching smoke from the burning tyres. Geordie was having none of it, no way was he going to be left behind; he grabbed Edgar by the scruff of his neck and pushed him to the ground saying "sorry but I want the bastard that shot me." Geordie just got a foot into the Range Rover passenger side of the car and was hanging onto the door climbing into the car as it began to move. Andy had his foot off the clutch and was pressing down on the accelerator, the back wheels of the Range Rover screaming as they tried to grip onto the asphalt road; the friction took hold and the black Range Rover went speeding down Brook Street.

Andy drove to the end of Brook Street. "Which way?"

"Go towards the City Centre," Peter said.

"Go right, head east," Geordie said.

"Geordie, get onto the airport and tell them to get the

Durham Police helicopter up. Let's see if we can get a bird's eye view," Peter said.

Andy came to another t-junction. "Right again, take the A696 towards the Retail Centre at Kingston Park," Geordie said.

Andy shot out of the junction and into the narrowest of spaces between the two way flow of traffic on the busy dual carriageway, cars were hooting their horns, putting their brakes on and drivers cursing at Andy as he started to speed up again.

"Light in the glove compartment," Andy shouted. Geordie opened the glove compartment and took the magnetic blue flashing light out, down with the electric window and banged the light onto the roof of the Range Rover and, not leaving hold until he was sure the magnet had stuck to the roof, Andy turned on the flashing headlights. The cars ahead of them began to pull over to give them a clear path.

Geordie lifted his hand to indicate something – he is listening to the Police channel.

"We are on the right track – a report of a white Audi A4 just up ahead, it has just ran a Mini off the road." Andy stepped on it.

"What is up ahead?" Andy asked, swerving around slower vehicles.

"We are coming up to Kingston Park; the traffic will be very heavy, in fact it will be down to a crawl to get into the Retail Centre."

The traffic was indeed slowing down. Andy wanted to keep moving, he wanted to see that white Audi and stay on its tail. "Hold tight!" Andy shouted as he turned off the road and mounted the pavement and drove along the footpath to get past cars slowing down. When there was a decent margin of space between the cars on the road Andy would swerve back onto the

CHAPTER 52

road and then onto the footpath when he got too close to the traffic in front of him.

"There it is!" Geordie shouted. The white Audi was driving down the middle of the road forcing traffic to either side; up ahead of the Audi the traffic was coming to a standstill.

"What is it?" Andy said.

"The Metro train – a level crossing, the red lights are flashing, the barriers are coming down. They will either have to or... Jesus!" Geordie shouted as the white Audi just went straight through the level crossing smashing the road barrier into small pieces and sending it flying into the air. The traffic ahead of Andy was stopped and pulled over to either side of the road; there was a clear but narrow passage through the stopped vehicles. Andy looked ahead and to his right – he could see the yellow train speeding towards the level crossing; the driver of the Metro train has green lights, he has a clear way and is travelling at eighty miles an hour hurtling towards the level crossing.

Andy was five hundred yards from the level crossing; the Metro train was roughly the same distance; Andy was not going to let the white Audi out of his sight. Now he put more pressure on the accelerator: the Range Rover responded.

"Oh my God!" Geordie shouted.

"Go for it!" Paul Bennet shouted. Peter just sat trying to keep calm and not taking his eyes off the Metro train that was going to smash them into smithereens, because by his reckoning they were dead on for speed to make a perfect meeting at the level crossing.

Trevor Carhill put his hands over his ears and his head on his knees and began to pray. Andy looked right at the Metro train and then straight ahead, then right again and then straight ahead again. He pressed harder on the accelerator; there was a small incline in the road up to the tracks of the level crossing. Andy hit it at eighty five miles an hour, the Range Rover took off, they were airborne. Andy looked to his right at the yellow mass of three hundred tons of metal hurtling towards them at eighty miles an hour. The driver of the Metro train stood up from his seat, mouth wide open in shock as he sees the black Range Rover sail by only feet in front of him. The Metro train flashes by, the Range Rover comes down onto the road bouncing as it hits the asphalt surface.

Andy has to think quickly: there is no more road, it takes a sharp bend and there is no way he can take that bend and stay on the road at the speed he is travelling. His only option to keep the vehicle upright is to go straight ahead. The Audi must have been in the same predicament when it went over the level crossing and not been able to take the sharp bend it had choose to go straight forwards, smashing through a small one rail fence that was the boundary mark for the huge car parking areas in the Retail Centre. There were several large stores that catered for parking in the out of town Shopping Complex. Luckily for the Audi and Andy and his passengers there were no cars parked in front of the unusual route the two speeding vehicles took into the car parking areas. Andy did not have to look which way the Audi had turned – it had left a trail of bushes, flowers and soil as it went through the small fence and over a planted garden before coming into the car park.

Andy followed the trail to the right. The Audi was up ahead trying to avoid a car that was trying to reverse into a space between two parked cars. Andy took a left and then a sharp right up the car park to the left side of the Audi. Andy could see an opportunity to gain on the Audi as it had to slow down to avoid a side-on crash into the reversing car. The car parks

CHAPTER 52

were full; Andy had to crane his neck to see over the top of the parked cars. The Audi was off again full pelt, they were running neck and neck with each other, six rows of parked cars between them. Andy had to brake hard and swerve into a narrow gap between two parked cars when a Volvo turned into the lane he was speeding up. As soon as the front wheels of the Range Rover were through the small gap between the cars, Andy nudged the steering wheel as he went through the parked cars giving them a glancing blow and pushing them to one side to make his access route a little wider.

The Audi had turned left and was heading back out of the Retail Centre car parks and onto the main road. The Audi turned onto the main road and accelerated, not slowing down at all when it came to a mini roundabout and going straight across it, causing traffic to swerve out of the way and come skidding to a stop. Andy was hot on the Audi's heels.

"Three hundred yards up this road from the mini roundabout is a major roundabout – if he turns left or right he is on the A1 Motorway," Geordie said.

"If he turns onto the motorway and we can keep him on the motorway, we will have him," Peter said.

At the main roundabout the police cars were just arriving and beginning to form a road block across the entrance onto the roundabout. A police Rover car was just pulling into the path of the oncoming speeding Audi; the Audi hit the Rover in the nearside wing sending it spinning into another police car. The Audi swerved a bit and then gained control again and went straight across the main roundabout and not turning onto the A1 Motorway at all. Andy had to swerve to miss hitting police officers who had run into the middle of the road to watch the speeding Audi disappear out of sight.

"This is Ponteland Road," Geordie said. "It goes on for a couple of miles all the way to the City Centre; we have about four roundabouts – we should be able to take them at one of them."

"Radio ahead and advise, Geordie," Peter said.

Traffic ahead of the speeding Audi was moving to one side allowing it access up the middle of the road. Andy had a line of police cars following behind him that had joined the pursuit, their sirens screaming and blue lights flashing, giving warning to everyone of the dangerous speeding convoy coming their way.

"They are not ready," Peter said as the Audi was coming up to the next roundabout. Just like the previous roundabout the police were not yet prepared as the convoy of vehicles was screaming their way. The police cars were trying to manoeuvre into position, police officers were guiding two police cars to move up tight against each other, nose to nose. The police cars were just closing the gap between them to form a solid barrier when, wham! the Audi hit both police cars on their front wings splitting them apart and sending them into a three hundred and sixty degree turn into the police officers and scattering them across the road.

The Audi kept on going, suffering very little damage compared to the police cars. Andy pulled closer to the Audi – he was within twenty feet of the Audi. Shali and Alama could be seen now, looking out of the back window at the black Range Rover bearing down on them.

"It is Shali and Alama," Trevor said, looking over Andy's shoulder. Trevor's blood began to boil – what he would not give to get his hands around Alama's neck. This was the first sight of the terrorists that Peter, Andy and Paul Bennet had seen – there they were in the flesh. Trevor did not have to say who was who –

CHAPTER 52

all four men knew the bigger man of the two was Shali.

Then suddenly Shali and Alama dived down out of sight; the back window of the Audi shattered.

"What the fuck?" Andy shouted. The big American Paul Bennet was hanging out of the back window of the Range Rover firing his gun at Shali and Alama in the Audi.

"Get back in here," Peter shouted, grabbing him by the waist and pulling him back into the car.

Shali did not need a invitation for a gun fight – the obstacle of the back window in the Audi was out the way now; Shali popped up, AK47 in hand and pointed it at the Range Rover. As soon as Andy saw the gun he swerved and went over the central reservation and onto the other carriageway. He was heading into oncoming traffic now. Shali let loose with a burst of fire – it shattered the windscreen of the police car that was directly behind the Range Rover, hitting the driver and the passenger in the head and the face; the police car was out of control, instantly shooting off to the left and hitting the kerb, sending the police car up into the air and flying towards a bus stop.

There were four people at the bus stop waiting: two men and a woman with a pushchair that had a baby in it. Luckily the noise of the chase had these people looking in the direction of the pursuit. One of the men grabbed the woman and pulled her to one side, the other man grabbing the pushchair as he dived to his right, lifting the pushchair off the ground as he went. Andy and everyone in the Range Rover watched in horror as the flying police car came down crashing into the bus shelter, destroying it completely. The guy with the pushchair was still in the process of diving out of the way, the man and the woman were clear. A sigh of relief when the guy with the pushchair came to the ground harmlessly, out the way of the deadly impact.

Now Andy was trying to avoid oncoming traffic.

"Stop this bastard, Andy," Peter shouted. "Get him off the road."

Andy speeded up, heading into traffic then swerved over the central reservation onto the right carriageway. Andy was up alongside the Audi, the Range Rover dropped back a couple of feet just so the front of the Range Rover was in line with the Audi's back wheels. Andy swerved to his left, hitting the back end of the Audi, trying to fishtail it off the road, the police cars behind Andy staying back, expecting one mighty smash up to occur any second up in front of them.

The Audi was away spinning. Andy put the brakes on; Nareem was a better driver than Andy had given him credit for. Nareem took the Audi in a complete three sixty and fishtailing out of it straightened the Audi up and was away heading still east down Ponteland Road towards the City Centre.

"We have got to get him at the next roundabout," Peter shouted.

Geordie turned and screamed, "What the hell was all that shit about, Yank? You trying to get us all killed!"

"I want that Shali," Paul Bennet said.

"We all want Shali," Peter said, "now concentrate on how to get him and stop arguing."

"Fucking crazy Yank," Geordie said under his breath.

The police were getting organised up ahead now, the Durham Police helicopter was flying up above the pursuit, giving information to the ground on the progress of the chase. The police had now stopped all traffic from driving on Ponteland Road. Andy pressed on the gas again and in no time he was up behind the Audi. Andy took the Range Rover real close to the rear of the Audi. Alama popped his head up and then back down

CHAPTER 52

again.

"If you want to take a shot," Andy said, "do it when we are this close, not when we are far back and not wildly – the bullets will fly into the footpaths and the civilians."

Alama came back up this time, weapon in hand. He was going to take a shot at them. "Andy!" Geordie shouted.

Alama's head and shoulders were up above the Audi rear window; he points the assault rifle at the Range Rover. Andy presses hard on the accelerator, the Range Rover slams into the back of the Audi. The impact makes Alama fall forward onto the boot of the Audi; he loses his grip of the AK47 when he puts his hands out to stop his face slamming into the boot of the Audi. The rifle falls to the road, the Range Rover drives over it; the rifle comes bouncing out from under the back of the Range Rover, smashing into pieces as it scatters over the road. Shali reaches up and grabs Alama and pulls him back into the car and down behind the seat.

"Get him now," Peter shouts. Geordie takes aim out of the Range Rover window. The Audi speeds up again. Geordie does not take the risk of shooting in case his shot goes wild and some innocent bystander gets hit.

"The next roundabout just up ahead," Andy says as he speeds up to stay with the Audi.

The Police now have a heavy presence at this roundabout and they have a road block on the left side of the roundabout leaving the right side open, inviting the Audi to go that way.

"What they doing?" Andy said, "they will go to the right and get away."

"That's what they want them to do," Geordie said. "They must be going to try a Stinger Trap." The Audi swerved over to the right, bouncing over the central reservation and heading up the wrong side of the carriageway.

"They are falling for it," Peter said.

Andy mounted the central reservation and followed the Audi but keeping far enough back to give the police officer enough time to retract the Stinger device before the Range Rover went over it and had its tyres punctured. The Audi was a hundred yards from the roundabout and when it got to just about fifty yards the Audi suddenly swerved to the left and over the central reservation onto the carriageway and then up onto the footpath. The Audi turned and began to drive at breakneck speed along the footpath; armed police officers were all along the footpath, some of them just had enough time to get off a few shots at the Audi but to no avail before they had to dive for their lives. The Audi headed straight for them; it would have mown down anyone in its way. Police officers were diving over fences and under cars, anywhere to try and get out of the way; one officer had to break through a shop window to gain safety from the unstoppable white menace.

Andy had to take the right hand side of the roundabout; he did not have enough time to take the same unexpected manoeuvre the Audi had taken.

"Tell these people these guys are not going to stop. They will die first – make sure they all know that," Peter shouted out.

The Audi skidded and swerved along the footpath and then back onto the car-free Ponteland Road after it had passed the roundabout.

"If these murderers get into the City Centre we have got real trouble," Trevor said.

"It will be crowded with Friday night revellers, real trouble," Geordie said, "and this is not real trouble now, we have another roundabout before the Central Motorway into the City Centre."

CHAPTER 52

The Audi sped off reaching speeds of seventy miles per hour. Andy was determined to stop Shali this time.

"I will get close to him, this time see if you can take out the tyres," Andy said.

Within no time Andy was back up behind the Audi. Geordie reached out with his gun and fired a couple of shots at the back tyres of the Audi. Paul Bennet leant out of the back window and let three rapid shots off, sparks flying up off the road surface as the bullets struck it, but none of them hitting their target. The Audi weaved from side to side to make for a more difficult target to hit; up ahead the helicopter was hovering about sixty feet above the road.

"I hope they are not going to be shooting at the Audi," Peter said, "we are right in the line of fire."

The following police cars were gaining on Andy and the Audi. Suddenly Shali just sticks the barrel of the AK47 out the back window of the Audi and lets go with a volley of shots, not aiming just shooting in the direction of the chasing cars. Andy goes to the right and drops back a touch. Luckily the following police cars did the same thing and the volley of shots did not hit anything vital. Alama took Nareem's rifle from the front seat and he aimed out of the side window and let a burst of shots off at the helicopter. A pinging sound and then sparks spitting off from the helicopter's tail arm. Alama has been lucky with his aim: the helicopter veers to the left and gains altitude quickly as it turns and flies high up out of harm's way, the bullets fortunately only striking the steel frame work of the helicopter tail arm and doing no real harm.

Geordie and Paul Bennet both fire at Alama; there is no risk now of hitting any civilian cars – there were only emergency and police vehicles on the road.

"What was that?" Andy shouts. "Was that a hand grenade?"

Sure enough it was – the grenade explodes just behind the Range Rover but in front of a police Range Rover. The police Range Rover veered sharply as the grenade went off, shrapnel from the grenade hitting the front windscreen of the police Range Rover, sending fragments of glass shooting into the faces of the policemen sitting inside the vehicle. The Range Rover instantly begins to roll over onto its roof and then back onto the wheels and then roof again and eventually sliding into a lamppost.

"The bastards," Geordie shouted, firing off a couple more rounds at the Audi.

Another grenade comes out of the back window of the Audi. Andy stays to the right of the Audi; the grenade explodes without hitting any of the following police cars this time and only punching a hole into the road surface, sending asphalt chippings flying. Up ahead is the last roundabout on the Ponteland Road before the Central Motorway.

The police have the roundabout blocked off with just enough room left between two police vans for a car to get through; the footpath either side of the roundabout has police cars parked on it to prevent the Audi going for that route this time. The police had decided to let the Audi through but this time they were guaranteed that the Stinger would disable them – if they had blocked the road off completely and the terrorists could not get past they knew it would end up in a gun battle. Andy could see the police plan and he began to ease off the gas. Peter would have liked the police to have blocked the whole road and had the shoot out with the terrorists, but on the other hand he understood their tactics.

The Audi travelling at sixty miles per hour hit the gap

CHAPTER 52

between the two police vans; the Stinger had already been deployed but as the Audi went over the Stinger Shali and Alama fired out of either side window and dropped at least two grenades. The officer who deployed the Singer was kneeling down ready to retract it as soon as the Audi past; he took a bullet into his right shoulder, the force of the bullet hitting him and sending him sprawling back over onto the road between two parked police Cars – the protection of those police cars would save his life.

"Shit!" Andy shouted, "windows up," as he pressed his electric window control button to close all windows on the Range Rover.

"Down," Andy shouted as he headed for the gap between the two police vans, speeding up as he got there and just scraping through when the grenades exploded. Both of the grenades, luckily for the black Range Rover, exploding beneath both police vans, the police vans lifting up off the ground and the force of the blast shooting out from under them and throwing both vans onto their sides as they burst into flames; pieces of metal debris flying into the side and back of the Range Rover, the temporary weight of the vans before they were lifted off the ground by the explosion keeping the outward blast low level.

Andy had ducked down behind the steering wheel. Geordie was down in the footwell of the passenger side, the three men in the back squashed down between the front and back seats of the Range Rover. The Range Rover was dented and holed in places, the paint work was burnt off but it was still functional. Andy could feel straight away the sluggishness and the stiffening of the steering as he sat back up and took control of the vehicle.

"Everyone all right?" he shouted.

"I am fine," the big Tynesider Geordie said.

"We all seem to be all right back here," Peter added.

Andy looked in the rear view mirror – the inferno of the two police vans was what he could see, the following police cars had just stopped in time or they would have been part of the burning wreckage in the middle of the roundabout.

"What we got to do to stop these bastards?" he said.

The Audi was now heading for the Central Motorway; it weaved from side to side as the air from its tyres gradually seeped out but its speed increasing rather than decreasing. Andy knew he was on a level footing with the Audi as the tyres on the Range Rover began to deflate as well.

The Audi was on the Central Motorway speeding into the City Centre. The Central Motorway had banks along its sides, sloping up at about forty five degree angles.

"What's at the end of this stretch of motorway?" Andy asked.

"This is only a short section," Geordie replied. "It only goes on for about half a mile with several slip roads leading off to different areas of Newcastle City. At the end of this road is a very large roundabout; it houses the local radio station building in the centre of it, it has six roads leading off the roundabout again leading to different locations in the City Centre, but if you were to go straight across the roundabout it takes you out onto the Tyne Bridge."

"The local radio station – how do you get access to that if it is in the middle of the roundabout?" Peter asked.

"You can only get there on foot – pedestrian walkway tunnels and foot bridges – deliveries are from a sub level. The entrance is beyond the roundabout," Geordie answered.

"The police have another road block set up further down this road and all the slip roads barred off," Peter said.

CHAPTER 52

"Peter, these bastards seem to know where they are headed," Andy said.

"If they do get into the City Centre it will be a nightmare, but I think this is their end coming up. Just in case though, Geordie, get in touch with the helicopter – get them to use the loud speaker and try and get the people off the streets and indoors," Peter said.

"He is slowing down," Andy said as he fought to keep the steering wheel of the Range Rover steady. Up ahead was an underpass where the motorway went under a road bridge; the whole motorway was blocked off with police and Army vehicles; up on the road bridge it was lined with armed Army and police officers, every vehicle had flashing blue beacon lights and every slip road off the motorway was blocked off with police vehicles.

"Hang back a bit Andy, this will get very hot," Peter said. The Audi did not slow down – its tyres were giving off smoke and were just beginning to catch fire from the friction heat. The Audi headed straight for the road block; they had decided they were going for it. Shali and Alama poked the nozzles of the AK47 rifles out of the side windows.

"Grenades," Geordie shouted as two black objects came out of the windows of the Audi.

"They are spent mags," Andy said. Shali and Alama had reloaded their assault rifle and were ready for the showdown.

"They are going for it!" Andy shouted.

"Get the fuckers," Trevor shouted.

It was Shali and Alama who fired first, blasting away at the road block, sparks flying off ricocheting bullets and car windows shattering. Police officers behind cover at the road block kept their heads down, the police officers and soldiers on the road bridge letting loose with everything they had. The front of the

Audi was peppered with bullet holes, a bullet ricocheting off the Audi bonnet and into the windscreen and shattering it; Nareem ducking his head just in time as he was showered in glass. Just as Nareem lifted his head a bullet creased his neck putting a gash in the flesh as it passed and went through the headrest of the seat and taking a lump of flesh out of Alama's right thigh. Both men were screaming with pain but the adrenalin pumping through their veins kept them going.

    The Audi swerved and left the road, going up the embankment, and kept on going along the embankment, the Audi lying over at a forty five degree angle as it went. It sped past the road block and under the road bridge; the Army and police officers running to the other side of the bridge to fire on the car as it came out from underneath the road bridge, the police that were behind the road block were now shooting at the Audi driving along the embankment, and then – one, two, quick explosions. Shali and Alama had thrown grenades out of the window as they passed the road block; they had missed the vehicles but the explosions from the grenades going off made the firing officers dive for cover and gave the fleeing Audi vital seconds to get back onto the road.

    When the Audi hit the road its tyres immediately began to catch fire, the smoke off the burning tyres acting as a smokescreen when the Audi came out from under the road bridge; police and Army alike just firing at the white blurred shape in the black smoke. Andy drove as fast as he could to the road block; he was not going to attempt to go up the embankment and around the road block like the Audi; he did not have the centre of gravity like the low Audi car, the Range Rover may have tipped over. Andy drove straight up to and into the road block; he hit the back of two police cars that were

CHAPTER 52

parked back to back and pushed them out of the way with the Range Rover and then put his foot down. The smoke and sparks flying off all four wheels of the Range Rover, it would not be long before both vehicles would be running on the steel rims of their wheels; the Audi still travelling at breakneck speed down the motorway, large lumps of burning rubber catapulting off the wheels as it went. Andy pressing on the accelerator to build up speed and catch up to the fleeing Audi.

A thousand yards down the road the Central Motorway comes to an end and they come to the Centre roundabout. The Police were arriving in force at the Centre roundabout and preparing for the oncoming terrorists. What was bothering Peter now was that he could see members of the public, civilians moving around as they passed streets. "God is there no way to bring this to an end before more people get hurt?" he thought.

"You don't think they are trying to get to the radio station?" Paul Bennet suggested.

"We will soon find out," Andy said, the rubber flying off the wheels of the Range Rover now and sparks streaming off them like four big grinding wheels cutting into metal. The Audi had shed all the rubber tyres from its wheels now as well and it was looking like it was running on fireworks, Catherine wheels, the Alloy rims making a white cascade of sparks spraying out from under them.

Andy was now getting closer again; he held the steering wheel with his left hand and reached into his coat with his right hand bringing out his firearm.

"Andy, what are you going to do?" Peter said.

"I am going to do what I should have done when this chase started." Andy pressed hard on the accelerator, the steel wheels not gaining much grip at first, they span freely throwing sparks even higher as the rotation speed got faster, the white hot wheels gripping after a second or two on the asphalt surface and the Range Rover moved off faster. Andy was going up the left hand side of the Audi; he wanted to get alongside so he could get a shot at Nareem driving and put an end to this once and for all.

The Range Rover was just pulling up alongside the Audi when the Audi veered right and onto the footpath hitting a litter bin and sending it flying into a shop window. Peter screamed 'God no' as he saw a man jump into a shop doorway to avoid being run down. The Audi was speeding up again to get away from the chasing Range Rover; the Audi was now fifty yards ahead of Andy – it was swerving, hitting and glancing off lamp posts, litter bins went flying over the top of the car as it careered down the footpath. All of a sudden it hit a railed off area on the footpath and then disappeared into the ground; the Audi was flying down concrete stairs, the Audi was going down the stairs that led to the pedestrian under pass walkway beneath the Centre roundabout.

"Where the hell have they gone?" Trevor shouted.

"They are going down into the underpass. This side, Andy," Geordie shouted.

Andy had seen on the left hand side footpath the same handrail set up as the one that the Audi disappeared down into on the right hand side footpath. Andy went for it: turning to his left he mounted the footpath and headed straight for the stairs, everyone in the Range Rover leaving their seats and nearly crashing their heads on the roof of the car as it suddenly dropped with a thud onto the concrete stairs. Andy had no control – he had to just hope for the best as the Range Rover slid down the stairs. It was a tight corner; to the right at the bottom of the stairs Andy could see the Audi bashing against the wall as

CHAPTER 52

it came down the stairs on the right and bouncing off the wall when it hit the bottom, sending the Audi in line with the subway tunnel, sparks spraying up as the Audi's wheel tried to gain grip on the concrete surface, and then suddenly it lurched forward and just fitted into the subway entrance.

Andy had to do the same thing – he knew he could not get the tight turn at the bottom of the stairs, he had to use the concrete wall to help him get the turn. The Range Rover hit the bottom of the stairs very hard, temporarily distorting the shape of the car and bursting the windscreen out onto Andy and Geordie; the windscreen stayed in one piece. Geordie pushed it back out of the Range Rover onto the bonnet; it smashed against the wall as the near side of the Range Rover slammed into the concrete wall and bounced back in line with the subway entrance, the impact causing Geordie to smack his head against the door post and gash his head. Geordie was knocked dizzy and drowsy, Andy screaming 'are you all right?' but getting no answer.

Andy put his foot down and when the white hot steel wheels got grip the Range Rover shot forward into the subway peeling the wing mirror off as it went, sparks and very hot shards of metal filings came billowing into the Range Rover off the Audi as it scraped along the subway walls. Andy pulled Geordie down into the seat and ducked behind the dashboard himself; he did not have to try and steer the Range Rover – the narrow subway was keeping the car straight, all Andy had to do was keep his foot on the gas.

Shali and Alama saw this as an opportunity to get the Range Rover knowing that Andy could not swerve out of the way. The two terrorists fired their rifles at the unmissable target of the Range Rover. Andy and the others in the car were already taking cover from the tirade of hot sparks spraying into the car, they could do nothing but just hope none of the volley of bullets hitting inside the car did not ricochet into them. Andy reached over the dashboard and fired rapid shots from his firearm at the Audi, knowing his shots were going in the right direction; Paul Bennet did the same reaching over the front seat, knowing that Geordie's head was down and he was safe. He fired several times, the noise off the gun fire and the screeching of metal along the concrete subway wall was deafening. Trevor and Peter covered their ears with their hands to dampen the ear splitting sound, smoke belched out of the subway, the smell of burning was everywhere.

 The Audi came spitting out of the subway like a cork leaving a bottle, sparks streaming from the wheels. It headed to the right to go around the building that was directly in front of them, then the Range Rover came spurting out of the subway, its sides polished silver from the scraping along the subway walls. Andy took the left to avoid going into the local radio station building, both vehicles battered and pieces falling off as they manoeuvred around the building. At the other side of the radio station building was more stairs leading down to a short subway; it was about thirty feet long and then you were out onto the road. The two vehicles screeching and screaming as steel and Alloy tried to make a purchase on the concrete footpath. The Audi hits the stairs and practically clears them coming down very hard just in front of the subway, one of its wings flying off from the impact of touch down. It seemed to bounce into the entrance of the subway, hitting off both sides of its walls as it disappeared inside, then the Range Rover seemed to leap from the top of the stairs and it came down real hard just in front of the short subway entrance, everyone in the car getting thrown from side to

CHAPTER 52

side, Trevor burning his hand on the hot surface of the car when he reached out to steady himself, the roof of the Range Rover hitting the roof of the subway as it shot into the entrance by the forward momentum of their speed.

The Audi shot out the other side of the subway, clearing four more steps and the footpath and landing onto a cobbled street and began to slide sideways down the street, Nareem desperately trying to straighten the car up as the Alloy wheels slid over the cobbles. And then the Range Rover came shooting out of the subway like a bullet from a gun, it also clearing the four steps and the footpath and sliding sideways down the cobbled street. Andy turned the wheel in the opposite direction of their sliding and the Range Rover began to straighten up. Nareem had gained some sort of control and the Audi was screeching down the cobbled street, plumes of white sparks spraying up from the wheels that were quickly reducing in size as the grinding on the hard surfaces wore them down. The terrorists had evaded all the police efforts to stop them.

"Where are we?" Peter shouted.

"Geordie, where are we?" Andy shouted.

Geordie looked through glazed eyes. "This leads to City Road," he sluggishly said.

Peter did not like what he saw when the Audi flew out across a junction and hit a passing police car in the rear, sending it spinning into a shopfront. There were people on the streets, lots of them running for cover as they saw the Audi hit the police car. The Audi regained control after the impact with the police car, Andy swerving around debris from the crash as best he could, trying to keep control on steel wheels was not easy. Both vehicles were back on asphalt roads now, a modicum of grip for the metal wheels.

"This could end in a catastrophic way," Peter said.

"We have people everywhere!"

"They are the Friday night revellers," Trevor said. "They will be heading for the quayside to do their partying."

CHAPTER 53

The people were scattering as the screaming vehicles approached, spraying hot sparks onto them. The Audi took a left down a street hitting several parked cars with glancing side swipes, the Audi's front end now practically stripped down to the engine. Peter notices a street sign, 'to the quayside' it read.

"That's where we are headed," Peter shouted, "the quayside," hoping the police would get it over Geordie's transmitter.

More and more people began to appear. "Please God don't start shooting," Peter said. A lot of the people were crossing the road up ahead of the racing cars; luckily the noise of the metal wheels grinding into the road surface warned them in time to get out of the way fast. The helicopter was hovering above the spark spraying cars, warning people over a loud speaker to leave the streets but most were taking no notice. It was a grand but dangerous spectacle to witness and a lot of the revellers who were several hours into a night's drinking could not give a damn anyway.

Down at the bottom of this road Andy could see the River Tyne; the road took a right bend at the bottom. Peter looked; he was getting desperate to stop this now before more innocent people got hurt.

"Take him into the water, Andy," Peter shouted, knowing that if Andy did exactly that they were going into the river as well. That was a sacrifice Peter was willing to take to stop this chase and avoid any more injuries.

Andy put his foot down and kept his hand on the horn trying to warn as many people as he could to get clear. Andy got alongside the Audi's driver side and threw the steering wheel over to the right, the Range Rover turned into the Audi and both vehicles slid into the steel roadside bollards, the Audi taking one of the bollards out of the ground completely and it went underneath the car as it slid towards the river. The Range Rover hit a bollard head on and it stopped the car dead in its tracks, setting off the air bags. People were screaming and shouting as the collision was taking place, most getting well out of the way; the quayside was a swarm of young people on a night out. The radiator burst and sent red hot steam billowing out from the engine of the Range Rover; the Audi went on sliding into more bollards that protected the entrance onto the Millennium Bridge, the famous 'Blinking Eye' over the River Tyne. How it missed any of the crowd of people who were watching the bridge opening was a miracle, the crowd scattering, pushing each other out of the way to get a clear run to safety, two guys opting to go into the river rather than be hit by the out of control car and be thrown into the river.

The Audi eventually came to a halt, its engine had given in. Everyone in the Audi and the Range Rover were temporarily stunned. A warning siren was sounding from the Millennium Bridge, alerting people that no one was allowed onto the bridge – the barriers were down, the bridge was opening. Shali was the first to come to his senses – he scrambled out of the back door of the Audi and onto the top of one of the bollards; he leapt onto the bridge walkway as it was in the process of lifting.

Shali turns and fires a shot from a handgun at the smoking Range Rover; Andy is out of the Range Rover and fires a shot back at Shali who is now climbing up the edge protection rail on the Millennium Bridge as it is lifting up to open and allow access to a passing vessel. The bridge is opening to let a pleasure craft through – the Pride of the Tyne makes regular trips up and down

CHAPTER 53

the River Tyne and one of the treats for the tourists taking the cruise is to witness the famous Blinking Eye Bridge opening to let them pass under.

The massive steel structure was just in the process of opening when the two cars came to an unscheduled stop at the bridge entrance. Andy was only interested in getting Shali – he shoots his gun, the bullet hitting the stainless steel framework of the bridge just inches above Shali's head; white sparks fly as the bullet ricochets off the steel. Alama forces his way out of the back door of the Audi and squeezes between the bent over bollard; he climbs up and onto the bridge structure following Andy. Trevor has his eye on Alama making a dash for it. Trevor was out of the car and away after Alama; Trevor wanted nothing else in this world but to get the man that he knew had killed his friend Brian.

"Trevor!" Peter shouted as he pulled himself out of the wrecked Range Rover. Trevor looked at Peter to say, 'there is nothing on this Earth you can do or say that will stop me going after this man'. Peter knew that; he took his gun from his waistband holster and threw it to Trevor. Trevor caught the gun and turned to make for the bridge at the same time. Alama was wounded – he was carrying his injured right leg. Trevor just missed grabbing his foot as he made a dive off the roof of the Audi. He fell down the mesh gate barrier and had to start again.

Nareem was out of the front of the Audi and running along the quayside and heading west, pushing through the people as he went. Paul Bennet hopped as fast as he could after Nareem, the crowds of people already noticing the drawn weapons and making a dash for safety in all directions. Nareem was running into people who were heading to see the Millennium Bridge open, crowds of people young and old dressed for a summer's evening out, men in sleeveless shirts and shorts, women in blouses and short skirts.

Paul Bennet stops and looks along the quayside at Nareem running as fast as he can.

"He is heading for the Arena," Peter shouts. Paul Bennet lifts his nine millimetre Glock handgun and fires two shots into the air. He shouts at the top of his voice, "Armed police, stop or I will shoot."

The people on the quayside needed no more warning – they were diving for cover; along one side of the quayside there is nothing but pubs and restaurants, the night time revellers dashing into these buildings for cover. Paul Bennet levels his handgun and takes aim.

"Take him," Peter shouts. Paul Bennet fires one shot: Nareem explodes into a huge ball of red liquid flame, a thunderous bang that sends him splattering, every ounce of his liquefied body over the pub and restaurant fronts.

"My God!" Peter shouted in shock, "they are not wearing flak jackets, they are bomb vests."

Peter looked over the River Tyne – he could see the all glass structure of the Sage theatre building. He did not need telling what would happen if Shali and Alama got in there with bomb vests on – the terrorists were on a suicide mission.

"Andy!" Peter shouted out.

Andy replied: "You don't have to tell me, they are wearing bomb vests." Andy had heard the explosion and seen Nareem disappear in a cloud of red liquid spray.

"Andy, you must stop him, he is heading for the Sage – it will be full of people. Andy, stop the maniac," Peter screamed.

The eight hundred ton weight Millennium Bridge that spans the River Tyne is two large steel arches linked together with

CHAPTER 53

forty millimetre thick steel tie rods. One of the steel arches when lying horizontal becomes the pedestrian and cycle way, its large curvature sweeping out from one bank side to the middle of the river and sweeping back to the opposite bank side. The other arch is in the ninety degree vertical position to the pedestrian arch and this is the resting and safe position for pedestrians and cyclists to cross, both arches meet at a pivotal point on each bank side of the River Tyne. When the bridge opens, two massive hydraulic rams at each pivotal point push the vertical arch section; as the vertical arch moves from the ninety degree angle it acts as a counter balance and the heavy steel link tie rods help pull the cycle and pedestrian horizontal arch over. When the bridge is open, the two large arches are like rainbows over the river. The pedestrian arch has a walkway footpath and a cycleway; they are separated by a dividing hand rail.

Shali was being pursued by Andy over the inner walkway section of the bridge arch. Trevor was after Alama who was climbing up the outer cycleway section of the bridge arch. As the Bridge was pushed by the large hydraulic rams to open it and as it rolled on the pivot points, the pedestrian arch got higher. On the inner section of the arch the edge protection handrail was becoming the deck as far as Shali and Andy were concerned; the rail that separated the cycle and pedestrian way was quickly becoming the deck for Alama and Trevor.

Shali had to start climbing now to advance over the bridge; he was looking back and down at Andy coming after him. Shali fired a couple of rounds at Andy, they ricocheted, pinging off the steel close to Andy. Andy returned fire, three rapid shots pinging and sparking as the bullets ricocheted off the steel work just above Shali. Alama fired up at Andy from his lower position on the bridge. Andy was being fired at from in front and behind –

none of the lethal rounds hitting home though.

Trevor aims the handgun he got from Peter and pulls the trigger – nothing happened: the safety is still on. Trevor has never fired a gun before in his life and he had no idea how to take the safety off. Bullets are pinging and sparking all around Andy; he has nowhere to hide. He just pulls himself as close to the steel bridge structure as possible. The tourists on the pleasure cruise all look up in amazement at what is unfolding above their heads; the Captain of the Pride of the Tyne pulls the throttle wide open for more power to get the vessel past and under the bridge as quickly as possible. A ricocheting bullet hits the cabin window, breaking it and making the Captain dive for cover. The Millennium Bridge Control Operator is in a panic – there is nothing he can do, he must let the bridge open to its full extent to allow the cruise vessel to pass, and on the other hand he has men climbing up the bridge as it lifts even higher. He was praying for the cruise vessel to get by so he could reverse the controls to begin closing the bridge to its rest position.

Shali had reached the top of the arch. He balances himself and fires his gun from his left hand at Andy, still not hitting Andy but getting damn close. Andy returns fire but Shali has cover now – he was starting to climb down the other side of the huge steel arch. Trevor was gaining fast on Alama. Alama turns to take a shot at Trevor and slips; he drops his gun so he can use both hands to hold onto the steel of the bridge. Trevor tries again to fire the gun – still nothing happens when he pulls the trigger. Trevor holds onto the bridge with one hand and throws the gun at Alama with the other, missing him by feet.

The cruise vessel is through the massive arches of the bridge and the bridge operator quickly reverses the controls and begins to close the bridge. Alama is just reaching the top of the arch

CHAPTER 53

as Andy is on the down side after Shali; Trevor is moving fast – he is crying with rage, he needs to get his hands on Alama. The dividing handrail that had been acting as a deck for Alama stops – there is a twenty foot gap before it starts again. This is the cross over section where cyclists and pedestrians could swap over to any side if they chose, obviously when the arch was down on the horizontal. Alama was stuck: he had nowhere to go unless he drops down onto the handrail below him, which is the one that Shali and Andy are using as a deck.

Alama decides to try and jump down. Trevor has a hand on the shoulder of Alama. Alama jumps. Trevor pulls back the bomb vest and a handful of hair rips off Alama. Alama drops down onto the inner hand rail; he squeals in pain as he hits the handrail hard and rolls over to the edge and just stops himself from going right over and falling into the river eighty feet below. Alama stands up, only to be flattened back down by the weight of Trevor's body hitting him. Both men roll over the edge of the handrail; Trevor holds onto Alama as they fall – they look like two sky divers holding hands in mid-air as they plummet eighty feet to the river. Crowds of people on the both quaysides yell and scream in horror as the two men fall and hit the water with a slapping splash. Trevor loses his grip on Alama when they hit the water hard.

Andy has to hold on with both hands as he climbs down the sloping arch; he pokes his finger through the trigger guard of the gun and hooks onto the steel mesh for more support. Shali has discarded his gun so he could hang on with both hands, his right arm not in good condition – Agustus the police dog made sure of that. The walkway arch is coming back down to its rest position fast now.

Trevor kicks his legs and breaks the surface of the water; he can see Alama dog paddling towards the large pivot point of the bridge. Alama pulls himself out of the water onto the huge concrete base where the massive hydraulic ram is housed as it pushes the big steel arches; Trevor is only feet behind him. Alama stands and is just going to make a dash for it when Trevor dives onto him; both men hit the hard concrete base that the pivot bearing shaft sits on. Alama struggles and turns to face Trevor; Trevor is still on top of Alama. Alama reaches up and gets his hands around Trevor's throat, trying to choke him. Trevor gets his hand under the chin of Alama and pushes his head towards the huge hydraulic ram as it pushes the bridge back to rest, the flat face side of the eight hundred ton pivot point coming to rest against the rest plate on the concrete base as the bridge closes.

Trevor pushes Alama's head into the narrowing gap between steel and concrete. Alama tries with all his strength to push Trevor off. Trevor is strong – he has the help of the drugs Dr Luke gave him to stem the pain and help him move around after his beating off the Kosovos. The gap between steel and concrete gets narrower as the massive hydraulic ram pushes the eight hundred ton bridge back to rest. Alama screams as the steel pushes down slowly and begins to trap his head; he yells and nips with his hands on Trevor's neck, blood coming through his fingers; Trevor does not ease off the pressure. Trevor could pull him back and save him, but Trevor thinks of Brian and the suffering he had to endure before he died.

Trevor pushes harder on the chin of Alama; Alama's grip on Trevor's neck loosens. Trevor looks Alama straight in the eyes. Alama's head begins to squash between steel and concrete, blood begins to run from his eyes, nose and mouth, his eyes pop out of the sockets as blood pressure behind them forces them out; blood begins to flood out from openings in the nose, eyes, and

CHAPTER 53

mouth and the sound of the skull breaking as it is crushed under the tremendous pressure, then a bang as the head bursts and sprays blood and brain matter all over Trevor's face. The massive hydraulic ram pushes home the last few inches squeezing the last drops of blood out of the crushed skull. Alama's head disintegrates into nothing. Trevor pulls his hand back; the decapitated body of Alama is lying in a pool of blood. Trevor just sits in a daze – he feels no sense of revenge or satisfaction.

Shali jumps from the bridge when it still has about fifteen feet to go before it is at rest. Andy loses his grip and slides down the handrail and jumps from the bridge when he is about ten feet from the quayside. Andy hits the ground hard, throwing his hands out to stop himself going flat on his face. Andy still has his gun in his right hand; he squashes his index and middle finger between ground and gun breaking them. Andy screams in pain but he gets up and onto his feet and is after Shali who is making for the steps up to the road.

"Andy, come in Andy, are you all right?" comes over the receiver in Andy's ear.

Andy sucks in air to breathe before he answers, "I am alive, Peter – just – and still after Shali on foot."

"Andy, you have to stop him. I think he is trying to get to the Sage and explode his bomb vest before we get him," Peter says.

"This place is overflowing with people, Peter, I cannot start shooting," Andy says.

"You have to make a decision, Andy."

"How is Carhill?" Andy asks.

"I can see him in the workings of the bridge, he looks all right."

Shali was running over the road now towards the towering concrete stairway that ran up to the high level car park adjacent to the Sage. The Sage theatre stands on top of a hill, the side of which is very steep in places. Concrete retainer walls have been built against the steep bank sides to stop them slipping away. The steps Shali was heading for were built into the retainer wall, about one hundred steps in all with a landing every thirty steps. The landings had seats on for people who were taking the long climb so they could rest before they tackled the next flight of steps, and at the top was the car parking area for the Sage visitors, the access to it from the road behind the theatre. The Sage theatre is a large modern glass building and to some it looks like a bumble-bee.

Shali was pushing people to one side as he started up the steps; there were droves of people coming down the steps. Shali barged his way through them as he climbed. The police helicopter flew low, warning people to get out of the way; for those people on the steps they could only either go up or down. Andy started up the steps after Shali shouting for the people to get out of the way and give him a clear shot.

Shali got to the first landing and picked the litter bin up and threw it down the stairs at Andy. There were people between Andy and Shali, the litter bin hitting a woman on her back and knocking her down the steps, Andy just catching the woman before she fell too far. A man coming down the steps confronts Shali, "what the hell do you think you are doing, you could have killed that woman!"

Shali punches the man in the face, sending him over the handrail and tumbling down the bank side. People begin to run back down the steps in fear for their lives; those who are on their way down turn around and head back up the steps. Shali is off again taking two steps at a time in his stride. Andy struggles to keep up, every muscle and bone in his body is telling him to

CHAPTER 53

stop and rest. Andy points his gun in the air and fires. People jump over the handrail – they prefer the bank side rather then being on the steps with Shali and Andy.

Shali reaches the second landing and throws the litter bin at Andy again. Andy has to stop and dodge to one side and parry the litter bin away, sending it rolling down the bank side. The people are leaving the steps in whatever way and route they can now, screaming and yelling as they go. Shali is slowing down, his energy sapping away every step he takes on the arduous climb. Andy is in the same boat: both men determined to see their goal through to the end – Shali to reach the Sage, Andy's goal is to stop him. Andy puts the gun in his left hand and chances taking a shot at Shali. The bullet goes wide of its target, spitting concrete up as it strikes a step five feet below Shali.

"Get him Andy, you must get him," comes over the transmitter.

"I am trying, I am trying," Andy repeats.

Shali goes straight past the third landing not wanting to stop and use energy throwing the litter bin this time. Andy was using his left hand to help pull him up the steps – he was nearly done for. Shali is down on all fours now as well, but he is at the top – he takes a split second to try and catch a breath and check on how close Andy is. Shali staggers onto the car park – the car park is full, every space is taken. That means the Sage is full, Shali thinks. Shali runs into the rows of parked cars to use them as cover from Andy shooting at him and they aid him as he leans on the cars to pull himself along.

Andy gets to the top of the steps, gasping for air, his legs refusing to hold him up but he has to force himself.

"Andy, shoot the bastard," Peter shouts.

Andy goes into the parked cars; he is in the same row as

Shali; he can see Shali up ahead of him. Andy leans his gun hand on a car and takes aim; he fires the bullet, hits Shali in the left calf. Shali drops to the ground and then immediately pulls himself upright holding onto a parked car, and begins to pull himself along again using the cars to grip onto. Andy aims again and fires – this time the bullet misses and hits a car. Shali is through the cars; just ahead of him are eight steps leading up into the entrance of the Sage theatre building. You can hear the music being played by the Northern Philharmonic Orchestra.

Shali staggers to the steps; dragging his injured leg behind him, he starts up the steps. Andy falls on the ground as he pulls himself out through the parked cars; Andy is beat, he can go no further. Andy raises his left hand, the gun is shaking. He brings his right hand up to help support and steady the gun; sweat is running into his eyes, he cannot keep still, he is breathing too heavy. Shali is half way up the steps and in front of him is the twenty foot high glass entrance doors to the theatre. Andy takes a breath and holds it – he steadies his hands and squeezes the trigger; the gun kicks in Andy's hands as it fires. Andy watches as everything seems to go into slow motion, the bullet just clips Shali on the shoulder lifting his shirt collar and then hits a man who is running to try and get safe in the leg, sending him tumbling down the steps in agony.

Andy wipes the sweat out of his eyes and takes aim again; he fires, click, click nothing – the gun is empty. Shali hears the clicking of the empty gun being fired; he is at the top of the steps now; he turns and looks at Andy as he lifts his left hand with the toggle detonator switch in it and his left hand thumb poised over the button.

Shali shouts, "for my brothers" as he stares at Andy. Andy is praying to God to put a live round in the gun he is keeping on

CHAPTER 53

firing. Shali begins to turn to make a run into the Sage theatre.

A dull thud sound – the massive glass door at the entrance to the Sage shatters. Shali looks in horror as his left forearm blows off from just above the elbow joint – there is not much blood, there is only red hanging flesh and bits of white bone sticking out. Shali stares at the stump on the elbow where his arm used to be and then thud – Shali's head explodes into a red ball of blood and matter, his headless body standing still for a second before it falls back over slamming onto the concrete floor.

Andy looks up behind him at the large tower block building a thousand yards away. Paul Bennet stands up from his prone position he had taken on top of the Baltic Flour Mill from where he had fired the Super Sniper Rifle.

Paul Bennet turned to Peter Gray and says," For my brother."

"The guy in the photograph?"

"Yes, Shali killed him. That's how they got their hands on the Sniper Rifle," Paul said.

"You took a chance with all those people on the aeroplane," Paul added to Peter.

"There were no passengers on that Jet," Peter said. "The Emirates Jet left Tel Aviv as scheduled but landed safely in Manchester Airport. The Emirates Jet that came to land at Newcastle Airport flew from RAF Brize Norton with a brave RAF flight crew who had volunteered to fly the mission, and that is another key on my rack," Peter said.

"A key on your rack?" Paul Bennet said, puzzled.

"Never mind," Peter said. "I know a certain doctor who will be interested to know you had a brother, Mr Bennet. Come in Andy, where are you?"

Andy rolled onto his backside and sat up. "Yes Peter, I am here," he said.

"Andy, get off your arse and get Carhill, then come and get me. I need my bed."